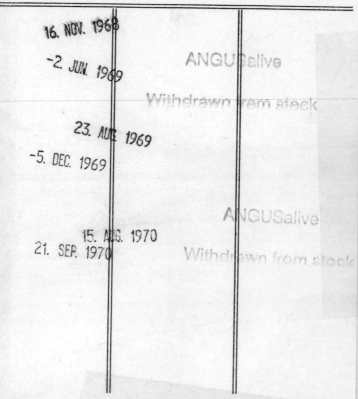

TOMORROW'S FIRE

A Novel of the Third Crusade

Tomorrow's Fire

JAY WILLIAMS

MACDONALD : LONDON

First published in Great Britain in 1965 by
Macdonald & Co. (Publishers) Ltd.
Gulf House, 2 Portman Street, London W.1.
Made and printed in Great Britain by
Purnell & Sons, Ltd.
Paulton (Somerset) and London

This book is for
CANDIDA
with affection and gratitude.

FOREWORD

In following Denys's journal it is well to remember that medieval chroniclers and clerks generally used the Roman system of dividing the months into Kalends, Nones, and Ides, with all the attendant confusion of reckoning days before and after those points. They also, not infrequently, departed from the classical system and thus produced an incredible chaos of what appear to be overlapping dates. I have tried by periodical comparison with the popular method of numbering the days of the months to keep the chronology clear. Most readers ought, perhaps, to ignore Denys's dates altogether; those who are curious to know the exact dates of his entries will find a splendid guide in the *Handbook of Dates for Students of English History*, edited by C. R. Cheney, and published as No. 4 in the Royal Historical Society's Guides and Handbooks.

Some readers may be vexed by my use of anachronistic words or phrases. However, a historical novel is, by its nature, a kind of anachronism in the first place, inevitably so since it is written at a great remove of time. The best one can do is give the illusion of being in a sort of living present, as if the historical novel were really a modern novel for its own period. If, therefore, whenever a disturbingly contemporary word or phrase appears, the reader will simply translate it for himself into its twelfth-century French equivalent, everything will then seem perfectly natural and proper.

The quotations from the Koran are taken from *The Meaning of the Glorious Koran*, An Explanatory Translation by Mohammed Marmaduke Pickthall, and are used by kind permission of George Allen and Unwin, Ltd.

I am deeply grateful to Dr. Leonard Maidman for providing medical information, to Gisèle Ganz for helping me to struggle through masses of medieval French, to Sue and Jeannie Krochalis for performing valuable research tasks, to my son

7

Christopher Williams for advice and information about ancient music and instruments, and to Norman Kelman for allowing himself to be used as a whetstone with his usual patience and acuity.

TOMORROW'S FIRE

This bed of straw my bottom frays,
Lord, not a penny in my purse;
Those who were friends in better days
Like dust before the wind disperse.
Poets, like paper, can't be thinner,
Or deep the sharpened pen may bite.
Tomorrow's hopes provide my dinner,
Tomorrow's fire must warm tonight.
*   —Rutebeuf (c.1240)*

CONTENTS

I

FRANCE

Little is known of the founder of the distinguished but now extinct family of Courtebarbe, Raymond Surplice, called the Irascible, beyond the fact that he was a vassal of Charles the Bald and married a werewolf. A man of great personal courage and a fearful temper, he appears to have established the fortunes of the house largely through tolls levied on wayfarers who were enticed into staying the night and were never seen or heard of again. His son, Rogier, called the Hot, became the first Seneschal of Courtebarbe, having had the foresight to abandon his family's allegiance to King Odo in favour of the more powerful Hugh Capet. He was rewarded with broad meadows and woodlands on the banks of the Thouet River. It is said of him, in the *Petite Histoire des barons de Poitou*, that he took the name Courtebarbe from his habit of tearing out the hairs of his beard when in a rage. However, there is a story that, having stolen six horses from a neighbour, William of Loudun, known as The Leopard, he is said to have boasted that he had "bearded the leopard for want of a lion". William, hearing of this, fumed, "I will give him a rope for a beard (*corde-barbe*)!" Whatever the truth of the matter, it is an indisputable fact that Rogier died in most unpleasant circumstances at the hands of the men at arms of several local castellans with whom he had had similar disagreements.

During the next two centuries the family prospered. The characters of the heads of the house changed with prosperity; from being contentious, short-tempered, and eager for gain, they began to develop a kind of prudence expressed in a fondness for comfort and contentment. It is reflected in the nicknames they acquired. Instead of the Irascible, or the Hot, the end of the eleventh and the beginning of the twelfth centuries saw a succession of Aimars, Raymonds, and Rogiers called the Cautious, or the Fat. Raymond IV, the Wise, refrained from joining the First Crusade. In the same way, his son Aimar the Silent refused to answer the feudal summons of King Louis VI, claiming a complicated and painful illness. As a result, while the domain of Courtebarbe knew a surprisingly long period of peace and prosperity, it did not expand. By the last quarter of the twelfth century this limitation of the size of the fief meant that its heirs, unable to move into the administration of other properties, had to wait patiently for the death of their father before claiming any lands.

The then Seneschal, Aimar V, had four sons. The first three so far followed a hundred years of tradition as to be called, respectively, Rogier the Slothful, Geoffroy the Sluggish, and Raymond the Motionless. The old lord, already in his seventies, showed no signs of decay, being of that lean type of man who desiccates with age, growing browner, drier, and more sinewy year by year. The three older sons, true to their names, found matters not at all uncongenial. They were perfectly content to wait, each with his wife occupying a chamber or part of a chamber in the castle, for as long as their father chose to live, providing he called them to a well-laden table three or four times a day. Hunting, hawking, and listening to an occasional minstrel gave them quite enough activity to fill up the hours between.

With the fourth son, Denys, it was another story. He was a restless, ambitious, active youth with a talent for poetry. There was also in his nature a good deal of admiration for gold and silver, and a certain impetuosity which made his father mutter that there may have been some truth in the legend about the wife of the first Raymond.

In his journal, fragmentary and casual as it is and lacking the refined polish of a finished work—for evidently it consisted of notes which he planned some day to make into a chronicle of his adventures on the Third Crusade—Denys says of himself: "I was never so unready for simple pleasures of the body that I would liefer lie down alone for weariness than wake in company. I would no sooner have some project in hand than my eye would be wandering, and my mother said of me that I was born under no star but a comet. I was constant only in my wish to learn the making of verse, and even there my patience often ran out so that I was fitter for short ballads than for epics."

If the prospect of waiting for his father's death to grant him a doubtful portion of inheritance was irksome to his ambition, his restlessness alone would have prevented his acceptance of so quiet and uneventful a life as that offered by the domain of Courtebarbe. Furthermore, to learn the mysteries of poetry, the enormous complexities of foot and rhyme, of the forms such as the *sirvente* and the *canzo*, of *accordanza* and *cazensa*, of consonantal rhymes and bastard rhymes and all the rest, it was essential for him to study with a master. Some art he had picked up from visiting minstrels, some from neighbours who trifled with song-making as a courtly accomplishment. But about the year 1180, by which time Denys was eighteen or so, he left home and went off to the city of Poitiers. The famous troubadour, Peire Vidal, was visiting there and Denys attached himself to him, spent what little money he had on presents of food and clothing, and when Vidal left to return to Toulouse, followed him there. In the next year he seems to have learned the basic rules of the poet's craft, first from Vidal, later from Peire of Auvergne and others at the court of the Dauphin, Robert I. Thus, travelling from town to town, from castle to castle, he assumed the life and title of a *trouvère*, the word by which poets were known in the northern parts of France, as they were called *troubadours* in the south. The root is the same: it means a discoverer.

His journal begins with a rather casual itinerary, and its first note of any length concerns one of those crucial turning points in his life which, somehow, were always to be bound up in one way or another with women.

*   *   *

Journal of Denys de Courtebarbe. Extract 1.

vi Id. Nov. mclxxxvii. On this day I commence these records from which, if God wills it, I shall some time make my chronicle. In the name of the Father, the Son, and the Holy Spirit, and imploring especially the protection of the sweet Mother of God, and of the estimable Saint Denys the martyr—like him, I have often enough walked with my head in my hands. . . .

Having served my apprenticeship with Peire Vidal, the king of folly and chief of poets, I took leave of him within the octave of Easter, in the year [1182] and journeyed to the country of Auvergne. Here, I fell in with Peire of Clairmont and by his means procured an introduction to the Dauphin of Auvergne, that gentle prince Robert whom no poet can think of without tears of joy and satisfied hunger. This noble gentleman, although poor enough so that none would ever hold him to ransom, living in a cheese-paring state and ever sewing new sleeves to his coats, yet welcomed in all who knew the mysteries of the Art and could make good songs. I made, in his honour, that sirvente which begins:

'A lord I know whose lands are full of sun,
    Whose coffers golden suns do ever spill . . . etc.'

which I may say in all due modesty is still sung by many a minstrel beyond the Loire without proper credit given to its author. I am not one of those who, dusty-throated, must hire another to sing for him, and I learned early to play both the harp and viol. For the sake of this poem and my own singing I was given a place at his court and there I dwelt for upwards of a twelvemonth, in peace and accord, with much merry-making although I had scarcely two deniers to rub together in my purse. We passed the time in making verses, in games and pastimes, in knightly sports now and then as riding to the quintain and the ring or practising that contest brought into the south by some knights who saw it done by the Moors, the behourd, which is a duel on horseback with blunted spears. There were nine of us trouvères at the Dauphin's court, and minstrels as thick as mice in a barn coming and going. We chose ladies for our loves according to custom, and if there was some lack of variety in our victuals, there was none of games of love.

I had, there, two good friends from whom I learned much. One was the noble Pons of Capduoil, a baron of Puy Sainte-Marie, of great stature and a man of much refinement. Lest the angels should envy perfection, God had placed in him a slight flaw which was that he was so stingy he would not give you a greeting lest he thereby wear out his words. In dicing he would borrow from his neighbours, and if he lost would cry mercy and lackaday, but if he won would vanish from the land for a fortnight until it had been forgotten. He would not use his own dice for fear they should be rubbed

16

smooth and lose their spots. Yet always he used great courtesy and bore himself nobly, smiling and large-hearted so
that if you drank with him in some tavern and he then
rose, saying, 'Alas, I have left my purse at home,' you found
yourself paying the charge with gratitude that such a man
should let you do so much for him. He made fine canzos,
and especially aubades which he sang so sweetly it would
bring tears to your eyes to hear him.

The other was Peire of Clairmont, who for his renown was
called Peire of Auvergne. Although of common blood he
was mild and fair of speech, goodly to look at in spite of a
bad complexion which was, no doubt, the result of that
softness of upbringing we find in the houses of burgesses. His
father had been a merchant and, as is their wont, had dressed
the child in red frocks and fed him on sweetmeats, the sur-
feit thereof coming out in boils and blotches on his face
when he was well grown. His songs were like those of a
nightingale, but, like a bird's songs, seemingly in another
tongue and hard to follow, so that I wrote of him:

> 'Peire of Auvergne has in his voice
> Both high and low notes at his choice,
>   His fame is transmarine;
> A silver stream his verses run,
> His words are fine and fair—yet none
>   Can tell you what they mean.'

I later learned that some attribute this stanza to Peire himself. Peace. I say no more.

I chose for my love Maurina, the wife of a castellan of
the Dauphin's, a little dark lively lady with a sideways look.
She said nothing, but her look spoke for her. She was a
good listener. Yet I could never get a yea or nay from her
to my pleas. I would compose a verse for her and sing it,
and afterward throw myself on my knees and swear I would
die for love of her, and she would but nod, soberly, as one
whose thought is elsewhere, touch my hand with her fingertips smiling absently, and say, 'Play on, fair Denys, you viol
well, by God's head.'

It happened that one evening in summer we all went out
to sit upon the grass outside the walls, and the Lady Joanna,

wife to the Dauphin, for sport said that we should have a Court of Love after the fashion of Queen Eleanor, she who was wedded to the king of England. Then Lady Joanna sat as Chief Justice, and chose three others of her ladies to be judges as well, and called thereafter for any who would submit their cases for arbitrament, of all questions of love. Bernard of Saint-Troye asked, Whether if a man has pledged his love to a lady and sworn to do all she asks of him, and if her first request is that, for love of her, he speak no more to her of love, he may honourably refuse? After some laughing argument the judges then said that a man must be bound by the law set down in the *Regulae Amoris*, to wit, 'That love must refuse nothing to love,' and that he could not in honour turn aside from the first task set him, were it to cast himself into the sea. But the Lady Joanna, in her harsh voice somewhat like that of a man, said, 'Nay, for stronger still is the law which says, That none loves truly if he does not obey the irresistible impulses of love. And therefore, since the lover's deepest impulse is to speak of love, to sing of love, to breathe sighs of love, no man can in all honesty be silent, and I judge that lady at fault who cruelly sets him such a task.' Then all applauded and said that judgment was well rendered.

And others propounded weighty questions of this sort and that, and all the while I could not keep from looking at Maurina with great tenderness. At last, I stepped forth boldly and cried the court's mercy, and begged a judgment. I said, 'My good judges, and you, Madame Justiciar, I ask that the court rule for me against a certain lady who will not say whether she loves me or does not love me. For consider, is not this the worst of cruelties that denies to say yea or nay, but leaves the lover hanging on a long rope so that sometimes his feet touch the ground and he may take breath and deceive himself that he still lives? For there is no greater torment than hope eternally deferred.' At this, indeed, the more part of the judges said that such a thing was much to be blamed, at which Maurina changed colour yet kept her eyes down and did not look at me. But the Lady Joanna glanced from under her dark and bushy eyebrows from me to Maurina, and I understood that she knew full well all that lay between us and of what lady I spoke. She said,

'Each case must be decided on its own merits, and in this case there is something unsaid which is not known to the plaintiff but is known to me. It is that the lady is beloved of another and loves him in return. Yet, being tender-hearted, she cannot confess this, and further it is truly said that whoever is not discreet is not worthy of love. Nor can she, in all gentleness, check the natural desire of another to tell her of his love for, says the *Regulae Amoris*, there is no reason why a lady may not be beloved of two men. And so I judge that there lies no fault in her, but the petitioner must, if he is a true lover, be patient and bear in mind the law, That the lover must in all things give way to the will of his lady.'

Then the court ruled that the lady should be acquitted, but although I smiled and bent my neck I was filled with jealousy. I determined that I would know what other man she had given her heart to. Accordingly, I took counsel with Peire of Auvergne and laid all bare to him and asked him for his help. And when he knew that it was the Lady Maurina I meant, he clapped me on the back, and shook his head and said, 'What? Then you do not know who her lover is? For in truth all the rest of the world knows that it is the Dauphin himself.'

At this, I was choked with bitterness, and tears burst from my eyes. I dashed my head against the wall and wept so that Peire was filled with alarm and brought me hippocras to drink and a wet cloth to put on my forehead where I had bruised it. And he comforted me as best he could, saying wisely, 'Who has no shield must bear the blows,' and 'What can't be cured must be endured,' and 'The pliant reed bends to the wind,' etc., etc., until for very weariness I begged him to be silent.

Now it chanced on the very next day some of us gentlemen were playing the game of *chicane* in which with wooden mallets a wooden ball is beaten from one end of a field to another. And as I came to strike the ball I saw that the Dauphin was standing before the stake. A rage of jealousy possessed me, and before I thought what I did, I struck the ball with all my force and drove it straight at him and hit him with it on the leg a little way above the ankle. He dropped his mallet and, clutching his shinbone with both hands, commenced to hop about crying aloud and speaking of me in immoderate and intemperate language. He was borne from the field by one of his squires. Shortly after, there came to me Pons of Capduoil, with a long face, and also Peire of Auvergne, and they both told me that for the friendship they bore me they judged it wisest if I should pack up my things and depart from the castle, for the Dauphin no longer felt towards me the affection he had hitherto displayed.

I took leave of my comrades with many sighs and tears, but I said no farewell to the Lady Maurina, although it was owing to her coldness that this misfortune had overtaken me. Pons of Capduoil, in parting, allowed me to press upon him my last sou, swearing he loved me well and would repay me in God's good time.

Of my wanderings during the next years I will not write at length. That winter I passed in the lands of Foix and Béziers. In [1184] I journeyed into the lands of the king of Aragon, nor did I return into France until [1185] and was robbed by the way. In the season of Christmas [1186] I was in Paris and there it chanced that as I came out from hearing mass, one day, I saw a poor man set upon by some thieves and beaten, and although I am prudent beyond measure I grew hot with anger and went to help him. I succeeded in chasing them off, and then, seeing that he was shivering with cold since they had stolen his cloak, I was moved to give him mine which was, in any case, old and threadbare. On the next day I fell ill, with coughing and sneezing and an ague from the cold air. Yet mark how the blessed Saint Denys, observing my good deed done without hope of reward, requited me! For that very day, the same man came to visit me in my lodgings and revealed to me that he was in truth a rich burgess of the town, and gave me money and sent wine and fire to cheer me. I made a song for him which gave him great satisfaction, and thus I got through that winter.

That which had driven me forth from my father's house in the first place remained with me all through these years, the restlessness which persuades me that there lies some unperceivable truth beneath and beyond that which we call poetry. I may write of this here for it is not yet my chronicle

nor would I dare otherwise say so, but it has seemed to me
that there was some larger way of poetry I might follow
instead of treading the track beaten out by a hundred others.
For all men know that there are certain forms which poetry
takes, with rhymes and metres and a certain measure, and
to learn this art I gave many years. There are figures which
must be used to describe how a poet feels when he is in love,
and then he writes a canzo; there is a morning song called
an aubade, and an evening song called a serenade, and
who would use the word 'dawn' in an evening song? No
troubadour would write of his true love in a sirvente, or write
of war and battle in a canzo. Yet it has seemed to me there
are things moving within me for which there is no kind of
song. As it has seemed to me there must be a kind of love
for which there is no accepted form. All men know the
forms of love. I have followed them as strictly as the forms of
poetry, like all my fellows. I have loved many a lady according to form, choosing her, writing songs to her, dedicating
myself to her, exchanging such small gifts as will not awaken
covetousness, and so on. Yet it appeared to me, each time,
that I had chosen wrongfully. Something within me whispered, even as I chose, 'This is not she.' Thus I go on searching for that one lady who will, perhaps, one day make herself known to me, as I search for that one verse which will
one day sing itself through my mouth.

Once, I was sitting in a shop which sold roast meat, with
a minstrel, one of that vulgar sort who wear red wigs and
juggle with knives, and sing base songs before the populace.
We had a small fire, and the sleet grated on the closed
shutter. He, idly plucking at his harp, spoke these lines
as if for himself:

> 'As long as kings and noble lords
> Whose mothers all wore golden gowns
> Must end at last between pine boards
> And others have their robes and crowns,
> I, the poor pitchman out of Rennes,
> Will I not die at God's command?
> Well, I have had my fun. Amen.
> Come, honest death, and take my hand.'

I asked him, as if in jest, where he learned this verse, and he shrugged and replied that he had made it out of his head, considering the time, the place, and the season of the year. I said to him that it had no proper style, no cadence, no metaphor, none of the dress of poetry, and besides was full of the common speech and low phrases. He answered that it was no matter to him, for many such stanzas came to him, as he said, from his heart, and were a great comfort to him. I said that if I were to sing such verses myself before some lord, all men of taste would laugh at me. He answered that that was of little moment to him for he cared not whether I sang them or no, and as for the approval of lords he would not give as much attention to it as to a fart but looked to his own approval. He said that he knew well how to earn money by jumping and turning the somersault, by snapping his fingers, whistling bird songs, making snails leap on the table, and singing the lay of Tristan, 'But,' said he, 'for my own pleasure my own measures, and not for any man else.' On the morrow he was gone, nor did we ever meet again. Yet, observe, I have not forgotten his lines. Was there something in them better than elegance? It irks me that I cannot answer this but find myself sometimes repeating them nonetheless.

*

iv Non. Mai. mclxxxix. On this day I sang before the great baron, Eustache de Gramonte, and was welcomed to stay in his castle which lies upon the banks of the Charente in Poitou. And straightway I chose as my lady his wife, Yolanda of Brissac, for her pale skin and golden hair and the wistfulness of her beauty. She accepted my homage. Nevertheless, it must be admitted that I sometimes thought she welcomed my company only as one who would listen to her complaints against her husband, a gross and hairy man. And although she was graceful, she shed water as freely from her eyes at the most trivial mischance as if there were a river in her head.

For two months I paid court to Lady Yolanda, giving her in my poems the *senhal* or secret name of Bel Vezer, which is to say, Fair to the Sight, and sighing after her and lavishing much attention on her. A little after Midsummer Day, when Baron Eustache being abroad with his hawks she and I were in the herb garden alone, I sang for her the aubade I had written, which begins thus:

'Why must the nightingale so soon depart,
And we our scented hawthorn bower fly?
The sun's first ray strikes sadness to my heart,
Ah, love farewell; the dawn invades the sky.'

There were six stanzas, and, by rule, the word 'dawn' appeared in the last line of each. Her eyes rolled up in her head from pure pleasure, and when I pressed her hand she agreed to grant me my chiefest wish. It was, that we should lie all night long side by side, body to naked body, chastely and lovingly, our souls rising to intermingle in bliss in the air above us (as is the way with true lovers). To this she blushingly consented, saying, 'Let it be on that night when my lord rides to Limoges to a conference of barons.' That befell on the eighth of the Ides of July.

And yet, we had no sooner lain down together on that night, than there came a stir in the courtyard with shouting, clatter of horses, and noise of gates, and it appeared that the lord Eustache had returned home. I began to assemble my clothing. But Lady Yolanda, having wrung her hands and wept for as long as it might take a hungry priest to say *benedicite*, began to push me towards the window. I informed her gently that there was no way to climb down the outer wall. She then opened one of the great chests that stood along the wall and which was half full of neatly folded linen. I crossed myself, commended my soul to the Virgin Mother, and climbed in praying that my lord baron would have no need of a clean shirt before morning.

By good fortune there was a little crack between lid and lip of the chest, and through this I could breathe. By it, also, I was not shut off from all entertainment but could hear what was spoken in the room. Thus, I heard my lady ask what it was brought him back that night all the way from Limoges. His reply was such that I came near betraying myself by a sudden start of astonishment.

He said, 'The king of England is dead. The news was brought us in haste by Aimar Taillefer, from Poitiers. He died two days ago, at Chinon, and Count Richard is now king. No man can say what will follow.'

I composed myself as best I could within my chest, to listen if there were any more, and then to wait until they were asleep so that I might steal out. But this news was like to make a change for me, a brave change, if so be Count Richard should recall the word he had once given me along with a certain ring. . . .

* * *

The encounter between Denys and Richard Plantagenet had taken place just a year before. It is necessary to describe the circumstances of the time so that the reader may understand how it happened that the prince of England, Count of Poitou, Duke of Aquitaine, and one of the most notable warriors in the world, should find himself under an obligation to a nobody of a strolling poet.

If the matter of inheritance had been a problem for the sons of Aimar of Courtebarbe, it was even more vexatious for thousands of others. It might be said that Europe was swept by a hurricane of conflicting heirs. Some struggled to secure what was rightfully theirs, others to anticipate by bloodshed what was to come, and still others with nothing at all tried to steal a bite from someone else's table. Richard Plantagenet, whose life was distinguished by extravagances of every sort, carried even this matter to excess. Although he had received Aquitaine and Poitou from his mother, Queen Eleanor, the exertions required to secure and hold these rich and luscious provinces kept him too busy ever to enjoy them. He was like some householder who from dawn to dusk toils to pay mortgages and insurance, wages an endless war against moles, cutworms, caterpillars, and mice, mows his lawn, mends his fences, weeds his garden, and thus never has a moment to sit down in the sun.

At the age of fifteen, Richard was formally invested with the Duchy of Aquitaine, receiving the ring of Saint Valeria and the lance and banner which were the emblems of his state. He did homage and swore fealty to King Louis of France, but the situation was somewhat complicated by the fact that his father, King Henry II of England, had earlier done similar homage in his son's name and could not bring himself to relinquish his guardianship over Richard's possessions.

In Henry's view, the hard-won Plantagenet holdings on the Continent—Anjou, Normandy, Maine, Brittany, and the rest —must be portioned out to his sons during his lifetime so that all men would know his intentions before he died. However, he was not yet dead, and he wanted it clearly understood that there was only one President of the Board with a controlling interest in the stock, and that his name was Henry II. It was a position nobody seemed able to grasp, neither his sons, nor his wife Eleanor, who detested him with the same fierce amplitude with which she loved her boys, nor his chief opponent and liege lord the king of France.

In 1170 Henry had had his oldest son, Young Henry, crowned king of England. He had no intention of relinquishing the crown himself; the act was more symbolic than anything else. Lovingly, he served his son on bended knee. Young Henry was used to adulation—he had a great many admirers, chief amongst whom was himself. He remarked that it was only right he should be so served, "Since," said he, "I am a king's son, while my father is merely the son of the Count of Anjou." It was obvious he would not rest content as a mere figurehead, a point of view his mother shared. Thus, a year after Richard's investiture as duke of Aquitaine, he and Young Henry, along with their younger brother Geoffrey, who held Brittany, banded into a league to force their father to give up everything to them. Eleanor was behind them, as was the king of France, to whom the energetic King Henry had always been irksome. There began a merry round-robin of marching, counter-marching, burning of castles, bashing of helms, surrenders and counter-surrenders, which was to last in one way or another for the next fifteen years or more.

To begin with, King Henry rapidly subdued the young princes. But meantime, a number of irritable barons had risen in revolt, some against him, some against Richard in Poitou, and some, for lack of anything better to do, against each other. The business was complicated by a good deal of skirmishing and plundering by bands of private mercenaries who, being unemployed at the moment, had to keep in practice for fear of growing rusty. Richard was sent by his father to overcome all the opposition, and in the course of some two years of brilliant campaigning succeeded in doing so. He then went a little further under his father's urging, and plunged into Gascony where he captured a number of castles and towns.

But meanwhile the restless barons, notably Vulgrin of Angoulême, Geoffrey of Rancogne, and Aimar of Limoges, rose up again behind him. The next two years were spent bloodying their noses and taking their strongholds away from them. After a short breathing-space another league was formed, this one organized by the troubadour Bertrand de Born, but with the same membership. Another couple of years passed in putting it down. Now, having had enough of this kind of external warfare, it was felt the time had come for a return to fratricidal strife and both Young Henry and his brother Geoffrey turned on Richard and on their father. But before this could go too far, Young Henry fell ill, and after considering the matter from one angle and another, determined there was little chance of overcoming his father, and accordingly died. He was followed, three years later, by his brother Geoffrey, so Richard, contrary to expectation, was left heir to the throne.

All during this period, Old Henry had never ceased from scheming and plotting, against his sons, against the kings of France—first Louis, then his son Philip—and against a variety of knights and nobles up and down the land of France. A modern statesman would naturally have made long-range plans, intelligently conceived and carefully executed. Alas, Henry was, like his contemporaries, a medieval personage, and thus simply behaved according to the requirements of the moment. The upshot was that tensions continued, fighting went on and on, and nothing was settled to the day of Henry's death. As for Richard, he found himself now going at his father's orders to fight against a couple of barons, now suddenly facing King Philip Augustus, now attempting to make peace between Philip and Henry, constantly misunderstood by everyone, and never with a week of rest in which he could pull off his armour and draw a tranquil breath.

Since he was a man of strength and courage and was to be found always at the head of his knights, it can hardly be said that his life was ever really out of jeopardy. However, in the midst of one of the most confusing of his campaigns, in the year 1188, he faced a moment of truly grave danger.

He had just put down the annual outbreak of rebellious barons headed, as usual, by Lusignan, Rancogne, and Angoulême, capping the affair by taking the absolutely untakeable stronghold of Taillebourg for the second time in nine years. No sooner was this accomplished than word came to him that Raymond of Toulouse, whom he had trounced some years before, was once again in arms and had seized some merchants of Poitou and handled them most discourteously, blinding and castrating some of them and executing others. There is reason to believe that behind this sudden outbreak on Raymond's part lay a certain amount of inducement by King Henry, still busy with his own schemes: Richard, carried away by the eloquence of the Archbishop of Tyre who had come to Europe to plead for help in the Holy Land against the growing power of the Infidel, had taken the Cross along with his father and King Philip of France, and it is suspected that Henry, who had no design whatever for going off to the East, sought for ways of dissuading his son from putting into practice what should have been no more than a politic announcement of good intentions.

Whether this was the case or not, Richard dropped everything and went galloping off to the south, where he briskly laid waste a part of Gascony, seized a number of castles, and finally advanced to the very walls of the city of Toulouse. This was more than anyone had bargained for. King Philip Augustus, in retaliation, entered Aquitaine and in a little over a month had snapped up almost everything claimed by England in Berry and Auvergne. Henry cried "Murder!" at this and began mustering his own host in Normandy, while Richard wearily turned round and trotted northward again.

Philip had taken the key city of Châteauroux, in Berry, leaving it to be guarded by a knight of great prowess, one William des Barres. It seemed to Richard a worthy feat to retake the city, and he sat down before it with his knights and a large body of those free-lances still called Brabantines even though most of them came from the marches of Spain and would have died of pneumonia among the marshes of Friesland.

Denys de Courtebarbe had voyaged down from Paris that mild summer, sampling the comfortable little castles on the eastern side of the Loire, from Auxerre to Vézelay and then

to Nevers where he crossed the river. The wines were strong
and rich, particularly the white wines of Chablis with their
subtle astringency; the country fare was copious, with splendid
hams flavoured with juniper berries, and jolly pies of game
and poultry. Denys had sold his viol in Paris and had taken to
the harp, instead, as being easier to play for his own accom-
paniment, and not once had he to draw his sword, for everywhere he found a hospitable reception for his singing and
poetry. However, he had the misfortune to come into the
duchy of Berry at about the same time as King Philip entered
it, and he found uproar and disturbance everywhere. He took
refuge in Châteauroux shortly after it fell into the hands of the
French, and he was on the point of retracing his steps to the
relative quiet of the eastern provinces when Count Richard
arrived before the city walls.

Richard did not actually have enough men to besiege the
place, and consequently there was a good deal of traffic in and
out of the city. One morning, therefore, Denys packed up his
saddlebags and set out through the Bourges Gate only a few
minutes behind a foraging party which had ridden out to pick
up what it could. He walked his horse a short distance along
the road and had turned in the saddle to look back at the
walls and towers of the town, when he heard whoops and
screeches and the clash of steel and found himself abruptly
caught up in the midst of a running fight, like a chip in a
whirlpool.

The foraging party had run straight into an ambush of
Poitevin knights and men at arms and was trying to get back
to the shelter of the walls. Denys dragged at the reins, caromed
off a man in a torn leather coat and managed to dodge a blow;
for an instant he was knee to knee with another man and then
he had pulled clear, off the road. He would have galloped
away then and there had not his attention been fixed on the
leader of the Poitevins.

He was a tall, broad-shouldered man whose reddish mail
was webbed with silvery lines where sword-strokes had gashed
away the rust and left the steel links shining. He wore no
helm and even his mail coif was thrown back on his shoulders
so that his long auburn hair streamed behind him. His teeth
shone in his beard, his eyes were wide with the madness of
battle; he laughed and shouted as his arm rose and fell with the

vigorous concentration of his fighting. He was a man who enjoyed his work and gave it his full attention. He swung a long-handled axe as lightly as a switch, its blade and haft plastered with blood, and his right hand was as dark with blood as if he were wearing a glove. To watch him was like watching an ancient epic come alive, the song of Roland or of Ogier, the very epitome of knighthood which devotes itself to combat.

Denys could not take his eyes off him. He guessed at once that this must be Count Richard of Poitou, and he knew why some who had seen him in battle called him a lion; the word sprang at once to mind, for he was irresistible, ferocious, and tawny.

There came suddenly loud whistles and battle-cries from the city. A small party of horsemen dashed out of the Bourges Gate. Count Richard drew rein, shading his eyes. The fighting ceased, and the men of the foraging party separated themselves from their foemen and drew off. Denys could see then that there were only three knights with Richard and eight or ten mounted sergeants in leather jacks and steel caps. Half a dozen dead men sprawled along the road, and two dead horses, while a third kicked and whinnied, trying to get to its feet.

One of the Poitevin knights said something in a loud, hoarse voice: "—ten to one—" Denys heard. The sergeants turned their mounts and broke away in a clump, back along the road at a gallop, one of them lolling forward over his saddle horn.

"Come back, you lousy bastards!" yelled a knight with a blue star painted on his shield. His voice cracked with anger. Richard laughed, swinging his axe.

In that space the men from the city had joined the remainder of the foraging party. They all together rode at Richard and his three. Still, Denys did not move, although he told himself that this was none of his business.

The air was full of particles of dust. Blades glimmered. There was a loud and terrible scream that made Denys start. It came not from a man but from a horse. He saw that Richard's mount had sunk down under him; the count threw himself free and rolled over in the road. He sprang up, holding his shield over his head. He had lost his axe.

A knight thrust at him with a lance. He caught the shaft and pulled the man towards him. They struggled for a moment and the wooden shaft broke with a crack clearly heard over the tumult. Richard leaped back, holding the lance-head as if it were a short sword, its banner fluttering over his bloody hand.

Denys caught a glimpse of his face. There was upon it a grim shadow. He no longer smiled, but now he looked more leonine than ever and more dangerous.

"Yield!" someone cried.

Someone else shouted, "Cut him down!"

Denys put spurs to his horse without further thought. He swept into the circle of men surrounding the count, slashed at one man even as his horse crashed into another and sent it bolting away. The knights wheeled this way and that in confusion. Denys halted beside the count and held out his hand.

"Up!" he snapped.

Richard vaulted behind him. At once, Denys swung his steed and was away up the road, Richard clinging to his belt. The others chased them for a bit, and then stopped and turned for the town, for the Poitevin sergeants who had run off now came cantering back along the road, waving their weapons.

Denys stopped and Richard slid off the crupper, wiping his face with the banner of the lance-head which he still held.

He looked towards the city and said, bitterly, "Guy, Elias, and Centol, all taken or dead. And a good horse——"

He glanced at the sergeants who sat motionless, most of them staring with stony faces at the ground. "Filth," he said. "But what can you expect?" He crooked a finger at one of them. "Give me your horse, you." Silently, the man got down and held the stirrup while his master mounted.

Richard now turned his eyes on Denys. They were blue as ice, with finely arched brows and long lashes. He smiled, and said, "My thanks. It's a nasty thing for a knight to be on foot. You know me?"

"I know you, Count of Poitou."

"Are you of gentle blood?"

"I am. I am named Denys de Courtebarbe."

"Ah! Your land lies where?"

"Not far from Saumur, upon the Thouet."

"You saved my life. I am grateful. How did you come to be there on the spot?"

"I am a trouvère. I left Châteauroux this morning because

it is a little too uproarious for me. I prefer the quiet life, my lord Count."

Richard chuckled. He pulled a ring off his finger, a rough amethyst set in gold. "In that case, come and see me when there is a little peace in my lands, trouvère," he said. "I am fond of music and poetry. Call on me for your reward. But see to it you have a good song ready."

"I will," said Denys, taking the ring and bowing courteously. He watched as Richard rode off, followed by his men at arms. He put the ring on his finger, thinking of the count's blunt-nosed lion face, his lively blue eyes, and his golden hair tangled with the rings of his mail coif and spattered with blood. That was a lord a man could follow, he said to himself. But also, a man to beware of. Who would venture to pat a lion?

It was of this incident that he thought now, huddled in the chest while Baron Eustache prepared for bed. His mind had turned to Richard from time to time over the past year, as in his travels he had heard news of him. Richard had tried to bring about concord between King Henry and King Philip and, for his pains, had found nothing but strife. It had been widely rumoured that the old king loved and preferred his youngest son, John Lackland, above Richard, his heir, and this had become openly evident at a meeting of the kings at Whitsuntide, when Henry proposed that the French princess, Aloysia, whom he had been holding in ward as Richard's betrothed, should marry John instead and be dowered with the Plantagenet lands in France. The upshot of this was that Richard had no choice but to join with Philip against his own father for the protection of his inheritance.

"Come to me when there is peace in my lands," Richard had said. Well, the conflict between father and son was finished, at any rate, provided Baron Eustache's news were true.

Denys yawned. It was stuffy in the chest. He heard the slap as Eustache flung his riding boots into a corner and the clinking and clanking as he threw his sword and belt over the perch on the wall.

Yolanda, her voice muffled, said, "How did King Henry die?"

"Wretchedly, so Aimar said," Eustache replied. "Is there wine in that pitcher?"

There came a gulping, like a hound drinking. He sighed, and belched. "God, riding gives me heartburn. I'm not as young as I was," he said. Denys heard the bed-boards creak as the baron lowered himself to the edge of it, and he could imagine the hairy belly bulging over his knees as he sat. There came a couple of sensual groans and a rasping sound which puzzled Denys until he realized that it was Eustache rapturously scratching his shins where his hose had chafed him a-horseback.

"Wretchedly," he repeated, as if he enjoyed the thought. "In Chinon. He went there after that last discussion with Philip, the one that came to a bad end. They say after he died the servants stole everything in the house and stripped his body so that he lay there naked. Some boy threw a summer cloak over him." He chuckled. "Aimar said they used to call him Henry Shortmantle, so he was living up to his name. *Living* up to it. Understand?"

He snorted and strangled with laughter.

"Well, God rest his soul, the old devil," he said, heaving himself into the bed and floundering around for a bit. To Denys, it sounded as though the bed were about to collapse. Then he added, sleepily, "That put an end to our meeting, in any case. Nobody knows what will happen now. Richard king of England! Tomorrow I'll get after my steward, and I want the castellans called in. . . ."

"Poor man," Yolanda sniffled, her gentle heart touched as ever by any misfortune even if it was not her own. "To lie all alone that way. Oh, dear, what a dreadful way to die." She saw herself, forsaken and stripped, a lovely and deserted corpse. "I must just get up for a moment and say a prayer for his poor soul."

"Shut your trap," said her husband, amiably. "You can pray all you like in the morning. Let me get some sleep. I've been two hours in the saddle."

There was silence, pierced now and then by a scarcely audible whimper from Yolanda, and an occasional snorting breath as Eustache composed himself to slumber.

Denys had a crick in the neck. He managed to get one hand up under his cheek and gently massaged what he could reach of his neck muscles with his fingertips. He would have to wait for at least another half-hour before he could be certain the baron was sound enough asleep to risk pushing up the lid of the chest. He wondered whether Yolanda had forgotten him entirely, and hoped that she had. The last thing he wanted was for her to come weeping and sighing over him at this hour and in these circumstances.

He tried to relax, and ran over a few verses in his head. Richard wanted him to bring a song. . . . One had to be careful what one said in a song made for a king. Barons were bad enough, counts and dukes touchier yet, but kings! An elegy on the death of old Henry? It would, perhaps, be wiser not to mention old men at all. "A king I know whose lands are full of sun. . . ." Good God, no. England was said to be as dark and wet as if it were at the bottom of the Narrow Sea. It was said that in England the only difference between night and day was that in the day you went out into the rain. English cocks gargled instead of crowing. "A king I know whose lands are wide and wet. . . ." That would not make him very welcome.

He thought of songs, and songs mixed up with rain. His mind touched lightly on that minstrel he had once met, the two of them sitting in the steamy chill of the cook-house while rain and sleet rattled outside. All that winter he could never quite get warm. Or his face would be hot from a fire but his back frozen.

He remembered how it had been when, as a boy of seven, he had been shipped off to the castle of his father's cousin, Raymond of Beaupréau, to serve as a page. Frozen fingers, cold nose, and six of them huddling together in the sheepskins to keep warm, shivering with chill and homesickness. Like mice, they were. Mice in a barn; I must remember that, he thought. Naked baby mice in a warm litter of wool, and playing innocent games to keep ourselves warm, the rubbings and gigglings and twitterings which helped you to forget the security of home, the lavender-scented linen, the mother's enfolding body. Lord Raymond's castle was cold, always cold, always full of penetrating dampness from its flooded ditches. But home, Courtebarbe? The river was somehow kinder there and the dampness known and affectionate with frogs and fish and long reeds that served as spears in the game of the four sons of Aymon.

The Four Sons. That had been his favourite of all stories.

Lying among the dry rushes on the warm stones near the hearth, in winter, with snow filtering softly down now and then through the smoke hole in the roof of the hall, a bearskin thrown over him, and his mother's foot in a soft leather shoe resting on his back and nudging him with gentle absent-mindedness from time to time, while the minstrel with harp on knee sang the Song of the Four Sons of Aymon. And he would think of his three brothers, already away in the world, serving their apprenticeship elsewhere as pages, the oldest one, Rogier, nearly old enough already to be learning the trade of arms. No premonitory fright touched him, then, that he would himself be so soon pushed out of doors, sent away to study the arts proper to a gentleman. He knew that it would come, one day, but he had had no understanding of the future; the future was only tomorrow, when he would track rabbits in the forest in the snow. The minstrel, a calculating eye on his host sang of Aymon, of how the Emperor Charlemagne with his own hands gave the accolade to those four noble brothers, Renaud, Alard, Guichard, and Richard, on Christmas day; of how Renaud angrily slew the Emperor's nephew with a chessboard, and how Aymon, proud vassal, turned against his own sons rather than betray his liege lord. And of how, dressed as beggars, the four came home to Dordone, and their mother, knowing them through every disguise, fell upon them weeping: "Renaud, my son, conceal it not, if in truth thou art Renaud then in God's name who is all-powerful confess it." And all those listening to the song sighed deeply, one great sigh in the hall, and tears glittered in his mother's eyes and rolled soundlessly down her cheeks. Denys, his head pillowed on his arms, watching her with one sleepy eye, would think, "Don't cry, Mama. All will come right in the end, and I will go to the Holy Land—I Renaud (but he was the eldest not the baby) —and in the end become a saint."

He grinned to himself. Little sainthood he found in Cousin Raymond's house. Only fetching and carrying, from the stables and kennels to the kitchen and bedchamber, always at someone's command: "Here, what's-your-name, hold this hank of wool. Come, child, pick up my stool, my linen, my needle, my spindle. Stand here with this cup. Run to the kitchen and fetch a sop for the babe." And so on, until in exhaustion he learned to doze standing in a dim corner at odd moments.

By the time he was eight, he had learned to feel in his sleep the approach of someone ready to give him a slap and wake him up with an errand. "But this is how you learn knighthood, in the discipline of servitude. A knight should be humble and serviceable. Let Jean the Farmer spoil his children now, they will pull the plough later. As for you, if you ever hope to wear belt and sword and govern men, you must learn to govern yourselves." Thus that good chaplain, Dom Felix, clucking at the pages and younger squires, with the odour of onions strong on him, for he ate them like apples for the sake of humility and the cold in the head which he had from September until May. Dominus vobiscum. Et tibi pax, Dom Felix, by God you must be melted away to pure onion juice by now if there is anything left of you at all.

There was this much better in Lord Raymond's castle, though, that he loved minstrels and trouvères and had more of them about him than Denys's father could abide. When Denys was eight he began to learn the harp and the viol and to copy the making of verses from some of these visitors. He heard many more songs, too, stirring and hair-raising ballads: the Song of William, the Song of Roland, the Song of Huon, and dozens of others, each with its procession of worthy heroes, each full of satisfying bloodshed, of cracked bones and spilled brains, of the heads of paynim flying through the air like footballs: Garin tearing out his enemy's heart with his hands, Jourdain shearing off the ear of the traitor Fromont. . . .

Jourdain. He had almost entirely forgotten that story. God, how it had terrified him once so that hearing it one time when he must have been about twelve he could not listen but had to put his fingers in his ears. But why? He could not remember it, he could recall no line of it, nothing but that one glimpse—was it perhaps a dream?—in which someone (perhaps not Jourdain after all?) struck with his sword at a gilded and bejewelled helm which turned the blade so that it cut off an ear instead. Why should it have frightened him so? He had heard many worse tales. What was an ear more or less, the ear of a traitor, that it should leave such a poison of terror in him?

He could see in a high-raftered iron hall, lighted by unearthly torches haloed with coruscations like those which appear when you clench your eyelids, a long festal table. And there sat

Fromont, with open red mouth and sharp teeth, licking out a tongue like a serpent's. A sword descending, himself holding it. There were jewels, great carbuncles, smaragds, uncut diamonds, beryls like drops of sea water, flying like spray.

Fromont, an unctuous fat man, offered him a plate on which lay a round-pointed breadknife and a napkin. He lifted the napkin and recoiled with loathing, for there was an ear on the plate. He threw it violently from him. Fromont was insistent. "Please take it," he said. "It's good for you. How do you expect to grow up to be a knight?"

"I don't want to be a knight," said Denys. He began to sob.

"Mother will be very angry," Fromont said. He took up a broom and began to sweep crystalline blood together amongst the rushes. The blood tinkled like broken pottery.

Jourdain dropped from the ceiling, landing lightly on the balls of his feet. "That's the way you do it," he said. "And swing, with the right arm, so!" He demonstrated, using a large wooden sword. "Do you see? Catch the bastard under the arm as he lifts his shield."

He winked. "If you use your sword properly you can cut him in two. That'll teach him. Understand?"

"I understand," Denys said. "But you're hurting my ear."

And indeed someone had pulled his ear away from his head until it was joined to him only by a long, thin, elastic cord of flesh. Staring from the corners of his eyes he could see it vanishing into the darkness. A cry of horror and pain bulged in his throat, and he clapped his hand to his head, whining, "Let go. Please let go."

He broke up out of the dream in bewilderment, remembering in a confused way where he was. The lid of the chest was open and someone was helping him out. He was so cramped that involuntarily he cried out as he straightened.

"Shh!" the other hissed.

"Is that you, lady?" he groaned.

"It is not," said the voice of Baron Eustache. "You were making enough noise to wake the dead. She can sleep through anything, but I'll be damned if I can. Look, trouvère, I've had a hard day, I have been two hours or more in the saddle. Get to hell out of here."

"My lord, I——"

Eustache thrust Denys's clothes into his arms, mumbling,

"Ah, Christ, my shirts——! Go! I'm too weary to harm you tonight. Besides, everyone knows about troubadours. . . ." He gave Denys a shove towards the door. "Whatever you do," he added, in a growl, "don't let me see your face in the morning."

He limped back to bed and was snoring before Denys had reached the bottom of the stair.

2

ENGLAND

Journal of Denys de Courtebarbe. Extract 2.

vij Id. Jul. mclxxxix. On this day I came to the city of Saumur where the Count of Poitou held court having come thither from Fontevrault where his father, King Henry, had been laid in the earth. Thinking of which, as I ascended the hill on which the castle stands, there came into my head the lines of that justly famed plaint written by Bertrand de Born upon the death of the Young King, Richard's brother:

> 'If all the sighs, the tears, the grey despair,
> And all the woes of which our age is wrought,
> And all the grief which mortal men must bear,
> Were heaped together, all would be as naught
> Against the death of the young English king. . . .'

There would be few such plaints written on the death of the old king but thanksgiving offered from many mouths, as when some ancient tower, a nest of robber folk, is at last overthrown. I heard on every side the rumours of Richard's clemency, as for example to William the Marshal, that strong warrior and foremost among knights, who had opposed him in the past out of loyalty to the king but whom he now freely pardoned and made great. And it was said that his bounty had no limits, that he gave as the saying is with both hands, at which my heart was much uplifted.

But there were many in line before me to taste of that bounty. It was none so easy to come near to the count (for so we still thought of him, as he was not yet king nor would be until he had gone to England to receive the crown). I dare swear every trouvère and minstrel and jongleur and singer and dancing wench in all the lands of France swarmed like bees to this new king bee so that not only could I not come within a hundred paces of the castle but that night I had to sleep under the arches of the Loire bridge for want of a better bed. It was woesomely wet, and during the night it rained and my harp had my cloak so that I sat and shivered and sneezed until daybreak. Then I was hoarse and gave up hope of singing, and that day the count rode forth with all his following and set out on the road to Séez. That was a five days' journey, and then five days more to Rouen, and throughout that time I hung upon the skirts of his train along with a hundred others living on crusts and hope.

Rouen is a great and fair city, the main part whereof lies upon the northern bank of the river Seine, with a bridge connecting it to the other shore where there is a fine suburb, and here I found lodging in the house of a merchant who was content that I should sing him such of those songs the Normans love best, mainly of war. For it is said, "The north loves war, but the south loves life." In the cathedral, on Thursday, which was the thirteenth of the kalends of August, Count Richard received the sword and banner of the duchy of Normandy. It was girded on him by the archbishop of Rouen, and all the people sang *Jubilate*. I came there to see if I might catch a glimpse of lord Richard, and so I did when he came out on the steps of the cathedral to receive the fealty of the people. Very noble he looked, in a fair long coat of scarlet and vair, crowned with the ducal coronet. As I stood in the great press that filled all the square I felt a heavy hand clap me on the shoulder, and turning I beheld Pons of Capduoil, whom I had not seen in six years. Now listen, and you shall hear how a great good came of this chance meeting through the benevolence of the holy Saint Denys and the intervention of Our Lady.

Pons and I embraced and made our way out of the throng to the river's edge where there were some small wine-shops for the sailors and fishermen who dwelt thereabouts. We sat down and when we had drunk together Pons told me that he had lately come from Beauvais where the lord bishop had given him good entertainment for upwards of a year, but they had had a falling-out over the matter of some fifty pounds, money of Paris, which had found its way from the purse of the bishop's almoner into the hands of the deserving poor. 'But,' I said, 'surely the bishop could find no cause for complaint in such a worthy act?' Whereupon Pons replied, 'You speak truly, Denys, it was a worthy act, and as God lives I could find no poor so deserving as myself. But bishops, as you know, are notably greedy and crabbed and I, being a large-hearted man, would no longer stay with him for upon my soul's welfare I swear I love charity above all else in a holy man.'

Then we spoke of Count Richard, and Pons told me he had hoped to get some gain from a song he had written in Richard's honour and this had brought him to Rouen, but now he saw there were trouvères gathered together in such profusion to that end, that he had determined to go southward once more, maybe into the lands of the Count of Saint Gilles, and to bring him that same song. I said that Count Raymond had no love for Richard even though he had sworn fealty to him, whereat Pons said he thanked God Raymond's name had the same number of syllables as Richard's, and it were no great matter to change one name for another in the song. He told me he was living in the house of a good soul, a weaver, who was greatly honoured to have a trouvère of such noble blood and reputation sleep beneath his roof and therefore would take no money although Pons pressed it upon him. Then Pons said he would not depart from Rouen until Richard left the country, for with all the knights and barons in the city there was much good sport in dicing and ball-play and jousting at which a man like himself might earn both money and knightly harness. He loved well the tourney and the behourd and, being tall and well-made, often overthrew his adversaries and took their armour and horses to ransom. As for dice, he was as fond of hazard as a monk of his beads. I said that I would come to see him in his lodgings on the morrow, and with that we took leave of one another. But first, coming to pay for the wine we had drunk, Pons cried alack! he had forgot his purse and had not a sou and, casting his arms about my neck with a smile, begged me to pay for both and he would well requite me. I had no money and so I left my dagger in payment, which had a silver hilt in which was set a splinter of the shaft of one of the arrows with which Saint Sebastian had been martyred, which I thought ill to part with.

That same day, Count Richard rode out to the fortress of

Gisors where, so I heard, he later met with the king of France and they pledged amity and an end to the strife between them, now that the old king was dead. And as they had before taken the cross, they now swore to go on crusade together in the Lenten season of the following year. It was said that as the count departed from Gisors the bridge of the castle broke beneath his weight and cast him and his horse in the ditch. Some said that this was an evil omen, but I thought myself it was no more than a tribute to Richard's great size and weight, beyond that of other men.

Now that same evening, having heard the news that Richard had gone to Gisors, I took counsel with myself to determine what I should do. Little profit it seemed to me would come of dragging behind him like the train of a lady's gown which gathers dirt and is good for nothing but to kick out of the way. There were but two choices before me, so it seemed, either to put aside further attempts to bring myself to Richard's notice, or else to go to England and there try to come nigh him when he should arrive. This latter seemed good to me, for by then there would drop off many of the court followers and trouvères who could not afford to pay for a boat over the Narrow Sea. But then, I reminded myself, I was in the same plight: as matters stood I could as soon fly across as buy passage. Accordingly, I knelt in my chamber and prayed to Saint Denys and to Our Lady to succour me, and so in much puzzlement and heaviness of heart went to bed.

The next day, about the hour of nones, the heat of midday having somewhat abated, I strolled over the bridge into the main part of the city, and went to the house in the weavers' quarter where Pons dwelt. As I drew near there came out into the street Pons and two other gentlemen in light summer mantles of gay colours, one of whom I knew to be the young knight Gervais de Tankarville, son of the grand chamberlain of Normandy, a most liberal and open-handed youth but much addicted to lust; the other I knew not. Pons greeted me and said that they were going to the house of Gervais to play at dice, whereat Gervais entreated me to accompany them if I would. We walked along together, singing merrily, and as we went Pons took me by the elbow and led me a little aside as if he would make water against the wall of a house.

He said to me, soft in my ear, 'These be covetous men, very hot for play. Have you any money in your bag?' For answer, I showed him that it was empty save for a holy medal of Saint Thomas in pewter which, for its resemblance to a silver penny, I hoped to pass off if I should find a taverner in too much haste to look closely. Said he, 'See, then, Denys, give me your purse and let you take mine which is full of money, as I know you are an honest man, and thus may I keep prudent in play, nor need you join in at all.' To this I agreed, and so we went on.

Thus we came to a fair house which the family of Tankarville maintained within the city and passed into a fine hall where were three or four other gentlemen already in play around a table. Gervais offered us wine and then, the play having finished, called for the dice and swore he felt lucky and would nick three throws out of three, 'For as I awoke this morning,' said he, 'I saw seven starlings in the garden that flew up four and three, wherefore seven is my number.' They all then cried out that one, William de Clères, should be the setter and place the stakes, and they all bet one way and another. Gervais said to Pons, 'Come, my true heart, Capduoil sweet friend, bet you along with me.' Pons, for answer, took out my purse and opened it with a rueful face, saying, 'As God lives, I have not a penny but I will make shift with what my dear companion Denys de Courtebarbe will loan me.' At this, I had no choice but to take out the purse he had given me and which was full of silver money, both of Tours and Paris, and gave him as he asked five deniers.

Then they played, and Gervais calling seven threw in the first throw with a six and one, and the second throw again with seven. They called for more wine, and the stakes doubled, Pons playing with what he had on the table, and again Gervais called seven and nicked, three and four, so that such good fortune I never saw the like of. They played on, and the play grew hotter, and they all pushed to the table so that I was justled somewhat aback and found myself standing alone near the door.

And at this moment there came a mist before my eyes, and methought I saw the image, as it were, or simulacrum of the good Saint Denys holding his mitred head between his palms, which same smiled at me and a voice said, low but clear, 'Fair son, go forth and take ship to England as you desire, for lo, the money lies within your hand.'

With that I was, as it seemed, transported into the street by no power of my own and so carried miraculously in the space of two days to the port of Honfleur, where I found a ship that was lading wine for Portsmouth and got passage for myself and the horse I had purchased before leaving Rouen. I commended myself into the hands of God and set sail upon the vast, heaving, and unfriendly deep.

How long we were upon the water I cannot say for I was the whole time in great perturbation of spirit, in dolorous fear of death, and vomiting in such wise that it seemed to me I would fetch up the soles of my feet through my mouth. But God preserved the vessel—and, indeed, the Master Shipman, who stood the whole time at the helm laughing so that I deemed he was out of his wits, said that this was a smooth and easy crossing and that these I thought to be waves were in reality no more than ripples such as you might find on a stew pond. Nevertheless, when I was once again upon the dry land I knelt down and gave thanks to Our Lord that He had seen fit to make me a man of noble blood and not a sailor.

It now appeared to me that the land of the English was not so wet as I had been told, for the sun shone and in the fields the reapers worked with their gowns tucked up into their belts. In Portsmouth I rested and refreshed myself until the earth ceased to move under my feet, and much did I admire this great and busy port. There dwell within it many a hundred men, yet for a wonder it had not yet received a royal charter which was a matter of some complaint among the folk. From here there runs northwards toward London a street going by way of Chichester and thence to Guildford, and I set out in company with some monks from the cathedral convent of Chichester who, having come to Portsmouth to buy ropes, tar, and other necessaries for the rebuilding of their cathedral which had lately burned, were now returning home. I could speak no word of their tongue, but their steward was of good birth and spoke French, and thus through him I conversed with them. I sang them songs by the way, and when we were come to Chichester they kept me with them and gave me lodging for the night and good cheer,

and when I set out again their abbot bade them wrap for me
a store of bread, cheese, and dried herrings to last me on the
road. He told me that when I should have gone over the hills
they call the Downs, an easy day's journey a-horseback, I
would come near the village of Pulborough to a newly-
founded convent of Black Monks whose prior would give
me shelter.

I rode over those Downs which are chalky hills, very rolling,
not very high, and wooded with a thick and ancient wood.
The day held fine and I was blithe of heart and heard larks
singing. At midday, being come upon the downward slope,
I ate of bread and cheese and looked abroad upon the vale
wherein I could see among the trees ploughed and planted
strips, grazing land, thatch, and the square tower of a church,
lying far below me. I thought this a rich and plenteous-
looking land. Then I remounted and came down the hill, my
reins slack, my head nodding from the heat of the sun and
thus, I know not how, missed the track and took a side-road,
yet I was not aware of it for all this country was strange to me.
So I came at length along grazing common whereon a flock
of sheep browsed and three or four fellows lay talking together
under the shade of a tree. I drew rein and hailed them,
speaking the name of that priory I had been told of: 'Hardham?' said I, as best I might for the barbarous difficulty of
the English word.

They got up and came towards me, and stood staring at
me. They were dressed cleanly enough in smocks with their
legs bound in the English fashion, wearing knives and carrying long crooks or staves. One of them, a great hulking man,
spoke in his villainous tongue, and the others growled. They
came still closer, and the first laid hold of me and pulled me
from the saddle.

I mislike to be so handled, and by peasants such as in
France would never dare do such a thing. I broke free of
his grasp and drew my sword, putting my back against my
horse. In soft language I protested this incivility to a traveller, meanwhile considering within myself whether it were
better to run against them or to try to mount and gallop off
before they could set upon me. They stood regarding me,
talking among themselves and bending on me such grim and
glittering looks that my heart sank and I was filled with regret

that I had ever left my own country to come among such uncouth fellows.

At this juncture there came the sound of hoofs, and I saw canter across the meadow a man on horseback with a falcon on his fist, and behind him a cadger with a perch of hawks across his pommel and another man armed with a short bow and sword. I knew the leader could only be a knight or squire from the peregrine he bore and thus I hailed him, saying, 'Good sir, if these be your dogs whip them off.'

When he had ridden up I saw him to be fair-haired and smooth of face, of a most mild and sunny appearance so that I could not help but be drawn to him. He greeted me, saying, 'Fear not, they are but men of my manor,' and turning to them with a smile spoke to them in their own speech, although somewhat haltingly as I judged. They thereupon, spitting on the ground and lowering, turned and went off.

He said to me that they meant no harm, it being no more than their rude English way. 'They are,' he said, 'as children, responding not so much to reason as to gentle words and affection, or to the rod if it be necessary.' I said naught to this but asked him whether it were far or not to the priory of Hardham. He laughed, saying I was well off the mark and had come two leagues from the high road. His name, he said, was Arthur de Hastynge, and he prayed me to come with him to his house where I should rest and we would take counsel over what were best to do. And seeing my harp which hung in its bag behind my saddle, he said that few indeed were the trouvères or minstrels who came to these remote parts, and that he would take it as a great favour if I would play and sing for him whatever I would. And so pleasantly and courteously did he speak to me that I could deny him nothing but went with him, nor did I guess that by this means I should be brought in the end to my desire in coming to England.

*   *   *

Denys's first impression of sunniness had been correct: Arthur de Hastynge was a man who had not lost his temper in twenty-five years. His was the kind of even, friendly disposition which suspects no evil of anyone; he was so in love with life and had so many things to occupy him that there was no room in his mind for envy, hatred, or avarice. He owed fealty by knight's service to the Bishop of Chichester for four hides of land, and, by one of those complicated arrangements common to the feudal world, held another virgate from the Abbey of Fécamp upon payment of the worth of two pigs and a sheep yearly. His neighbours were companionable people: on one side the lands of Maude Fitzleroy, a vassal of the de Hauterives, and on the other the industrious family of de la Lye, great menders of fences and solid trenchermen. Arthur lived in a snug, damp manor house, half stone and half wood-and-daub, well guarded by a businesslike palisade. He was unmarried, but from time to time had carnal relations with a willing and handsome widow who was one of his tenants, and who substituted this kind of frolic for the payment of her rent. His mother, a rather formidable old woman who was reputed to be a hundred and three years old, kept a sharp eye on his steward and saw to it that there was no cheating in the accounts, so that Arthur was in moderately good circumstances, his lands being worth something over the twenty pounds valuation of knight's fee.

He had been made a knight by his lord, the good bishop, when he was twenty-two years old. In the three years that had passed since that time he had drawn his sword only twice: once during a raid by outlaws which had been successfully beaten back, and the second time when he had been attacked by an infuriated and insane gander in a villein's farmyard. On both occasions he had acquitted himself with his usual good-natured courage. In spite of the quiet tenor of his life he took the institution of chivalry quite seriously, and greatly enjoyed hearing the tales and songs of the champions of Christendom. Like most of those who wore the noble belt and spurs, he could neither read nor write but never felt the loss. He had, however, one serious shortcoming which he managed successfully to conceal from everyone simply by never mentioning it: this was that he was terribly near-sighted.

He was much taken by Denys, an attraction which increased with acquaintanceship. Having no sense of humour himself, he took a wistful pleasure in the other's wry wit. But also, beneath Denys's mocking tales and careless way of speaking, he felt a warm luminosity which touched his own delight in the act of being alive: joy in warm sunlight, in the smells of cooking, in a caress, a bird's song, the feel of supple leather, the freshness of rain dropping through leaves. They belonged, for all their differences, to the fellowship of those who are aware of the world, rather than those who go through it as through a desert searching only for something to relieve their thirst. And finally, as one who had never gone farther than fifty miles from his home, he admired Denys who had travelled from Normandy to Spain, and from France all the way to England, who was footloose and carried all his possessions in his saddlebags.

Denys was not reluctant to stay on at Hidehurst (for so Arthur's manor was called). Richard was not yet in England. The road to London was apt to be longer and more difficult than he had anticipated. He had no friends in England and it occurred to him that it would do no harm to begin making some. Quite apart from all this there was his liking for Arthur, a quite genuine and spontaneous response to the candour and warmth of the other youth. Accordingly, he made himself at home and at once endeared himself to the ancient Lady Elizabeth de Hastynge by kissing her withered cheek with as much ardour as if she were Yseult the Beautiful.

"I hope you won't mind," Arthur said, shyly, "but I've invited my neighbours to dine with us. After all, it isn't every day that a famous troubadour comes by."

"Nothing would give me more pleasure than to sing for you and your guests," said Denys. "However, I'm afraid I'm not really very famous."

"You have the modesty true chivalry demands," Arthur said. "But we're not quite so barbaric here as you might think. Even in this remote corner we've heard your name, along with those of Peire Vidal, Arnaut Daniel, and Bertrand de Born."

Denys could not help flushing with delight. "You're very kind. I shall do my best to see that you're not disappointed," he said.

When they sat down to dinner the hall was full. At the high table, Denys sat at Arthur's right hand, and there were also the Lady Elizabeth, and Arthur's two most important neighbours, Lady Maude Fitzleroy, and Robert de la Lye with his wife, his son, and his daughter-in-law. At the top of the lower table were Arthur's steward, his chaplain Dom Anselm, Lady

47

Maude's chaplain and two of her women, and a number of Arthur's more well-to-do tenants. Everyone was on his best behaviour and there was only polite small-talk in low voices until the ale and wine had circulated several times and the beef and mutton had been cleared away to make room for dried fruit, nuts, and apple tart.

Robert de la Lye let his belt out a notch and discreetly broke wind. He was short and square, as wide as he was thick, very red in the face with bristling eyebrows and a large, grey, old-fashioned moustache of the kind the Normans used to call *grenons* and which a later age was to label "handlebar". "A delightful dinner, my boy," he said, in a rasping bass voice. "Perfectly delightful. Why the devil can't we eat like this at home, Beatrice?" he added, turning to his wife.

She made a faint bleating noise.

Arthur rinsed his hands in the basin held by his body-squire. "Thank you, Robert," he said. "That's a real compliment, coming from a man who knows the pleasures of the table as you do."

Robert chuckled. "From anyone else that could be taken as a kind of insult," he said. "My dear boy, that beef was like butter. I'm very partial to a bit of beef. But I've sold my cattle, you know, and turned to sheep. Much more profitable, hey, William?"

His son, William, was a hard-featured young man with dirty fingernails. He had managed to get through the entire dinner so far without saying a single word beyond brief requests that his cup or his plate be filled. He now uttered a grunt, "Mm-hm," and reached for another apple, which he broke in half with one twist of his muscular farmer's hands.

"Right," said Robert, proudly. "As he says, just look at the differences. Half a beef herd must be killed for the winter salting at Martinmas, but with sheep, now, we've found we can get enough cheese and wool to pay for their keep. Still, I'll have to come over here once in a while, Arthur, so that I don't forget what beef tastes like. I'll wager you haven't any beef like this in France, Sir Denys."

Denys said, "I had been told, sir, that the English beef is the best in the world. I doubted the boast, but now I know it is true."

It wasn't much, but it was the best he could do in a conversation of this sort.

Lady Maude Fitzleroy, at his side, said, "You are either an incorrigible flatterer, or you have really travelled enough to be able to form such a judgment. The best in the world? Truly?"

Denys turned to look at her. "Madam," he said, "as for the second, I have eaten dinner in more castles, towns, and villages than I can count. As for the first, if I were a flatterer I would be distrained to honesty before your eyes, for flattery dies in the face of true beauty."

He felt a little better with that speech. As for her, she blushed all up the length of her long, slender neck, to the roots of her pale, straw-coloured hair, half-hidden by a light veil. She had the most beautiful complexion Denys had ever seen, and very round, large, artless blue eyes.

She replied, "I must be careful of you, I see. I'm afraid you're something of a courtier, and we are all simple country-folk."

"Lady," he said, "I'm neither a courtier nor a plain liar. I am a Frenchman, and where ladies are concerned I must tell nothing but the truth."

"What'd he say?" croaked Lady Elizabeth, pulling her son's sleeve. "Henchman? Whose henchman?"

"He says he's a Frenchman, mother," said Arthur.

"Splendid! Of course he's a Frenchman. Why shouldn't he be? With that curly hair and handsome face? Damned if I wouldn't turn French myself if I were thirty or forty years younger." She shrieked with laughter at the thought, showing five or six large yellow fangs, all she had left. "Here, Frenchman, never mind making eyes at that girl. Tell us the news from France. What do you think we gave you dinner for?"

"Yes, Denys," Arthur said, "do tell us what's been happening. The last word we had was over a week ago, when we heard of the death of King Henry."

This was one of the things they had all been waiting for, and Denys obliged them with as full and interesting an account as he could give. They hung raptly on his words. "Naturally," he said, when he had done, "I can't tell you what's happened in the last few days. Things move rapidly, you know. But the rumour was that Count Richard would be in England by the middle of this month. If that is so, I'd like to get to London by then."

49

"You have business with the king?" asked Maude.

He nodded. "If I can ever come close enough to talk to him."

Robert de la Lye hummed through his nose. "So the kings have sworn to go to the Holy Land in Lent, have they? Hmm. Hmm. I wonder if Richard will actually go? Our good master the late king took the cross in '87, didn't he? But I'd swear on my immortal soul he had no more intention of going than he did of giving away the throne to his sons. Who ever knew what Henry was going to do? He'd look one way and strike another. I'm still paying off the debts I incurred for the Saladin tax and the last scutage. A nice, cheerful, thoroughly religious way of adding to the treasury, that's what it was, his taking the cross. And do you mean to tell me Richard isn't his father's son?"

"I'm sure he's very like his father," Arthur said, gently. "On the other hand, from all I've heard of him, Richard is a true knight with a high sense of honour."

"Oh—honour!" Robert snorted. "You're living in the past. Chivalry . . . Whatever Richard is, he isn't Sir Tristan——"

"No, from all I've heard he certainly isn't," cackled Lady Elizabeth, who had been listening with her hand cupped around her ear. "Tristan indeed! He likes the young men, nice and smooth, no beards, that's what they tell me. Why, he never said boo! to his father's lying with that French princess—what was her name? Adelaide——"

"Alysia, Mother," Arthur said. "And I really don't think——"

"You needn't shout at me. As I said, Alysia. Never said a word, although he was supposed to marry the wench himself. He was too busy fondling the pages, I dare say."

Arthur reddened. "Whatever he does, it's his own business, Mother. And he'll be anointed king before the month is up, so that it isn't very polite to talk about him that way. As for the crusade, I'm sure if he swore to go, he'll go."

"Now don't misunderstand me," Robert cried. "Don't think I'm against crusades. Not at all." He cracked a walnut fiercely with the hilt of his dagger and went on, with his mouth full, "We've got to teach those infidel dogs that they can't trifle with us. We'd have them over here raping our women

50

and burning our houses if we didn't. No, no, it's the proper thing for a Christian king to do—go over there and rape their women and burn *their* houses. Absolutely, my dear boy. Nobody's keener on freeing the Holy Sepulchre than I am. I've got my principles, same as anybody else. If it's got to be freed, it's got to be freed, that's all there is to it. I'm only saying that a wise man won't lay any bets on Richard doing anything heroic or chivalrous unless there's good sound profit in it."

He held his cup to his shoulder so that his squire could fill it. "Eh, William?" he said.

William, whose mouth was full of raisins, nodded. He patted the knee of his plump, giggling wife, and winked.

"You mark my words," Robert went on. "Whatever happens, we're going to have to pay for it. We've just finished coughing up the shield-tax for old Harry's last expedition to France. Now he's dead, God rest his soul, and we're going to have to tighten our belts again."

He clapped his ample middle mournfully, and Denys could not help laughing.

"My dear sir," he said, "I'm sure that everything you say of Count Richard is true, but I have seen him in action and I tell you he loves to fight better than anything else in the world. He will go to the Holy Land if only because the fighting's better there. As for your point, Arthur, I think he is perhaps more drawn to knightly deeds than his father was."

"I hate to discuss politics with my guests," said Arthur, hastily. "I beg you not to debate this any longer or our party will end in a quarrel. Denys, come, sing something for us, won't you?"

The others joined in, and Denys, who needed little urging, thrust back his chair and took his harp from a page. The lower table fell silent as he tuned it. He looked about with a smile and touched the strings.

He sang, to begin with, some of those merry dances so popular in the southern lands, *baladas* such as "Happy am I", or "Come, take my hand", lilting and lively, which soon had his audience beating on the tables and tapping their feet. Then, striking a bold and jolly theme, he sang that sirvente written by the Monk of Montaudon:

51

> "These things I hate: low, vulgar company,
> A belted knight who has no courtesy,
> A nagging wife, a jealous concubine,
> Too much of water and too little wine . . ."

Those at the high table laughed; those who knew a little French at the low table laughed also; those who knew no French laughed loudest of all, glancing sidelong to be sure their appreciation was noticed.

Now, changing his mood, Denys sang some of his own songs, a love song he had written to the Lady Maurina long before, another for which he had been awarded a golden loving-cup at the court of Aragon, a more recent canzo composed at Gramonte. By now, the whole hall was hushed and tears stood in many eyes, and here and there hands or knees touched, and the room was breezy with sighs.

Denys looked meaningfully at Lady Maude. "To conclude," he said, "I would like to sing my newest work. You may know that we trouvères sometimes set ourselves the problem of rapid composition, trying to see how swiftly we can write both words and music. Well, this is a song I composed this very evening, during dinner."

There was a respectful intake of breath from everyone. He went on, "It is in the form of an aubade, or morning song, and, as you will hear, the word 'dawn' appears in the last line of each stanza. That makes it more difficult. I have dedicated it to—a lovely lady whom I shall call Bel Vezer, Fair to the Sight."

He then sang:

> "Why must the nightingale so soon depart,
> And we our scented hawthorn bower fly?
> The sun's first ray strikes sadness to my heart,
> Ah, love farewell; the dawn invades the sky."

There was a long hush when he had finished, better than any applause. Then the applause broke out thunderously. Arthur called for his cup and had it filled with wine; he took a gold ring from his finger and dropped it into the cup and passed it to Denys.

"Drink, Denys," he said. "You have shown us what a

master is, and we are all grateful. I'm sorry the gift is so small, but you must be satisfied with our thanks, and admiration."

"I'm more than satisfied if I have pleased you," said Denys, glancing at Maude. She was pink as a morning sky herself.

"Pleased us? It was grand, my boy, simply grand!" said Robert. "And damned clever, too. You troubadour chaps amaze me. I've often felt I could compose a song myself, you know, if I had the time. But then I think, How do they start off? I mean, thinking up all those words and tunes and things."

"It's not difficult when you know how," Denys said.

"Ah, there you are. It's all in the knowing how. I suppose you trained for it from childhood and all that sort of thing? Well, there you are. Some of us must plant corn and keep flocks and make the world wag, though. What do you say, William?"

William wiped his mouth with the back of his hand.

"Grmf," he muttered, and reached for the tart-dish.

Robert eyed him fondly, and turned back to Denys. "Now you, Denys, you'd probably be lost if you had to look after a farm, eh?"

"I'm afraid so," said Denys. "Very true."

"It must be a wonderful life, though," said Robert's wife, Beatrice, unexpectedly. "I mean, wandering around . . . seeing the world . . . singing before kings and—and——"

"Shut up, my love," Robert said, heartily. "What do you know about it? I'm sure Sir Denys isn't interested in your notion of a wonderful life."

"No, Robert, I can't agree. There's a good deal in what your lady says," Arthur put in, softly, so that the rebuke was not evident. "I sometimes feel awfully pent up, here. Not that I'm not happy, you understand. I love my land, as we all do. On the other hand, I do sometimes feel that a knight shouldn't spend his life sitting in one place."

"Knight errantry again!" Robert exclaimed.

"No, no, not exactly," Arthur protested. "I think we tend to forget that our duty calls us to the banners of our lords. We've begun to feel it's more profitable to pay for mercenaries than to appear ourselves—all these taxes seem easier to cope with, in spite of the expense, than to leave home and fight abroad. And so we get so—so—well, concerned with our own limited little world that we forget there's a wider world outside.

Denys sees that wider world. I'm sure it makes a grander, better man of him than I can ever hope to be."

Denys put his hand on Arthur's shoulder. "That, in any case, could never be so," he said. "Oh, I'll admit there are certain advantages to travel. It's amusing enough to see strange lands. But I often grow weary of it and begin to long for a haven, a place of my own, roots—I sometimes weep, remembering my home, where there's no room for me."

Arthur said, earnestly, "I'd like you to feel you can stay here for as long as you wish."

Their eyes met, and they both smiled.

Maude touched Denys's hand and he turned to her. "I hope you'll let me follow Arthur's example," she said, "and make you a tiny gift, too."

She took a thin gold chain from around her throat, as she spoke. It was studded with polished ovals of rock crystal. She held it out, timidly.

"Lady," said Denys, his hand closing over hers as he took the chain, "I shall wear it as your favour wherever I go. It shall be a keepsake and a reminder of you, in battle or in peace."

"In battle?" She sighed, dropping her gaze. "Oh, how terrifying. But how splendid to think of it. Your song—that aubade—it was so lovely. Did you really compose it during dinner?"

"Yes, I did," Denys said.

"How in the world could you manage? Thinking of those beautiful words while we were all eating and drinking——"

"It wasn't easy. It takes a certain spur, what we poets call inspiration."

"Oh. I see. The inspiration of that lady you spoke of, whom you no doubt left behind in France?"

"Bel Vezer is not far from me at this moment," Denys said, lowering his voice.

"You mean that she is in England?"

"Lady, she is what makes England a garden for me. She is England. Need we fence? She is here." He pressed her hand.

She said, faintly, "Everyone is looking at us."

He released her. "Does that disturb you so much?"

"It's very public." She looked straight at him with those

enormous, innocent blue eyes. "You mustn't think I'm un-grateful. But it's the first time anyone has ever made a song for me."

"Does it displease you?"

"Oh, no. It doesn't displease me at all. But I—I'll have to think about it. I'd like to thank you properly——"

"You have already thanked me more than sufficiently." He weighed the chain in his palm.

"I hope you'll come and visit me," she said. "My lands lie next to Arthur's, and my house isn't very far away. Perhaps you can persuade him to bring you to see me. Perhaps in my own house I—I can express my thanks more fittingly."

He bent his head. At that moment Arthur spoke to him and he turned away from her. But he was well pleased with his evening, so far, and quite resigned to spending the rest of it listening to Robert de la Lye.

*   *   *

Wilkin the Fisherman and Ernald the Smith sat in the thick lower branches of a gigantic oak tree which overhung the forest path. Balanced between them was an anvil. It had rained during the night and the branch was still slippery, and they had some ado to keep the anvil steady.

After a time, Wilkin said, "I dunno."

"What don't 'ee know?" Ernald said. "Hold un steady, man."

"I don't know as it's right to drop un on master's 'ead."

"O' course it's right, thou gert lunk."

"Be 'ee certain 'e'll come this way?"

"Certain sure."

"Ah."

They savoured the fresh morning air, saying nothing for a while. Then Wilkin muttered, "Well, I dunno."

"What don't 'ee know?"

"'E be none so ill a master, as they go."

"Ah, true. A good master 'e be. I'd clout any man as'd say different."

"Well, then?"

"Well, but," said Ernald patiently, for he had explained this whole point over and over again, "look you. Master be lord o' the manor, bain't 'e?"

55

"Ah, so 'e be."

"And we be 'is men, bain't we?"

"True for you, Ernald."

"Well, then. Men must fight masters. It be the principle of the thing, man, that's what," Ernald said, and this ended the argument.

It would have ended then in any case, for at that moment Arthur came into sight, deep in talk with Denys, switching the heads off tall weeds with a willow twig as he walked.

"You see, people are so hard to convince," he was saying. "Everyone will agree to something in principle, but then when you try to get them to carry it out in practice, they balk and find all sorts of excuses. Now this business about the lord's responsibilities to his tenants——"

At that moment, they passed under the oak. There was a swish and a thump which shook the ground. Denys, whose reactions were somewhat swifter than Arthur's owing to the more random nature of his life, seized his host by the arm and jerked him off the path. They both stared about. The anvil lay deep sunken in the soft moist earth; it had missed them by inches.

Arthur peered at it. "Dear me," he said. "What's this?"

"It appears to be an anvil," Denys said, drily. He had his drawn dagger in his hand and was looking up into the oak.

"But that's absurd," said Arthur. "How could an anvil fall out of a tree?"

"I imagine those types up there can tell us something about it," Denys said. "Perhaps you'd better tell them to come down. I don't speak their language, you know."

Arthur could see nothing but the green blur above. However, he said sternly, in English, "Come down at once."

Rather sheepishly, Ernald and Wilkin dropped to the ground and stood patiently, with their heads hanging.

Arthur squinted at them. "Ernald the Smith and Wilkin the Fisherman," he said. "What on earth are you up to?"

Wilkin nudged Ernald, who said, "'Er slipped, my lord."

"Slipped? I should think it did. But I didn't realize one sat in trees with anvils. Eh?"

"Ah," said Ernald. "Not generally, 'ee don't."

"Well, speak up, man."

"We was tempering un, my lord."

56

"Tempering the anvil? In a tree?"

"Ah, that's what. They do say, by custom, like, that the oak be the smith's tree. And if 'ee take anvil and bathe it in the dew off the oak leaves about Saint Swithin's Day there'll come naught but good luck to the work."

"I see." Arthur shook his head sadly. "My good fellow, what do you think Dom Anselm would say to such heathenish goings-on? To say nothing of the fact that the dratted thing might have killed me? You'd have been in sore trouble, if that had happened. You know that, don't you?"

"Ah, my lord, indeed we does," said Ernald. "But 'tis custom, like."

"Yes, yes. Custom. Of course. Well, take your anvil and get along with you," said Arthur. "And try to be more careful next time."

They touched their foreheads respectfully, picked up the anvil between them, and went off. Arthur looked after them and sighed. "They are such superstitious children," he said. "How I wish I could civilize them."

"Superstitious? Is that what you call it? Murderous, I should have said," Denys grunted.

"Oh, no, not at all. It was an accident," Arthur said. "You see, everything goes by custom in this part of the world. And the custom is that if you bathe an anvil in the dew of oak leaves around Saint Swithin's Day it will bring good luck to the smith. One of those men was the village smith."

"Saint Swithin's Day was a week ago, I believe," Denys remarked.

"Ah, well, he said *about* Saint Swithin's Day. At least, I think that's what he said," Arthur replied, uncomfortably. "No, my dear Denys, you mustn't have such suspicions. They are really good, simple people, just dreadfully ruled by custom or by ancient superstitions, and obstinate as the devil in the bargain. They call it independence, of course. But there's no harm in them."

"I wouldn't say it was so good and simple of them to have tried to kill me when I first arrived here. You remember, I had merely asked a couple of your hinds the way to Hardham Priory and they dragged me from my horse and wanted to beat me. No harm in them——!"

"Oh, that." Arthur chuckled. "Yes, I meant to tell you

57

about that. It was a misunderstanding, you see. Osric told me about it later—he is one of the shepherds. I was embarrassed—well, you see, it was the fault of your accent, Denys."

"My accent? I don't follow."

"You asked for Hardham. To them, it sounded as though you said, 'God damn!' They thought you were being gratuitously rude. They're awfully touchy about the Normans, even after a hundred and fifty years. I think they still resent my speaking French at home. Anyway, you see, it wasn't anything serious."

"I'm glad you can be so cheerful about it. If you hadn't come along just when you did someone would have been killed. And do you honestly believe those fellows in the tree didn't intend to squash you flat?"

Arthur looked shocked. "Heavens, no. Nothing of the sort. Intended to squash me——! My dear Denys, I'm the lord of the manor. They may be simple and hag-ridden but they aren't rebels. They accept authority in spite of their stubbornness, and they know perfectly well that I have the strongest feeling of protectiveness for them. They return it with loyalty, the kind of sturdy, devoted loyalty only the English are capable of. I mean, after all, our whole system, our whole way of life is founded upon mutual respect and interdependence, isn't it?"

Denys balanced his dagger in his hand. In spite of Arthur's words he kept a sharp eye on the underbrush on either side of the path. "What about what you were saying a while ago?" he said. "About people not carrying their principles into practice? Aren't there some who don't go along with—mutual respect?"

"Yes, I know. That's what I was saying, isn't it? It's too bad, but there *are* barons and knights who are selfish. They know what chivalry requires of them, but they are proud instead of humble, greedy instead of generous; they injure women and oppress the meek. But Denys——! That doesn't mean that chivalry doesn't exist. It doesn't mean that chivalry is empty and useless, does it? Take away the Order of Knighthood and society would fall to pieces.

"The same is true of the relationship between master and man. All this——" he waved his hand, "this would return to the ancient forest and anarchy, if we didn't support one another. The knight's duty is to govern, to protect, to uphold.

The peasant's duty is to grow food, to cultivate the land. We go hand in hand, like brothers, all under the king's protection, and God's."

His face shone, and his gentle brown eyes, straining to focus on Denys's face, brimmed with earnestness.

Denys smiled at him. "Yes, you're right," he said, unable to contradict his friend. "And you do try to put it all into effect, don't you?"

"I do my best," Arthur said. "They *are* short-sighted, you know. I try to make provision for the lean years. I try to pay high wages to my shepherds and ploughmen and carters and dairywomen. I try to end each year with a little profit from the corn, the swine, the cheese. It's very difficult, you know. They are usually satisfied if their bellies are filled today. Why, do you realize that in the ploughing alone—well, you know, you have to give the oxen a three-minute breather after every fifty paces or so, but if the bailiff didn't keep his eye on the drivers they'd all lie down and doze for an hour. They object to the gift days, but they don't realize it's for the good of all to get the fields ploughed and sown without waste or loss of time."

He went on enthusiastically, giving lists of figures, quantities of produce, income realized, expenses for the year, and so forth, while Denys, nodding affably, began looking for the forest to end and Lady Maude Fitzleroy's grazing land to come into view.

Arthur said, "Oh, dear, I'm afraid I'm boring you. But when I get started on the subject——"

"No, really, I'm very interested," Denys said. "And I do think you're right, in principle—there's that word again! I was just wondering how much farther we have to go."

"Not far. Oh, would you mind awfully if I turned off for a moment here?" They had come to a grove of willows and a rough log bridge beneath which a brook chuckled and gurgled. A narrow, overgrown trail led along the far bank, off the path. "I must just look in on the Archangel Gabriel and give him his pittance."

"Eh?" Denys was a trifle taken aback. "The archangel?"

"Gabriel. He lives off this way on the edge of the stream. A thoroughly daft old man, of course, but quite sweet. I give him a penny a fortnight for his keep. Since we were passing this way anyway, I thought I'd stop."

Denys followed him along the trail. It ended in a clearing much trampled, where there was a tiny hut of woven wattles plastered with mud with a rude cross planted in the earth at its door. An exceedingly dirty old man, whose face was like a withered winter apple entangled in the mattress of his hair and beard, sat fishing on the bank. A small, shining trout lay beside him half wrapped in leaves, and in a wooden bowl were worms. His hearing must have been good despite his years, for his head was cocked over his shoulder and he watched Arthur and Denys come into view with the wariness of an old and well-trained hound. When he saw who it was, he grinned toothlessly.

Denys wondered what the proper form of address for an archangel was. But Arthur said, without hesitation, "Good day, your Celestial Highness."

"Ah, good day, good day. It's that young knight—what's-his-name? The names of these mortals slip my mind. Triviality anyway. Come and sit down."

They settled themselves beside him. He moved his rod lightly, letting the worm drift with the current. A dragonfly hovered close to the brown water and darted off, glittering. Tits chipped and gossiped in the thicket, and a missel thrush, somewhere far above in a tree, began his call, "*churr!*" like a boy hitting fence palings with a stick.

Denys lay back, propping himself on his elbows, to stare up into the leaves. Arthur said, "I've brought you your penny, your Celestial Highness."

"Many thanks. You're a good boy. Who's the other one?" asked the archangel. Denys thought idly that an angel ought to have at least enough miraculous power to know someone's name. But perhaps that kind of thing wasn't important enough to him.

"A friend," Arthur said. "How's the fishing?"

"Poor. The hot weather makes 'em lazy, you know. All they want to do is lie under the stones. If I were younger I'd tickle 'em up. As it is, I don't care enough about it."

Denys said sleepily, "I didn't know archangels went fishing."

"When we are in human form, my boy, we behave as humans. I was once an abbot, and then I behaved like an abbot. I know it's hard to believe that an abbot and a human being can have anything in common. . . . ."

"On a day like this I can believe anything," Denys replied. "I can see why you'd rather be the Archangel Gabriel and sit here and fish, instead of an abbot in a cloister busy with administration and discipline."

The archangel chuckled. "It isn't quite so simple," he said. "But you're a bright lad. Just for that, how would you like me to read the future for you?"

"No, I don't think so," said Denys. "Suppose my future was that I were to die tomorrow? How could I enjoy today? It would be two days spoiled instead of one."

The archangel fixed a bloodshot but penetrating eye on him. "You won't die tomorrow, nor the day after," he said. "You'll go farther than you think, but you won't find what you're looking for. However, if it's any consolation to you, you'll find something else which is equally precious, only you won't know you have it until you come near losing it."

"I don't think I like that future," Denys said. "Mayn't I have another?"

At that moment, the line tightened. The archangel, all his attention on the water, made certain the hook was fixed fast and then pulled. Up came a second fish, twisting and flapping. He knocked its head against a tree root and looked it over.

"Lovely thing," he said. "How fine it is to be able to enjoy one's nourishment both aesthetically and palatally. What a bounty there is on earth! When I was an abbot, I was blind. My devotion was turned inward to things of the spirit. I did not realize that the things of the spirit only exist because of the world, and not in spite of it. Inward! What an accursed word that is, anyhow. It allows us to mistake self-love for the love of God, and to find our own inner darkness more illuminating than God's sunlight."

He wrapped the trout in leaves, dipped it into the stream, and laid it beside the other. "That is why I forsook the heavenly courts," he mused, half to himself. "First to suffer as a man, then to find joy as a man. For, after all, these things are barred to angels. There are some drawbacks to living in a state of perfection."

He stretched out his skinny bare legs with their twisted toes and black nails, and hunched forward, folding his arms over his shrivelled belly. "In doubt, torment, and uncertainty we come closer to the meaning of joy."

Arthur said, "Yes, I remember your telling me about it. The hours you spent trying to answer that question. . . ."

"What was the question?" Denys asked.

"It came to me in the midst of the lesson, one day," said the archangel. "Out of a clear sky. I was listening to the reader drone on, and watching the faces of my monks, row after row, some dull, some mild as sheep, some gaunt and hungry, a few attentive. The reader read, 'And he commanded him, saying, of every tree of paradise thou shalt eat: But of the tree of knowledge of good and evil thou shalt not eat. For in what day soever thou shalt eat of it, thou shalt die the death.' And suddenly, the thought flashed into my mind, If God is indeed omniscient, then He knew that Adam would eat of that fruit. In that case, what need of the commandment? Or, if He did not know that Adam would eat, then He was not omniscient. In that case, how could He be God?"

"Yes, I see what you mean," Denys said, thoughtfully.

"I could not get it out of my head," the archangel continued. "I went to my study and sat alone, staring out the window. What could be the truth of it? If God knew all things, then He knew Adam would eat the fruit of knowledge. Then was it not sheer cruelty to command him not to do so? Or if He did not know, since Adam had free will, then He was not all-knowing but blind to the consequences of His acts as any dull-witted father who forbids his son to drink wine and thus plants in him an unquenchable thirst.

"I said to myself, 'This is a mere quibble. Faith is all.' Yet I remained antinomially transfixed like a beetle on two pins. 'You are coming dangerously close to heresy,' I warned myself, and for this there was no cure but penance, bread and water, even flagellation. But between blows, I could not help thinking, 'Does God know that I am beating myself? Does He know why?' It was like the toothache. But where could I find a theologian skilled at such dentistry.

"In this torture I passed my days. I forgot the hours, the rules of my order, the management of my abbey. I could neither eat nor sleep. I grew thin as a rail, all skin and bone, nor could I even pray, for in each prayer which spoke of God's love or God's mercy I saw concealed hypocrisy. Is God so loving? How then could He permit injustice and evil to flourish? Is God so merciful? How can He allow some of His children to die lingering deaths in agony? Is God omnipotent? How then can the devil so often cheat Him of souls?

"I wandered forth from the abbey, in my darkness. I slept for very exhaustion on the bare ground and lived on crusts pressed upon me by kindly passers-by. One day, I came into this very wood, to this very place. I fell to the ground, close to death, despairing and depleted. At that instant, a voice spoke to me, calling upon me by name: *Gabriel, Gabriel! Chief among My archangels*, it said."

He paused, the fingers of one hand buried in his white beard. Denys, fascinated, said, "And the voice revealed the answer to you! What did it say?"

The old man smiled faintly. "It said, 'Take a stick, tie a string to it, put a hook on the end of the string, bait the hook, and fish in this delightful stream.'"

Denys blinked. "Oh," he said. "And you did?"

"I did. For I realized that archangels need not know the answers to questions which concern mere mankind. An archangel, like his God, simply *is*."

He picked up his fish, and stuck the end of his rod into the soft earth. "I'm going to sleep for a while, now," he said. "When I awaken, I'll cook my lunch. What more could any-one ask? God bless you both. Run along, now."

Arthur got to his feet. "Goodbye, your Celestial Highness," he said. "I'll see you again in a fortnight. Don't forget to visit me if you need anything before then."

"I have everything I need," said the archangel.

As they walked back along the stream, Denys said, "What an odd chap. But as you said, awfully nice."

"England is full of odd people," Arthur murmured. "It's one of our charms. But I do like Gabriel. It is rather comforting to think that on the Day of Judgment he will be one of the seven angels with trumpets heralding the world's end. I imagine he'll blow reluctantly."

Denys laughed. "I was interested in the prediction he made for me. Do his predictions often come true?"

"I really can't say. He hasn't made very many. He told me last year that I must prepare to hear new songs which would draw me to follow the singer, but I haven't——" He stopped short. "Good heavens," he said. "Of course. He meant you."

63

"Hmm." Denys rubbed his chin. "Perhaps he did."

"Why, then what he said about you—about finding what you're looking for. *Are* you looking for something in particular?"

"Yes," said Denys, and then paused, at a loss. How could he explain something so vague, so intensely personal? Much as he liked Arthur, the other was not a poet and could hardly be expected to understand a search for poetic form—a search which, in any case, had an inexpressible goal. Or, to put it another way, when he could explain the goal, he would have reached it. But there was another desire, almost equally strong, which could be voiced. He said, "I'm looking for a place of my own."

"Land?"

"Yes, land, money. In the plainest language, I'm looking for a fortune. I was pushed out of the nest, you might say. Father has a good many years in him still, I dare say, and when he dies there isn't going to be enough for four in any case. My brothers are quite satisfied to live happily together on whatever there is, but I want—more. I've always wanted more."

"More?"

"More than I had, more than there is." He made a restless movement with his shoulders. "Anyway, my own lands and my own house where I can live as I please and spend my own money in my own way."

Arthur nodded. This much, at least, he could understand perfectly. It was the whole of life for him: a piece of earth rich with its crops, sleek cattle, men labouring, oneself in the midst secure in one's own place. He could imagine himself roving as Denys did—indeed, the thought was growing more attractive by the hour—but he could not conceive of himself as landless. Whatever happened to him, he would be attached, as by an invisible leash, to that stake in the fertile earth which was his domain, and more profoundly, to the responsibilities he owed both to those below him and to his feudal lord. He had his place in the ladder of things between those who held it up and those who sat on the upper rungs; it was not mere resignation to the way things were, but a satisfying feeling that this was the way things ought to be and that within this frame a man always knew where he was.

He said, coming straight to the point, as always, "It's easy to solve, Denys. Why not hold land of me?"

Denys stared at him.

"I've got more land than I know what to do with," Arthur went on, untruthfully but enthusiastically. "You could have the two virgates bordering the de la Lyes' land, with the mill and the stream. There's a foundation, where there used to be a castle which King Henry ordered demolished after the troubles fifteen years ago. We could easily build you a nice manor on that spot. And you'd have the mill revenues to start off with. What do you say? Wouldn't that be grand? And I'd be a very easy lord to get along with."

Denys had to smile. He clapped Arthur on the arms, and said, "Nothing would please me more. But it wouldn't do, Arthur. Don't look so crestfallen. I know perfectly well that you can't afford to give me seisin of any of your land; you haven't that much. And to tell you the truth, I want more than sixty acres. I'm greedy. I haven't your capacity for contentment. If I can get to see Richard I think I can at least make a start. He owes me something."

Arthur looked crestfallen but at the same time a trifle relieved. The mill was, after all, an important part of his revenues. "I think I understand what you mean," he said. "But it is too bad. I'd have loved having you for a vassal. However, if you're relying on Richard to pay you money he owes you—well, what Robert said at dinner last night was perfectly true. The treasury is almost empty, and I'm sure Richard is going to have to scrape for funds."

"It isn't that sort of debt," Denys said.

The forest had thinned, and they came out of its shade on the flank of a low hill where sheep grazed among the ferns. A little farther they passed the long, narrow, cultivated strips worked by various tenants, and soon after came in sight of Lady Maude's home farm with the manor house beyond it, surrounded by its palisade.

They found her in the dairy supervising the pressing of cheeses. She dried her hands on a towel one of the maids brought her, and greeted them. As was the custom in England, she kissed them on the cheek, and Denys, catching her by the hand, said, "In France, Lady, we think the lips more courteous."

"We aren't in France now, sir," she said, primly. Nevertheless, she did not move away and he kissed her lightly, catching a fresh milky smell from her clear skin.

She sent a little page running to get wine and wafers, and led them through the courtyard into a small, pleasantly shady garden where country flowers and herbs grew side by side, and around the edges a dozen apple trees. An up-ended section of a log served for a table and there were three simple wooden benches. They sat down together, and in a moment or two the page came scurrying back with a napkin over his arm as if he were a table-squire, and with him another lad. They poured the cool wine and passed around a dish of cakes, and then vanished behind the trunk of the largest of the apple trees where they could be heard whispering and snickering as they ate the crumbs.

"We stopped by the way to visit the archangel," Denys said. "Do you know him?"

"Oh, yes. Isn't he a dear?" said Maude.

"Some of the things he said I can't get out of my mind. That question of his—how *do* you answer it, I wonder?"

"What question?" asked Maude.

Arthur said, soberly, "Is God omniscient, or not? You know, Denys, I doubt it's a gentleman's business to concern himself with such matters. After all, look what happened to poor old Gabriel. He was a gentleman, you know, the second son of an earl. You can only guess it from the fact that he still speaks courtly French. And there he is, living like a wild animal in a thicket and all because he couldn't get it into his head that a gentleman—whether he's a knight or a cleric—ought to leave things as they are."

Denys said, "But he doesn't seem dissatisfied with his lot. He seemed rather happy."

Arthur nodded. "It's all very well now, in August. But can you imagine what it must be like for him in January? I see to it that he has firewood and a warm cloak, of course, but I hardly think it's an ideal life. A gentleman, after all, should have a certain amount of humility . . . and tact. And a question like that one smacks to me of arrogance. It's like asking whether the good Lord is a fortune-teller. God gave us the world and we ought to accept it with thanks and not go prying and poking into corners."

Maude said dreamily, "But, Arthur, living in the woods like a hermit is so romantic. It's just the sort of thing knights are always doing in the ballads. Lancelot, in dear old Walter Map's beautiful tale, went off and lived in the forest when Guinevere wouldn't have him; why, he was just like Gabriel—'wild was he as any beast/and all his senses perishèd.' And Tristan, too, in that new chanson written by Elias de Borron, went mad for love of Yseult and wandered away."

"Yes, but Gabriel didn't wander away because of a woman," Arthur said. "That's really off the point, Maude."

"Oh, I don't know. I think she's got a good point," Denys put in. "When you come right down to it, there's something heroic in what he did. I'm astonished it doesn't appeal to you, Arthur."

Arthur grinned. "Why are you both bullying me? It's quite simple, what I believe. Only it's awfully hard for me to put these things into words. Chivalry isn't that kind of heroics— running off because you can't answer a silly question about religion. It's courage, above all else. If you can't find the answer to something like that, well, you just face up to it and manage to live with it somehow. But *I* think his responsibility was to his monks and his abbey. He should have stayed there no matter what it cost him."

Denys put a hand on his friend's knee. "You're a man in a thousand, Arthur," he said. "By God, I admire you. You make me both ashamed of myself and proud to wear a belt and sword."

"I'm sorry. I certainly didn't mean to make you feel ashamed," Arthur muttered. "Anyway, let's not talk about it any more. There was something I wanted to ask you about— that prediction Gabriel made. I was wondering whether I could be of any help in getting you to see Richard?"

"I don't know," Denys said. "How do you mean?"

"Well, you see, my liege lord is the Bishop of Chichester, and he and I are very close. Ever since my father died, when I was first made *armiger*, the bishop has thought of himself as in loc— er—*locus*—what do they call it——?"

"*In loco parentis?*"

"Yes, that's it, like a parent, you know. And so he's been awfully good to me, and so I thought perhaps for the coronation he might be going up to London and could put in a word for you."

"That's very kind of you, Arthur."

"Why do you have to see Richard so desperately?" Maude asked. "Or would you rather not talk about it?"

"I don't mind talking about it at all," Denys said. "If the story won't bore you." He sipped his wine and launched into the tale. "You see," he finished, "I feel he owes me something, if it's no more than a place as a trouvère at his court." He pulled open the strings of his purse and fumbled inside. He found the ring and held it up. "It's a pretty bauble, anyway. I've been keeping it so that I can identify myself when I see him. But if all else fails, I suppose I can sell it for a couple of marks."

Maude's eyes were shining. "It's simply too thrilling," she gasped. "You saved the king's life——"

"He wasn't the king then," Denys put in.

"—at the risk of your own. And you've been so modest, talking about how Arthur makes you feel ashamed, while all the time you did something so knightly and gallant——"

"Oh, heavens!" said Denys. "You're making me feel horribly embarrassed. It wasn't anything like that. I didn't even think of what I was doing, I just don't like to see a man outnumbered and alone. I'd have done the same thing for one of the other side if Richard and his men had had him surrounded."

Arthur said, "My dear chap, you've no need to explain to *us*. Everything you say makes it perfectly clear what you did and why. And I think it's disgraceful the way Richard has forgotten you. We absolutely must get you an audience."

"I can do it," Maude said, abruptly.

They looked at her in surprise.

"I'm sure I can manage it," she said. "Oh, please don't stare at me like that. You see, my grandfather, Henry Fitzleroy, was the bastard son of King Henry the First and the Welsh princess Nesta. He was settled on these lands after the king's death and became the vassal of the de Hauterives. I am the ward of William de Hauterive, and one of his best friends—and one of my father's, too—was William the Marshal. I've known the Marshal ever since I was a little girl. Goodness! I can remember how much in love with him I was. He was the perfect knight, and so strong, and so excellent in tourneys and in battle. When I was about twelve, while my father was still alive, he used to come down to the de Hauterive

castle in Burton for feasting and hunting, and he used to say,
'My little maid, if your father can't marry you off you can
always have me.' I haven't seen him for years, it's true, because he's been in France so much, but I'm certain he'll
remember how he used to promise me anything I wanted.
And I know my liege, William de Hauterive, will help. He is
a man of some importance. What do you think, Denys?"

Arthur cried, "What does he think? Why, it's a marvellous
idea. William the Marshal! He's one of the most notable men
in the kingdom. Why, everyone knows the story of how he
once had Richard at his mercy and spared him. The only
man who could beat Richard in a fight! You told us yourself
that one of Richard's first acts was to send him to England to
take charge of things. He must be in London now."

Denys pursed up his lips. "It certainly sounds feasible."

Maude glanced at him. "You don't really want to accept
help from a woman, do you? You sound very cool."

He raised his head. "My dear lady," he said, "that's not it
at all. I meant what I said last night. Did you think I was
joking? I have your favour here, around my neck, under my
shirt. It is my place to do your bidding, to serve *you*. And here
you are, proposing to help me in a way I can never repay."

Arthur coughed. "I—uh—if you'll excuse me," he mumbled, "I think I'd better—I'd better see to my horse."

He got up hastily and left them without looking back.

Maude giggled. "He's forgotten you walked over," she said.

"He's pure gold," said Denys. He moved closer to her and
took her hand. "Bel Vezer," he said, tenderly.

She turned her head away. "If I can help you it will be as
much as I can ask," she said, almost inaudibly. "You have
already given me more service than I deserve—writing that
song to me——"

"I shall write you a hundred," he said. He pressed her hand
to his lips. "What song can do you justice? I came to England
thinking to find a foggy land where the sun never shone, and
I find it is the very birthplace of the sun. All I ever learned as
a trouvère can't help me now for there aren't any words with
which to praise the sun itself."

He leaned still closer, slipping his arm about her pliant waist.
His lips were at her ear. "Warm me once with your eye," he
said.

She turned her face and they were mouth to mouth. "Oh, dear," she whispered. "Nobody's ever talked to me this way before." And with a sigh of melting delight, she sank into his arms.

It was in the very middle of that kiss that the thought came to Denys that he might marry her. Lord of the manor of Fitzleroy, vassal to the de Hauterives, friend of William the Marshal. . . . It hadn't occurred to him before, but now suddenly it seemed perfectly possible.

He drew away. She opened her eyes languidly and said, "What's the matter?"

"Nothing, sweet lady, except my own amazement that I should be so fortunate," he replied, and fell to kissing her again, with a certain pensiveness.

* * *

Journal of Denys de Courtebarbe. Extract 3.

That thought which had come into my head, that I might wed the Lady Maude, would not leave me although I resolutely put it by. I was like some money-lender with a jewel left him in pawn, now contemplating it with precious care, now thinking of selling it for gain, anon taking it out to cherish it in the light, then locking it up straightway lest he be tempted thereby.

Now I would think on her fair lands, rich fields, meadows, cattle, and many tenants, turning over in my mind what could be the annual income, speculating on wood and water, for there is a good knight's fee in her manor or I will never draw breath more. Then I would ask myself, Is this the way of true love to think of gain? What need has a trouvère for marriage, or how could I settle in this remote and rustic place to be an outlandish English vassal? To wed? Yes, but on my own terms when I come to hold my own lands, then to make some good and advantageous marriage; such a thing would be fair and right. But the Lady Maude I had taken for my Bel Vezer, my lady love, and as the *Regulae Amoris* says, 'Between husband and wife there can be no true love.' But then again I would think how kindly a thing it might be to be Arthur's neighbour and we two be such friends as the heathen Damon and Pythias as are told of in

70

Holy Writ or some such place. And again, I would find that
nagging query in my mind, like the worm at the heart of
the blossom, asking myself, Is she indeed the one, is she my
love in truth, or do I once again deceive myself? And if she
is not, then all other considerations are vain.

But she is very fair and full of courtesy, and tender to be
with, although it may be she talks overmuch of chivalry and
the dues of knighthood. This is not a great flaw in her, however, and only such a one as might have come from
having her wits addled by a superfluity of romances, for I
have learned she has her clerk read to her nearly every evening out of some book, or will herself read, for she has been
taught the art of letters which, on my soul, is a great wonder
for an Englishwoman.

Thus have passed some two weeks, not wholly in such
speculation on my part, but in merry-making and jollity,
riding out with the hawks, walking in the fields, feasting and
dancing to such rude music as Arthur or his neighbours may
assemble, going among the labourers in the fields (for so
Arthur will do by cause, as he says, of his responsibilities as
their lord), and sometimes visiting now in one place, now in
another. We went up in company to the town of Petworth
where there is a fair house belonging to the de Percys, good
friends of the Lady Maude's, whose liege lord, William de
Hauterive, is related by marriage to Agnes de Percy. Arthur
took me also, one day, to that Priory of Black Monks at
Hardham which I had missed on my road from Chichester,
and there on the walls of the church I saw most marvellous
paintings, as clear as life, of the Last Judgment with the lost
souls struggling in torment so that it made your flesh creep,
and many other delightsome pictures as well.

I have grown ever more fond of Arthur, for although I
cannot agree with him in all things yet there is a sound,
solid core to him such as is rare enough in these days when
many wear the belt and spurs but few live up to them. He
is such a one as you would want at your back in a quarrel,
one who having given you his friendship would never take it
back no matter what the provocation. I know well that so
long as he lives I shall never need starve or go threadbare.
He loves well to listen to my singing, and in return has
given me, besides his friendship, new clothes to my back,

new furniture for my horse, a little sumpter to bear my bundles, and a gift of two pounds Angevin money against the day when I must go on to London.

On a day as Arthur and I strolled together, it being very warm and clear, he took me along a stream where he had osiers planted, and he discoursed to me of how they cut them for withes and how skilfully the tenantry plaited them to make fishing-traps and baskets and the like. We came into a clear space where there was a pool and there were some children playing, tousle-headed brats in ragged shirts, dirty and shrill-voiced. I saw that two of the bigger ones had set upon a small one and were beating him, and tying up his wrists with string made from the willow bark. Now I like not to see such things for they remind me uncomfortably of those days when I served in my childhood in the castle of my lord Raymond de Beaupréau, when I was bullied and beaten by the older pages and so tormented that I would not have given a berry whether to live or die. I started forward but Arthur was before me and had pulled off the bigger boys and held them, each by an arm, looking sternly upon them yet holding them, I saw, neither cruelly nor ungently.

He said to them that this was most discourteous for two to set upon one, and asked them what they played. One of them, who had a pleasant, cheerful face spotted with freckens, and a wide grin, gapped where his front teeth were gone, said freely (so Arthur told me later) that they did play a game called Knight and Peasant. Then Arthur, stroking the boy's hair, told them that this was an ill game for it did not beseem knights to mistreat a peasant so, but rather that knighthood bore with it the shield of honour, to guard the lowly and care for the helpless, and he went on and told them of the Knights of the Temple who lived by a strict discipline as monks, and of the Knights of the Hospital of Saint John who cherished the sick and wounded, and said to them that he himself so long as God might leave his soul in his body would never raise a hand against one of his peasants, whether free or unfree. I understood none of their talk but saw his face soften as the boy replied to him, and he let them go with a deep sigh, patting their heads and watching them as they ran off into the wood. I asked what had been said, and he told me. I said, 'That was well done, and such as I expected of you, for few knights care so much for the welfare of their tenants as to watch even over the doings of their children.' 'Yes,' said he, 'but what am I to do with them? They are all simple, and I know not what good my care does. For when I had done speaking, the child said innocently, "But my lord, *we* were the Peasants, and that one we were beating was the Knight."'

I laughed at this until the tears rolled down my cheeks, but he shook his head. After a time, however, he fell to laughing also, and then he said that it was his curse to be so serious and that he must come to me and be my scholar and let me lesson him how to be more light of heart. And so I wished I might do, but I saw well he would never be more light of mind in such matters as duty or honour, nor would I have had him otherwise.

There came another day on which, Arthur being busied at some affairs with his bailiff, I walked into the woods and came to that clearing where dwelt the hermit who called himself Gabriel. He was on his knees at his orisons, and when he saw me he nodded, smiling, as one who should say, 'Anon, anon,' so I sat down with my hands behind my head, leaning against a tree, and fell to day-dreaming. There passed through my mind tags and poems, snatches and bits of lines, and all at once a most strange notion so that I sat erect. For I thought, Since love is uncertain, fierce and unconstrained, why should a love poem be straitly confined within a form? Why should I not write a poem to Love without rhyme, without a strict count of syllables to each line, a poem as wild and free as love itself should be?

I struck my forehead to jar loose such madness. How could such a thing be? Such a poem would be no poem at all but mere words. Nor should love be fierce and unconstrained, for all the labour of lovers has been according to the laws of love as set down in many a chanson and tract, as for example in the courts of Queen Eleanor when she reigned in Poitou, and in those of the Countess of Champagne, and many another. All reason and precedent was against such a thing, both in love and in poetry, for as love has certain laws so has poetry also, and without law we should be as brute beasts.

Still, I could not abolish the thought, saying, New laws

might be made, as the laws of metre and consonance were first made. Why might I not make laws of my own, that as I searched for she who was to be my true love, so might I search in metaphor and in swift-running lines for words to tell of her. As the brook which ran before me babbled without form, or as birds sang from their hearts without form, so I might sing. As I sat wrestling thus within myself, the hermit came and sat beside me and asked what was troubling me.

I replied that it was naught he could comprehend, whereupon he answered, 'My son, all things are comprehended in the mind of God, and as we archangels, like men also, are a part of the mind of God so may we partake of that comprehension, as each drop of water is as wet as the whole stream.' Thus encouraged, I poured out to him what was in my thoughts. He sat with his knees drawn up and his chin upon them, in deep contemplation. Then at last he said, 'Have you ever heard of that part of Holy Writ which is called the Canticle of King Solomon?' And when I said, that I had not, he recited to me as follows, pinching the bridge of his nose between thumb and finger and with his eyes closed in the effort of memory:

'Thou hast wounded my heart, my sister, my bride,
Thou hast wounded my heart with one of thy eyes
And with one hair of thy neck.
How beautiful are thy breasts, my sister, my bride,
Thy breasts are more beautiful than wine,
And the sweet smell of thy ointments
Above all aromatical spices.
Thy lips, my bride, are as a dropping honeycomb,
Honey and milk are under thy tongue;
And the smell of thy garments
As the smell of frankincense.'

When he had done, his words yet hung glowing in the air and it seemed to me that all other poems faded and were ashen for a space. Then I said, 'Is that truly in Holy Writ?' 'Yea,' said he, 'it is, and I have heard it argued by many exegetes of great wisdom that this Canticle from whence it comes—and it is of great length, all of the same kind—

74

represents the love of God for His Holy Church, or the love of Our Lord Jesu for the soul of man, or, as I was told by a wise Jew, the love of God for the pure intellect. How say you, trouvère?'

I said I had no knowledge of such things, but as he yet pressed me, I said that it seemed to me the most precious of all love songs I had ever heard. 'And though it may be pure blasphemy for me to say so,' I added, 'yet may my soul be damned everlastingly if there be aught else in that poem than a man's love for his lady. This King Solomon,' I said, 'must have been the most excellent trouvère in the world, every whit the equal of the great Count William of Poitiers.' Whereupon the hermit said that I must not ask for my soul's damnation but that in all other matters he inclined to agree with me.

There was little else I could say for the great confusion of my wits and so I rose up and took my leave. But before I departed he said to me that life was brief and we might not meet again and that he wished me well. He bade me kneel down, and gave me his blessing, and said, 'Think on this, trouvère, neither God nor good poetry are to be sought by forms alone.' With that I left him, thinking that whether he were an archangel or no, he was both wise and holy enough for a man.

And on the morrow, it being the xix of the kalends of September, or in vulgar reckoning the 14th day of August, the word was brought to Arthur as he sat at meat that King Richard had landed in England on the preceding day at the harbour of Portsmouth where he had been greeted with great rejoicing, and after receiving the homage of the town had ridden with all his train to Winchester. Then I knew that the hermit had foreseen this happening and had thus bidden me farewell.

Yet there were surprises in store for me. For when I said to Arthur that the time was come when I must leave Hidehurst and bid him adieu, he said that we should not yet part for he had determined to go with me. On this, my mouth hung open as I had been struck with God's levinbolt. He said, lightly enough, that I had so filled him with the traveller's itch that he would not rest until he had made the journey, for he had never in his life seen the city of London nor any place more remote than Chichester or Southampton. Nor was that all, for on the next morning came the Lady Maude riding to his door, having also heard the news of the king's arrival, and said that now was the time come when she might help me as she had promised, and that she would give me no letters nor writings but would come with me herself unto William the Marshal and beg him to fetch me into the king's presence. Tears came to my eyes, and I gave thanks to Our Lady and to the blessed Saint Denys for sending me such true friends.

We did not start out at once, for there were many things to be set in order by both Arthur and Maude in their households and estates. Meantime, other tidings came to us, how Queen Eleanor had been released from her long imprisonment by William the Marshal and had met her son, Richard, at Winchester, and there embraced him whom she had not seen for near upon fifteen years so that all who witnessed it wept. Also, William de Hauterive told us that the king had ratified the promise made by his father to William the Marshal that he should wed Lady Isabelle de Clare, the daughter of the earl of Striguil, saying, 'By God's legs, my father only promised, but I give freely both lady and land.' The wedding would be held upon the 21st day of August, after which they would retire to the manor of the lord Enguerran d'Abernon, in Surrey. Accordingly, after some deliberation, we decided that we would go thither some two or three days after the wedding, rather than to London, and see what chance and the word of the Marshal would bring us.

*

xi Kal. Sep. On this day we set out in company, Arthur with his squire, a youth named Peter de Cotes, Maude with a serving woman and one of her household men, and myself. We rode singing, laughing and telling tales. Arthur was flushed and joyous as a child, ready to smile at anything. The sun shone, the small fowl called in the hedges, and our hearts were high.

So we came at length to Stoke d'Abernon, passing by villages whose names amused me: Mickleham and Effingham, Brockham and Fetcham. For with my scant English I thought the word 'ham' to mean that which we eat, and

such a profusion of hams, I said, spoke well for the English
bellies, but Arthur told me that in the Saxon tongue this
meant only 'village'. We lay that night in a town the name
of which I have forgot, and on the morrow went forward
to the castle of the lord Enguerran, and here we met with
that mirror of chivalry, the noble, the courteous, the valiant
William the Marshal.

What shall I say of this lord, whose name rings throughout
the world and whose deeds make him a model of knighthood?
Fair to look on although somewhat broad of girth, in the
prime of life, soft of speech and modest, yet proud of bearing,
all these he was. From a poor, penniless bachelor who made
his living by tourneying, he had come to that eminence
where now he stood at the king's right hand. But where
many another would have grown haughty and swollen with
importance, he remained gentle and serviceable, greeting the
Lady Maude with great affection, embracing her, and before
she could speak putting her in mind of the last time they had
met five years agone when she was but a little maid of
twelve and he had come to England to visit his sister, who
was the wife of Robert de Pont-de-l'Arche. He welcomed us
all, and when he heard Maude's plea that he should inter-
cede for me with the king, he said, 'Ill seems it to me that
a gentleman to whom Richard owes his life should stand
and wait in antechambers. I will set this matter aright, and
great pleasure will I take thereby.' He then told us that he
would go to London for the king's coronation which would
be held within the nones of September, although the day had
not yet been fixed upon, and that after that ceremony he
would himself take me before Richard.

He kept us by him that night, and we feasted with him and
his lady who was both beautiful and wise, and met there also
with a certain Hugh de Hamelincourt, one of the Marshal's
old companions, a man of much valour but a certain hardness
of head. He, however, told many tales of their adventures
together when he, and the Marshal, and the renowned
knight Baudouin de Béthune had been comrades-in-arms.

We heard of the days when the Young King had been
placed by the late King Henry in the Marshal's charge, and
how they had gone from tourney to tourney winning a
sufficiency of honour and ransoms. By his own reckoning,

the Marshal had taken part in no fewer than six score tournaments in those times. We heard the tale of the tourney between Anet and Sorel, in which so many knights of France, Flanders, Champagne, Normandy, Anjou and England had fought that the ground was clogged with broken lances and the horses had much ado to run among them. And in this tournament, the Marshal and the Young King arrived late and found their way barred by Simon de Neauphlé, a very worthy knight, with a following of men-at-arms. The Young King would have turned back, but William dashed forward so that the rabble opened a path for him. He seized the bridle of Simon de Neauphlé and galloped on, dragging Simon's horse behind him and followed by the Young King. As they rode, they came where a rain gutter thrust out from a house into the road, and Simon was caught on it and pulled from his saddle and so remained hanging on the gutter. But the Marshal knew nothing of this and rode on to their camp. Here he called to a squire, 'Take this knight.' 'What knight do you speak of?' cried the Young King, behind him. 'This one whom I lead,' replied the Marshal, and then turned and beheld the empty saddle, whereat the Young King was much amused.

Then we heard also, from the mouth of the Marshal himself, the tale of how he had had Richard at his mercy, which was a great deed. It befell during the month of June, shortly before King Henry's death when he was at war with King Philip of France, and his son, Count Richard, fought on the side of King Philip. King Henry had taken refuge in Le Mans, and there he had been besieged by certain barons of Poitou and France. One of the faubourgs of the city was set aflame, and although the English fought well it seemed the city would surely fall. The Marshal told us that when he urged the king to flee, Henry cried, 'Christ, I will no more honour You, who take from me all I hold most dear on earth, and suffer me to be shamefully beset by that stripling traitor!' And indeed, the Marshal said, it was a woesome sight to see the father so bearded by his son. They then rode out of the city, nor did they wear their mail coats for very haste, and they had gone no great distance when there came behind them a troop of riders with Count Richard far in advance. Richard wore only a haqueton of leather and carried a mace but neither lance nor sword, so impetuously had he ridden after them. William turned back and thus they came face to face whereon Richard cried out, 'By God's legs, Marshal, would you kill an unarmoured man?' 'May the devil kill you, not I,' said William. He thrust his lance into Richard's horse and turned and galloped away. Thus did he save King Henry from capture.

And he went on and said to us, leaning his cheek on his hand and with the other hand rolling up crumbs of bread upon the table, that shame was it to behold that sick and weary king driven like a stag before the hounds and brought to bay in Chinon. An old wound of Henry's opened in riding and a fever filled his blood. Then he was summoned to parley with King Philip and there forced to accept terms which stripped him of his lands for Richard's sake. Nor, said the Marshal, to be honest, was it wholly Richard's fault, for his father had often played him false and had threatened to take from him his rich provinces to give to his younger brother, Count John, who was his father's best beloved. But, said the Marshal, it was not this parley which brought the king to his death, but another thing. For he had bargained that they should give him a list of all those who had deserted him to join with King Philip. And when the names were read to him, the name of Count John stood at the head of the list.

Then I asked the Marshal how it had fared with him after the old king's death, for all men knew that Richard could not bear to be unhorsed or bested in combat. He said, 'When he had looked upon the body of his father, which lay in Fontevrault Abbey, he summoned me and looking evilly upon me said, "Ha, Marshal, the other day you wished to kill me, and you would have done so had I not turned your lance with my arm." I know Richard well, nor does he ever tell the truth save when it pleases him, and also he likes bitter japes and to put men to the test, but I would have none of that. I said, "My lord, I never had the intention of killing you, neither did I try to do so. For if I can strike straight with my lance in the tourney, so can I in war, as well you know. I might as easily have driven it into your body as that of your horse. But for the slaying of the horse I think I did no wrong, nor do I repent of it." On that, he smiled and said, "Marshal, I pardon you and hold you in no rancour." '

With his fingers, the Marshal flicked away the morsels of bread, and said, 'I tell you, he is a worthy king for all his faults. For he might have swept me away as I sweep away these crumbs, but he is large-hearted and liberal as befits a king. Nor will he have forgotten you, trouvère, I will stake my head on it. Only,' and with this he bent a sober look on me, 'be wary of his moods, for there is some demon in his blood makes him sudden as the sea wind. Not for naught did Bertrand de Born call him Richard Yea-and-Nay.' And those words of the Marshal's I strove to remember.

Then on the morrow we took the road for London and with us went Hugh de Hamelincourt to bear us company, with letters to lodge us in the house of Richard Fitz-Renier, who was the Marshal's dear friend, until the coronation should be past.

London is a great city to behold, not as fair as Paris, nor with so many fine churches—for they say of one who is fortunate that he is as happy as is God in France—but in London you may see a surfeiture of merchants, and of stalls and warehouses with goods from every country of the world. The houses in London are mainly of timber in their lower parts, with much whitewashed plaster in the upper, and this is kept very cleanly so that it makes a brave display. Not so the narrow muddy lanes and streets which are dirtier by far than those of Paris, and with the linen and furs which are washed in the gutters there is a great stench. Yet I believe London is more orderly than Paris, chiefly because it has fewer of those brawling scholars and vagabond clerks who, with their syllogisms, arguments, thievery and drunkenness, create uproar and unrest, so that a gentleman has much ado to walk safely abroad.

Hugh de Hamelincourt took us to dine at a cook-shop at Saint Botolph's wharf, which is very famous for such dishes as capon in crust or English lamb, the best in the world. We went out then along the river, which was clear and gravelly with pretty banks of grass, and rode through the hamlet of Charing to Westminster where lay the great, fair house of Fitz-Renier. Here, for the Marshal's sake, we were shown good cheer, and Lord Richard Fitz-Renier himself, one of the viscounts of London, kept us by him and made us welcome.

*

ii Non. Sep. Three days agone did King Richard come into his city of London. And yesterday we all saw him crowned in Westminster Abbey, the first time I ever saw the anointing of a king.

The lord Fitz-Renier took us into the abbey and there we stood by a pillar in a great crush of people while into the church came the procession: first, two noble barons with the cap of maintenance and the golden spurs, then William Longsword, a bastard of King Henry's who is now earl of Salisbury, with a rod on which was a golden dove representing the Holy Ghost, and with him William the Marshal, wearing the earl's coronet of Pembroke (although he had not yet been formally invested with the earldom which he received through his wife) and bearing a sceptre on which was the Cross. Then came three more noble gentlemen with the three swords of the kingdom, and twelve others with the royal vestments in a great coffer, and behind them the earl of Essex with the crown. Then came in Count Richard himself, walking under a silk canopy held aloft on four lances borne by barons, and with a bishop at either elbow.

Most kingly did he look, most to be feared and revered, taller by half a head than any around him, walking with a long stride so that the churchmen must skip two steps to his one. Power looked to be contained in him and my heart went out to him so that I was ready to lay my hands between those of such a lord.

He sat down upon a low chair before the throne, which stood in the nave, and there received his election from the clergy and the people, for such was the ancient custom of the English. The church was sweet with the smoke of incense and full of the glow of tapers upon rich garments and golden copes, so that I thought I had never seen so brave a sight in my life. Richard swore an oath to maintain Holy Church and his people, and then, while prayers were offered, he went behind a curtain where he put off his robes and was dressed in a shirt. The archbishop of Canterbury anointed his head, his shoulders, and his chest with the holy oil and bound his head in a chrism cloth. He was clothed in a fair tunic and dalmatic, in sandals of gold and the cap of maintenance, and invested with the sword and spurs of his royal knighthood. He then came before the high altar and I saw him take up the crown and give it into the hands of the archbishop of Canterbury. I know not whether at all coronations this is done, but certainly it seemed to me a thing most fitting for a man such as Richard to do.

Then said Baldwin, the archbishop, that in God's name he must not presume to wear this crown unless he meant to keep his oaths, and Richard answered that with God's help so would he do. The crown was placed on his head, the sceptres in his hands, and he was led to the throne while the sound of the Te Deum rose joyously. Thus was Count Richard made king of England.

*

Nonae Sep. On the morrow after the coronation, I was brought by William the Marshal into the presence of the king.

Richard held his court in the great hall of the Old Palace of Westminster. He sat upon a chair of ivory, the arms and legs cunningly carved in the semblance of the heads and feet of boars in most seemly work. That end of the hall behind his chair was screened off with crimson-dyed hangings, so that the dresses of the barons and their neck-chains and jewels showed fair to see. Yet Richard, crowned with the crown of England over the chrism cloth which he yet wore and must wear for seven days more, and robed in scarlet diapered with gold, outshone them all. His head trembled slightly, from the malaria which he had once had, but this tremor, which would have seemed weakness in another, gave him a grim dignity beyond his years.

He greeted the Marshal and regarded me with an unrecognizing eye. The Marshal said, 'My lord, here is one that has a claim on you,' and taking from me the ring Richard had given me put it into the hands of the king.

'Nay,' said Richard, 'I know this not.'

'My lord,' I said, 'it is your ring, given me when I saved your life before Châteauroux. You bid me come to you when there was peace in your lands, for my reward.'

The king placed the ring on his finger, looking down at it. I could not forbear a sigh, for I saw both ring and promise reft from me, and no profit thereby.

Then the king said, 'It is in my mind that I promised somewhat to a trouvère if he would bring me a good song.'

'My lord,' I said, 'I have made a song and will sing it.'

He frowned. 'How know I that the song is yours? Many jongleurs there are who sing, and who can tell whose the song? If you are in truth a trouvère——'

'I swear by Holy Rood,' I said, 'I am Denys de Courtebarbe, he to whom you gave that ring.'

'Ring?' said Richard, quick and sharp. 'What ring? I saw no ring.'

I cast a glance of despair at him and at his barons, and saw naught but chill regards. As for the Marshal, he stared at me as if uncertain whether he had to do with a madman or a cheat.

Then said Richard, 'If you are indeed a trouvère you will write me a new song in that space between now and when I go to dinner, having no converse with any man, shut up in a chamber alone, and bring it forth and sing it to me when I sit down to meat. And I will set you your theme. Will you accept this challenge?'

I had little choice but to agree. Then Richard said I should make him a sirvente in which two opposites should be combined in one harmonious whole. I was conveyed into an upper room beside the solar and shut up therein. They gave me a harp—for I had not brought my own—and a loaf of bread, some cheese, and some wine. Now was I on my mettle, for I saw well that if I could not come forth with some good song to please the king I should be cast out, beaten, or lose nothing but my head. I set to work and by sundown I had finished. Many now know the song I wrote, the sirvente which goes thus:

> 'Most do I love when winter's fled
> And singing birds swoop on the air,
> When all the earth is garlanded
> With flowering hawthorn in her hair.
> Then do I find my spirits soar

To hear the lively trumpet sound,
Where tents like mushrooms hide the ground,
And valiant knights come forth to war.
Then am I quick to take the field,
To hear the clash of lance on shield;
Better to me than meat and bread
Are cries of battle everywhere.
Great strokes provide great feats of arms,
The trampled grass with blood is wet,
On every hand rise new alarms
When men in springtime are well met.' (etc.)

I sang the whole over five or six times until I had both melody and words fixed in my head. And by then, a servant came to conduct me down to the hall where the boards had been spread and a good company were already seated at the low tables and the high. I came before the high table and placed my harp on my hip. The king motioned to a herald who stood at his right hand, and the herald raising his staff said, 'Noble lords, barons, knights, it is the king's will that you listen.'

Then the king said, 'Let that stranger stand aside for the moment, for there is new come into my lands the notable and famous trouvère Arnaut Daniel, who begs leave of me to sing a song he has written for my pleasure.'

There rose up from a place just below the salt that man pre-eminent among poets, he who had invented the sestina, most learned and gentle of men whose name was as well known to me as my own. I had never before seen him, and great was my curiosity. He was tall but slight of build, careworn, with large haunted eyes like those of the melancholy stag. He took up a harp inset with plates of precious amber and set about tuning it with the key, what while I stood clownishly staring and wondering how I could follow this prince of troubadours with my poor song. Arnaut smiled at me and bowed to the king, and then commenced singing in a pure, high voice:

'Most do I love when winter's fled
And singing birds swoop on the air,
And all the earth is garlanded. . . .'

And so on, to the very end of my song, word for word, note for note.

I felt that I had lost my wits. All became dark before my eyes, and when I could see again the first thing I saw was the king laughing. A great roar of laughter burst on my ears. All that company of lords, knights, squires, and ladies, laughed and applauded.

But for me there was only rage. I ground my teeth and stared into the eyes of Arnaut Daniel, and said, 'That is my song and you have stolen it, how I know not, but by damned trickery.'

With that, I turned to leave the hall. But there came the herald and caught me by the arm and turned me round. He brought me up to the king's side, and the king, with tears of merriment in his eyes, embraced me, kissing me on both cheeks.

'My poor Denys,' he said, 'you have suffered enough for this jest. Indeed, Arnaut was hidden by my orders in the solar and listened as you rehearsed your song until he, too, had learned it. Thus did he steal it, and you should think it no shame that it was first sung for you by such a master.'

'And upon my soul,' said Arnaut, coming to take me by the hand, 'it is the best of songs and my one wish is that I might in truth have written it myself. Forgive me, Sir Denys, for this deceit.'

'He had no choice,' Richard chuckled. 'All were in on it, even to my good Marshal, who protested but in the end went along with it.'

I could not speak. I looked at the king and remembered the words of the Marshal, and thought to myself that this was a sorry sort of jest to play on a poet, and a small-minded and evil way so to use me.

Richard set a heavy arm over my shoulders, saying, 'My lords, now will I make known to you that this man indeed saved my life when I was in great peril, at the risk of his own. And he has met my challenge and written a song in such wise that few could equal him.' And he took from about his neck a chain of soft gold in flat links, each link set with a ruby or a cat's eye, and put it about my own neck.

'You shall remain with me and I will reward you as you deserve,' said he. 'Go, sit down and feast with us. And it is my will that you shall be a member of my household. Does this please you, trouvère?'

I was all perplexed and torn two ways, by his open-handed praise and generosity, and by his spiteful humour, so that I knew not how to take him. But I bowed low, and all I said was, 'Great thanks, my lord.'

*　　*　　*

"So that I did not know how to take him. . . ." This was to be the keynote of the days that followed.

For Richard was a man full of contradictions, swayed by impulses which appeared sometimes to be no more than whims, seesawing abruptly between extremes. He was England's king; he had at last taken the place of the father with whom he had so often quarrelled, so often been reconciled, so fiercely hated and so humbly submitted to, yet all his efforts were now bent towards leaving England as quickly as he might. He was expert in the use of arms and seemed to love all warlike exercises, he was renowned for his skill in battle and siege, yet he shunned tourneys, and although his companions from France waited for him to hold at least one tournament in celebration of his coronation, they waited in vain. His reign began with that leniency he had displayed towards William the Marshal and extended to nearly all those who had refused to abandon King Henry during the recent conflict, yet, when three noblemen who had gone over to Richard's side and had been bereft of their lands in consequence asked him for justice, he played them a cruel trick. He restored their lands to them, and then, having satisfied the letter of their request, immediately despoiled them again, remarking coolly, "Such is the reward of traitors."

Every monarch turns before the wind of many influences, some good, some bad. The trouble was that in Richard's case you never could be sure which would blow the strongest from day to day. There was, on one hand, the upright and honourable William the Marshal; on the other was William Longchamp, Richard's chancellor, as different from the Marshal as a man could be. He was dwarfish and lame, the son of a labourer, malicious and subtle, a man of whom it was said that he used both hands in the dish with equal dexterity and could move from place to place by the devil's help like a flash

86

of lightning. Another who swayed Richard was his brother,
John Lackland, that strange and self-centred youth, his father's
favourite, yet foremost among those who had rebelled against
the old king. No honour, it seemed, was too great for Richard
to give him, but none could say precisely where John's own
affections lay, apart from himself. But more insistently than
any other wind blew the mistral of that southern queen,
Richard's mother, Eleanor of Aquitaine.

At the outset, almost in the moment of his landing in England, her power was clear. It was she who had urged, and
obtained, the release of all who had suffered imprisonment
under the old king. As Richard was leaving Winchester, news
had come to him of a raid on the Welsh border and he had at
once turned aside, quite ready to forsake the road to his coronation in favour of a bickering. Although no other could
persuade him, Eleanor had swiftly caused him to change his
mind and go on to London.

For good or ill, her hands had shaped his life and his destiny.
He had always been the darling among her children, that one
with the greatest breadth of spirit, most generous, most cul-
tured, and perhaps most intelligent. Young Henry's enormous
charm had never been sufficient to overcome a kind of awe-
some stupidity in his nature; Geoffrey was crafty and selfish;
John was like his father, energetic and egotistical, but in him
old Henry's force became mere arrogance, his statesmanship
mere guile. In the marital war between Eleanor and Henry,
she had made her sons her allies. Young Henry and Geoffrey
were dead, and she herself had been punished with fifteen years
of imprisonment for setting them in rebellion. She had done
her best with Richard, and now at last he sat in his father's
seat.

She had loved Henry deeply and passionately. But she
was the descendant of a vigorous line and had had no intention
of living an uneventful life as a mere decorative object. She
had planned many moves with Henry, and tried intrigue on
her own account; after a few years the king had refused to
consider her participation in affairs of state as anything more
than meddling and had shut his ears firmly to all her sugges-
tions. Eleanor was a cultivated woman while Henry had little
time for such fripperies as poetry or art. She loved splendour
and elegance, and Henry was a man of action, one who

transacted his business—and even ate many of his meals—standing up; he was plain-living, coarse, stubborn, rude.

These differences, profound as they were, might somehow have been resolved had it not been for the fact that Henry was also as lecherous as a sparrow. What was worse, he had not even had the decency to conceal his promiscuity: his illegitimate sons were given preferments, and his affair with Rosamund Clifford, which had lasted for ten years, had been an open scandal. Eleanor was no prude; like most intellectual women she was simply proud. She had ended by detesting Henry as passionately as she had loved him. The Plantagenet had stalked through her dreams with muddy boots, eyeing her stonily, threatening her with his maleness. And this had been her son's legacy from her: scorn and contempt for his father mixed with a loyalty both feudal and filial. There was something more. Richard was unable to enjoy the sensual love of women which should have been natural to such a brawling, masterful, vital man, but turned instead to other men for his enjoyment. To Eleanor, this made little difference so long as he was resigned to marriage and to the dutiful begetting of an heir to the throne. However, it aroused a certain distaste among a few of the clergy who went around muttering about "the sin of Sodom", and it made things awkward for some of his friends, who either had to reject his advances or to deny rumours that they had accepted them.

All these contrary forces made Richard a difficult patron. Denys found himself confronted by a certain ambiguity in their relations from the start, a pattern which tended to repeat that disagreeable beginning with its mixture of outrage and gratification.

He had spent a final day with Arthur and Maude, bidding them farewell and accepting their congratulations. Arthur, blinking myopically, embraced him and said, "There will always be room for you at Hidehurst. If, for any reason, things don't work out at court you will come home to me. Will you promise?" "I promise," Denys said, with a smile. Maude gave him a parting kiss on both cheeks, and said, "Now that you have found your place beside the king, you'll forget us simple countryfolk."

"Lady," said Denys, "I owe everything to your kindness. Do you take me for an ingrate? I will come back to Sussex as soon as Richard will allow me."

"You will be welcome," she murmured.

"There are some things I cannot say as yet," he continued. "But if matters go well, it may be—there is something I will ask you——"

Her neck and cheeks became very pink. "Be sure I'll answer you," she said.

He nodded. "Well," he said, "I will send you a song to keep you in mind of me."

"We won't need that," Arthur said, stoutly. "Oh, excuse me, I didn't mean it that way, Denys. I meant, we'll think of you without any reminding. Good luck, and God keep you."

They parted then, and Denys moved his few belongings into Westminster, where he was given lodging in a corner of the Old Palace. That evening, the king called him up to the high table and asked him to sing for the company, and when he had done so to great applause Richard dismissed everyone and commanded Denys to remain. They withdrew to the upper end of the hall, which was curtained off by a great crimson hanging, and Richard, tossing aside his mantle, dropped in a chair and stretched out his long legs.

"Come, Denys," he said, "let's be friends, let's get to know one another. Tell me about yourself."

"Well, my lord," Denys began.

Richard interrupted. "Oh, no titles between us, please. You're not one of my great vassals, you're a poet. It's only with men like you, and Arnaut Daniel, and Peire Vidal, and so on, that I can feel truly at ease. You don't know what a burden it is to be a king! If I could only have remained Count of Poitou, if I could have held my court at Poitiers the way my great-grandfather did, with trouvères and musicians. . . . Did you know that I've written some songs?" he asked, rather shyly, biting at a hair of his moustache. His head shook gently, which made it look as though he were begging Denys to say yes.

"No, I didn't, my lord," Denys said.

"Please call me Blondel," Richard said. "That's the name I've written under. Do you know Peire Vidal?"

"Yes, my—Blondel—I served my apprenticeship under him and first learned the art of poetry from him."

"Isn't he a marvellous man? Mad as a March hare, of course. Do you remember how he used to carry that enormous pavilion about with him everywhere, and claim it had been given him by the king of Aragon because he was of royal blood? He said that every woman he met fell madly in love with him, and that he had to fight his way through mobs of insanely desirous wenches whenever he set foot in the street."

"Yes, I remember once——" Denys began.

Richard said, laughing heartily, "He came in panting, one day, covered with scratches, complaining that he had sung a mere two lines of a new song and straightway every woman within earshot had tried to catch him and bed him. This was when I was at my mother's court in Poitou. And so I remember Marie of Champagne challenged him to sing the whole song to her to see if she could somehow find the strength to withstand his allure."

"How did he get out of that?" Denys asked, greatly amused, and not daring to feel annoyance at the king's interruptions.

"Oh, the rascal, he was clever, he began to sing and pretended that his voice was gone; he said he had grown hoarse from shouting for help. With that, my mother had him turned out of doors, for she said he was not only a liar and a braggart but that any man who cried for help when women tried to kiss him was too discourteous for her to bear. Come and sit beside me."

Denys did so, and Richard touched his hand. "Would you like to hear one of my songs? But if I sing for you, will you promise to tell me exactly what you think, just as if I were one of your fellowship?"

"Of course, Blondel. I am always honest with other trouvères."

"Yes, or I will call you *Renier*, as I did Peire."

"'Foresworn'?" Denys raised his eyebrows.

"He also promised to tell me the truth about my songs, and then pretended to faint with a joy too great to be borne when I sang, and said he was left too drained and limp to give any criticism. He was such a fearful liar. Have you seen him lately?"

"No, Blondel."

"Nor must you lie to me. I can't bear liars." He lay back in his chair, and lolling so was like some huge feline only partly domesticated, his heavy-lidded eyes half closed, the fingers of one hand tangled in his short beard showing a glint of a gold ring against the red-gold hair. "My father lied to me, too. He taught me that it was part of the kingly art, you know. Did you ever meet him?"

"No."

"No. . . . I thought you might have, in his expeditions up and down my lands. Poitou and Aquitaine had barely a yard of unscorched ground by the time he finished with them and died."

Denys moved uncomfortably on the low stool where he sat beside Richard. He wasn't at all sure he liked being made the king's confidant in this way, although it was flattering enough.

Richard patted him on the knee. "Have you everything you need?" he said. "Don't hesitate, my Renier, but tell me whenever there's anything I can do. I promised that you should be rewarded. Perhaps you think the memory of a king is short? No, I haven't forgotten that I owe my freedom, or perhaps my life, to you."

"Well, I—mm—I haven't much money," Denys muttered.

"You shall have money. Remind me tomorrow. What else?"

"You're very kind," Denys said gratefully. "I did want to talk to you about a lady."

"Ah?" Richard abruptly sat erect. "What lady?"

"Her name is Maude Fitzleroy. Her home is in Sussex. She is perfectly charming, and a friend of William the Marshal."

"I see. So that's how William came to bring you to me."

"Yes, and my problem is very simple. I'm the fourth son of the Seneschal of Courtebarbe, which means that I have no prospects. And yet I'm in love with her, and I think she's, well, not indifferent by any means."

"Is she a ward of mine?" asked Richard.

"Oh, no. She's the vassal of William de Hauterive."

"Well, what do you expect me to do?"

"I thought, if you could support my suit . . . if you had no objection. . . ." Denys fell silent for the king's face had become rather hard and cold.

"I have no objection," Richard said, after a moment. Suddenly, he smiled, one of his warm, flashing smiles. "Let me think about the matter. Maybe I can help you. You may go now. I'm feeling rather tired."

"Thank you, Blondel," Denys said. He got to his feet and, taking Richard's hand, kissed it.

He lifted the corner of the canvas drapery. Richard said, "You won't have to worry about it for a while, in any case. I'm going north to Hertford and Northampton tomorrow. I'll want you with me."

There was something disturbing in his tone, reinforced, rather than diminished, by his smile, and Denys went off to his box of straw feeling slightly uneasy although he couldn't have said exactly why.

Nine days later his uneasiness was becoming desperation. In the king's train he had gone from Westminster to Saint Alban's, from Saint Alban's to Silverstone, from Silverstone to Northampton, and thence to the manor of Geddington. The two pounds Arthur had given him to tide him over were gone, spent on new clothing suitable for the court, on new harp-strings, on necessaries, and on stabling and fodder for his horse and sumpter. The king, busy with charters and state affairs, had said nothing further to him nor had he even been asked to sing at any dinners; Arnaut Daniel had been given that honour on several occasions, and on others ordinary minstrels had been selected. Even more chilling had been an incident on the second day at Geddington; summoning his courage, Denys had waited for the king to finish signing some papers and had accosted him as he left the council room, bowing and saying, "My lord, I have learned a new song by the trouvère Blondel, if you will allow me to sing it to you tonight," and Richard, looking absently at him, had said, "I know no one named Blondel," and had stalked away.

Denys hung on at Geddington because he didn't know what else to do. He was tempted to leave, to rejoin Arthur in Sussex, but he was ashamed to own defeat so quickly. He toyed with the idea of coming straight out with a proposal of marriage to Maude, but his pride forbade such an action. He pondered bitterly on the fickleness of kings, and meanwhile rode to Northampton where he found a goldsmith to whom he sold the jewelled neck-chain Richard had given him, for fifty shillings, a fraction of its worth.

He had two friends who made things bearable for him.

Arnaut Daniel was unfailingly kind and complimentary, and they soon became very intimate; they spent many hours together discussing the forms of poetry, mutual friends in the profession, and other shop talk. From Arnaut, Denys heard that Peire Vidal had gone to Marseilles where he was living under the roof of Lord Barral of Baux, who cherished him and supported him. Another old comrade, Peire of Auvergne, had won the Sparrowhawk at the court of Puy Saint-Marie for his canzo, "Nightingale, I beg you go", which had ravished the senses of all those who heard it. To Arnaut, Denys once confided what he had so far told no one else: his dream of finding a new and utterly different kind of poetic expression.

"I know just what you mean," Arnaut nodded. "That is why I invented the sestina, with its complicated structure. I thought the answer lay in a more difficult shape for a poem. For just as a cathedral is greater than a village church, I reasoned that the beauty of a poem must lie in the amount of work needed to write it. I was wrong."

Denys sighed. "Gold is softer than iron," he said. "I know a hermit who once told me not to search for what I wanted in form alone."

"Yes, he's quite right. It is as if one were to elevate wood-chopping over embroidery simply because it's heavier labour. And I have seen simple village churches where God dwells more happily than in many a cathedral. All I got for my pains was the accusation that I wrote in a style that was too complex to imitate—in fact, I began to find it too difficult for my own uses! Then, I began using far-fetched metaphors, casting further afield for the strange, the outlandish, the unseizable, the inexpressible——"

> " 'I am Arnaut who piles up wind,
> Courses the hare against the ox
> And swims against the stream,' "

quoted Denys.

"Thank you. It's good of you to remember that. I was never satisfied with it, myself. But you know, any number of trou-vères have said that my words were too obscure. My old friend Thibaud, the Monk of Montaldon, made fun of that poem you've just quoted. He said, 'Arnaut has indeed given us something new: love-making under water. I never even knew he could swim.' "

"But does it matter what other poets say? Or what anyone

says?" Denys cried. "I met a man once, a common jongleur, who wrote a poem which sticks in my head to this day. And he said he didn't give a damn for what anyone thought, he wrote his poems for his own pleasure."

"Yes, and no doubt he was happy doing so," said Arnaut. "I am a weaker man. I want my poems to be heard, and to awaken in those who hear them the sadness or joy I feel when I write them. My God, Denys, if I were condemned to live shut up in a tower to sing my songs to the four walls, or to the birds, I would sooner die. It would be as terrible a sentence as to be condemned never to write another poem."

"But there must be an answer!" Denys said, passionately. "Our poetry seems to me so dry, so sterile—monotonous! Always the same images, always the dawn, the evening, the nightingale, or the cries of the battlefield."

"When you find the answer, let me know," Arnaut chuckled. "What else is there in life but love and war?"

"Oh——!" Denys shrugged. "Love and war are proper enough subjects. But there are others, aren't there? And it's what we say about them that means more than the subjects themselves. That jongleur, that same fellow I told you about, he sang me a poem which he called a Lament. He used the rough form of the *planh*, the same kind of thing Bertrand de Born used when he wrote his Lament on the death of Young Harry, the same thing half a dozen poets have written on the death of the late King Henry. But do you know what his lament was about? You'll never guess. An old whore bewailing her lost youth!"

"What?" said Arnaut, raising his eyebrows with an incredulous laugh.

"That's right. And it was good, Arnaut. Damn good! It went through you like steel, like a shiver. I wish I could remember his exact words, but they're gone like the youth she wept for."

"But—no one writes poems about whores," Arnaut protested.

"He did. And another about all things ending in death. 'In the end the wind takes all.'"

"That's a good line."

"Yes. And a quatrain which said—although I can't remember at this distance the rhyme or metre—'Thus we regret our happy youth as we squat on our haunches around a little fire of dry leaves, ourselves aflame so young; so quickly burned out.' "

"Mmm. An interesting image. You could do something with an image like that," Arnaut murmured.

"You see? But imagine if, when Richard asked me to quickly furnish him out with a nice new poem, I had written something like this:

> "'As long as kings and noble lords
> Whose mothers all wore golden crowns
> Must end at last between pine boards
> And others have their robes and crowns——' "

He could not finish, but burst into laughter.

Arnaut snorted. "He'd have had your head."

"And so I gave him one of our standard works," Denys said, sourly. " 'Two opposites——' The same theme Bertrand de Born has used, and Guilhem de Saint Gregori, and Bernart de Ventadorn, and I don't know how many others—'In the fair springtime I love to hear the clash of arms, the cry of war, the screams of the dying . . .' and so on, and so on."

Arnaut tapped him lightly on the arm. "You mustn't run yourself down," he said. "It was a first-rate poem. And you needn't think that Richard's ear is so dull or his sensibilities so blunt that he didn't recognize it. He's not a fool in spite of his size and his warlike appetite. Perhaps you don't know it, but he's written some very passable poetry under the name of Blondel."

"I know. What am I to make of him, Arnaut? He is sometimes so generous, and then so beastly. He is noble and greathearted as he was on the day I saw him facing a dozen men who wanted to kill him. Then he will be small and nasty, as he was yesterday when he pretended he didn't know who I was."

Arnaut said thoughtfully, "You know the saying, 'No land without a lord, no man without a master.' We must each of us give our fealty to someone."

"Have you?"

"To Richard? No. I am the man of the Count of Perigord who is Richard's vassal."

"Richard is worth following," Denys said, with a sigh.

"You know the Song of the Four Sons of Aymon?"

Denys sat up straight, smiling. "Know it? I should think so! It was once my favourite of all the old chansons de geste."

"Oh? Mine, too. You know, I wrote a new version of the adventures of Renaud, the oldest of the sons."

"I didn't know that. You must sing it for me."

"I will. What I wanted to remind you of was the words of old Aymon: 'Better to be a noble vassal than a lord of men.' "

"I remember. 'Shame to that man who dies not for his lord.' "

"When you find someone fit to be a king, and if he draws you, then you should go, you should do homage with an open heart. What do you think Aymon would have said of Richard?"

"I suppose he would have chided me for trying to find fault with a lion. I suppose he would be right."

"If you're uncertain, why not leave Richard? You can always find a patron, Denys. You have a reputation——"

"Thanks. I don't know why I don't leave. Partly, because I think he owes me something for saving his life. There, that's candid, isn't it?"

"But there's more to it than that?"

"Yes, he *does* draw me. He attracts me—this same image comes to mind—like seeing a lion as a household pet and wanting to stroke it but being frightened of it. . . ."

"In any case, there's no hurry. You needn't decide today," said Arnaut.

"I want to find out all about him," Denys said. "But you're right, not now. I want to hear your song about Renaud de Montaudon before I hear anything else."

And this conversation, while it didn't really solve anything for Denys, made him feel much better.

His other friend, curiously enough, was Hugh de Hamelincourt.

Hugh was twice Denys's age. He was a blusterer. He had a bad habit of repeating himself. He was solidly conservative, and regarded anything new with intense suspicion. He was scarred and furrowed like an old tomcat, and affected rough clothes and bad manners. He lived by a simple principle: that the duty of a knight was the trade of arms, and he would have no truck with mercy, compassion, humility, or other nonsense of that sort which he termed "clerical twaddle".

And he accompanied his endless tales about his adventures with digs in the ribs, nudges, and pokes of his short, powerful fingers, all of which was exceedingly painful.

But whatever he was, he was not a bore. His stories were frequently comical, always scandalous. With William the Marshal and Baudouin de Béthune, another grizzled ruffian whom he called "Bobo", he had knocked about tournaments, courts, and camps of war for twenty years; unlike the other two he had nothing to show for it, for he was addicted to gambling and would bet on which flower a butterfly might light upon, or how many times a priest would stumble over a word during mass.

Furthermore, every day he gave Denys a good work-out with sword and lance. It helped pass the time, and provided Denys with plenty of exercise and fresh air. While they stayed at Geddington he had a post planted in a field and wrapped in sacking, and this was used for sword practice; at the other end of the field he had a small gallows planted with a ring hanging from a cord at the end of its arm, and this served as a quintain for practice with the lance. Hugh, apparently tireless, would whack away at the post with grunts and curses and set Denys to doing the same while he watched with a bilious eye and chewed his moustache and said, "Lift your shield with that stroke! Put your shoulder behind the sword!" The splinters flew, and Denys would feel that his arms were ready to fly off as well. Or, mounting their horses, they would canter at the quintain and try to catch the ring on their lance-points. After an hour or two of this kind of exertion, dripping with sweat and exhausted, Denys could forget his problems in the simple physical pleasures of a bath, a cup of wine, and utter relaxation. In a languorous stupor he would sit on a bench with Hugh and listen to the stories of his exploits and be content for a time.

They were sitting thus, one day, in the warm sun surrounded by the thrumming of bees, and Hugh had fallen silent. Great piled masses of clouds lay on the horizon—the English sky was almost never empty—and somewhere not far away someone was sharpening a blade with a steady *wheet-wheet*, a soothing, monotonous sound like the note of a bird.

Denys said, idly, "I've been thinking about swordsmanship. I've got a sort of an idea, Hugh."

"What's that?"

"Well, you see, what about using your sword blade instead of your shield to block your opponent's slash? He strikes at you and expects you to ward the blow on your shield, and you catch it on your blade instead."

Hugh blew out his cheeks. "Use the sword blade as a shield, what?"

"Exactly."

"And then? If you caught his stroke on your blade, how would you strike back at him? With your shield?"

"Absolutely. You'd step in close and bash him with the point of the shield."

"Can't be done," said Hugh.

Denys raised his head. "Why not?"

"Why not? Why, my dear old gossip, it just wouldn't work, that's why not."

"I still don't see your objection."

Hugh clicked his tongue. "Look here, my dear chap, it's never been tried, has it?"

"Not so far as I know."

"Well, there you are."

"There I am where?"

"Perfectly clear. It won't work."

"But how do you know?"

"Well, if it would work, somebody would have done it, don't you see?" He shook his head in kindly admonition. "You young fellas are all alike. Too bloody restless. Always looking for something new, some new way of doing things. You take this bee Richard has in his bonnet, now, for instance."

"What bee is that?"

"Haven't you heard? Arbalests. Cross-bows, these English call 'em. The Italians have been using them for some time, developed 'em out of regular siege ballistas. Richard's mad for them. Claims he can make a stronger supporting force out of his infantry by backing up the spearmen with arbalestiers, or whatever the word is."

"And you don't think it's a good idea?"

"Good? Good?" Hugh poured a cup of wine straight down his throat and almost choked in his agitation. "My dear fella, it's preposterous! It's downright dangerous! In the first place, who cares about infantry as a supporting force? Rabble is what they've always been, and rabble is what they are. Throatcutters. At the first sign of trouble they run. Why, I remember a tournament Bobo and the Marshal and I went to—have I told you about this, eh?—where Simon de Neauphlé showed up with three hundred foot, mostly spearmen. The Marshal and Young Harry were ahead of us, and Simon tried to bar their way. Harry wanted to turn back. By God, the Marshal rode his horse right into those dogs and they turned tail and ran. He captured Simon, too. What the hell good was all his infantry then?"

"But why is it dangerous?"

"Why? My good old gossip, have you ever seen what one of those arbalest bolts will do to chain mail at close range? I have. Sling-stones, ordinary arrows, are just not in it, believe me. How far do you think the Marshal would have got if Simon de Neauphlé's lot had had cross-bows? Those things in the hands of peasants would make them the equal of mounted knights. It would mean disaster, absolute disaster. A couple of hundred of them—all right. But Richard is talking about thousands. I presume he'll buy them in Italy and then teach our fellas how to use them. If he does, he's just giving them a bit, bridle, and saddle for their masters, that's what."

"I gather you don't think much of Richard as a military leader, then," Denys said, slyly.

"Ah, now, hold on. I wouldn't go so far as to say that," Hugh replied, clasping his hands over his stomach. "Don't think much of him? No, no, I'd never say that. He's young, you know, but he's damn good. You know about the taking of Taillebourg, of course?"

"The impregnable fortress?"

"That's it. High on a crag; nobody ever believed it could be taken by siege or storm. He marched up, burned the countryside and ravaged it, attacked the main gate, burst it in, and made himself master of the place. Less than a week. Incredible! He's got all his father's ability that way, and more. But I don't know whether he's got everything his father had up here." He tapped his forehead.

"He didn't like his father very much, did he?"

"Like him?" Hugh glanced at Denys, and then guffawed, jabbing him in the ribs. "Hated the old man's guts, my dear fella. And you know, I'm afraid the feeling was mutual. It didn't start out that way. Old Henry had a good deal of affection for Richard. It was *her* fault." He jerked his head in the general direction of London, where Queen Eleanor had remained at home. "Richard was her favourite. Since Young Harry was to receive England, she gave Richard Aquitaine and Poitou. Well, that was all right, you know, but Henry had no intention of letting his sons grow more powerful than he was. He thought of family above all. Wanted to let the youngsters see what was in store for them, but he meant to keep the generalship in his own hands. Quite right, too. You can't have three or four rulers on the same throne. After all, he wasn't the sort of man to retire in the prime of life. But *she* conspired with the princes and persuaded them that their father meant to cheat them out of their proper inheritances. That's what started the trouble. Henry finished it. Fifteen years in prison, and now it's her turn to rule the roost, eh?" He poked Denys with a forefinger like the butt of a lance.

Denys moved unobtrusively away. "Then you don't think King Henry really lied to Richard? You think he meant him to have Poitou and Aquitaine?"

"Kings don't *lie*, my dear fella," Hugh replied. "They evade, and conceal, and equivocate, and all the rest of it, but they don't *lie*. That's statesmanship, that's what it is. Henry was a master at it. By Christ's rood," he added, shaking his head in admiration, "if he said 'Good morning', you began to shake in your boots wondering what devilry he had up his sleeve. You take the case of the French princess, Alysia. She was betrothed to Richard when she was nine. This was supposed to tighten the bonds between England and France. Henry took her and raised her—keeping her as a hostage, you see. Well, every time the king of France demanded that she and Richard be married, Henry found some reason for putting it off. She was too valuable to him as bait. He held that marriage over King Louis's head, and then over King Philip's when the boy came to the French throne. But the fact is, when the girl was old enough, he seduced her himself, made her his mistress, and even, so they say, got a brat by her. He was an old devil, he was."

He sighed heavily. "I was faithful to him, all the same. And so was the Marshal. For all the wicked ways he treated William, the Marshal would have cut off his hand sooner than turn against him. And I'll give Richard his due—he tried his best not to break his oath of fealty. The trouble was, Henry put him in a quandary. He put everybody in a quandary at the very beginning."

"What do you mean?"

"Ah, well, Henry did homage to King Louis of France for Aquitaine and Poitou, you see, when the princes were only boys. Then he had the princes do homage to France for their holdings—Young Harry for Brittany and Anjou; Richard, who was about twelve, for Aquitaine and Poitou. Well, then, of course that made it seem as if there were two dukes of Aquitaine, Richard and his father, just as it looked to Eleanor and Young Harry as if there were two kings of England. France assumed that the sons were the real vassals, but Henry assumed that he was the vassal and that it was understood his sons would be his heirs. It made a fearful mess. Richard had a narrow line to walk, between his allegiance to his father and his oath of fealty to France. That's why he had to side with both.

"You know the story of how Richard came riding out after his father at Le Mans, without a lance or even a mail coat? Why do you suppose he did that?"

"I hadn't thought about it," Denys said.

"Why, he wanted to show that he had no intention of *attacking* his father, only of protecting him. That's why he was far in front of his own men. The Marshal knew it, too. And so he struck down Richard's horse; he might jolly well have slain Richard, you know."

"I see," Denys said, thoughtfully. "Richard must have been frightfully torn between the two loyalties."

"He was trying his best to satisfy both sides right up to the end," said Hugh. "He was trying to make peace between them at Gisors just before Henry died. He'll make a good king one of these days," he went on, emphasizing his words by jabbing Denys on the thigh until the pain was almost unendurable. "Got a lot to learn. But don't get the idea he's not a real fighter. He may have some idiotic notions, but he'll get over them."

"You were loyal to his father," Denys said. "Where do you stand with Richard, Hugh?"

"I? I was his father's liegeman, and I'm Richard's."

"No question about that?"

Hugh stared at him, his florid face grave. "You're not

serious, my dear fella. One must live up to one's blood, after all."

The phrase struck an echo deep in Denys. It returned to him again and again, nagging for recognition for the remainder of the day, but it wasn't until he was lying in bed that night that he remembered. When, as a boy of seven, he had been sent off to the castle of Beaupréau to do his service as a page, his mother had said to him, with her hands on his shoulders and her face close to his, "Do well, and don't shame us, my dear boy. Live up to your blood, to your noble lineage. Remember, you are serving a hard apprenticeship, but it is for the best thing in the world and some day we will see you wearing the belt of knighthood."

Her voice had broken. His father had taken him by the shoulder. "Come along," he had said, but not harshly.

Denys had clung to his mother, dry-eyed, speechless, and filled with terror.

His mother, embracing him once more, had pushed him off. "You must be brave, or mother will be very angry," she had said. "Go with your father."

He had known that this was coming. It was as inevitable as each day's sunrise. But now the dreadful moment was upon him; he who had always been obedient to his mother could not make his fingers unclench from her dress, could not make himself move to follow his father. His mother had opened his hands and his father had taken him by the arm and pulled him away. He had heard her sob, achingly; he was the youngest and last of her sons.

In the courtyard his father had lifted him into the saddle and had mounted his own horse. They had ridden out side by side, with six men at arms and a squire behind them. When they had passed over the causeway and left the river, Denys had burst into tears.

His father had growled, "How the devil do you ever expect to become a knight? Your brothers made no such fuss. Shut up, and dry your eyes; the men are watching you."

"I don't want to be a knight," Denys had whispered. But he had stopped crying and had mopped his face on his sleeve.

So that was it. It had gone deep, it had penetrated him and become part of him, something to be resisted but also to be obeyed. "Better to be a noble vassal ..." He was both the son of Aymon and Aymon himself: his mother's darling boy but also her fruit, and that obligation of blood to which she had submitted herself had been transmitted to him. Let him be as footloose as he would, there was no leaving this burden behind, it was a stone chained to his ankle: the necessity for finding a lord whom he could follow, the need to give loyalty and service and to have it received.

In any case, he thought, turning over and composing himself for sleep, the decision isn't up to me now, but to Richard, for it was he who cast me off.

But in the morning the wind had shifted once again.

Denys had barely finished his breakfast when a page came to summon him to meet with the king at Pipewell Abbey, which was within the manorial demesne. He found Richard in the refectory, a large, high room with a splendid vaulted ceiling. It had been swept and cleaned and the floor strewn with fresh rushes. Richard stood at one end gesturing with a riding crop as he directed the hanging of canvas curtains behind the dais and the arrangement of chairs and benches.

He gripped Denys's shoulder. "My dear Renier," he cried. "How good to see you again! Where have you been keeping yourself? Forgive me; I'll be with you in a moment. You, there! Move that armchair forward to the edge of the dais." He turned to his chamberlain, who stood at his elbow leaning on a polished staff. "I'll have the chancellor at my right— he can sit in the folding chair—and the archbishops on my left. Put a stool over there for the chancellor's secretary. Be sure that the Bishop of Durham sits right before me on the lower bench; I have a reason for it. Come, Denys, let me talk to you."

He drew Denys to a broad window-seat which looked out into the cloister. They sat down together, and Richard, with his most charming smile, said, "Now don't begin by frowning —I have seen little of you lately, and the fault is mine. There is so much to be done! And so little time. I gave my word to meet Philip in France in the spring, and there are a thousand things to attend to. You do forgive me, don't you?"

"My lord, forgiveness is not in a servant's power," said Denys. He had planned to be stand-offish, but the insistent warmth of Richard's manner melted him. The king's blue eyes were clear and guileless, and Denys could not find it in himself to disbelieve a word of what was said to him. "It's enough for me that you should see me now," he added.

" 'My lord?' " Richard said, as if hurt. "I thought we were friends. You must call me Blondel."

"In public?"

"Oh, no, of course, I see what you mean. Now tell me, you have everything you need? Enough money?"

"Well, I——" Denys began.

"I know how improvident you trouvères are!" Richard laughed. "You needn't try to excuse it. What else should a poet be but extravagant? I'll see that it's taken care of. And have you a new song for me?"

"Why, I have had——"

"I shall expect to hear it at dinner tonight." Richard patted Denys's knee. "And you and Arnaut are getting along well together, aren't you? He's such a talented man. I wouldn't blame you for feeling jealous of him. Now, let's get to business. I have summoned a council for this morning. They'll be arriving at any moment. I want you to sit in a corner—say, here in this window seat—and watch and listen."

"I, my lord?"

"You, my friend."

"But I don't know anything about——"

"Be calm. This council is in the nature of a fund-raising affair. Now, I anticipate a certain amount of resistance to my requests, especially from one or two gentlemen who can well afford to pay whatever I ask but who think they can't. I want you to take careful note of everything that is said, and particularly of anyone who shows fight. You will talk with me later and we'll settle which ones need attention."

Denys's heart sank. "But, my lord," he protested, "if it's a matter of challenging them—I mean, I can handle a sword or a lance but I'm hardly a champion——"

Richard stared at him. Then he burst out laughing. "My dear, good Denys," he said, "not *challenge*. Most of them will be clerics. I want you to write satires against them. A few lines, picking out their frailties and flaws, a biting couplet or two which can be sung or whispered—that sort of thing sometimes does more good than any pressure, to make a man see what a fool he's being. You're champion enough for that, aren't you?"

Denys could not conceal his blushes. "Yes, I can manage," he said. "So long as the blows are limited to metaphoric ones."

"Good man." Richard got to his feet, for his chamberlain was hurrying towards him, and there was a stir of arrival at the door. "Come to me when the council's over."

The benches quickly filled. There were noblemen in jewelled belts and rich tunics, the earls of Essex and Leicester and Striguil, the king's brother Count John, the chief justiciar of England, Ranulf de Glanvil, and several others. There were bishops, abbots, and priors from every part of England, some grey and gaunt, some sheep-faced and docile, some portly and well-fed. On the dais with King Richard were his chancellor, William Longchamp, whose lively eyes raked the assembly as he sat hunched in a little folding chair, and the archbishops of Rouen, Trèves, Dublin, and Canterbury, their garments stiff with gold and precious stones. The chamberlain struck his staff on the floor and slowly all grew quiet.

Richard sat erect, his thumbs hooked in his belt, his golden moustache lifting to a little smile, the crown gleaming upon his ruddy hair. Even seated, he towered above the others on the platform and dominated the room.

"Well, my lords," he said, "I suppose you're wondering why I called this meeting."

He regarded them benevolently, and reached out a hand into which the chancellor put a sheet of parchment. Richard glanced at it.

"I have here," he said, "the treasurer's report for the fiscal year which will end on the 24th of this month, just a little over a week away. I know you'll forgive my anticipating the date but we're a trifle pressed for time. According to this report, the revenue for the year amounted to—or will amount to—£48,781, nought, nought. An accounting of the Royal Treasury, taken on 15th August, showed a balance of £66,666 13s. 4d. However, as you know, the coronation proved rather costly, although I'm sure you'll all agree it was well worth the expense for the sake of putting our best foot forward and starting off the reign with the best possible augury for a prosperous future. Furthermore, I have restored to the Queen Mother her dowry so that she need no longer rely on the Exchequer. It's my hope that this will maintain her in her proper state and will make up somewhat for the indignities and outrages to which she was subjected for so many years. I'm certain none of you will find anything to object to in that."

He paused and glanced over his audience. No one stirred.

"This will leave us," he continued, "with a total balance of something under fifty thousand pounds, give or take a few shillings. Quite inadequate, as I'm sure you'll agree, for a Christian army going to free the Holy Land."

The justiciar, de Glanvil, a very old, bald man with a silky white beard but still vigorous and straight of back, said, "Then, my lord, it is your fixed intention to go to the Holy Land at once?"

"Not to the Holy Land," Richard replied. "That is, not at once. I have pledged my knightly word to King Philip to join him at Easter in France, and to set out then. Which reminds me that from the treasury balance we must deduct the sixteen thousand-odd pounds due Philip under the terms of my agreement with him at Gisors, in July. That was the price of his resignation of claims to the lands he took from my father in Aquitaine and Poitou. But surely, my lord justiciar, you wouldn't have me break my oath or refuse the Cross I took so many years ago?"

"Your father also took the Cross, my lord," de Glanvil said, stubbornly. "But he recognized that his kingdom had a prior claim on his attentions. I myself took the Cross four years ago, and yet I feel that England, on the threshold of a new reign, needs its government."

"De Glanvil," said Richard, thoughtfully, "I would not for worlds stand between you and your duty to the Holy Sepulchre. It will be difficult to find someone to replace you."

He turned to the chancellor. "William," he said, in a soft voice, "make a note that I release de Glanvil from his obligations to the Crown upon payment of—hmm—fifteen thousand pounds."

Longchamp nodded, and gestured to his secretary. The ex-chief justiciar sat down again looking grim.

"That will help pay Philip," Richard went on, with a frank and ingenuous smile. "As it happens, I already have a couple of men in mind for the post of chief justiciar. My dear de Glanvil, it will take two to fill your shoes." He held out his hand again, and the chancellor handed him a sheaf of parchments. "By these charters, I hereby appoint William de Mandevill, earl of Essex, and Hugh du Puiset, bishop of Durham, to

serve as chief justiciars, jointly. Furthermore, in token of my
affection and in keeping with his high office, I have hereby
given Hugh du Puiset the earldom of Northumberland."

The bishop rose from his place on a bench just before the
dais, sleek, round-headed, slab-faced, smiling. "My lord, I
am grateful," he said.

"Yes, Hugh, and you will have the opportunity to put your
gratitude into more concrete terms," said Richard. "You took
the Cross, as I recall, and you must understand that that places
me in a dilemma. I need you here at home, and at the same
time I can't deny you the fulfilment of your vow to go on
Crusade."

There was a silence, and the bishop slowly sank down again.

Richard shuffled through his papers. "As it happens," he
said, cheerfully, "I have here letters patent from His Holiness,
Pope Clement, granting release from the vow of the Cross to all
those who in my judgment are needed to conduct the affairs of
the kingdom at home."

He looked up blandly. "It must be understood," he went
on, "that in such cases, the Crown will require some compen-
sation. Hugh, my dear friend, I'm sure you can find ten
thousand pounds for what amounts to relief from a vexatious
burden."

The bishop grinned broadly, for he had been expecting a
much more exhorbitant figure. "Willingly, dear cousin," he
said. "It's worth it to have seen the magic of kingship in
action."

Richard's eyebrows lifted. "Magic? I don't follow."

"Why, right before our eyes you have transformed me—
an old bishop—into a new young earl," said du Puiset.

There was a good deal of laughter, in which Richard joined.

"Well, well," said the king at last, "now that the ice is
broken, I hope it's clear to all of you assembled here that you
may show directly to my treasury your pleasure at being
left safely at home in your dioceses, abbeys, or castles. And
before the week is out, please. A crusade, my friends, is not
come by cheaply. I must have a war-chest sizeable enough to
carry on a real war. This is not going to be a forty-day feuda-
tory squabble. Those of us who go to the East are going to stay
there until we have retaken the Holy Sepulchre and broken the
Saracen power completely."

His face had become stern and his geniality was, for the moment, gone. He thumped the arm of his chair with one large freckled fist so that the wood creaked.

The archbishop of Rouen, raising a thin, white hand, said, "I applaud your zeal, my lord. But may not zeal be carried sometimes to excess? Surely, a kingdom deprived of its king is like a body from which the head has been shorn, whereby, from a superfluxion of the vital fluid, i.e., blood, we witness the degeneration of the members and the termination of existence? If you set no term to your absence, and if it should stretch, let us suppose, beyond a year, what excesses, what rival comminations, what factionalism, what——"

"Spare me, reverend sir," Richard broke in. "Any more polysyllables and I'll have a splitting headache. I will leave a sound set of administrators behind me. They will include, in addition to the two chief justices, William Marshal, earl of Striguil, whom you all respect and admire, Geoffrey fitz Peter, William Brewerre, Robert of Wheatfield, and Roger fitz Reinfrid. You may as well understand once and for all that I don't intend to come home until I have accomplished my vow. I didn't say I would go and fight Saladin. I said I would go to the Holy Land and rescue it and the Holy Sepulchre of Our Lord from the infidels. There's only one way to do that and that is to smash those savage atheists once and for all, to demolish their power and to disperse them!

"The mistakes made in the past were simple ones. Previous crusaders made truces with the infidels. They made bargains with them, and were satisfied to hold bits of land in Syria or Palestine. And what happened? A strong leader like Saladin was able to rise, to consolidate his forces, to divide them and deal with them bit by bit and finally to destroy them.

"There's an empire over there for the taking, my friends. Pope Urban II realized that back in the year 1095. Didn't he say, at Clermont, 'Set out on the road to the Holy Sepulchre, take the land from that wicked godless people and make it your own. That land which is flowing with milk and honey, more fruitful than all others, as it were a second Paradise of delights.' Ah, yes, I can hear you smacking your lips. Well, the idiots who settled over there—no, don't look shocked—*idiots*, like Louis of France who let himself be diverted into attacking Damascus, a thoroughly unprofitable undertaking, or

Baldwin, who made truces as fast as he broke them, or Guy of Lusignan who let himself be trapped at the Horns of Hattin— God's legs! Imagine such folly, to be cut off from water and surrounded on a dry rock! God knows what he thought he was doing up there. I understand that when the Saracens captured his knights they were all prostrate on the ground; not one was wounded, they were simply exhausted. What could be expected of such blockheads except that they should lose everything that was won in the First Crusade?''

His face was glowing; he stared into some distance perceived only by himself, his eyes wide, his teeth shining in his beard.

"I'm going to get that empire," he said. "I'm going to hold it. There isn't room for negotiation with the Saracens. I won't bargain with 'em. I'll sweep them away. But to do so, I'll need money. I intend to sell anything I can to get it. I'm open to any reasonable offer. There are good lands available, Crown privileges, Crown demesnes, exemptions, anything you like if you've got the money. By God's legs, if I could find a buyer for it, I'd sell London!''

When he had finished there was a good deal of applause and then a gabble of excited talk until the chamberlain pounded the floor with his staff and brought silence.

Richard said, "Are there any more questions before I get down to further specific details?''

The archbishop of Canterbury, as rubicund and burly as the archbishop of Rouen was pale and bony, said, "My lord, I've heard rather disturbing news that you intend to use a certain weapon, a weapon so terrible that I can scarcely bring myself to speak of it.''

"You mean the arbalest," Richard said, calmly.

The archbishop drew down the corners of his mouth. "Exactly. The arbalest. I have heard the rumour that you intend to purchase several thousand of these devices. I would be gratified at the assurance that this rumour is false.''

"The rumour is false," Richard answered.

The archbishop sank back, folding his hands within his sleeves.

"I do not intend to buy several thousand arbalests," Richard went on. "I intend to hire several thousand arbalestiers, or crossbowmen, mostly from Genoa. They're the best, I hear. They'll probably join me in Sicily, or at Acre.''

The archbishop's face became so empurpled that one of the monks started forward in terror, ready to catch his master should he topple over in a fit.

"My lord," gasped the archbishop. "Sir! I protest! This weapon you speak of is anathema. Most reverend lord of Rouen! My lord of Trèves! You spoke with me about this matter. I appeal to you."

The archbishop of Rouen said, shakily, "It is as he says, sir. Although none may dispute that war must be waged by the use of implements or, as it were, contrivances for the better execution of the task, *ex necessitate rei*, nevertheless there exists some unlawful machinery so fearful in its effect, so inhuman and noxious, that in short——"

"In short," thundered the archbishop of Canterbury, finding his voice once more, "the Church of Our Lord Jesu Christ, full of charity and love for God's creatures, cannot be prevailed upon to sanction its use, as a matter of principle. I remind you, my lord, that the second Lateran Council fifty years ago expressly prohibited the hand-ballista to be used by Christians. And I would add that in the army of the Cross it would fill me with horror to see pilgrims operating such hellish instruments."

"Apocalyptic," whispered the ancient archbishop of Trèves, faintly. "The end of mankind. It is said that the machine will shoot a bolt no longer than a man's hand a distance of five hundred paces with such violence that nothing can withstand it."

In his most winning and persuasive tone, Richard said, "My lords, my lords, I share your abhorrence of this weapon. Nor will I excuse it, as I might, by saying that war is hell. However, let me bring to your attention two points. In the first place, the arbalest will not be used by English or French troops—at least, not by any large numbers of them. What blame there is must be laid to the Italians who have developed the weapon and perfected it, and who employ it daily. The Church's very just censure must, therefore, fall upon their heads. And since they will use it in any case, what harm can there be in employing them to use it against the Infidel?

"In the second place, let me ask your reverend lordships whether the saving of human life is of no concern to you?"

They looked at him in puzzlement. "How can you speak of

saving lives by using the arbalest?" said the archbishop of Canterbury, at last. "It's a contradiction, surely——"

"Not at all. Consider: if by using the arbalest I can shorten the time it takes to defeat the Saracens, I will be saving the lives of Christians who would otherwise fall in battle. Indeed, I will be saving Saracen lives as well, for when they see themselves hurled back on every front, they will surely surrender more rapidly than otherwise. Then you gentlemen can go to work on them and save their souls. Surely, that's a consideration?"

The archbishop of Canterbury, who was no fool, glanced sharply at the king but could detect no trace of irony in his expression.

The archbiship of Trèves said, "There is meat here."

The archbishop of Canterbury nodded. "We will discuss the matter, my lord, and inform you of our decision within a month."

"I thank you, most reverend lords," Richard said, gently. "That will be splendid. Within a week, then, as you say. I'm certain you'll all see the logic of my arguments long before then."

He reached out a hand and the chancellor gave him another sheaf of manuscript.

"We will now come to the next item on the agenda," he said, briskly. "The question of Crown benefices which may be granted to ecclesiastical feudatories upon payment of the proper fee. . . ."

*   *   *

Journal of Denys de Courtebarbe. Extract 4.

. . . . But when the king spoke of going on Crusade, and replied to those lords that he would meet the king of France without fail at Easter and for this purpose he had determined to go into Normandy before Christmas, then all at once I grew cold from head to foot. For until this moment I had not thought about following Richard all the way to the Holy Sepulchre. I had known that he meant to go, but as is ever the way I had put the knowledge aside in favour of more pressing matters. Suddenly, there was naught more pressing.

Let none believe I am without religion. My respect for all

the saints in heaven is boundless, and I am filled with love
for the martyred Saint Denys my patron in especial, and for
Our dear Lord Jesu also. Nevertheless, it appeared to me
that to go oversea and perish in Syria fighting against Saladin
was not my destiny, for I have never been a warrior and have
small affection for deeds of bloodshed. There came into my
mind all the tales I had heard of the demonic ferocity of
the Saracens, how they flayed their captives alive or spitted
them on stakes, of the heat of the deserts which cooked
men's brains inside their helmets as they were a dish of eggs,
of the scorpions and venomous serpents and lions and more
fearful beasts like the cockadril, which lures men to its jaws
by weeping tears, or the catoblepas which strikes men dead
with its look, or the elephant which has no joints in its knees
but is as great as a mountain and can mash whole armies
beneath its feet. In truth, although I have spent many years
in travel and like well to see new places, such sights and
adventures are not agreeable to a poet.

And there was this, also: that although Richard blew warm
towards me today, who was to say he would not blow cold
tomorrow? And ill it seemed to me to think that I might
find myself shouldered aside in that distant land and be
penniless and forsaken with no friend or hearth to turn to.

As if to drive home this nail with another, there occurred
that selfsame night an incident which brought me to a decision.

I had met with the king as he commanded, after his
council, and obedient to his will had made four or five little
satires against men whom he considered to be slack in
responding to his need for money. I will not set them down
here for they were nothing, being but good workmanlike
carpentry, witty enough but of no substance. These he bid
me tell one of his clerks, who copied them out fair and spread
them abroad. As we sat at dinner that night, they were
speaking at the high table of the king's plans, and Richard
said that those who thought he did ill to look for so much
money even at the expense of his royal living knew nothing
of war or the requirements of war, for, he said, he cared not
an egg for good opinions or fine display but wars were won
by that captain who could longest keep a strong army in
the field. Then Count John, his brother, looking sidelong,

said there had come to his ears that evening a verse which much tickled him concerning a certain baron, and then quoted:

> 'Well does he *brew*, but when friends call
> Turns a deaf ear; himself drinks all.'

Which most of the company understood clearly to be levelled at William Brewerre, one of those whom the king had appointed to be one of the council, but who had shown little enthusiasm for paying what the king asked for an earldom to go with this honour.

Then there was laughter which pleased me even though none knew I had written the verse, and there spoke up Nicholas Dulworth, who was one of the king's chaplains, a very pretty youth, slight and rosy and scarce old enough, one would have said, to know his prayers. It must be said that this Nicholas was often beside the king, and was very intimate with him and was often fondled by him, and sometimes took liberties none other would have ventured upon. He said that he too had heard some verses on the subject of one who took all and gave nothing, and then repeated some barbarous doggerel of which I recall only:

> 'Honours of England, honours of France,
> How he makes the piper dance;
> Little he cares for consanguinities
> So long as he may swallow counties.'

Now this lumbering rhyme was directed at Count John, to whom Richard had given the county of Mortain in Normandy, and the English counties of Nottingham and Derby, with many other holdings besides, and in particular the Honour of Gloucester by wedding him to Isabel, the daughter of the earl of Gloucester. This the king had done despite the prohibition of the archbishop of Canterbury who forbade the marriage because the lady Isabel and Count John were related by blood.

Nicholas had been lounging behind the king's chair, doing him the pourer's office, and when he had said these verses he uttered his sniggering laugh, meantime looking from the corners of his eyes at the count, whom he little liked. But all at once the king, with a brow grown black as thunder, picked up his goblet and dashed its contents in Nicholas's face, and as the clerk staggered backward, hurled the goblet itself at him which, catching him on the side of the head stretched him out senseless on the rushes. And while everyone gaped, the king said only, 'Fetch me that dog to a kennel.' Then, to his brother, heartily, 'Come, John, drink to me,' and so the matter was passed over.

But I thought to myself, if such is the fate of a king's favourite for the sake of one unfortunate rhyme, alas for me if I should make a whole song which displeased him. The longer I considered of the matter the less I liked it: if it were simply to stay in England or France with him, I would need only ride a league to find another lord, but if he should shuffle me off under the walls of Acre I would be a stranger far from home amid alien disasters and surprises.

On the morrow the king was going out once again to Pipewell Abbey to hold a second council and I approached him humbly to ask if I should go with him, whereupon he said, coldly, that he should have no need of me and added that I should beware how I wrote verses other than those he commanded of me. Then I understood that he thought I had written the verse against his brother. I said, 'My lord, I swear to you by God's Mother and my soul's welfare that I did not write those lines Nicholas spoke last night. In truth, my lord, it is insulting that you should think so, for if I knew no better than to rhyme *consanguinities* with *counties* I would deserve to have my harp broken about my ears.' At this he grew softer and more moderate and asked my pardon, and said that he was all distraught for labour and worry. He said that we should be going on to Dodford and Warwick in two days and he would have more leisure to speak with me, and asked me if there was aught I had need of. Then I said, 'Only a little money, my lord,' at which he laughed and derided me for a spendthrift. He said that he would give order to his purser to give me two marks, and so took leave of me. I was then ready to beat my head against a wall, for I had so far had not one penny of him and had no choice but to sell my sumpter together with his saddle that my other horse might eat.

That day I fell desperately ill of a languor and sluggishness, together with such faintness and lassitude that I might not walk but took to my bed. . . .

* * *

"Actually, I wasn't all that sick," Denys confessed. He and Arthur were sitting close to the fire, listening to the rain which lashed against the house, drowned the courtyard, and turned the fields and orchards of Hidehurst into a shining lake of mud. "Not physically, anyway. It was another kind of sickness. I don't know how to explain it, but I had a dreadful sinking sensation at the pit of my stomach. It was like the very first time I stood up in a hall full of people and sang one of my own songs. I saw myself, all at once, in the place of that poor devil Nicholas, doing something that displeased Richard, and being beaten half to death and thrown out to fend for myself. And there I'd be in some dismal foreign land. . . . Well, I decided I needed time to think things over. Richard plans to go to France some time early in December. That gives me more than two months in which to make up my mind."

"So Richard went off to Warwickshire without you?" said Arthur.

"He was as gentle and careful with me as a woman," Denys said. "Walking on tiptoe and speaking in a hushed voice, you know. He said that when I was well enough to travel I should go back to London by easy stages. He himself suggested that if I wished, I should come down here to stay with you for a few weeks until I was completely recovered."

"What do you think he'll do if you decide not to return to him?"

"I don't think he'll do anything. I think, if I have not returned by the time he goes to France, he will have forgotten me completely."

Arthur shook his head. "I don't believe Richard's mind works like that, from all you've told me. He's devious. I suppose that's how a king should be."

"I know one thing," Denys said, spitting thoughtfully into the flames. "If anyone can defeat Saladin, he's the man. Devious, subtle, forceful, furious—I've seen him in a fight, and I've seen him handle a room full of churchmen and barons, all pretty tricky types themselves, and I admire him. I respect him, too. And I feel myself drawn strongly to him. But I don't know whether I like him."

Arthur sighed. "I wish everything were simple. I wish you could forget your problems and settle down here. And at the same time, I must admit, a strange thing is happening to me. I—well, the more you tell me about Richard and his plans, the more I feel—I'd like to go to the Holy Land with him."

"You?" Denys said in astonishment. "You of all people, pack up, leave your land and wander to the East? Arthur! Are you feeling quite well?"

Arthur smiled ruefully. "I know how strange it must sound to you. You know, going to London was a curious and interesting experience for me. Mother said an odd thing: when I got home I asked her how she'd been and she said, 'Don't you worry about me, my lad, I've made up my mind not to die until you settle down for good.' I thought she was just jealous about my leaving her, or possessive, or something like that, but perhaps she saw into some part of me I wasn't even aware of myself—not until this moment."

"When the climate is as filthy as this, I don't wonder at your feeling restless," Denys said, with an effort at lightness.

"You're right not to take me too seriously. I can't really see myself chasing to the ends of the earth," Arthur said. "But you know, it isn't restlessness exactly. I've everything I could want here. And I like the climate. It suits me. I don't think I should care for it very much in a place that was too dry. It's just a passing fancy, I suppose." He rested his arms on his knees and peered into the fire. "I keep thinking about strange sights, people unlike ourselves, foreign tongues, places where perhaps they've never heard of bullocks, or wheat, or ploughs; the most commonplace things of ours would be alien to them, and what they take for granted would be amazing to me. It's so queer to think of it! And then I think—don't laugh at me —how splendid it would be to be one of the chosen band that might liberate Jerusalem once again. You said Richard could do it, didn't you?"

"Yes, but——"

"It's what I think, too. How marvellous it must have been for those who followed Godfrey de Bouillon when he entered

Jerusalem as its liberator, ninety years ago. What rejoicing there must have been in heaven. What pride they must have felt, those knights who wore the Cross!"

"Hmm. From all I've heard they were too busy gathering up plunder to feel anything." Denys regarded Arthur with a worried frown. "I thought you told me that a knight's chief responsibilities were his land and his dependants."

Arthur nodded. "But first, he is responsible to God."

"You were made a knight by the bishop of Chichester, weren't you?" Denys said. "Is that what he told you, by any chance?"

Arthur blushed. "Let's not quarrel," he said, earnestly. "After all, Denys, you've seen something of the world. But for me, London was dazzling, overwhelming—all those people, all the sights, the bustle, the churches and buildings and markets! Do you know, I saw two women dancing on swords and juggling knives and cups, and singing at the same time? Maude and I visited Gracechurch Market—they have things displayed from all the counties in the south and east. Then we went to Newgate, where there's a market for the northern and western counties. I saw some little men wearing coloured skirts and deerskin cloaks, and they were no taller than my shoulder! They were from the distant north. Then the Cathedral at Westminster! And when we had our dinner at St. Botolph's Wharf there were Italians chattering away at the next table, do you remember? One of them had a bird on his shoulder which cursed like a man."

Denys chuckled. "Yes, I remember," he said. "Chichester has a fine cathedral and a market, and Portsmouth and Southampton have good ports, and you must have seen women dancers at fairs——"

"No, never," said Arthur. "I've never seen anything like London. We saw people from Norway and from Flanders, and we even saw two Saracens. Saracens! At least, I think they were—they had dark skins and pointed beards, and wore strange round hats and long cloaks——"

"Jews, maybe," said Denys. "Arthur, you're like a boy. Go to London, again, if you want to travel. But the East——?"

Arthur sat silently for a while. At last he said, "Tell me, Denys, when you left home. . . . I know you went because you wanted to be a trouvère and to learn that art, but did you anti-

cipate anything else, any adventures? Did you feel any sense of
—I don't know how else to put it—knight errantry?"

"Knight errantry? Of course not." Then he hesitated, and
thought for a moment. "I don't know. I'm not sure what you
mean. The Four Sons of Aymon . . . perhaps they were in my
mind. Or another chap, Jourdain, in the Song of Jourdain de
Blaivie."

He stopped short. Jourdain? Why should that come into his
head? He could not remember any details, really, except something about a traitor named Fromont who had had his ear cut
off, but why, or by whom he did not know, and some vague
recollection that Jourdain, the hero, had travelled to the East
or to Spain or somewhere where there were Saracens. He shook
his head. Anyway, Aymon and his four sons were clear enough
in his mind: their brave deeds had furnished his young imagination with ample fuel.

He said, reflectively, "I used to make up stories in my head.
I would be one of four noble brothers, and I used to imagine all
sorts of adventures. In fact, I have three brothers, you know,
but they aren't very adventurous. They simply wanted to stay
at home and take things easy. But in my imagination we were
four paladins who overcame pagan sorcerers and fought giants
and met wondrous ladies who loved us in a pure and gentle
fashion. . . . I'll be honest with you: I don't know. Maybe
something of all that childish whimsy was somewhere inside
me. But my case was so different from yours, Arthur! I was the
youngest, I had no prospects except the Church or service under
the banner of some knight. You were an only son, your father's
heir. Why should you feel any restlessness?"

In spite of himself, he couldn't keep a note of bitterness out
of his voice. Arthur clasping his hands under his chin, said,
"Do you regret your life?"

"No, I don't regret it. I hope to change it, in some ways,
some day."

"I know how you must see me," Arthur said. "I know how I
see myself. Lord of Hidehurst Manor, with nearly thirty souls
in my keeping. I didn't always feel so paternal.

"I didn't have much freedom when I was a child, Denys. I
had a brother but he died in infancy. So I was my father's only
hope. He had worked hard for this land, he had given himself
to it. My great-great-grandfather won it after Senlac Field; he

fought under Duke William's banner when they beat King Harold. Then for fifty years, he and his sons had to fight to subdue their own tenants, who quite naturally hated them. By my grandfather's time, they had learned to work together and my grandfather was accepted by the farmers in the same way as the thegn who had held all these lands before us had been accepted. My father could put real effort into improvement, and we began to show a profit. He looked forward to seeing me a baron, widening the holdings, hiring more retainers and men at arms, spreading out. . . .

"I wasn't sent away, as a child, as you were. I served as a page here at home, but I also served as my father's assistant. I learned early how to get in the hay, how to judge the times for sowing and reaping, how to look after cattle. Only later, when I was fourteen, I was sent to the house of my uncle, Ralph de Hastynge, to be a squire and to learn the trade of arms. I was there for three years, and they were happy ones. It was a cheerful place; my uncle loved good food and drink, and my two cousins were merry men, several years older than I and fond of practical jokes, gambling, and women. I found out that one of my great-uncles had gone to the Holy Land with the crusade of King Louis and had died there, before Damascus. I saw his sword and helm, which had been sent home and hung upon the walls of my uncle's house.

"*That* is when I was restless, Denys. When I had a free moment I'd stand and look up at the sword and helm, a little rusty, quite black with dust and cobwebs, and think of the places they had seen, the long way there and back, the adventures they had taken part in.

"But I hadn't much time for restlessness. Well, you know how much there is to be done when you're learning the profession of arms. And when I returned home there was twice as much work to be done as before, and when my father died there was six times as much. I had to make up my mind."

He pulled at his lip. "No, that isn't quite right, I suppose. My mind was made up for me. It was either take on the responsibilities, or chuck them. And I couldn't do that, you know. I had to take them on."

Denys nodded.

"But sometimes I remember that sword and helm," Arthur said.

"You can't help remembering things," said Denys, absently.

They sat in silence. The rain had slackened, and now the gutters and eaves could be heard, a chorus of gurgles and babbles, and a musical irregular dripping. Denys glanced at his friend out of the corners of his eyes.

It's my fault, he thought to himself. What if I had never come along? If I had never dragged him to London. He has no business away from here; he would go away on impulse and regret it all his life.

But suppose, he thought, just suppose Maude would marry me? I'd stay here, then, and be his neighbour. No nonsense about sailing off to the gates of Jerusalem.

Either take on the responsibilities or chuck them?

He thought of Maude's fair hair and innocent blue eyes, and of her creamy smooth complexion, like none he had ever seen before.

Ah, well, he thought, there are responsibilities a man need not utterly fear to accept.

He rode the long way round to the Fitzleroy manor. The morning was cool but the air was still full of moisture through which the stubble meadows and the forest appeared hazy and indistinct, all colour blurred and softened. He rode into the courtyard and a snub-nosed page who knew him winked impudently and led him into the house.

Maude was with two of her women embroidering a wall-hanging. It was coarse linen, worked in wool with the story of David and Goliath: a smirking little David confronting the giant, then the great headless body and the shepherd boy holding the head by the hair with the stone standing out between its pop eyes, and then David before King Saul who, leaning sideways, had the abstracted expression of a man trying to suck a seed out from between two of his teeth. Maude stuck her needle into a corner of the frame and sent her women away.

"It's charming," Denys said.

"I hope it will keep some of the draughts out of this room," Maude said, in a rather flustered manner. "So you're back. Oh, dear. How—how wonderful." She had almost said, "How frightening." She looked about distractedly. "Would you like some wine?"

"No, thank you."

"I hope there's nothing wrong. I mean, you haven't quarrelled with the king or anything, have you? It's so unexpected."

"I fell ill, and begged for leave to rest a while."

"Oh, I hope it wasn't anything serious."

"I wanted to see you again."

She grew very pink. "I'm forgetting my manners. Wouldn't you like some wine? You wanted to—you mean, you weren't ill at all?"

He laughed at her confusion. "I was a *little* ill. But my heart was cold, there with the king. It needed warmth. Like a bird, chilled by winter, it sought the sun."

He took her in his arms, to give her the kiss of greeting. She said, faintly, "But it's been raining all week——"

He kissed her tenderly. And as he did so, a pang of misgiving struck him so that he drew away from her again.

She opened her eyes, and sighed. "I am glad you're back. I have missed you. And of course," she added, still blushing, "it isn't raining now. Oh, Denys, say something else."

They sat down together in the window seat. "Maude," he began.

"Have you brought me a new song?" she said, over-hastily.

"Yes, any number of songs. I have something to ask you," he replied.

She sat very still, with her hands clutched together in her lap.

"My blood is ancient," he went on, after a moment. "The family of Courtebarbe is honourable, but not very rich. I have no prospects. I am a wanderer, homeless, with nothing to offer. Therefore, I really shouldn't be asking you this. I can't very well go to your lord, de Hauterive, and drive a bargain with him for you. At least, not until I've spoken to you. Could you marry a landless man?"

Her eyes had been growing rounder as he spoke. "Oh," she said. "I thought you were going to ask me something else."

"Eh?"

"Never mind," she said, quickly. Her face was burning. She looked down at her hands and said, "I can't make choices. I must marry whomever my liege, William de Hauterive, commands me to marry."

"I see. And you have no preferences whatever?" He smiled, with a touch of irony.

She raised her head. "Denys," she said, "I'm only a girl, and a country girl at that. I'm not very clever, either. Do you want me to be honest with you? It's been frightfully exciting, having you as *my* trouvère, calling me Bel Vezer and writing songs to me, and telling me all these lovely things. Nothing like this ever happened to me before. I don't know very much about courtly love, but it's given me a feeling of being part of a larger, more delightful world in which all sorts of wonderful things happen: courts of love, tourneys, games, dances. . . . It's been like one of the old romances, the tales of ancient chivalry. But people don't marry simply because of love."

Denys could not argue that point. "I know it," he said. "But still, you ought to know where your own inclination lies. I think I can say that the king himself is my patron. Arthur is my friend. De Hauterive may be brought to see that there would be some advantages to my holding your manor. But you can tell me what you yourself desire."

She said nothing for a long time. Then, in a low voice, she answered, "My husband ought to be a perfect, chivalrous knight, one who gains renown for his deeds of arms, who comforts the weak, cares for the poor, and holds his honour stainless."

Denys opened and closed his mouth once or twice. Then he said, rather helplessly, "I would hope to be worthy of you."

"Oh, Denys!" She took his hand in both of hers. "I didn't mean that you weren't any of those things. From all you've told me, from all Arthur has told me, from all I've seen, I know that you are kind, and brave, and honourable. But—but compared to William the Marshal, for instance, well, you haven't done many deeds of arms. And—that isn't the most important part of it, really—well, you have done so much travelling I simply can't help wondering whether you'd ever be able to——"

"Settle down?" Denys suggested, drily.

She nodded. "Yes. And with me."

He thought of throwing himself on his knees, of embracing her, of pouring out such a flood of eloquent nonsense that her doubts would be swept away. Instead, he sighed and stood up. "Perhaps you're right," he said.

"Now you're angry."

"I'm not. You're a wise girl. I haven't any idea whether I could settle down. I could lie to you and say that it would be easy. It might be, at that. I'll tell you this, whatever else, I feel you've made me aware of something I'd forgotten: the obligation of chivalry. Whatever is decided, I fancy I'll remember what you think a man of knightly birth should be like."

"Thank you, Denys," she said, softly.

She walked with him down the outer stair into the courtyard. One of her servants, at her nod, brought Denys's horse.

"Shall I see you again, soon?" she asked.

"Tomorrow if you like. I have not yet sung you those songs."

He was about to mount, when she caught his sleeve. "Oh, there is something you can do for me," she said. "You know Gabriel, the sweet old archangel who lives in the wood; the weather has been so bad and I'm afraid it's going to get worse, and I thought of sending him something comforting. What do you think?"

Cares for the poor, Denys thought instantly. "A splendid idea!" he said. "Blankets, a warm cloak, some bread and meat—I'll take them to him now, if you like. I can ride back along the wood road."

"That would be lovely."

He was carried away. "I'll tell you what, I had another idea, too," he said enthusiastically. "Do you think he's a holy man? I do. I feel he's got more true religion in his little finger than most clerics have in their whole bodies. And I've thought about him, in that rough hut with a wooden cross in front of it, and thought that he ought to have a better cross, a good one, a crucifix that an abbot would be proud of."

Maude's eyes shone. "Oh, that's so true. You're right." Her fingers tightened on his arm. "It's fine of you to have thought of it, Denys. Have you got such a crucifix?"

"No, but perhaps I could ride to Chichester and have one made."

"I'll give you one," Maude said, with determination. "I've a beauty in my chapel. My father had it made when the chapel was enlarged."

"I'll replace it," Denys said. "I'll get you another one even finer."

He went with her into the chapel, which was built alongside the manor house. It was a small place, only large enough for twenty people or so to kneel in, but it had a handsome stone font and an altar with wooden panelling. Three slits of windows let in the light. On a beam near the door hung a polished wooden rood, nearly three feet long, bearing a suffering Christ of pure silver.

Maude lifted it down; it was so heavy that she nearly dropped it, and Denys had to take it from her. He lugged it out to his horse, and for a while he was at a loss how to carry it, but eventually a villein brought a piece of rope and they hung it from the saddlebow. Maude had a cloak and some provisions brought, and Denys strapped them behind him. Before he mounted, Maude put her arms around his neck and kissed him.

"This deed will count for you," she murmured.

He swung up into the saddle and trotted off. His brain was in a ferment. She was without doubt intelligent and good, very fair to look at, sweet to hold and to kiss, but at the same time he asked himself whether she wasn't a little crazy. He did not particularly want to behave like someone in a chivalric romance. On the other hand, while he could never be a Tristan or a Lancelot, surely it was all to the good for him to follow her wishes? Giving old Gabriel this rood, for instance—that was a good thing, wasn't it? Honour, meekness, charity, courage— what was wrong with living according to such ideals? They were the very things he admired in Arthur. "He'd make her a better husband than I would," he mumbled to himself, bending his head to avoid low-hanging wet leaves. Still, if in the end her desire to marry him grew strong enough, it might overpower any other considerations her liege lord might have. And there was always the chance that she would grow out of her romantic notions. After a while he began to whistle.

He had a bit of trouble with Gabriel, because the old man at first did not want to accept the gifts.

"I already have a blanket and a cloak," he said. "Young what's-his-name gave them to me, that young man who holds Hidehurst Manor. More than that would be ostentatious."

"You can always give them to the poor," Denys said.

"And I have a rood, as well," Gabriel went on, waving his hand at the two sticks tied together and planted at the door of his hut. "All this silver and gold—pure vanity. People throw it about to satisfy their own pride, to make themselves feel important. Do you think the Lord God needs a show of magnificence to make Him feel important? Nothing men can make can equal the creations of God, which He accomplished with only six days of labour and very little expense of energy."

But Denys was not going to be talked out of his good work. "You'll hurt the Lady Maude's feelings," he said. "I can't imagine an archangel going out of his way to give someone pain, particularly a lovely girl. Besides, it's a handsome object——"

"Not as handsome as a tree, or a bird," grumbled Gabriel.

"Poverty can be just as ostentatious as magnificence," Denys said, pointedly.

There was a silence. Then the archangel said, reluctantly, "I suppose you're right. My protests are a form of pride, aren't they? I ought not to care one way or the other. Very well, hang the thing on that tree branch next the hut."

Denys did so. Then he took his leave of the old man, and rode home through the forest filled with a glowing sense of virtue which remained with him for nearly an hour.

In spite of his concern, Denys had almost completely forgotten Maude's high ideals until, a few days later, he was forcibly reminded of them in the middle of a clear, bright, gold-and-blue afternoon. Enticed into idleness by the fair weather, Arthur had joined him in an open meadow and they were slowly and lazily shooting arrows at a butt and drinking new perry from a wooden pitcher they had set close at hand, when Maude came cantering out of the woods. They waved to her, and she sprang from her horse and came towards them, unwinding her veil. Her cheeks were glowing as much from excitement as the ride.

"Have you heard the news?" she cried.

"What's happened?" Arthur took her hand. "War? Pestilence? Or something good for a change?"

"Evidently you don't know. One of my people, Perkin, heard the herald in the market at Petworth. You'll never guess—a tourney!"

"What?" Arthur looked his surprise. "A tourney? Here in Sussex?"

"King Richard has begun importing ideas from France, eh?" said Denys.

"No, it is being given by William de Braose, at Bramber," Maude said. "It's in honour of the king's accession to the throne."

"A tournament! Well, upon my soul," said Arthur. "It will be well attended, that's certain. I've never taken part in one, and I'll take oath there must be a hundred knights in the shire in just my position. A tournament! What fun! When is it to be?"

"Friday week," Maude replied. "Everyone is to gather on Thursday. There will be two sides, the herald said, and knights are to say whether they will fight with the defenders or the challengers." She turned to Denys with a bright smile. "Isn't it wonderful? It's like being part of that larger world we were talking about. We've never had so much excitement here. The herald said that there will be six knights of Poitou, guests of de Braose, who will lead the defenders. Maybe there will be someone you know—perhaps even someone from your own family."

"Heaven forbid," Denys said, before he could stop himself. "Oh, I don't mean that. It's just that I can't imagine one of my brothers getting up energy enough to climb into the saddle."

Maude laughed as if he had made a joke, although he was perfectly serious. She said, "Well, I can't stay. I must be getting home. I simply had to ride over and tell you about it. Shall we all go to Bramber together?"

"That would be grand," said Arthur. "We can take pavilions and pitch them in a pleasant spot I know on the hill above Wiston. We'll make an outing of it."

"Good!" She put a hand on Denys's arm and smiled up at him. "We were speaking of deeds of arms only the other day. My lord, de Hauterive, will be there although he will not ride in the tournament himself, but he will be watching. I'm certain you will draw his attention. I know that you are capable of some worthy feat. And I—I'll be watching, too."

She blushed and turned away. Then she swung round and thrust her veil into his hand. "Will you wear this for me?"

He touched it to his lips. "I will wear it, Lady," he replied, gravely.

She drew a deep breath. "Oh!" she said. "It's like the Song of Lancelot. Thank you, Denys."

She ran to her horse and sprang into the saddle. With a wave of her hand she cantered away to the woods.

"Well!" said Arthur, blinking.

"Well?"

"Well, things appear to be more serious than I thought. Between you and Maude, I mean."

"Serious or not, that girl's utterly mad," Denys said. "I'm going to pack my things. I'm leaving."

Arthur caught hold of his jerkin. "Leaving?"

"I have no intention of fighting in a tourney and having my head split open, or worse."

Arthur looked at him, aghast. "You're joking."

Denys groaned. "I don't know whether I am or not. God! I remember one of those interminable stories Hugh de Hamel-incourt used to tell, about the days when he and the Marshal and Bobo chummed together. The Marshal had done some exceptionally lively work in a tournament and it was decided that he should have the prize, so a couple of barons went looking for him. They found him in a smithy with his head on the anvil and the smith, with pincers and a hammer, trying to get his bashed and dented helmet off his head. Not for me, thank you."

Arthur bit his lip. "I know you don't mean it, Denys. Stop trying to pretend you're a coward. Is it that you don't really care for Maude?"

Denys sighed. "Arthur, my friend, don't begin making up stories in your head. I see what you're thinking—that I've been trifling with her affections like any troubadour, and now I'm looking for a way out. Isn't that it? You needn't look so shamefaced. The fact is, I'm very fond of Maude. The fact is—well—I've asked her to marry me."

Arthur's face lighted. "Really? Why, that's marvellous! I had no idea. What did she say?"

"She said that the decision rested with de Hauterive."

"Quite right. Oh, I see, so that's why she said he'd be there and watching."

"She also said that her husband must be a perfect, chivalrous knight, who performs great deeds of arms and so on." He shook his head, twanging his bowstring fretfully. "I don't know. I really don't know. Sometimes I think she's delightful, just the girl for me. And you know, you've been urging me to settle down here; I almost think I ought to take you at your word. Then, along comes a thing like this tournament and I think she's daft, she's living in some sort of dream world. Well, I'm not. It isn't that I'm afraid of a brawl. If it were war, a matter of life or death, I think I'd be able to face it. I've been in some tight spots, you know. But this kind of game where you coldbloodedly fight someone you hardly know for no reason at all——"

"I see what it is," Arthur said, with a smile. "You're just nervous. I can't blame you. I'm nervous myself. One wants to do well, and there will be ladies and noble barons watching. But you've got nothing to worry about."

Denys looked tragically at him. "My hands," he said, in a hollow voice.

"Your hands?"

"Exactly. I'm a trouvère, Arthur. What if I lost a finger, or had my hand smashed? I'd never play the harp or vielle again. It isn't a matter of my livelihood, but of my very life. Playing and singing and making poems and songs are as important to me as the land is to you."

"Oh, I say. I never thought of that," Arthur said, in dismay.

"Besides, I haven't any armour," Denys added. "I've never owned any. Not even a helm."

"That's easily taken care of. I have two or three suits of mail—one was my father's—and a helmet I can loan you. But the other——" He snapped his fingers. "Denys, I have it. I know how you can ride in the tourney and do well before Maude and still not worry about accidentally injuring your hands."

"How?"

"Tilt with me!" Arthur laughed aloud. "That would solve it. We'll ride on opposite sides and find one another at the very onset. You can overthrow me, and then retire honourably. There! It's all settled."

"Wait a minute. It's not settled at all. What about you? You're dying to get into this game, and you'd be out of it before it properly started."

"It doesn't matter all that much. Far more important for you to do well. Isn't it? After all, I've not got to appear to advantage before de Hauterive. Or Maude, for that matter. No one will think anything of it if I'm unhorsed. Oh, it's a splendid idea. Come on, let's find that armour and try it on you so that the smith can make whatever alterations may be necessary."

Denys reluctantly gathered up the bows and arrows and followed his friend. He had the glum feeling that perhaps he should have left well enough alone, without putting in the dramatic business about his hands. At the same time, he was profoundly touched by Arthur's willingness to sacrifice himself for friendship. He knew very well that he might have raised the question whether this was a completely honourable scheme, but such a quibble would only have given Arthur pain and would have solved nothing, since Arthur was quite ready to overlook even his honour for the sake of his friend's need.

What a man he is! Denys thought, not without a twinge of shame. And not for the first time, added to himself, He's the one Maude's looking for, her model of chivalry.

It has been variously suggested that the tournament was invented by Emperor Henry I, called the Fowler, who first taught his vassals to fight on horseback, or by the illustrious Geoffrey de Preuilly from whom are descended the counts of Tours, or by the Saracens (who, being instruments of the Devil, might have been expected to invent devilish games). But the truth is that wherever there exists a military caste good for little but warfare, games always evolved quite naturally which are designed to test and improve their skill with arms. Said the chronicler Roger de Hovedon:

'A knight cannot shine in war if he has not prepared for it in tournaments. He must have seen his own blood flow, have had his teeth crackle under the blow of his adversary, have been dashed to earth with such force as to feel the weight of his foe, and disarmed twenty times; he must twenty times have retrieved his failures, more set than ever upon the combat. Then he will be able to confront actual war with the hope of winning the victory.'

The logical force of this statement is as inescapable as the conclusion that a knight who took his work seriously must have spent most of his leisure time in convalescence.

The problem was that tournaments were expensive. Many of the entrants fended for themselves, but a certain number of the most noble and important had to be entertained by the giver, fed, bedded, and, in the case of those who had neglected to bring their own physicians, given medical attention. At least one great feast was expected, at which victors and vanquished could join in eating and drinking themselves into a convivial stodge. In consequence, only wealthy men gave tournaments. Furthermore, they had to be holders of plenty of land, for until the invention of the lists—that is, enclosed fields within which the mock combat could be held, an improvement which did not come until a later century—the tourney required ample open ground for its proper enjoyment. Temporary shelters, called "forts", were built in strategic places to serve as bases of safety like those in a game of tag; from their walls the ladies and heralds could watch, and in them wearied knights could catch their breath and take a little refreshment. Both sides were at liberty to ride about the territory engaging in single duels or multiple combats, and by rule a man who surrendered had to ransom himself either with money or his horse and armour, a system which allowed a strong but penurious fighter such as William the Marshal had been in his youth to build a fortune out of the monotonous regularity with which he overthrew his opponents. It must be obvious, however, that for the steady losers this only added to the costliness of the game. In France, tournaments were a kind of luxurious vice to be ranked with sumptuary excesses like the wearing of jewels in battle, an extravagance for which the French knights were famous. In England, on the other hand, they were a rarity, partly because of the English dislike for show—a certain rustic simplicity which persists to this very day, so that uncouth tweeds and ill-fitting hats are the surest badges of the county nobility—and partly because of the Saxon stolidity which manifested itself in a bull-dog distrust of anything frivolous. Eventually the Crown imposed an entertainment tax upon participants. Then the Church banned tournaments as immoral, declaring that those who rode in them would surely go to hell. This was the turning point: at once tournaments became immensely popular in Britain. Nevertheless, the English denied that they received any pleasure from them, only maintaining stoutly that it was an Englishman's right to tourney if he chose, and that in any case England's victories had been won on the jousting fields of Eton.

William de Braose's tournament, however, took place long before that day had arrived, and for more than half of the entrants it had a refreshing novelty. On the day before the event, the fields and meadows between Bramber and Steyning blossomed with many-coloured tents, and every house and cot accepted a squire or knight who preferred not to sleep under canvas. Forests of pennons and flags sprang up and the air was clamorous with neighs of steeds, shouts of vendors of sausages and pies, clanging of anvils, and the last-minute hammering of carpenters. Bramber Castle was crammed to the roof of its old-fashioned Norman round tower with visitors, including the six distinguished Poitevin barons who had come to England in order to patch up their past quarrels with Richard, now that he was king, and to see what might be contrived in the way of future plots against him with disaffected English knights. The heralds whose duty it was to make up the rolls of the two sides recorded the names of sixty-eight knights and squires for the defenders, and sixty-three for the challengers by sunset, with several more men expected before the last moment Friday morning. It was a splendid turn-out, and de Braose had every reason to feel proud of himself. His only disappointment, in fact, lay in the king's response. He had hoped that Richard would attend, but instead the king had written to him that he was greatly annoyed at the holding of a tourney in these days when every Christian knight ought to be bending all his efforts toward preparing for the Holy War, and he added, characteristically, that as an expression of his displeasure he was levying a fine of five thousand pounds on de Braose, to be added to the war chest of the crusade. De Braose paid, and accounted himself lucky it was no more.

Late Thursday afternoon a thick sea fog rolled in over the Downs, and by evening it had turned to rain. But during the night it stopped and the stars came out, and Friday morning, to everyone's relief, dawned bright and mild. The ground began to dry and the tents steamed in the sunlight. Soon after the hour of the tierce, the riders began to arm, struggling head-first into their mail coats, dragging on the smooth, heavy, fine-mesh mail hose, buckling on spurs and belts, tying padded arming caps over their heads and pulling up their mail hoods, fastening the thongs of their helmets under their chins. No sharp or edged weapons could be used; the essential arm of the tourney was the lance, with blunted head, from which the sport took its other, equally common name of hastilude, or spear-play. One of de Braose's expenses, accordingly, had been to provide a number of spare lances, newly trimmed out of larch wood or fir, and to stack them in readiness in the various forts.

The two sides drew up in several long, ragged lines, facing

each other across a few hundred yards of level ground. On one side of them rose the round-backed humps of the Downs, crowned by inestimably ancient rings of trees or circular earthworks; on the other side lay the shining river Adur, cutting its placid way through the hills to the sea, which was near enough for its brine to give a tang to the air.

Denys, in the front rank of the challengers, shifted uneasily in the saddle. His armour fitted well enough, but its unaccustomed weight was a burden, as was the shield slung around his shoulders and the long lance, the butt of which rested on his right toe. The rings along the edges of the mail hood chafed his cheeks and caught painfully in the stubble of his beard. He held his helmet on his saddle bow for he could not bear its stuffiness yet. He sighed, and puffed, staring at the opposite lines and finding Arthur, at last, on the very end. He squinted, shaking his head in puzzlement. Arthur had not brought his squire. Instead, one of his villagers, a man named Ernald the Smith, stood beside him, a huge hammer slung from a strap over his back. This man had made himself useful putting up the tents and helping prepare dinner on the previous day, and Arthur had explained that he wanted him as a footman, "In case," he said, winking at Denys, "there should be any trouble in the onset, any great press that might prevent my getting into the fray. Ernald," he added, "is very strong, and young Peter de Cotes is terribly inexperienced, after all." Denys understood that Arthur was taking no chance of being diverted from their plan, but still that unkempt and hairy smith looked a little out of place. Some of the other riders had brought footmen along with their squires or valets, but for the most part these were neatly got up in padded gambesons and coloured hoods and were clearly professional men at arms.

Denys fiddled with Maude's scarf, which was tied around his arm. She was up on the platform of one of the forts, undoubtedly straining to see him. He blew out a great breath. All during the ride to Wiston, where they had camped, she had been warmly, even worshipfully, affectionate, hanging on his every word. At dinner she had seen to it that he had plenty of food and drink, taking slices of meat from the carver and laying them on his manchet of bread as tenderly as if she were tucking him in, holding his goblet up for the pourer, and prattling cheerily all the while about tournaments of which she had read and heard, and great wounds given and received, until Denys thought that he would lose his mind. This morning she had been quiet and thoughful, saying little, seeming nervous and distraught as if she were beginning to worry about him, and this had had the effect of upsetting him still more, since he was beginning to worry about himself. He was by no means happy with this tournament, with the plan they had made, or with anything.

He glanced again across the meadow, and slowly put on his helm, knotting the laces with slow, clumsy fingers. Then he decided that perhaps he'd better move to the end of the line so that he would be opposite Arthur and wouldn't have to ride diagonally across the field. He backed his horse and began to walk it behind the waiting men, and at that moment the trumpets rang out harshly and the first rank, with a shout, trotted forward.

Denys pulled his horse's head around sharply. He had not anticipated the difficulty of seeing through the small eye-slits of the helm. He had trouble orienting himself at first, and then when he had made out where he was in general he couldn't find Arthur at all. He groaned and began to curse, wishing he had practised a bit inside this helm. There was a great deal of activity just ahead of him, men cantering back and forth yelling challenges at each other, and one man already down and being dragged aside by his captor. After a moment's thought, Denys rode cautiously to one side in the hope of discovering his friend.

Arthur was having a problem of his own. He had brought Ernald the Smith with him, quite simply, to act as his eyes. He did not want to tell his squire, Peter de Cotes, that he was nearsighted for he knew perfectly well that Peter would be unable to keep his mouth shut about it. But he was certain that Ernald had a humbler, simpler loyalty, the quiet devotion to their lords of which the Saxon villagers were capable. Besides, since he was only a peasant, Ernald asked no questions but was content to do as he was bid. "Keep your eye on Sir Denys," Arthur told him. "You can see the red and white bars we painted on his shield for a device. When the trumpets sound, run forward ahead of me and show me where he is."

He would have been dreadfully shocked if he had known what was in Ernald's mind. Being a man of strict principles, Ernald had by no means given up his notion of killing his overlord. The fact that the attempt with the anvil had missed only troubled him very slightly; he had thought, in his slow and deliberate way, of two or three other plans meanwhile, but this great sham-fight was made to order. In the confusion, it ought to be easy for him to bash Arthur over the head with the sledge hammer he had brought along. All he had to do was wait for the proper moment. Meanwhile, there was this matter of leading Arthur to fight his visitor, that soft-spoken and pleasant foreigner. When the onset was blown, he shaded his eyes and looked at the spot where Denys had been. It took him a full minute to realize that the shield with the red bands on it had disappeared.

He rubbed his jaw thoughtfully. There was no getting around it, the shield was gone.

Arthur leaned over and said, "Well, Ernald? What are you waiting for? Off with you, man."

"Ah," said Ernald. "I be just going, my lord."

He started off at a ponderous lope. Armoured men were engaging one another: here two cantered together with a thud of lance against wooden shield, there a couple, having broken their lances had taken up maces and were zestfully battering at each other; a riderless horse stood patiently as he had been trained while his master, on foot, defended himself against a mounted man; several, who had broken their lances without final effect, were making for the nearest fort to rearm themselves. Ernald slowed, and finally stopped, at a loss.

"What the devil's the matter with you?" Arthur demanded. He did not usually swear, but he was beginning to be uneasy over the long delay. "Where's Sir Denys?"

"Sorry, my lord," said Ernald. "Yonder he be."

He pointed a massive arm. A man with red and yellow stripes painted on his shield went trotting past. Ernald put his fingers in his mouth and gave a shrill whistle. The rider stopped and turned his helmeted head towards them.

"Go for 'im, my lord," Ernald cried.

Arthur dressed his shield and set his lance at rest under his arm. He could dimly make out the dark blur of the other man and horse. His opponent prepared himself. They clapped spurs to their mounts and cantered towards each other.

Ernald stood watching with open-mouthed absorption. His eyes slowly filled with alarm and astonishment as he saw his master miss the other man by a good three feet and go riding on, towards the far end of the meadow.

He gulped, scratching his head furiously. Gripping his hammer, he began to run after Arthur.

Denys had been growing desperate. He was beginning to sweat, which made it even harder for him to see through the eye-slits of the helmet. An utterly unscratchable itch had developed under his right arm. He stood in the stirrups looking this way and that for a sight of Arthur or the villein who had accompanied him.

He heard a muffled voice shout, "Hola! Turn and defend yourself." Through his own helm and that of the shouter he could barely make out the words.

He sank into the saddle. A knight with a fan-shaped parchment crest fastened to the top of his helmet was gesturing at him with his lance, a dozen paces away. As soon as he saw he had Denys's attention, he called, "A little more space, sir, if you please," and wheeled his mount in a wide circle, bringing his lance into rest as he did so.

Denys gritted his teeth. "Very well," he muttered, into the close darkness of his helm. "If I must, I must. God help us both."

He became very cool. He set his own horse into a trot, bringing it round in a semicircle until there was sufficient distance between himself and the other, and lowered his lance, pointing it to the left across his horse's neck. The days of exercise with Hugh de Hamelincourt came to him: "Don't choke the lance, my dear fella! Light but firm. Use your elbow only to guide it. Eye on the ring and to hell with everything else." He fixed his concentration on the other man's shield, fiercely, and that triangle of painted wood and leather became the hub and vortex of his universe. The very smallness of his field of vision was now a help instead of a hindrance. He kicked his horse into a canter and hurled himself, his whole being, straight at the target.

He felt the shock of the encounter in his back, as he was driven against the cantle of his saddle. His right arm hummed from the blow, and he became aware that he was holding no more than four feet or so of his splintered lance. He blinked sweat from his eyes and saw his foe lying face-down on the trampled ground, a little way from his mount.

A great sense of relief and triumph welled up in Denys. He dismounted, murmuring, "Well, well, well." He rolled his fallen opponent over with an effort, unlaced the fan-crested helm and pulled it off to give the fellow air. He remained frozen, staring down at the all-too-familiar face of Baron Eustache de Gramonte, whom he had last seen in a bedroom in the middle of the night and never wanted to see again.

Of course! One of the six barons of Poitou. And, he thought wildly, I had to beat him. Why couldn't he have beaten me?

Panic started the cold water running down his ribs. As gently as he could he set the baron's head on the ground. He started for his horse; then, bethinking himself, laid aside his shield with the tell-tale red and white bars so that de Gramonte would not recognize him if they met again. But there were still men charging about seeking encounters, so he picked up the baron's own shield which was decorated with a diapering of blue and white diamonds. He remounted and rode away. He could not help looking behind him although he had to twist around in the saddle to do so, and caught a glimpse of someone halting his horse beside the baron's recumbent body. He turned round again with satisfaction, and found himself to his horror cantering straight into the middle of a violent six-sided combat.

This particular fight had been started, quite inadvertently, by Arthur.

When he had followed Ernald's pointing finger and had ridden at what he thought was Denys, he had been appalled to discover, when he got closer, that instead of five red and white horizontal bars his antagonist's shield bore several red and yellow ones. Involuntarily, he jerked his lance aside, but in any case he had misjudged his mark and he passed the other man by a wide margin. In his confusion he kicked at his horse, raking it with the spurs. It broke into a heavy gallop. Too late, he saw shapes looming up before him and pulled on the reins; his horse swerved and crashed sideways into another steed. The man on the other horse had been on the point of riding against someone else. He lost both his lance and his balance, gave a screech, and grabbed at Arthur, who also dropped his lance. They wrestled for a moment, grunting and panting, until Arthur succeeded in getting one hand free, swung his mailed fist and gave the other a buffet on the back of the helm that made it ring like a bell. Slowly, and with dignity, the fellow toppled over and landed on his head beside his horse.

The third man, enraged at the interruption, thrust at Arthur with his lance and hit him a glancing blow. A fourth man, at that, crying, "Shame! Two against one?" joined in, and a moment later three more rode up from opposite sides and, with joyful shouts, hurled themselves into the fray.

Arthur, defending himself with his shield, plucked up his mace where it hung from his saddle-horn and exchanged a couple of blows with first one man, then another. This was splendid! This was something like it! He laughed with glee, threw up his shield to catch a stroke and gave as good as he got. At these close quarters he could see as well as he had to. Someone else rode up alongside him; he caught a glimpse of a shield diapered with blue and white and dashed his mace against it. The other man yelled something, caught him by the arm and dragged him from the saddle. They fell together, struggling.

Ernald had finally caught up with his master. He unslung his hammer and danced around on the edges of the combat, mumbling to himself. He saw Arthur engage the knight with the blue and white shield, saw them go down together and roll on the ground, saw them pull apart and rise. He saw that the other had wrested Arthur's mace away from him and was swinging it back for a blow. He saw, too, quite clearly, that his master was in danger, and that the honour of Hidehurst Manor was at stake. He swung the long-handled sledge-hammer and hurled it.

It turned, once, in the air. This was all that saved Denys's life. The handle rapped him on the helm, as a man might flick at a gnat with his finger, but it was enough to stretch him senseless at Arthur's feet.

Arthur stared down at him, and then peered uncertainly around. The fight was over: the other victors were already looking to their prisoners, and Ernald came up wearing a pleased smirk.

"Was that your hammer?" Arthur asked.

"Ah, my lord, it were."

"Well, what did you mean by it? Don't stand there gowking and gaping. Why did you do it?"

"Eh, my lord? Do what?" said Ernald, in puzzlement.

"The hammer! The hammer! What the devil do you think I'm talking about?"

"Ah, my lord, if 'ee don't know, 'ow should I?"

Arthur sighed, and pulled off his helm to cool his face. "Why did you hit this gentleman on the head with your hammer?" he said, slowly and distinctly.

"Why, 'e were about to kill 'ee, my lord, that's what."

"I see. Very praiseworthy of you. Many thanks. But," said Arthur severely, "you must never again interfere in a combat between me and another gentleman unless I tell you to, unless you see that I'm really in danger, that is, if it's not a tournament. Do you understand?"

Ernald shook his head from side to side.

"Never mind," Arthur said, wearily, and knelt to remove the fallen man's helmet. When he had pulled it off, and saw Denys's face, white and still, he cried, "You idiot! See what you've done!"

"It's 'im," Ernald said, happily. "That un 'ee wanted for to fight. Ah, so all's well as ends well."

Arthur stooped over Denys, and to his relief felt his friend's warm breath upon his cheek. "He's alive," he said. "Help me lift him across his horse's back and we'll take him to the tents."

As they drew abreast of the large yellow pavilion in which the Chief Herald and the Marshal of the Tournament sat, a stout, red-faced knight—no other than Eustache de Gramonte —burst out of it with such fury that he all but ran into Arthur's horse. He was followed by the Marshal, John de Albini, and another man, a knight with a long, mournful face, and long, mournful moustaches.

"I tell you that is not the man who overthrew me, damn it!" roared de Gramonte. "I will award him a horse, but he's not entitled to my armour or to a ransom, and I won't pay it."

"But my dear Eustache," said the Marshal.

"None of your endearments. The proof of the pudding is that the man who overthrew me took my shield and left his. There's his damned shield, barred red and white, hanging from my damned saddle. Can't you use your eyes?"

Arthur interposed gently, "Sir, forgive me, but I think this is the man you're looking for." He indicated Denys, who hung across the saddle of his own horse supported by Ernald.

"Who the devil are you?" de Gramonte demanded.

"I am Arthur de Hastynge, and this man is my friend, Denys de Courtebarbe. That is his shield. And that explains why I didn't recognize him when we encountered. Your blazon must be lozengy of azure and argent, is it not?"

At the name, the baron's expression had hardened. He came forward and lifted Denys's head. "By God's beard," he said, "it's he. Denys de Courtebarbe. The trouvère. Well, I'll be damned."

Denys's eyelids fluttered. He opened his eyes, looked into the face of de Gramonte, groaned hollowly, and closed his eyes again.

"So you beat him, did you?" said de Gramonte. "Congratulations. I hope he dies of it."

"Sir," Arthur said, stiffly, "I don't like your words or your attitude."

"Sir," replied de Gramonte, "I don't know what business that is of yours."

Arthur flushed. "First, it's my business because Denys has done me the honour to call me his friend. And second, it is the business of every knight to see that the precepts of chivalry are obeyed. I appeal to you, Sir John. Is it not clear to you that Denys must, by this gentleman's own statement about his shield, be adjudged to have overcome him?"

De Albini, passing a hand over his white hair, said, "It is so, although since he did not stay to accept the surrender, he must be accounted to have shared it with Montgomery, here——"

"I don't give a damn for either of 'em," snapped de Gramonte. "That one didn't even fight with me, and as for this trouvère, he's a home-wrecker, a snake, a villain, and a damned rogue, and I won't give him a penny either."

"In that case, sir," said Arthur, "I will undertake to prove upon your body that my friend is neither villain nor rogue, for your words are neither chivalrous nor fitting for a man of honour to utter." He reached for his mace. "Mount, sir."

Denys opened his eyes again. "No, no, no," he mumbled. "No more honour, for the love of God. Arthur, I beg you to put your mace away. And you, my lord baron, please don't be so belligerent. I'm sorry I overthrew you. It was a mistake. I have paid for it, I assure you. I relinquish any claim to ransom I may have."

He beckoned feebly to Ernald. "You," he said, "help me sit up in my saddle. For God's sake, Arthur, let's go home. I've had enough of tourneying for one day."

The ride home was rather quiet. No one had much to say, and Denys was still feeling slightly fuzzy from his knock on the head. Maude and Arthur spoke occasionally in subdued tones, and Ernald rode in disgrace at the tail of the procession. Their road divided beyond Pulborough, and before they parted Maude said, "Will you come to visit me tomorrow? I must— perhaps there is something we ought to—I must talk to you."

Denys kissed her hand. "I will come, lady," he said. "I must have a good night's sleep, to recover my wits."

Early the following afternoon Arthur reminded him gently of his appointment.

"I know," Denys said, rather sulkily. "And I'm not sure I want to keep it."

"Not keep it? Why, what's the matter? Have you changed your mind about Maude?"

"I haven't made up my mind about Maude, to begin with."

"I thought you told me you had asked her to marry you," Arthur said, reproachfully. "Now I'm all mixed up. Surely, she thinks——"

"I know what she thinks. I did ask her to marry me. But seeing de Gramonte again—that whole incident—has started me thinking," Denys replied.

What he did not add was that the tournament had reawakened all his uncertainty about himself and Maude. If this was the sort of thing her taste for chivalric deeds was going to plunge him into, then he was by no means certain he would be able to put up with it. A young, idealistic, high-minded girl was all very well for someone like Arthur, for instance, but Denys asked himself sourly, rubbing the lump on the back of his head, how long he could survive such ideals.

He went on, "You haven't asked me why de Gramonte was so angry, or why he called me all those names."

"It isn't a friend's place to ask such things," Arthur answered.

"He was my patron. Then, one night, he found me hiding in a chest, naked, in his bedroom. I had been in bed with his wife," Denys said bluntly.

Arthur looked a trifle disconcerted. After a moment, he said, "I'm sure you had a good reason. She probably led you on."

Denys could not help laughing.

"In any case, what's it got to do with Maude?" Arthur continued. "Now do stop laughing and be serious."

"I am serious," Denys said. "I'm a restless, wandering sort of fellow, Arthur. We troubadours vow ourselves to the service of love. I have a vague image in my mind of the lady I must serve and love forever—we all have such a dream, all of us who make songs—and, I will be candid with you, I can't decide which is more important for me, to settle down comfortably and be a vassal and hold land and a wife, or to search on for that lady to whom I must swear fealty."

Arthur shook his head. "I think I understand you," he said. "But it's hard. I don't know anyone like you, Denys."

He paced away and came back again. He put his hands on Denys's shoulders, and said, earnestly, "I'll tell you what I think, may I?"

"Tell me."

"I think that although you are a trouvère, you are also a man of honourable, knightly blood. Having offered marriage to Maude, you can't turn and walk away from her. It would be like slapping her in the face."

Denys nodded. He had known before Arthur spoke what he was going to say. He was firmly caught in the trap of friendship, that sticky snare men lay for themselves against all inclination and desire, solely because they are afraid to be alone in the world. There was, Denys saw clearly, another image in his mind beside that one of Love: the image of himself, mirrored in Arthur's eyes. If he were to shatter it, he would live the rest of his life with its splinters in his heart.

He said, "I suppose you're right. Will you come with me?"

"If you like."

"Let us go, then."

They walked through the woods together, under mossy branches rustling their drying leaves. The wood seemed more open in places, less green and more grey, readier to echo the calls of birds, chillier in the shadows with the first hints of frost. They crossed the log bridge, and Arthur said, "Let's turn aside for a moment and see how the archangel is."

"Do you remember the first time you took me to see him? It seems years ago," Denys said, as he followed Arthur along the overgrown path. "I wonder if he really has the gift of sight? Remember, he said to me, 'You'll go further than you think but you won't find what you're looking for'? How did he know then what I was looking for, when I'm not even sure I know myself?"

"I never disturb myself too much over prophecies," said Arthur. "It's all I can do to decide what the weather's going to be from one month to another."

They came to the clearing. "It's quiet," Arthur said.

Denys stood beside him. It was unnaturally quiet, as if this part of the forest lay in ambush, all breath held in menace. Denys clutched his friend's arm.

The door of the hermit's hut was torn from its leather hinges and lay cocked at an angle. His cooking pot was upended over the strewn remains of a fire. He himself lay a short distance off, on his back, looking at the sky, and a robin stood unconcernedly, running its beak through its breast feathers, preening and combing itself, on one of his legs. The bird shook itself, eyed the intruders calmly, and with a flirt flew off.

Denys swept out his sword. "Put it up," Arthur said, softly. "There's no one about. He has been dead for quite a while, long enough for the birds to grow used to him."

They went to him, one on each side. One of his arms had been nearly hacked off so that the white collarbone protruded from his rags. His chest was all one gore of blood, clotted and hard, and as they drew near the flies went busily up from him.

"Christ!" said Denys. "Who would do such a thing?"

"Reevers—wild men of the woods. Outlaws, maybe," said Arthur. "Hopeless to search for them. They wouldn't wait about. But why? What would they hope to steal from him? Unless they did it just for sport."

Denys looked about the clearing. He said, bitterly, "No, not for sport." As he had expected, Maude's silver crucifix was gone.

"I should have heeded him," he groaned. "Vanity—that's what he said. It was my own vanity, wishing to do good, wanting Maude to think well of me. My God! I gave him his death, that's what I gave him."

Arthur shook his head. "That's not so, Denys."

"You think not?"

"He had the power to refuse. It may be that he foresaw where it would end. It may be that he wanted death."

"You don't believe he was an archangel," Denys said, harshly. "He was a mad old man. Of course! Or why should God, hanging here on this tree and watching, let him die without blasting his murderers?"

"What do you think he himself would say of this?"

Denys sheathed his sword. "I know what *he* would say," he replied, at last. " 'I forgive those who struck me.' He was capable of saying such a thing and meaning it. But not I. If I ever find those who did this thing—if I ever see that silver rood again—may I rot in hell forever if I do not cut to pieces whoever has it in his possession, guilty or not."

Arthur said, heavily, "We are closer to Maude's house than to mine. Let us get some men and bear him to holy ground and bury him."

When Maude heard what had happened, she straightway sent four of her hinds with a cart and horse to fetch the old man's body. Then she led Denys and Arthur into her hall and had wine brought for them.

Denys drank off a full goblet. Slowly, he tipped the dregs into the small fire which burned in the centre of the hall, and listened to them sizzle. Then he said, "I am going away."

The other two watched him in silence.

"I am going with King Richard to the Holy Land," he said. A little strangled sound came from Maude.

"I owe this much to the old man's soul," Denys went on, fixing his eyes on her. "And it's the better way. Much the better way."

Arthur said, "Very well. Then I'm going with you."

Denys said, gloomily, "You're insane. I was afraid of this——"

"You told me that you feared to be cast adrift by Richard, and find yourself friendless in a strange foreign land. I made up my mind then, I think."

"I can't stop you," Denys shrugged. "You're old enough to know your own mind."

Maude said, suddenly, "No, Arthur. Not you."

They stared at her. She was white, palms pressed to her cheeks.

"What would I do without you?" Maude whispered. "We've grown up together. We've lived as neighbours all our lives. If you think Denys would be lonely, what about me? Don't you think I have a soul?"

She burst into tears and cast her arms around Arthur's neck, burying her face against his chest. Arthur looked helplessly at Denys.

"It's you she wants to marry," Denys said, biting his lip to keep from smiling.

"Me? Marry me?" Arthur stared down at her blonde head. He held her gently away, and said, "Is that so, Maude?"

"You're a fool." She choked out the words. "And he's a bigger fool. It's just that I—things would be so dull and empty ——" She jerked her shoulders free. "Yes, you idiot. It was you I was worried about during the tournament. I was certain Denys could take care of himself—that was only a game, a game of being fond of a trouvère. But suddenly, when it was you, I was afraid you'd be hurt. And I was so proud of you when you did so well." She covered her face and began to weep again. "I know it's immodest of me . . . and unmaidenly."

"Well, upon my soul," Arthur mumbled. He put his arms around her and kissed the top of her head with an astonished air. "But this makes no difference, my dear," he said. "I must go with Denys. I *want* to go; I want to be among those who take the Holy Sepulchre from the infidels."

She sniffled, and took his face tenderly between her hands. "In that case," she said, firmly, "you owe it to your blood to leave an heir behind."

It was a point Arthur could not dispute. Denys turned and left them, feeling lighter of heart than he had in many days, and they did not even know he had gone.

3

SICILY AND CYPRUS

Journal of Denys de Courtebarbe. Extract 5.

Kalendae Dec. mclxxxix. Arthur and the lady Maude were wedded on the kalends of November, All Saints Day, in the chapel at Hidehurst. There were present both lieges, William de Hauterive, who gave Maude upon payment of the marriage fine, and the bishop of Chichester who made them man and wife. There were few guests but those noble, and afterwards we drank the bride-ale with decorum and little drunkenness, and even that little not marked by any unseemly behaviour.

Then, word having come to us that the king had gone to Canterbury upon the twenty-fifth day of the month in preparation for voyaging oversea to France where he intended to hold the Feast of the Nativity, Arthur and I went in company to that city, a journey of three days a-horseback which we accomplished with no difficulty since the weather held cold and fine with only a little rain so that the roads remained firm. In Canterbury we found Richard busy about his affairs and in high spirits for that he had amassed a very great sum for his war chest, nor was all the money in but more daily expected. He had in hand, for instance, a settlement with William the Lion of Scotland over the question of his homage, which I will describe as showing Richard's statecraft. These Scottish lords, sitting upon the northern border of England, had long bickered with the English kings over their holdings and allegiance, with many raids and sorties on both sides. In the reign of old King Henry, the Scottish leader, this same William the Lion of Scotland, had invaded the English lands. He had been captured when surprised in a thick mist by twice his number of English knights, and had bought his freedom by doing homage to King Henry and surrendering a number of castles and towns. But this homage, the Scots said, had been extorted by force, and they waited restlessly for the chance to raid into England and recover their possessions. Now King Richard showed both chivalry and such subtlety as befitted a king, for he offered freely and generously to quitclaim to William whatever King Henry had taken from him, to renounce the liege homage of the Scottish lords and to restore those lands formerly held by them within the English border. In return, William would pay over the sum of ten thousand marks of silver. Thus did Richard set at naught the schemes of those unruly northerners and quiet his borders during the time of his absence from the kingdom, and as well won such loyalty of the Scots king as he would never have had by force of arms. This agreement was, in fact, settled less than a fortnight after our visit to the general satisfaction of all men.

The king was very friendly to me, and inquired after my health and showed such solicitude as made me believe that my absence had but fortified my place with him. There had come to Canterbury upwards of a hundred knights and squires of the southern counties, and we all there took the Cross together in the cathedral and swore to accompany him on the crusade. I saw Hugh de Hamelincourt again, and also Arnaut Daniel, who embraced me with great affection and said that we should meet in France, for he planned to go at least as far as Vezelay with the king, although not to Marseille. And I was shown much honour there, for Richard had me sing to the company one night after dinner, and I sang three songs, among them an *ensenhamen* on the subject of advice to ladies whose lovers went to seek the Holy Sepulchre. I was much applauded and got many rich presents, for Richard gave me a goblet of pure gold, and then other barons, not to be outdone, gave me gifts as well. That night, too, Arnaut and I engaged in a *tenso*, or debate, upon a question put by the noble Roger de Préaux: Which virtue ought to be accounted best in a knight, bravery or liberality? Now, as all men know, this game is one requiring the utmost skill, and Arnaut and I so acquitted ourselves in extempore making of verses, myself taking the side of liberality and Arnaut that of courage, that never before was heard such shouting, pounding on the tables, and exclamations of wonder and delight.

Before we departed, I heard also that the archbishops of
Rouen, Dublin, and Canterbury (the old archbishop of
Trèves having died and his successor not yet named) had
agreed that the king should use his crossbows in the holy
war, and had procured letters from Rome granting this
exception to the interdict of the Lateran Council. Richard
himself practised almost daily with his new toy so that he
might, as he said, familiarize himself utterly with its abilities,
and he showed us how easy it was to aim the device by
looking along its barrel as it was held against the shoulder,
and thus taking a sight to the target, unlike the ordinary bow
which can only be aimed by judgment and the guesswork
of experience. With the arbalest he sent six shafts, or bolts
as they are called, into a wicker butt full of earth, all of them
hitting within a span of each other at a distance of fifty paces
and driving in up to the very nocks. 'I will show the infidel
good sport with this weapon,' he said, rubbing his hands.

He told us that he would cross over to Calais before mid-
December, and that he would meet with King Philip Augustus in France upon the first day of April as he had sworn
before the French envoys, and we all swore that before that
day we would join with him. Whereupon he took leave of
us, and in parting from me said, 'Do not fail, trouvère, to
make your tryst with me, for there is much glory to be won
in God's service, and wealth besides, enough to make you
richer than in my service.' I replied, 'My lord king, I
ask no more than to serve both you and God at the same
time,' on which note we parted on the best of terms. . . .

iii Id. Feb. mclxxxx. There has been little to write of this
past winter season, we keeping close to the fire for cold and
wet and passing the time in idleness. But I would here set
down a certain incident which deeply moved me, and which
has much changed my view of journeying to the Holy Land.
If, till now, I have been determined but still lukewarm in
my enthusiasm, I now feel somewhat of anticipation stirring
in me so that in truth I look forward to the springtime and
the first step of our voyage.

Soon after we returned from Canterbury, Arthur's mother,
the old lady Elizabeth de Hastynge, died of a fever brought
on by the winter chill. It was told me by some that she
had been born at the beginning of the reign of William Rufus,

but I do not see how this can be unless she was a very old woman when Arthur was born. I think, rather, that she only appeared old as is sometimes the way with these English-women of rustic families because of the weather, like as excessive wet in a garden will at first make the flowers appear fresh and fair, but in the end will mildew them. Arthur mourned for her, but I do not think he mourned as much as he would have were he not solaced by his new wife.

And indeed this marriage looks to be a singular one, for they two have been cooing as doves in a cote, more like lovers than husband and wife. And certainly it is strange to see them holding of hands, whispering in corners, languishing over each other with eyes like calves', and to think that they have known each other near upon all their lives and been close neighbours, and yet not to have thought of wedlock until I came hither.

And for this, they have been well grateful to me, and thus come I to speak of Christmas Day. This season, which in England they call Yule, was marked by a great feast which Arthur gave for his tenants, both free and unfree, with fires burning in the courtyard and a whole Mart-ox roasting, and withindoors more baking and roasting, and barrels of warm ale with apples bobbing in them which the people sought to catch in their mouths, their hands behind their backs, and many were soused but got no ill thereby. The whole manor was decked in evergreen boughs and hung with mistletoe, which they told me was a holy plant, although I think myself these Saxon farmers keep it holy from pagan days, for there is much paganism in England. There came in maskers who played the play of Saint George and the dragon, dancing very skilfully with swords in their hands and bells on their ankles. And we all sang and made good cheer and were very merry.

There came riding over Robert de la Lye with his folk to drink the Yule ale, crying, 'Waes hail,' as is the custom, which is to say, 'Be of good health,' wherefrom the drink itself is called the Waessail bowl. And he invited us all to come to him on Epiphany to feast on mutton. Then he asked me jestingly how I did, and whether I was turned into an Englishman since I said, 'Waes hail,' and 'trinc hail,' with the rest. And I replied that I was liker to turn to a mushroom since I seemed to flourish although there was no sun.

Then he clapped me on the back so that I came near falling flat, and cried out that I was a good fellow and would be a better when I had eaten more beef, at which I remarked that in that case we had better bring some to him for his good fellowship at Epiphany. And this I said because he often spoke of his sheep and how much cheaper they were to keep than oxen, but he did not despise to eat of Arthur's beef. Yet he took no offence, being at bottom a good-hearted man, and laughed with the rest and said we should get little enough of either beef or mutton when we had journeyed into Syria, but that we should perhaps make shift to eat Saracen flesh.

Then we came to talk of the crusade and Robert spoke long and soberly of it. He told us that his great-grandfather had gone with Count Robert of Flanders on the first crusade and after suffering many hardships had come at last to Jerusalem, and had won much plunder from the pillage of the city when it was taken from the infidel. And he had decided to return with Count Robert to England, bringing his wealth with him in despite of many who were, he said, no better than thieves and tried to spoil him of his goods on the way, but being capable of his hands and swift to strike hard blows had come back at last and, with his riches and the good repute in which he stood with the count, had been seized of that very land which now the de la Lyes held.

I asked him whether he would go again with the king or no, and he replied that he was very snug where he was nor would not set foot outside his country save if he were dragged. So long as he might pay the shield-fine, said he, others could go in his place either to free the Holy Sepulchre or to fight in France. But, he added, this was not to say that he was disloyal to God, or the king, or to his liege lord the bishop of Chichester, but only that some must remain at home and see to it that the land did not perish. But for those who, like myself, had nothing to keep them by the fire the crusade gave opportunity for striking at once two blows, for religion and for oneself. For, said he, on that first crusade had gone all the younger sons and landless men, Baldwin of Lorraine, Bohemond of Taranto and his nephew Tancred, and many another, and all of them had become princes and barons in the lands of Outremer.

And he went on to give many other examples, as that of Guy de Lusignan, who from a poor knight of good family but a thin purse had become king of Jerusalem, and Reynald de Chatillon, a mere penniless adventurer who had made himself lord of Outer Jordan and had proved so valiant a defender of God that when he had been taken prisoner at last at the Horns of Hattin, Saladin had with his own hand vengefully stricken off his head. And he finished by saying that as for Arthur, he knew not why he should forsake his native place and go abroad to seek his fortune, but that in my case it would bring me no loss and in all likelihood much gain.

Arthur said, gently, that it was not to seek his fortune he was going but to do his best endeavour as a pilgrim to regain the city of Jerusalem from the hands of the unbelievers, whereupon Maude gave him a look compounded both of affection and melancholy. However, said he, all else that Robert said was doubtless true, and that he himself believed I should take no less than a barony in Outremer. To this end, he said, he felt it was wise that I had determined to go, and also he was glad that the talk had come round to this matter for he had it in mind to make me a gift, and now that we were speaking of the crusade the moment was ripe. He rose and went to a chest behind his high seat and took therefrom a linen bag and another parcel wrapped in cloth. These he laid upon the table, whilst we all craned to look. He unfolded the parcel and brought out of it a fair sword in a leather sheath, the pommel heart-shaped and the hilt wrapped in leather studded with silver nail-heads. Out of the bag he took an open helm of iron, a little out of the fashion, pot-shaped, with a nose-piece in the Norman style. 'These are for you, Denys,' he said, laying them before me. 'They were my uncle's that I told you of, who went to the Holy Land.'

I sat for a space like one amazed, and at length I said nay to that, that I could not accept such a gift.

'Ah, but you must,' said he, with a smile, 'unless you wish rather to give us pain, Maude and I. For we have planned it for many weeks and begged these of my cousins. Come, take them with our love, and may they bring you good fortune over sea.'

I rose up at that and embraced him, and I could scarce speak for pure gladness at such friendship, the more so when I remembered how he had spoken of these arms, seeing them on the wall when he was a youth, and of how they meant such knight-errantry to him. And to speak truly, I found in myself a resolve growing, that I would not demean them but would wear them with such honour as I might.

That very night I bore these arms to Arthur's chapel and placed them on the altar. I knelt down and remained for a space, between prayer and thought. As I knelt there, it seemed to me that I could hear plain the voice of the hermit, Gabriel, telling me that I should go far and find something precious, and I knew that it was foredoomed for me that I should not rest yet but should look upon the Holy Land. What could that precious thing be (which he had said I should not know I had until I came near losing it) save the salvation of my immortal soul? At which my heart gave a leap within my breast, and I thought, What if I and I alone should be fated to be an instrument in rescuing the Sepulchre of Our Lord? It appeared to me that a glow of light rested on both sword and helm, and I fell upon my face and swore that I would have no more doubts, and that I would act worthily as should best accord with Arthur's gift.

Thus, in such refreshment of spirit, all things being joyfully at peace within my breast, I now wait for the spring season when we shall cross over the Narrow Sea to join the king, and if there is any hesitation within me it is only that natural queasiness which rises in me when I recall the last time I voyaged by ship across that heaving water. If such are the obstacles which are set in my way, then with the help of the Blessed Virgin and Saint Denys I will do my best to overcome them. But would it were possible to come to Jersualem by land!

*

Journal of Denys de Courtebarbe. Extract 6.

In the latter part of June we crossed over the Narrow Sea and met with King Richard at Tours, but could not come nigh him for two or three days because of the press of knights and the confusion of preparation. Then, through the good offices of William the Marshal, who was yet with him for the signing of charters and other necessary business, we came into the king's presence and were received with courtesy. Arthur had brought with him that great sum of money promised to the war-chest by his liege, the bishop, as well as his own men and those of Fitzleroy Manor and six free archers from the parish of Fittleworth who had enlisted under his banner for three halfpence daily and their food and drink, and all this gave the king much satisfaction. As for me, the king offered that I should ride in his train and have eightpence a day with my keep which was most generous, even though I misdoubted of ever receiving a penny of it, and so after debating of the matter with Arthur, it was decided.

On vi non. July we arrived at Vezelay and encountered the army of the French king, and there I saw such a crowd of men as surely never were gathered together in one place before. Such a multitude could not be counted, of knights, barons, squires, sergeants, of archers and slingers and spearmen, of sutlers and servants, of baggage wains and siege machinery, so that as far as the eye could see this great camp stretched. The king's chief arbalester, one Turpin, a man experienced in war, told me that he had made a count and estimation of this great host, of both English and French captains and their followers, and that the total could not be below eight thousand men all told, of whom more than a thousand were knights and squires.

Two days we were at Vezelay and by now Arthur had ceased mourning and longing for his wife whom he had left with child, and went about in a very ecstasy of astonishment and wonder. To me was given the honour of playing and singing before the two kings, and I saw for the first time King Philip, called Augustus, of France, a man of twenty-five years of age and thus some eight years younger than Richard yet appearing his elder. He was tall as Richard although not so well-formed, his hair thin and wispy, his complexion ruddy and marked with boils that indicated a choleric disposition. In all ways he was very kingly although not to be compared with Richard, for where Richard was large-handed and seemly, Philip kept his own counsel and appeared both mean and secretive. He had very piercing, hard eyes of a blue-green colour, and seldom blinked as other men do, so that when he turned them upon you you could not help but be disconcerted and soon found yourself shuffling and twitching like one afflicted with fleas. I have heard he loves to be served by insignificant men of whose loyalty he can be assured, since he loans them what stature they have and can easily dominate them, but of this I cannot now judge. He appeared well pleased by my singing yet he made me a present only of a plain silver goblet of little worth. . . .

We departed from Vezelay on the morning of the iv non. July and passed through the lands of the Duke of Burgundy and then by way of Lyon and Valence, and everywhere we went, so great was the multitude of our army, the townsfolk and villagers flocked out to marvel. Many cursed us most villainously for trampling their fields, and many were the squabbles along the way, for some of the pilgrims did not scruple to steal or pillage what they would in despite of the commands of both kings. Thus, more often than cries of joy we heard execrations, and wishes that we might sooner go to the devil than to the Holy Land.

At Lyon we had a lamentable occurrence when a bridge across the Rhône gave way and many were flung into the water. Some saw in this an ill omen, but others said that it was rather a good one since only two out of all our company were known to have been drowned and this showed that our losses in the war would be few. By King Richard's command many small boats were brought by the fishermen and others of that region, and thus the rest of the army was ferried across the river.

We reached Marseille at the end of July, and here I had a most joyful surprise for I met with two old friends I had little thought to see again. Pons of Capduoil had come hither in the company of William de Tankarville, grand chamberlain of Normandy, the father of that young Gervaise in whose company I had last seen him dicing. For, said he, he had been so lovingly entreated by Gervaise that he had remained in Rouen, and they two had become fast friends, and he had yielded to de Tankarville's urging that he accompany them on the crusade. Then he reminded me that I owed him somewhat from that game of hazard, and I, using those same words with which he had so often cozened me in the past, putting my arm about his shoulders, said, 'Fair

Pons, alack! I have left my purse at home, but give me a
a little time and as God sees me I will well requite you.' At
this, he laughed, although somewhat greenly. And thus the
matter rested.

The other old friend was my one-time master, the famed
Peire Vidal, prince of trouvères. He was living in great
splendour and luxury at the court of the lord Barral de Baux,
Viscount of Marseille, and now you shall hear how by such
folly as was customary with him he came to leave this snug
nest and set out with us on the crusade.

The lord Barral de Baux was a man full of courtesy, easy-
going and ever ready for laughter, and he held Peire in great
esteem as much for his many follies that he spoke and did as
for his songs which were the delight of all who heard them.
They called each other by such names of endearment as
good companions use, as 'Renier' and 'Mariner' and the
like, and it was said Peire could go in to the lord Barral
wheresoever he was, whether in his bedchamber or the
bath, and thus many in Marseille sought Peire's favour in
the hope that he might do them some good. So he had
friends and was in high favour. Now Barral's wife was called
Azalais, a fair woman but somewhat too minded of her
dignity, and Peire was mad with love of her. He wrote her
many songs, and sighed for her, and kissed the grass she trod
upon, and composed a lament upon the death of a flower
she wore in her bosom. He sometimes lay at her feet panting
like a dog, and sometimes carried about with him morsels
from her dish, saying that since her fingers had touched
them they were holy to him. Lord Barral made merry over
all this, and fell into such fits of mirth that he rolled upon
the floor. But the lady Azalais liked it little, although she
dissembled and made a jest of it.

One day, Barral having risen from his bed but his lady
remaining therein, Peire crept into the chamber and found
her yet asleep. And, so he told me, he was so overcome by
the sight of her rosy beauty and her naked breasts and her
shoulders white as milk, that he kissed her on the mouth.
She, thinking it her lord, returned the kiss and opened her
eyes, reaching up to draw him to her, and found Peire instead, whereupon she made an outcry, screaming that they
should bring hither swords to cut him down, and so raved

that, said Peire, he was both deafened and blinded on the
spot and could neither run away nor stand still but fell into
a faint. Noble Barral made light of the matter, and chid his
wife for noising abroad what should have been laughed
aside as of no moment, but she, full of fury and the desire for
revenge, told Peire privily that she would send men to kill him
if he so much as set foot once more within their house. And
once or twice, so he fancied, he had been followed by sinister-
looking fellows and now could not sleep in comfort, wherefor
he packed up all his goods, his many suits of clothes, his
armour and banners and harps and veilles, his rose sugar in
boxes, his knick-knacks and gleanings of a hundred courts,
all this he baled and stored away in the warehouse of a
merchant for whom he had done some services, and taking
only the bare necessities of war, and his great striped pavilion
which he said was given him by the Emperor, came with us
on the ships when we sailed for Sicily. But he left behind
him in Marseille a goodly song which many sang, that one
which begins, 'For nothing but a kiss She drove me from
her land.'

Richard the king had commanded that his fleet should
meet with him at Marseille, but as the vessels did not appear
after a fortnight had passed he hired two busses very large
and well furnished, and twenty well-armed galleys, and in
these set sail. As for the French king, he cared little to trust
himself to the waves and so departed by land, although his
ships coasted the shore so that now and then they might
transport him when he wearied of riding. On the day after
the Assumption of the Blessed Virgin, we all embarked, I in
the king's ship, and Arthur in one of the galleys, and we
embraced and said that we should meet in Messina.

After a day or two, I ceased to vomit and found that I
could stand and walk about the ship and even take some
pleasure in the sea wind, although I could not forget the
great deep of water which lay beneath the frail planks of the
vessel, nor did I ever grow accustomed to that uneasy movement underfoot where there should have been solid ground.
To give us all relief, the king broke the monotony of the
days by putting aland, now and then, and riding some miles,
and I went with him whenever I could. In this fashion we
came to the city of Genoa, a fair city but very full of stinks,

and here the French king lay ill. Then we went to the port of Ostia, and thence to Naples and Salerno.

On xi kal. Oct. we came to a town called Mileto, which is in the southern part of Italy called Calabria, and the king went ashore to ride. I was with him, and two or three archers, for he liked not to have a great following when he thus travelled, saying that in this way he was as free as any poor man and could better amuse himself. There is, in him, a wild streak which seeks adventure, and on this journey it was satisfied. For as we passed through a village he heard the cry of a falcon coming from one of the cottages, and reined in his horse saying to me, 'May I never know paradise if I see not what mischief is here.' He dismounted and went into the cot and came out shortly bearing the falcon on his wrist, with the villein behind him, speaking in his own tongue very angrily. 'Rogue!' cried the king, 'should a knightly bird be left in such foul hands?' And he made to mount. But then the villein whistled, and out from the other houses came a swarm of the ruffians with sticks and knives and fell upon us. There might you have seen such a deed of arms little worth such wretched clowns, for the king drew his sword and, disdaining to use the edge, beat about him with the flat of it until the blade broke. The villeins had drawn back leaving two of their number stretched upon the road, and Richard sprang into the saddle and bade us follow him. Although they threw many stones at us, one of which sore wounded an archer, we escaped by galloping through the thick of the mob. Yet alack! the king had lost his falcon which had its neck broken by a blow from a club, and much did he repine its death.

That night we crossed over the water from Calabria to Sicily, sleeping on land near the Pharos, which is a beacon which lights ships through that rocky strait. And on the morrow, we sailed into the harbour of Messina, all our vessels decked with shields and banners, the trumpets blowing, the sailors and archers cheering, and the king standing up in the prow of our galley, *Sea-Cutter*, clad in a scarlet mantle oversewn with golden flowers, his crown on his head, most royal to behold. He leaped ashore and embraced King Philip Augustus, who had come there before him. There, too, we found the fleet which had sailed in on the day of Holy Cross, having been delayed upon the way by stopping in Portugal where they had been besought to give aid in a battle against the infidels who hard pressed the Christians of that land. They brought with them more men of war, horses, and provisions which were very welcome.

Now, the season of navigation being all but past, it was decided that the army should winter in Sicily. The king of France was lodged in the palace of King Tancred of Sicily who was then in his city of Palermo, while King Richard was given the fair house of the chamberlain of Sicily, in a vineyard outside the city walls. As for the army, the French set up their tents near the city, or lodged in its suburbs, but the English encamped on the shore and to the south, being much annoyed by the insults and persecutions of the people, both Lombards and Griffons as they were called. And from this cause came such strife as threatened to end the crusade before it had well begun, with Christian fighting Christian, and many lives lost that should have been sent against the accursed infidels.

* * *

The trouble had really begun a hundred and thirty years before, when Roger de Hauteville and his Normans came thundering into Sicily and made it their prize. The Normans were renowned for their energy and ambition; they had briskly made mince of all opposition with their long lances and deadly axes wielded from horseback, and had then settled into the seats of government, using intelligent persuasion or bribery where possible, and vigorous tyranny when necessary. As a result, although Sicily had become a united, independent, and relatively prosperous principiate, the bitterness of its conquest was preserved by many of the common sort much longer than was strictly reasonable. After all, it was they who had felt the real weight of oppression, their soldiery who had been trounced by the rawboned men of the north. Tolerance was practised by the Normans, and all races and creeds, Christians and Saracens, encouraged to live together amicably and contribute of their best to the new rulers; unfortunately, a great many people were unable to extend this tolerance to their own conquerors. The small Saracen population placidly accepted any change. However, the Sicilians of Greek descent, called

Griffons, had a long-standing antipathy to rude northerners, while those of Italian descent, the Longobards, could never forget that their ancestors had been beaten by the Normans. Both nurtured the legend that the Normans—and hence the English as well—were born with tails which they kept coiled up inside their breeches. When the English arrived they were greeted with derisive cries of "Tails! Tails!" Luckily, most of the pilgrims could not understand the local dialect. Nevertheless, fights started even when translations were not available, since the locals were able to find other ways of showing their hostility.

Denys, who wanted nothing more than to pass the winter in peace and to look at the craggy, breathtaking scenery, became the innocent implement of the most climactic of these quarrels, one which began with an exceptionally trivial cause: a penny.

Arthur had pitched his tents with a number of other English knights in an olive grove on the shoreward side of the city. Denys moved in with him, since Richard's quarters were overcrowded, and they were often joined by Pons of Capduoil, Peire Vidal, and Hugh de Hamelincourt; the latter had come over with the fleet and had soon found Denys who greeted him with joy. Hugh explained that he had grown bored in England and had decided to "follow the dice", as he put it. "All the gamblers worth betting with have come along with Richard," he said. "England is a perfect shower these days. Not at all my cup of wine. The Marshal has become an executive, you know. And Bobo has gone back to his estate in France. And so I thought I'd see what I could pick up here, don't you know?"

The five spent an agreeable couple of weeks together, sightseeing, gossiping, drinking the local wine, and now and then exchanging blows or insults with groups of toughs from the city who were determined to pick quarrels. The air was restless, full of unease. Some of the citizens began work on the walls, repairing weak spots and raising the height in places as if preparing to resist attack. Others, however, set up booths and stalls and kept open market, getting staggering prices for fresh bread, fruit, and wine from the hungry crusaders. The distinction between the two kings was evident from the first: in the face of thievery, murder, and rape, Philip turned his back, but Richard at once erected a gallows and proceeded to hang anyone caught breaking the peace, man or woman, native or foreign. So energetic was his justice that he quickly earned the soubriquet of The Lion, a nickname which, with slight variations, was to stick to him. Philip, on the other hand, was referred to as The Lamb.

Early in October Denys and his friends went into the city to buy some provisions, as their own store had nearly run out. They passed Richard's gallows on which a couple of bodies dangled rotting in the sun, and Pons pointed out that one of them wore a surcoat with the red cross of the French on its shoulder. "As far as Richard's concerned, there is only one army with one commander," he said. "God knows what he thinks King Philip is doing here."

"There will be trouble, you mark my words," said Hugh. "And I don't mean from the Longobards or the Griffons alone. Have you heard about Richard's squabble with King Tancred?"

Tancred, the new king of Sicily, was cousin to the late king, William, who had been married to Richard's sister, Joan. William had bequeathed to the king of England a splendid gold table (some said it was only gold-plated), twelve feet long, along with three gold tripods, a silken mess-tent large enough to shelter two hundred knights, two dozen golden cups and dishes, and a hundred galleys with all their tackle and supplies. Richard had, of course, demanded that this bequest be paid over to his war-chest, and had asked that his sister Joan be sent to him along with her dowry and a golden chair as befitted her rank.

"Tancred did a good deal of hemming and hawing," said Hugh. "Can't say I blame him. It's a sizeable chunk of property. Still, there's no doubt Richard is entitled to the legacy even though it was technically left to his father, old King Henry. Well, when the Queen arrived a few days ago she had nothing with her but the furnishings of her bed-chamber. Richard was in an absolute rage—well, you can imagine. He has that sword with him, you know, the one he claims belonged to King Arthur, which he was going to present to Tancred; I understand he picked it up, swung it round his head so that everyone scattered out of the room, and then pitched it through the window. It killed some gardener chap or other. Afterwards, Richard was sorry and got it back and had a smith straighten out the cross-guard and polish off a few nicks and dents. Yesterday, another ship showed up with a couple of chests aboard containing a million of those rotten little gold coins—what d'you call 'em?—terrins. I don't think Richard's going to settle for that trash."

Pons spun a silver denier in the air. "He's much too finicking —I'd settle for a million of anything."

"And you think there will be trouble?" Arthur asked. "It's shameful. Isn't it? I mean, after all the kings are Christians, and belted knights. They should have no differences. I don't understand it. Here we are going to fight the Saracens, and so far we've had deaths from a collapsing bridge, from quarrels with townspeople in France and Italy wherever we've passed, and from endless little rows with the Sicilians, and we're still miles away from the Holy Land."

"Not everyone is as deeply religious as you, my English friend," said Peire Vidal gloomily. "Only yesterday, I had some little speech with an attractive child, one of these black-haired, black-eyed local girls, pointing out to her that since I was a soldier of the Cross she owed it to herself for the sake of piety to walk up into the hills with me—to show me some of the churches and chapels hereabouts which I understand are very fine——"

"And she knocked you down," Denys said, sympathetically. "What a damned shame."

"And she no more than a child," Pons added.

Arthur smiled, rather sadly, and shook his head. "I don't think you should do that sort of thing, Peire," he said. "It seems to me that nothing but ill-will can come of it."

Peire clapped a hand to his forehead. "My son," he said, hollowly, "you don't understand poets. We must have love; it's meat and drink to us. And in my case, I must have understanding as well. But what misfortune dogs my steps! I could name a hundred women, all high-born, rich, fantastically beautiful, who have thrown themselves at me, but none of them has really understood this tattered soul within my breast which yearns for tenderness."

"Some of them have thrown *you*, I understand," Denys said, unkindly, for he did not like to have Arthur mocked. "I've heard Richard's story of how his mother had you pitched out of Poitiers for insulting Marie of Champagne."

"Oh, Richard! Richard!" Peire shrugged. "My God, what

a man. Pours out money like water and takes it in like a sponge. A Patron of the Arts! Have you ever seen him fussing over the table decorations before a dinner, or twitching the hangings on the walls just *so*? Like some frippery chatelaine preparing for a banquet! But try to get a penny out of him when you've done him a favour, it's easier to squeeze red blood from a turnip, to coin a phrase. He owes me twenty pounds in promises. Luckily, I needn't depend on him for my living; Barral was more generous, and I didn't leave Marseille empty-handed."

"You were lucky to leave Marseille with any hands at all," Denys said, drily.

Peire rolled up his eyes. "It was worth it," he said. "My God, it was worth it. One kiss from those divine lips! In any case, I was getting bored with the whole business."

Pons linked arms with him. "Since you carried away so much wealth," he said, softly, "perhaps you wouldn't mind loaning me a few deniers? De Tankarville owes me quite a bit, but I hate to press him . . . you understand, don't you? He's a man of exquisite sensibilities. . . ."

They entered the city by the southern gate, threading the cramped streets where, in places, they had to go single-file for lack of room. High tenements built of brick after the ancient fashion and daubed with filthy whitewash towered up three or four storeys, plunging the streets into shadow from which the walkers would emerge into squares where the light was abruptly dazzling. Smouldering glances followed them as they strolled, and now and then someone would spit in their direction or mutter the cordial hope that their souls would fry in hell.

They came at length into the market square, the roar of which had been audible for the past five minutes of their walk. It was thronged with peasants and fishermen, who had their wares laid out on the stones or in small booths made of rough planks laid across bricks, and with townspeople and country-folk, among whom were a number of men at arms, archers, squires, and knights, who stared and pointed and pushed and bargained. Denys bought a hind-quarter of very suspicious-looking beef; Arthur filled a bag with almonds and dried figs as well as with small oranges, a marvellous delicacy which he had here tasted for the first time in his life. The others chaffered over olives, sweetmeats, and weevily flour, and Pons bought a goat which he claimed to know how to butcher and cook. As they were forcing their way out of the crowd, jesting at Pons and telling him that the goat was really a Saracen in disguise, and that it probably contained a devil, and that it smelled too horrible to eat, a ragged fellow came up to Denys and bowed low before him.

"Mon cher Signor, adlige Ritter, most noble lord," he said, grinning. "Out of your bounty, give a poor minstrel a single olive, a drop of oil, or better yet, a penny for bread."

Denys had thought, at first, that he was a native beggar. But looking at him more closely he saw that the man wore the tattered remnants of a haqueton with a red cross sewn to it, and that under his arm he carried a scratched harp. He had an impudent face with a sharp, jutting chin which gave him a vulpine air, and his eyes, small, wicked, and restless, glittered with some secret merriment.

"You are French," Denys said. "Or are you?"

"I am anything your lordship wishes," the other replied. "But for God's love, unless you wish me to be a disembodied spirit, give me a penny."

Denys pulled a coin out of his purse. Arthur, more generous, was about to give the man something more, but Pons touched his arm and shook his head. "You'll have us surrounded by a hundred beggars if you do," he muttered.

The minstrel caught the penny Denys flipped him, and turned at once to a woman selling small rolls of bread. Arthur and the others started off, but Denys lagged behind, listening.

"Beauteous and lovely madonna," the ragged man was saying to the woman, who was lean, and lank, and sunburned, with a huge brown wen on one cheek. "Gnädige demoiselle, how much for the bread?"

"Two pennies," she growled.

He held up the penny Denys had given him. "One."

She shook her head.

He put his hand on one of the rolls, looking more wolfish than ever, and held the penny under her nose.

She began shouting at him in a mixture of the local dialect and bastard French, waving her arms and shaking her head. He stepped back a pace, but he had neglected to let go of the roll. She tried to snatch it from him, screaming still louder abuse. Several of her neighbours abandoned their places and joined her. One of them struck at the minstrel with a cudgel.

It was as if, with that motion, the gates of hell had been flung open—a hundred yelling, demoniac faces appeared, gaping, jag-toothed, white-eyed, a hundred clutching hands, a hundred knives and clubs. The minstrel went down as if in quicksand, shrieking for help.

"Good God, they're killing him!" cried Arthur.

Denys had already sprung into the mob, brandishing the quarter of beef. He felled two people before losing his slippery weapon, grabbed someone else by the hair and dragged him out of the way, punched a woman on the nose, and finally won to the minstrel's side. With an effort he cleared enough space around himself so that he could drag his sword out of its sheath. He held it up in time to parry a blow from a club with it, and thrust wildly in return. Somebody screeched.

Pons had abandoned his goat and waded into the fight with his sword in one hand and his dagger in the other. Hugh's sword was swinging methodically, and he was talking as he struck about with the flat of it: "Oh, you would, would you? There's one in the eye for you, old cock. That'll do for you, friend. Etc." Arthur was struggling with a fat man from whom he finally wrested a knotty cudgel; he cracked the man over the head and began drubbing the nearest shoulders and heads. Only Peire Vidal was not fighting. He had prudently crawled under a booth where he munched on a handful of olives and sang softly to himself.

Pons had been shouting, "Pilgrims! To arms, pilgrims!" and all over the square weapons were drawn as the fight spread. Denys, standing astride the fallen minstrel, was soon joined first by Arthur, then Hugh and Pons, and among them they drove back the crowd. Things hung for a moment upon a dozen breaths, the people snarling but afraid to charge the swords; then Pons roared like a tiger and threw himself forward, sweeping his blade like a switch. The crowd broke. They went streaming out into the alleys and side-streets, carrying along with them most of the other citizens and leaving the square to the crusaders, the wounded, and the dead.

Denys wiped his sword with the hem of his shirt. A few paces away a man whimpered and cried, hugging his blood-soaked chest with both arms. Hugh walked over and calmly kicked him in the face; he jerked backward, cracking his head against the stones, and lay silent.

"Bloody bastards," Hugh said. His eyes were glazed and red and it was only slowly that he drew free of the rage of battle, pulling himself together like a man coming out of a five-mile swim, shaking the sweat from his face as if it were sea-spray.

Peire Vidal crawled out, dusting himself off.

"What the devil were you up to?" said Pons.

"I was encouraging you with a song of battle," Peire replied.

Denys bent over the minstrel. "He's still breathing," he said. "Pons, you're the biggest. Get him up over your shoulder."

"Where's my damned goat?" Pons growled.

Arthur, white-faced, was shaking his head as he squinted at the man Hugh had kicked. He straightened, rubbing his hands on his thighs and murmuring, "Jesu, forgive us all."

Peire said, "Since we have been left victors on the field, brethren, let us give thanks and collect the spoils." He picked up a little barrow with two wheels which had been tipped on its side, and began to load it with food.

Pons pulled the minstrel to a sitting position. "He's shamming," he said. "I've had harder beatings in tournaments. Come out of it, you fool, or I'll try clouting you once or twice myself."

The minstrel opened one eye with a piteous groan. "Are they all gone?" he said. "For Christ's sake, gentlemen, don't add to my bruises."

"Come along," Hugh broke in. He had a cut on his cheek, and kept mopping at it with the back of one hand, dripping blood and sweat upon his gambeson. "This was only the beginning. The wogs'll be back, mark my words. Back to camp, chaps, or we'll be trapped in these narrow streets. Hey, all of you!" He bellowed at the top of his voice, and all over the square men turned to look at him. Some of them had been helping themselves to food, as Peire Vidal was, while others, slowly recovering their wits from the fight and its sudden end, had been staring about or talking to each other in dazed and frightened voices. At Hugh's shout, they began to drift towards him.

"Clear out!" Hugh roared. And to Denys he said, "Leave that man where he is, unless he can walk by himself. Off we go, quick step!"

"Can you walk?" Denys asked the minstrel.

The man sprang nimbly enough to his feet.

Denys caught Arthur by the arm. "You look like a ghost," he said. "Are you all right?"

Arthur nodded. "I'm all right. Let us go," he said.

With their weapons in their hands they made their way out of the city. Peire, with Pons's help, trundled the barrow. "You'll thank me for this tomorrow," he said. The houses where they passed were all shut up, and the windows empty of faces, but deep in its bowels the city hummed ominously, like a stirred hive.

Denys helped Arthur, who stumbled from time to time. He looked sidelong at his friend's pale face but said nothing.

The minstrel stopped short. "Mother of God!" he exclaimed. "My harp. I've forgotten my harp."

"Never mind that," Denys said. "If you go back you'll be killed this time and no mistake. I'll get you another harp. Can you sing?"

"Like any bird," said the minstrel, cheering up. "My name is Giraud of Evreux, dear master. Fair Signor, I will make a song in your honour which will rival even the songs of Peire Vidal—in fact, I must confess to you that I am Vidal's friend and was for many years his jongleur——"

Denys snorted. "In that case, I'm sure you'll be glad to see him again. That's he, pushing the barrow behind us."

The minstrel shrugged, unruffled. "Well, a man can make a mistake. The fellow I worked for *said* he was Peire Vidal."

"He was probably right," grumbled Peire. "I, the descendant of emperors, pushing a nasty little barrow full of vegetables in the company of sots and degenerates——? I am doubtless an impostor."

"You'll be only a respected memory if you don't hurry," said Hugh. "That was just the beginning. We haven't seen the end of this day's work, by a long shot."

As an old campaigner, he knew what he was talking about. Word of the brawl had spread through the camp, magnified by rumours of all sorts: that the townsfolk had killed a hundred pilgrims, that they were burning some soldiers alive in the market place, that they were planning an attack on the camp. In vain, some of the more level-headed barons tried to calm their followers; the Norman men at arms of de Tankarville, ever turbulent, made a sortie against the gates of the city, which were shut against them by terrified and angry citizens. Many of the English, both knights and common soldiers, went to join the Normans. It was only when King Richard appeared and rode through the ranks, beating about him with a short truncheon, that the riot was quelled.

But not for long. Richard went to the palace where Philip of France was staying, to discuss the matter and determine ways of keeping the peace. Early the next morning the two kings met with the archbishop of Sicily and the governors of Messina, the military commander Jourdain du Pin, and the admiral Margarit of Brindisi. In the streets outside the palace, crowds gathered yelling challenges and surging back and forth with knives, swords, and pikes in their hands. Some of them went to the various gates and exchanged uncivil remarks with the crusaders. The uproar grew so great that Richard could hardly hear himself talk, and consequently he began to lose his temper. Jourdain du Pin and Margarit went out into the street, ostensibly to quiet the mob, but instead they maliciously spread the word that the king of England was being obstinate and threatening. They returned to the council chamber saying smoothly that all was well, but not half an hour later an English knight burst in and told Richard that some of the citizens had made a sally against the tents of Hugh le Brun, lord of Lusignan, and that there was hot fighting afoot. Richard became thoroughly enraged, as much at this duplicity on the part of the Sicilians as at Philip's irritating calmness; the king of France with a supercilious smile pointed out that none of his people were involved in the disturbance, and that his relations with the Sicilians had always been, and still were, perfectly amicable.

Richard rode out with his bodyguard and made his way to the camp. What he found was a small and limited fracas: a score of townsfolk squabbling with the sergeants and spearmen of the Lusignans. But the rest of the camp was seething, and more people were coming from the city while others lined the walls, cursing and waving weapons. Richard stood in the stirrups and shouted at both sides to stop. For answer, someone threw a stone which hit him on the chest. Richard's control over himself, never too great, vanished at this final indignity. He drew his sword and charged the Sicilians. They scattered before him as if he were an army.

He was like a magnet, drawing to him all the iron within reach. Shouting with anticipation, the Poitevins sprang to arms, and then the Normans, the Gascons, the men of Anjou, and the whole host of the English. Knights mounted, whistling for their followers, yelling their battle-cries; horns blew, and footmen came rushing from every side, mad for the chance of loot if they could once get into the city. The Sicilians ran back to the shelter of their walls and the gates were slammed shut. Arrows, lances, and stones began to fly from the battlements.

Richard by this time had forgotten where he was; he knew only that he was in battle. He pursued the citizens and behind him streamed the host. Some began hammering on the gates, while the archers and slingers tried to return the fire from the city, sheltering behind the shields of the men at arms. The king rode round the walls and found, near the shore, a small postern gate for the use of the fishermen. Some of his men pulled the mast out of a boat drawn up on the shore and with it beat in the gate. Richard was among the first to enter. Scores of townspeople ran belatedly to defend the streets leading from the postern; others climbed up to the roofs and dropped tiles and stones indiscriminately on their neighbours and the invaders. Three knights got their deaths in those streets but the rest, yelping hoarsely behind the king like hunting dogs, won through to the sea-gate, hewed down the citizens who tried to oppose them, and pulled out the gate bars so that the army could enter.

The desire to destroy swept through the host. Having struck one blow, no man could keep from striking another; having seen an enemy fall with a split skull, and felt the delicious satisfaction of slashing without restraint into the pleasant resilience of human flesh, none had the power to stop himself from slashing, and slashing again. The crusaders poured through the streets, dragging out the women as prizes, ripping down hangings, bursting open doors and shutters, and killing whomever they caught. Knots, eddies, or whirlpools formed in every open space around some unfortunate, outnumbered ten to one and cut to pieces or trampled to death; an immense howling filled the air, a kind of insane laughter. By noon, all was over. The city was in the hands of Richard's men, and his banner floated over the walls. The people had fled out to the countryside, or lay hidden in corners, or stood about in surrender while the crusaders counted over their loot and indulged their appetites.

Denys leaned on his sword, panting. He and Arthur had run out of their tent at the first alarm and had been caught up in the frenzy of the assault. Their horses had been picketed close by and they had mounted and ridden stirrup to stirrup to the city. It had been a matter of curiosity more than anything else, for amid all the tumult it was almost impossible to know exactly what was going on. They had been checked with the rest at the walls; then, riding around in the confusion, they had been carried into the city when the gate was opened. And thus, suddenly, in sheer self-defence, they had found themselves fighting, carried from one sword stroke to another, as a man idly rowing finds himself in a strong current, begins to row in earnest, and is thrust into a paroxysm, an exertion, and an agony of rowing in which there is not and never has been anything in the world save rowing. And like such a man who, landed at last on the shore, drenched and shivering with fatigue, sees the dreadful weir from which he has saved himself and has not even strength or emotion left to say "Thank God!" so Denys stood, sucking in air in great gulps and staring blankly around him. There were gaps in his memory, and hurtful images, and terrible sounds that still continued. His arms ached, as did the muscles of his jaws and the roots of his teeth. A pungent smell of blood filled the air, mingled with dust and the scent of burning wood.

He saw Arthur near by, resting his shoulders against the wall of a house, his knees sagging. Still in the same numbness he remarked that his friend's surcoat was splashed with blood and that blood clotted his mailed arm to the elbow. He shook himself. He stumbled to Arthur's side, and clutched his shoulder.

"Are you wounded?" he gasped.

Arthur raised dull and stupid eyes. "Butchery," he said. "Not my blood."

Denys wiped his face, shaking his head again in a vain effort to clear it. He repeated, "Are you hurt? What's the matter?"

"The matter? I don't know who I killed, that's what's the matter," said Arthur. "God forgive me. I don't know."

"Pull yourself together," Denys said roughly. He pawed at his friend's sticky surcoat and looked owlishly at his own wet hand. "They began it. Christians? They didn't act like

168

Christians. They deserved whatever they got. You can't get round it."

"You don't understand," Arthur said. He pushed Denys away, and then caught hold of him like a fretful child. "I couldn't see. Don't you hear me? *I couldn't see!* Dear Jesu, I never thought it would be like this when I came. I thought we would face the Saracens and that it wouldn't matter that my eyes are bad. I would ride at them and God would show me where to strike."

"Your eyes?" Denys said, thickly.

Arthur was biting at his lip. "I couldn't tell, for the dust and the screaming and everyone—I don't know whether I killed one of them or one of ours. I might have killed one of my own men from home. I might have killed you. I went mad. I chopped at everyone I saw. I couldn't see a face, or what anyone wore, or——"

Denys, in a panic, held his hand up before Arthur's eyes and passed it back and forth. "Do you mean you're wounded?" he said. "You can't see my hand?"

Arthur seized his wrist impatiently. "Of course I can see your hand," he said. "I've always been this way. I can't see anything clearly more than ten paces away. It's all blurred. And even closer sometimes, if I'm tired. . . . I've never told anyone. I was too proud."

"Blessed Mother of God," Denys whispered. "The tournament . . . then you didn't recognize me because you couldn't see me. And other times——"

He broke off and looked about. As he had expected, their horses stood patiently, as they had been trained, not far off among a dozen others whose riders were busy elsewhere, or dead. "Come along," he said. "Let's get out of here. We're going back to the tents."

He helped Arthur into the saddle. They rode out through a cloud of sunny dust and blue smoke which mercifully obscured much of what was happening, although it could not clog their ears to the whoops and screams and crashes of victory.

The camp was a relatively silent and peaceful place. Denys fetched water and washed the blood from both of them. He got a skin of wine and drank deeply, and saw that Arthur drank. They pulled off their surcoats and mail shirts and sat down on the ground before the tent, the hot sun, now overhead, baking comfortingly through their quilted jackets. Arthur had become quite calm. He said, "I'm sorry I was so upset."

Denys gave a mirthless bark of laughter. "Upset? I was more upset than you."

"It was knowing that we were attacking a Christian city," Arthur said. "That, and the fact that I was carried away by killing. I didn't think you could enjoy killing other men. And suddenly, it was over, and I began to understand that I didn't know whom I had killed."

Denys stood up. "We're going home," he said, grimly. "I think we've had enough of the crusade. We can take a boat for France——"

Arthur shook his head. "No," he said, "I can't do that."

"Are you mad?" Denys cried. "What do you mean?"

"I think you know. I made a vow to go with the king to the Holy Land. It would not be knightly of me to turn back, whatever the reason."

"And do you owe nothing to your wife? To the child that's coming? To your land? You're as good as blind. Do you want to go into battle without knowing who will strike at you, or from which side?"

"I don't want to," Arthur said simply. "But I must. It won't be quite like this when we get to Syria. You know that there will be proper battles in which I can fight, if I ride directly at the foe. I'll stay away from cities. Surely at close quarters I'll be able to tell an infidel from a Christian? In Messina I couldn't tell one from another. No one could. But at close quarters, I'll see their armour, their faces, their weapons. . . . Won't I?"

"You're an idiot," Denys said, in a rage. "By Christ, you're an utter fool. Peire Vidal is a fountain of sanity compared with you. If you won't think of yourself, think of me. I'll have to chase after you, and guard you as if you were a blind baby——"

The instant the words were out, he could have bitten off his tongue. Arthur blinked up at him with a woesome expression.

"Of course not," he said. "I couldn't expect you to do that, Denys. We shall have to part."

Denys sank down on his knees with a groan. "I'm a bigger fool than you are," he said. "I only said that because I'm afraid you'll be hurt. Do you really think I'd leave you?"

"But you——"

"But nothing. What sort of a traitor do you take me for?"

Arthur smiled. "I'm sorry, Denys, I didn't mean to insult you. You do understand, don't you? I can't go sneaking home. A knight has only his word. One pledges fealty to one's lord and one is expected to keep that pledge. God knew perfectly well that I couldn't see as well as other people, yet He accepted my oath. That means I must live up to it and trust in Him. Doesn't it?"

Denys nodded.

"You will show me the Saracens, and I'll ride at them. God will be my shield. After all, Denys, He didn't allow me to be hurt today, or even yesterday in the market place."

"Yes. I know."

"And I'll make one more vow," Arthur said, gravely. He drew his sword with some difficulty, for the blade had not been cleaned when Denys had sheathed it for him, and it stuck in the scabbard. He plunged the point into the ground and knelt before the hilt. "I swear," he said, "that I will never draw my sword against a fellow-Christian. I will not draw my sword again until we come to the walls of Acre, and then only against the infidel. You witness it, Denys?"

"I witness it," Denys said, with a horrible sense of hopelessness.

Perhaps the most far-reaching effect the taking of Messina had was upon the relations between the two leaders of the crusade. King Philip was furious. It would be uplifting to report that his was the moral indignation of a Christian sovereign, or the outrage of a kindly soul. However, his anger was simpler and more practical: he was annoyed because Richard had planted his own banner upon the walls of Messina, and not the banner of France. Technically, Richard held England as the fief of France; furthermore, the two kings had solemnly sworn at Vezelay to divide equally any spoils taken on the crusade. From Philip's point of view, therefore, Richard was behaving selfishly as well as disloyally. Exceedingly impolite words were exchanged, and it took all the tact and statesmanship of the royal advisers on both sides to restore peace. In the end, Philip's banner was set up alongside Richard's, and new oaths of allegiance and profit-sharing were taken. Nevertheless, much of the later discord which broke out between the two camps was the direct result of this rupture, and even the war which, after the crusade, was to flare out between England and France over the holding of Normandy has been attributed to the same cause.

But for now, as Denys noted in his journal, things grew quieter and the crusaders settled in for the winter. An informal truce kept both camp and countryside from their weapons, while Richard busied himself in negotiations with King Tancred, first over the matter of Queen Joan's dowry, and second to come to a substantial accord which would prevent an alliance between the Sicilian king and Philip of France, an alliance which might squeeze Richard out of what he thought of as his proper place as military leader of the crusade. For headquarters, he had a wooden fort built on a hill facing the city, using some of the beams from the siege machines, and he threw himself into the planning and overseeing of this work with his customary enthusiasm for new projects. When it was done, he named it "Kill Greek", so that simply speaking of it was both an insult and a reminder of how swiftly and dreadfully he had dealt with the citizens of Messina. Eventually, he settled with Tancred for forty thousand ounces of gold, a third of which he at once gave to King Philip as a peace-offering, even though the money was not a prize of war but the settlement of his sister's dowry. The plunder which had been taken from Messina by his followers he ordered returned for the sake of harmony. This caused a good deal of grumbling, particularly from knights who hadn't bargained for a long stay in Sicily when they had left home; some of them, like Hugh de Hamelincourt, had already diced away everything they had taken in loot. But Richard calmed everyone by giving out of his own treasury lavish gifts of money, jewels, neck-chains, gold cups, and the like so that even the lowliest foot-soldier had a handful of sous with which to toast the king's liberality. Although he was careful with money and shrewd at business, he knew the value of generosity. Richard's ends were always more valuable to him than his means.

While he was in the giving mood, the king did not forget his trouvères. Each received a purse, and Denys, who had accustomed himself to living on promises while stoically tightening his belt, found himself with fifteen marks of silver. He was so unbalanced by this abrupt prosperity that he hired Giraud of Evreux to be his minstrel.

The man had shown up after the taking of Messina with a new harp, which he explained airily he had found abandoned by some unfortunate townsman. He had a few other keepsakes from the same source: a silver bowl, a few rings and brooches, a new pair of shoes, a Saracen dagger with a jade hilt studded with pearls, and an ink-horn cunningly made of ivory carved with mythical beasts, such as the elephant and the giraffe.

Pons, to have some sport with him, said, "You claim to be a minstrel. Well, let's hear you sing something."

"Whatever your most exquisite lordship desires," said Giraud. "A love song? A song of battle? A gay dance tune?"

Pons, grinning at Hugh de Hamlincourt with whom he had a small side-bet on the issue, said, "Oh, no. I'm in the mood for something grander. Sing us that part of the song of Guillaume where Count Vivien first leads the Franks against the infidel."

"Hmm." Giraud touched his harp with a hesitant finger. "Very difficult to recall." Then he sang:

> "Forth from the bosom of his surcoat red
> He drew his banner with its fringe of gold,
> He laced it to the nails below his lance's head
> And raised it high, that to the wind it spread
> And *Montjoie*! cried, the battle-cry of old.

"Is that what you meant?" he said.

"Not bad," said Pons, a little taken aback.

Hugh reached out a cupped hand. "Two deniers, old boy," he said to Pons.

"Give us something from one of our modern masters," Denys said.

The minstrel nodded, and began:

> "Of chivalry and love I am the flower,
> Bravest among the brave—in lady's bower
> Is none more courteous and more debonair,
> Nor on the battlefield of greater power——"

He had to stop for the roar of laughter. This was one of Peire Vidal's more modest and self-effacing songs, and Peire himself said, "Very well sung. If I weren't so stingy I'd throw you a largesse."

The minstrel bowed, smirking like a hungry wolf. "Anything you require, hochgeboren *milites*—call out what you will."

It became a game. "Let's have a bit of *Amis and Amile*." "Something by Count William of Poitiers." "Do you know Folquet de Marseille's 'If I must leave thee'?" To each suggestion the minstrel responded with the proper chords and the right verses. What was still more surprising, considering his dirty and unprepossessing appearance, was his voice, which was clear, faultless, flexible, and sweet. He finished by singing one of Pons' aubades, and followed this with "Most do I love when winter's fled," the sirvente which Denys had written at King Richard's challenge.

Then he said, "Noble masters, forgive me but my throat is dry and my fingers somewhat cramped, or I'd be glad to go on until the end of winter."

They took the hint and brought out a couple of skins of wine, and when they had finished these Giraud curled up in the lee of one of the tents like a dog and spent the night. Thereafter, he was always around, unobtrusive but available, useful for running errands, and good for relieving the long stretches of boredom. When Denys received his money from the king, he said to Giraud, "I'll pay you a penny a day, and feed and clothe you. You'll sing my songs and any others I may call for. I don't know how long the service will last, but then nothing in life is certain, especially on a journey like ours. Are you satisfied?"

"You will find me unbelievably loyal, noble master," said Giraud.

He had his faults. He could not help stealing, but he was very inept at it and he was always caught and beaten. Pons beat him for stealing a shirt; Peire Vidal beat him for drinking half a skin of wine and refilling it with water; Hugh beat him unmercifully for trying to steal his spurs. Denys beat him for his own good. "You began the whole uproar in the market place in Messina by trying to steal a roll of bread," he said. "Will you never learn?"

"Dear master," wept Giraud, "I'm just no good. I've been thrashed for my sins in Paris, in Rouen, in Poitiers, in Cologne and Worms, in Genoa and Pisa, and in two hundred other cities. I can't help myself."

"Well, don't boast of it," said Denys, severely. "Try to mend your ways."

He was readier to forgive Giraud for his flaws since it was through the minstrel that he met Elena, the daughter of Francesco of Gazzi.

He had been working on a new song, a sirvente which would describe and celebrate the union of the two kings, praising their virtue in putting aside their earthly crowns to secure the crown of God and win His lands for Him again. Richard was planning a great Christmas feast in "Kill Greek" fort, and Denys hoped to be able to present his work on that occasion. He had finished the rough draft and now, with a little more than three weeks left, he wanted to discuss the music with Giraud. He was accustomed to going for solitary walks in the countryside, in spite of the danger of which Hugh had several times warned him that vengeful peasants might fall upon a lone crusader. He enjoyed these walks and liked to be able to declaim or compose aloud without being disturbed by listeners. He had found a spot in the stony hills a mile or so south of Messina where there was a ruined, ancient temple of the Greeks, and here he climbed and sat, looking out over the shaggy rolling earth with its clumps of low-growing, gnarled trees, to the glint of water beyond, and then the dark loom of Calabria upon the horizon. It tickled him that although it was so close to Christmas the weather was as mild as early autumn in Poitou, and in his snuggery among the broken columns with the hill at his back he was even protected from the damp and penetrating wind that sometimes blew from the north.

He took Giraud with him on this particular day, mounted on a spare nag. They rode up into the hills and walked their horses the last of the way. They hobbled them among the terraces of the ruins, and sat down on a flat yellow slab warmed by the sun. They spent an hour or more on the song, and Giraud began to sing it over, ornamenting it in his own way to Denys's admiration. They ate some bread and cheese they had brought, and Denys lay back with his hands behind his head, looking at the sky, while Giraud wandered off softly singing over the first phrases of the song.

Denys had fallen into a light doze when he was awakened by a clamour which brought him to his feet before his eyes were fully open. He could hear Giraud bawling, and another voice, a woman's screaming imprecations. "Oh, Lord," he thought. "He's tried his hand at rape."

He ran toward the voices. Beyond a smooth ridge of greenish stone the ground sloped away in a series of weedy terraces; he scrambled over the ridge and clattered down into a shallow sort of cup, or hollow, among the rocks, the gravel sliding under his soft shoes. He found Giraud half doubled up with his hands over his head, hopping about while a tall, strapping girl whacked at him with a stick.

"Stop!" Denys cried, hoping she knew at least that much French.

She did stop, frowning at him. Giraud smeared at his cheeks which were blubbered with tears.

"Clown! Blockhead!" Denys said to him, angrily. "Do you want to bring a wasp's nest about our ears? And didn't you have sense enough to see you couldn't master a girl half a head taller than you?" He turned to the girl, forcing a smile. "Crazy," he said, pointing at Giraud, and then twiddling his fingers at his temple in the universal sign language. "He would not rape you."

"*Stupro?* Rape? That one?" The girl burst into laughter. "I break him in six pieces," she said, in passable French. "He took my basket."

She turned a fierce eye on Giraud who shrank back. Denys now saw that the minstrel was holding a woven wicker pannier half full of what appeared to be roots and weeds. He held out his hand. Giraud sullenly put the basket into it.

"What in hell was the point of stealing a girl's basket?" Denys demanded.

"I thought it might come in handy some day," Giraud whined.

Denys gave the girl her basket, and said, "I'm sorry. This man is my servant, and I'm to blame. I was napping and I didn't know anyone was about."

"It's nothing," she replied. She smoothed down her robe and picked up her shawl, which lay among the bushes. She smiled, showing small, white, even teeth, as she wrapped the shawl about her shoulders and tied it around her waist.

Denys said, "You shouldn't be so far from home. It's dangerous in the hills. Armed men——"

She giggled. "Your man did not hurt me," she said. "I'm strong, eh? And I am not far from home." She crooked a finger at him. "Come. I show you."

He joined her. She clambered on an upthrust point of rock

and motioned to the valley below. He saw tiled and thatched roofs, white walls, the dark stripes of gleaned fields, the even rows of an orchard, all neat and tidy in the distance. "My house," she said.

"I see. Your father's a farmer?"

"Yes."

"What were you doing up here?"

She stirred the contents of the basket. "*Kappari*," she replied. "I pick the plants and plant them down there in my garden. In summer, we get buds. Put them in sour wine—in, hmm, what you call?—vinegar. Very good." She rubbed her stomach.

"I see. And you're not afraid up here alone?"

"Nobody hurts me," she said, laughing again. "My father is strong man, big, important. And my brothers, very rough. They can eat you."

She looked sidelong at him. There was an air of innocent energy about her, of inexhaustible mirth and freshness, that made her face most attractive.

"But maybe they don't want to," she said.

She jumped from the rock and took a few strides down the hill.

Denys said, "Wait." She stood, poised, arching her eyebrows. "I—er——" he said. "Do you come here often, gathering—ah—*kappari*?"

She pouted her lips in a soundless whistle. Then she said, slyly, "And you? Do you come here?"

"Oh, yes. Every day."

"Ha! Then maybe I would be afraid to come," she cried. She shouted with mocking laughter, and ran off down the hill like a young wild goat.

Denys returned the next day but there was no sign of her. He scoffed at himself for feeling drawn, however casually, to a peasant girl. He tried to work on his song, but could not collect his thoughts. He grew angry, at her for daring to disturb him, at Giraud for starting the whole business, at himself for being an ass—a lustful one. He mounted his horse and rode away, rode in a circle and returned to the ruins but still she hadn't come. He told himself that he would return once more and if she did not appear, he would forget her.

The following day, as he sat alone on the broken steps of the temple trying desperately to set the metre of a line, she came strolling up the hill chewing on a straw, her skirts swinging in a rhythm that put all poetic rhythms out of his head.

"Ah!" she said, pretending to a vast surprise. "You are here?" Then she could not help grinning. "What you do?" she said. "Pick *kappari?*"

"I am writing a song," he answered.

She had a trick of wrinkling up her nose like a child when she didn't quite understand something. She said, "I think you big liar. I don't see any pens or paper. Maybe you write with a stick on the ground?"

"Sit down," Denys said. "I'll sing it to you."

After a moment's hesitation, she sat on the edge of the slab, not too close to him, with her elbows on her knees.

Denys wished he had brought his harp. He cleared his throat, and sang:

> "Why must the nightingale so soon depart,
> And we our scented hawthorn bower fly?
> The sun's first ray strikes sadness to my heart,
> Ah, love farewell; the dawn invades the sky."

She gave a long sigh. "It's very pretty," she said, softly. "I don't understand all. Who is Nightingale? He's soldier, eh? And enemies come in the country so he must go and fight?"

Denys bit his lip. "You're enchanting," he said. "No, the nightingale is a bird—I don't know what you call it—a small bird, a sweet night-singer. This song is about two lovers who have spent the night together in a bed of flowers, and while they lay in each other's arms the nightingale sang to them. Now it is morning, the sun comes, and the bird flies off, and they must take leave of each other too."

"Ah, I see," she said. "Very sad. But if they like to lie together, they do it again next night, eh? So is not so sad."

"I never thought of that."

"You are a knight?" she asked, hugging her knees.

"Well, no, not exactly. I'm an armiger. I have been given the sword and spurs, but I've never received the *adoubement.* You know——" he made a chopping motion with his hand. "The blow of knighthood."

"You are land owner?"

"No. I'm the youngest son of a knight. I'm only a poor poet, a *troubadour*—you know that word, don't you? I don't know where my next penny is coming from. I warm myself by the hope of tomorrow's fire, and think about tomorrow's dinner to fill my belly." He laughed bitterly. "Does that disappoint you?"

She shrugged. "My father is rich. He owns many fields, olives, other kinds of trees, sheep, goats. He puts his hands between those of Gaucelm de Rametta." Abruptly, she bent forward to stare earnestly at him. "You came with the English king, Richard? Is true he has a tail?"

"No, it's not true," Denys laughed. "Even I haven't a tail."

"Ha! I knew was a lie."

She jumped to her feet. "Many lies. Is a lie, too, that you are all going to save Sepulchre of Our Lord Jesu. You want take away our lands. No?"

Denys stood up, too. "Certainly not. We *are* going on crusade."

"Then why you kill people in Messina?"

"They began it. They weren't very friendly, were they? Besides, you can't expect an army to act like a convent of monks."

He stopped, and drew a breath. "You and I needn't be enemies," he said.

She stared at him and her expression changed, her eyes clouded and her lips trembled as if she were about to cry. Then she turned to go. He was at her side in an instant and took her by the wrist. She spun round and there was a dagger in her other hand, a slender but solid nine inches of grey steel. He felt the prick of it through his quilted jacket and his shirt.

"Let me go," she said, between her teeth.

He did not move, but looking into her eyes saw that she would have no hesitation in stabbing him.

He said, "I won't harm you. Just tell me—why did you come here again?"

She said nothing, only pressed the point of the dagger more firmly against him so that he winced away from it and let go of her.

"Well? Why don't you answer me?" he said, sharply. "You came because you wanted to see me, as I wanted to see you.

Isn't that so? Why? Because you wanted to discuss the crusade with me?"

She sucked in a long, shuddering breath. Her jaw had begun to shake uncontrollably. Suddenly, she dropped the dagger and seized him by the arms, caught him tightly to her and lifted her face blindly to his mouth.

They moved apart at last, rolling away from each other on the soft turf, and she sat up. She drew the bodice of her gown together and giggled at him.

"You pretty," she said. "You marry me?"

Denys blinked up at her. "You're delicious," he said. He pulled her down, and embraced her again.

"Listen," she said. "Maybe you think your blood too good? My father is rich. He is headman of our village."

"Darling, I'm not a snob. My own great-great-great-grandmother was a werewolf." He bared his teeth at her. "They say that my great-great-great-grandfather finally brought her into the church for the christening of her son, and when a drop of holy water fell by accident on her hand she vanished out the window."

She shivered. "Don't joke about such things," she said.

"I'm not joking. It's all in the family history. But I just don't want to marry anybody."

"You marry me," she said with calm certainty.

He pressed her hand to his cheek.

"You can still go on crusade," she said.

"Oh, shut up," he said. "Come and kiss me."

The sun was almost overhead. She pulled away from him. "I must go home," she said. "You come back here?"

"Tomorrow."

She straightened her gown and brushed herself off as best she could. "Not tomorrow," she said. "Is Saint Margareta's day. Next day, maybe."

"What do you mean—maybe?"

"Oh . . . I think about."

She ran off down the hill.

"Anyway, I won't marry you!" Denys shouted after her.

He rolled over and lay on his back, grinning at the sky.

*   *   *

Journal of Denys de Courtebarbe. Extract 7.

I learned that her name was Elena, and that her father was one, Francesco of Gazzi, a land-holder in the fee of Gaucelm de Rametta, who was one of their barons. Rich enough was this Francesco, with many men in his pay to till his fields, and tenants of his own, yet he was of base blood and did no knight's service. And now was I held in a cleft stick, for upon my soul I loved Elena well and took much pleasure in companying with her, yet I could not think to wed the daughter of one who, in our land, would be but a mucky peasant with the dung of the cowyard clinging to his boots. Now I would think on his acres and count up what profit he might take in a year, and anon berate myself for such folly, for whatever dowry he gave Elena there would be no land in it and if the fief was heritable (which I did not know, but supposed) it would surely pass to his sons.

Each time we met, she would renew her urging that I marry her, and each time I put her by. This did not stand in the way of our dalliance but did in fact put such a spice upon it as ginger on mutton, ever renewing what might otherwise grow too bland a taste by familiarity.

I said to her, 'In God's name, my dear, why do you press on this suit? What is there for you in marriage with a poor devil of a trouvère should make you so hot after it as a bishop after benefices?'

In her scant French which came so quaintly off her tongue, she replied that I was a pretty man and one that liked her well in all things, and that she was no more than a servant in her father's house and would have a house of her own and be her own mistress.

And no help for it but that she must forever be urging it on, with smiles and caresses, or anon with shrewish curses and threats. My heart misgave me once or twice and I swore never to go more to that heathenish temple on the hilltop where we met, but I could no more hold myself back than keep from pissing when the need was on me.

None knew of our meetings. I took Giraud with me no longer, but finished my song and had him learn it. I made no doubt that Arthur would look at me down his nose if he but knew where I spent my afternoons, even though he was not the man to chide me for it, but I would not tell even him. As for Elena, I know not what she told her father and brothers, but one way or other she came each day to the trysting place and we disported ourselves if, on some days, only for a brief while. Thus matters went for near upon a fortnight and we came to Christmas. On the fourth Sunday of Advent she came not although I waited until the sun was going down, and the next day, it being the day before Christmas, I waited in vain again, and left in a rage vowing that all was at an end. And high time, too, I said to myself, for I was becoming so beguiled by her that I might have found myself saying yea to her demand from pure amazement of spirit.

On Christmas Day King Richard held a great feast in his keep of 'Kill Greek' to which were bidden every knight, baron, and noble lord in the whole army, whether English or French, Poitevin, Norman, Angevin, or Gascon. A countless multitude there were, for several hundred had come from England and as many with the king of France, and near two hundred more from other lands. All were seated within the great hall of the fort (and indeed, there was naught else within but that hall, for the kitchens were without, in penthouses, nor were there other offices or chambers), and I cannot tell the numbers of tables set upon trestles that they might sit at their ease. Round about in the countryside sat the common folk, for King Richard let the heralds cry that all might eat at the king's bounty, nor were there many who passed it by. The weather was fine and far from chill, so that archers and spearmen made the earth their table with no discomfort. All were merry, withindoors and out, and I swear there was no living ox or pig for forty miles round about, nor any farmer that did not count over the king's pennies and keep his Christmas cheer out of Richard's purse.

We trouvères were seated all together, and Richard showed in what honour he held our profession for we were near the high table where the two kings sat, with two of Richard's squires to pour wine for us and wash our hands. Arthur and I were thus separated, for he sat nearer the end of one of the low tables, but he had some friends from his own country and I knew he was not lonely.

Then might you have seen a wondrous sight, when all this

company sat down together, with crowds of valets and servers in coats of many bright colours, and great profusion of wine and viands. All the dishes and platters on which the food was brought were of gold and silver, and the wine was poured from vessels studded with precious stones and wrought with the images of men and beasts. And each man of that whole assembly received a cup to drink out of, according to his rank, of gold, silver, horn, or wood, and these were given to us as gifts from the king, for Richard counted that day lost on which he gave nothing away.

While we feasted there came in jugglers and dancers to amuse us, and when the feasting was done and more wine poured, the king begged us to bring forth our wares. And Pons sang in a voice that was like the amorous cry of a bull, and Peire Vidal had his own jongleur sing for him that was a man he had brought from Marseille and who indeed sang very passably. Then Giraud came up from the corner where he had been picking bones and at my bidding took his harp and sang my new sirvente: 'When from the Holy Land the cry was heard.' He was like the nightingale, drab and little to look at, but so honeyed of voice that tears fell from every eye, and when he was done there was a great noise of applause and I was acclaimed on every hand for the excellence of my song. Giraud was made to sing again, and I received rich gifts, money, a golden cup, a platter of gold, and I know not what besides.

I carried these things back to the tents, with Hugh de Hamelincourt and Arthur to bear me company, and I wished to reward Giraud but could not find him. And now, hear what evil was done to profane that holy day, for towards evening some Genoese and Pisan sailors, heated with wine, fell upon the guards of King Richard's fleet and fought with them, and several were killed and many hurt on both sides before an end was put to the matter.

Nor was this all; for the next day, tempers still running high, more sailors met and went to the wharves and taunted the guards, and once again fighting broke out. And as it befell, this became a cause of both good luck and ill for me.

I was that morning idling at the tents, watching Pons and Hugh at dice along with several others, among them the young Gervaise de Tankarville, who had already won renown for his relentless pursuit of women, there being no Saracens as yet for him to chase. Arthur had gone to that part of the camp where there were some English knights from his country of Sussex, for he was, at this season, grown homesick and longed, he said, to hear talk of simple things, corn and cattle and the management of land.

Now as we sat, there came to our ears an uproar in the distance, and soon after a man we knew, Baldwin de Carreo, a knight very apt with his hands and of a blithe humour, rode by laughing. I went and asked him what was toward, and he said that the sailors were at work once more celebrating Our Lord's Nativity with knives, clubs, and swords all up and down the waterfront. The Genoese had gathered in a crowd earlier and went swaggering to the moorings where they strutted, thumbing their noses, and spitting at the English guards and calling them tailed men and the like, and it might have come to no more than this save that a certain man who was, they said, a Norman minstrel, had come up reeling with drink and shouted out some song in the Italian tongue in which were verses most derogatory to the men of Genoa. And this had so infuriated them that they had set on him, at which the fleet guards ran to his help, and so battle was joined.

I had not seen hide nor hair of Giraud since his singing at the feast, and I guessed this must be he, for if he had a genius at song he had an equal genius for being where brawls started. I got to my horse, therefore, and rode out to the shore. All was confusion, for many in the camp had come to watch and mock, and here and there from this mockery came other sudden fights as it were grass fires springing up and soon quenched. Now the harbour at Messina is formed by a long curving bar of land shaped like a sickle which runs out to enclose a wide basin sheltered from the force of the sea, and the ships were moored on the inner side, nearest the city. But at one end, as it were the handle of the sickle, there were moored merchant ships and others not of our fleet. I rode first past this part, which was nearest our camp, and as I pressed forward between the low huts of fishermen I came suddenly where some French archers were chasing a man, beating at him with their bow-staves, and some striking with swords. He was all muddied and streaming with blood, his cloak in tatters, and the stump of a broken sword still clutched in his hand, but it was clear he was no common sailor, for there was gold about his neck and his torn clothes were of good quality.

My first thought was of prudence, for this was none of my quarrel, but one of the archers, coming close, thrust his bow between the man's legs and brought him down, and the rest, roaring with drunken laughter, began to kick him. This was a sport I took no delight in seeing, and I put spurs to my horse and rode at them. They scattered before me, and when they thought to stand their ground, one or two hastily stringing their bows, I cried that King Richard was coming and would have their necks stretched on his gallows for this work. So greatly was his name feared that they drew off without more ado. I lifted up the man they had felled and wiped his face and asked him how he did.

He said that he did well enough considering that they had all but murdered him. He begged me to bring him to the house of one, Turhan de Aragona, that was a merchant in the city of Messina, where he was lodged. I took him up on my horse's crupper and, for his better comfort, went at a walk holding my sword in my hand lest we be attacked. He showed me what way to go, and so we found the place, which was a tall house in a narrow street, the front shuttered and silent. I pounded on the door, and there came one to open it who looked at me in fright and would have slammed it again but the man I had brought shouted out in the Sicilian speech, whereupon the servant flung wide the door and hastened to help him dismount. Between us, we got him into the house and up a stair to a fine, large hall, elegantly furnished, with tapestries on the walls, chairs with leather seats, and several great coffers handsomely carved. There came in to us a swarthy man, hook-nosed and bearded, who seeing my man held up his hands and cried out, and for a brief while there was so much din in the chamber that I was fain to hold my ears. At last, my man turned to me and took me by the hand and said that he owed me his life. He was, he said, a merchant of the city of Genoa, by name Gian-Maria Scasso, who had come hither to do some business with King Richard. When he had heard they were fighting at the harbour he had feared for his ship, which was not yet unladen, but coming near the press he had been separated from his two servants and then set upon by the archers. He then asked me what reward I would have. But I was now considering what might have befallen my poor fool of a minstrel, Giraud, and bowing said that I was not so greedy as to take money for a man's life, but must depart. He kissed me on both cheeks, and said that if ever I needed aught I must come to him, or, if he could not be found, to this Turhan de Aragona who was his dear friend—waving at the bearded man who bowed low before me—and that whatsoever might be done for me would be done. Then I thought to myself it was none so ill to have him in my debt against some future need, and so left them.

When I returned to the harbour the fighting was done, for both the kings had ridden out together and put an end to it. I searched about and asked of many I saw but could get no news of Giraud, and at last I returned to the camp. I had no sooner seen to my horse and unsaddled him and cooled him, than Pons came up to me looking at me with fondness and drew my arm through his, and, 'Fair, sweet Denys,' says he, 'are we not friends?' I was instantly on my guard, and replied warmly that indeed we were and had been for a long while. 'I have been telling them so,' said he, 'and of all our ventures together, and how often we have dipped in each other's dishes and stood fast by one another.' And he laughed, and went on, 'Even of that time you cozened me when I gave you my money to hold.' I said I minded myself of it and was certain he had no hard feelings, considering of the many times I had paid for his drinking and supping, and how I had even given up my dagger with the relic of Saint Sebastian in the hilt for the sake of his drinking in Rouen. 'Yea, good is it to have such a comrade,' he cried, 'and well I knew I could trust you. For see, I was in play with Hugh de Hamelincourt, and by my hand, he bewitched the dice so that they fell always to him so that I got deeper and deeper in debt and knew not where to turn to find surety to play with. Then I knew that if you were here you would not begrudge me, and the long and short of it is that I have gambled away all those goods you got at the feast, the golden cup, the golden platter, six rings, four neck chains, and twelve brooches of gold and silver.' And he began to laugh heartily and said, 'It was such a jest made us all merry, and when I think of it I cannot forbear to laugh again. But look you, Denys, as God sees me I will repay you fifty-fold, for they were but pretty toys after all, and not such things as should come between friends. Nor look you, I would not have taken them from one I did not love well.''

At first I knew not whether to curse or spit for very rage, but looking at his face, open and handsome, with no malice in it anywhere, I could not keep from laughing myself at such friendship. And so we made it up, but I thought, God save me from any more such love or I should be driven to beg my bread in a ditch.

As for Giraud, in three days' time he returned. A sorry sight he was, all covered with bruises and stripes, his face swollen to make three of it. At first he would say nothing of where he had been, but when I taxed him with having caused the rioting at the moorings, he told me all. At the feast, the king had sent him a pitcher of wine by a page, and he had gone off to enjoy it. And so from one thing to another, so that he walked in a cloud of wine fumes and scarce knew what he did from that moment, until the sailors had begun to beat him. He had shammed dead and crawled away between the feet of the quarrellers. Then Richard had come, and separated the combatants, and some sergeants had dragged Giraud before the king, accusing him of having begun the matter with his singing. But the king had known him and had bidden him to the house of the chamberlain of Sicily, where Richard yet lodged. There he had been washed and dressed in a fine coat, and made to play and sing before both kings. And Richard had cherished him and made much of him, and given him gifts, and made him his bedfellow. But then a devil had entered him, for being in the king's bed-chamber he could not keep his hands from certain trinkets he found lying about there. When this had come to light all that had saved him from death was the king's favour, by reason of Giraud's sweet singing of certain songs by the trouvère Blondel (for Giraud knew as well as I who the trouvère Blondel was). So he had been beaten and thrust out of the house, and counted himself lucky he kept his head on his shoulders. This story made me somewhat uneasy, for I knew Richard's humours and feared that some day he might cast the blame for this mischief upon me. Yet I took Giraud back, especially since Arthur, who was ever soft-hearted, pleaded for him.

And now I have only to add that this very day, the last day of the year 1190 as I sat in our tent writing down these notes, there came a little ragged boy, brown and dirty, who bore himself like a young lord despite his grubbiness, comes swaggering into the tent with one hand on his hip and says to me, 'Denys de Courtebarbe?' I answered that I was, and he hands me a dried bunch of leaves clinging to a stalk. I scowled at him thinking this was some game he made of me, and jumped to my feet, saying, 'What's this, then?'

'*Kappari*,' he said, grinning like an ape, and held out one hand impudently, for a penny. . . .

* * *

Arthur was worried. For weeks Denys had been acting very strangely, and at least part of Arthur's trouble lay in the fact that he didn't know what to do about his worrying, or how to express it. Watching his friend mooning about with an abstracted look, or listening to his aimless, disconnected talk, he had many times cleared his throat in preparation for some sort of direct question, but he had never quite been able to get it out. "Is something wrong?"—that would be easy enough, but supposing Denys were to say, "No"? Or supposing he replied, "Yes" and nothing more? Could one be blunt enough to ask, "What?"

It would be easy, he thought, if only they were in the middle of a conversation, and Denys said that he was upset about something; then it would be quite proper to ask what it was. But you couldn't just leap into this sort of thing cold-bloodedly. There might be something very private that was bothering him, something he didn't at all want to talk about. Meanwhile, Denys stared into space with his lips moving slightly, or vanished for hours every day and returned smiling vaguely and looking rumpled, or sat at his dinner with a bit of meat turning cold and grey between his fingers without seeming to notice anyone or anything. And they never seemed to have any conversations, only desultory talk. Arthur was too good-hearted a soul to feel hurt by this; instead, he grew more worried.

If Denys had had any notion of his friend's state of mind, he would have been astounded. As it was, he didn't realize that he was acting oddly for he was busy with a new and absorbing problem, a problem in poetry.

Once, sometimes twice a week, he met with Elena. They had given up the ruined temple for the weather was more uncertain now, and she had led him, instead, to a tiny hut made of stone higher in the hills. It had once been used by a hermit, she said, a very holy man who came to Sicily many centuries before, floating over the waves in a stone coffin, and who had been taken up to heaven in a thunderstorm after performing many miracles. The place still had a faintly eremitical smell, although that may have been only goats. In this snug retreat, Denys and Elena spent their time making love and quarrelling.

They really had very little in common, aside from the temporary pleasure they took in each other's flesh. And yet they could not relinquish each other. It went deeper than the quenching of their appetites. For Elena, Denys had become a goal to be reached, an obstacle to be overcome, something to be fought with and subdued. He was not her first man—coupling was as natural as breathing in her fierce, rocky country, heated by a southern sun from without and by volcanic fires within. But he was the first man she had wanted to possess; he seemed as precious as a relic, a delightful thing from another world. The extravagance of his speech, the tilt of his head, the way his eyes flashed or brooded, all this was endlessly entertaining. And besides, she was sick and tired of being little more than a servant in her family's house. She was tired of doing her mother's bidding. She was tired of being clouted, no matter how amiably, by her father. She was weary of her two brothers and their strutting, and their heavy-handed humour, and their barnyard morals. They had looked for husbands for her, but so far she had not proved docile enough for most of the local men. It had never occurred to her—or to anyone she knew—to keep track of such trivial things as birthdays; otherwise, she would have put it that she was nineteen years old and with no prospects. It seemed to her that if she could cajole Denys into marrying her all these vexations would disappear.

As for Denys, he had been without a woman for a long time.

But more than that: he was tickled by her vitality, by the extremes of her moods, and the lavishness of her passions. He was like a man who, after days of greasy stew, sits down before a plate of crisp celery. There was no question of love. Love was a matter of dedication to an ideal mistress. This was appetite, and Elena excited the palate of his art as well as that of his senses.

For it had come to him, all at once, that it should be possible to write a kind of poem specially suited to her. Not for her the set measures of the canzo, or the skilful aubade in which the word "dawn" appeared metronomically, or the intricate rhymes of the sestina woven together like an oriental tapestry. No, none of these, nothing that he had ever learned except perhaps the rhymes he had once heard sung by that minstrel, long ago, in a cook-shop with sleet driving against the shutters: a poetry made of common speech, salted with slang, natural in its rhythms. *Natural*—precisely! That was the word, and it described Elena.

But how did one set about writing "natural" poetry? The two words were mutually exclusive, as if you were to say "light darkness" or "dry rain". Poetry had its own nature, was shaped by its own laws, stood alongside life, as it were, reflecting it in a more stately, more glorious manner, like a golden mirror; not lightly was it called "art" and thought of as a mystery.

The problem possessed him, and drove almost everything else out of his head. He had rarely been so happy, or so distraught.

Nothing would come right. It was simple enough to put down phrases of common speech, but he could not get them to ring *poetically*. They did not flow readily into melody that could be sung. He was constantly being seduced into forms he knew: he would begin breaking new ground and then, drawn by the need for a rhyme or led by a cadence he would find himself, all at once, upon a familiar, well-trodden path. Tags of the verses of others floated through his head in spite of all he could do; he found himself muttering lines or phrases hopefully, and then puzzling over whose they were, his or another's.

> "And I am girt with joy on every side,
> But she is joy who doth all else o'er-ride."

Surely that was Bernard de Ventadorn? And in any case it

was so flat, so bloodless compared with Elena herself, bursting with vitality. How could you say of her:

> "Lady, that day when first I saw your face,
> When first on me you let your beauty shine . . ."

(Was that William of Poitiers? Surely not. Peire Vidal? Or his own?)

It wouldn't do. It wouldn't do at all. Those set phrases were stale; no fresh wind of life blew through them. "And, in the end, the wind takes all." Whose was that? Ah, yes, of course, that starveling minstrel in the cook-shop, and in the end the wind had taken him, as well. Damn all winds, damn all metaphors, and damn all poetry!

By the end of the month, he had composed four lines.

> "Oh western wind when wilt thou blow
> That the small rain down can rain?
> Christ, that my love were in my arms,
> And I in my bed again."

He sang them over and over to himself. He wrote them down on a scrap of paper and stared at them. He was not even sure what they meant. He thought of showing them to Peire Vidal, or Pons, to see what they would think of them, but he could guess their reaction. "My dear Denys, that's not poetry! Very good stuff, of course, but after all. . . ." Only one man, Arnaut Daniel, would know what he was getting at, but Arnaut was in France. In despair, he crushed up the bit of paper and threw it away* and tried to put the wretched verses out of his mind. And then, like a bear feeling the stir of spring, he came back into the world again.

He became aware of the taste of food, and was conscious of the weather. There were long blanks in his memory of the past weeks, and he was interested to hear the news: small things, chiefly, as that Ralph de Clairaux had fallen from a boat while fishing and drowned in the harbour, that an English knight had been hanged by Richard for the theft of some plate from a Sicilian nobleman, that Hugh de Hamelincourt had, in a rash

---

* It is my belief that it fell into the hands of Giraud, who popularized it. This would explain how, passing from mouth to mouth, it at last appeared in the sixteenth century as the work of an anonymous contemporary—J. W.

moment, staked his winnings, including more of those fine things which for a short time had belonged to Denys, on the spin of a single coin, and lost. Also, word had come that Queen Eleanor was on her way to Messina, having crossed the Alps in January in spite of her age—she was now sixty-nine—and that she was bringing with her Princess Berengaria, the daughter of King Sancho of Navarre, the famous jouster. It now appeared that the old contention with King Philip was to be revived, over the question of Richard's betrothal to the French princess Alysia, Philip's sister. For it seemed that Queen Eleanor had made up her mind that Richard should marry Berengaria, and whatever that spry, scheming old woman decided generally became law for Richard. In all likelihood, King Philip would not seriously oppose the match; however, Richard had had information that there was dissension at home between his Council and his brother, John, and it was said he was contemplating leaving the crusade and returning to England. It was felt, said Hugh, as they all sat talking about the matter around a light lunch, one day, that King Philip might only give his consent to the marriage between his vassal, Richard, and Berengaria, on condition that Richard made no bones about continuing on his way to the Holy Land.

"After all his talk, and his promises, and his collection of a war chest, and his speeches about totally destroying the Saracens you mean he'd call the whole thing off?" Denys said. "I can believe many things about Richard, but hardly that."

"I doubt he's got any such intention," said Hugh, complacently. "It's a matter of principle with Richard to give King Philip as much trouble as possible. Keeps him on his toes you see, and prevents him from interfering with Richard's main purpose."

"What main purpose is that?" Arthur asked.

"Being accepted as commander-in-chief of the crusade," said Hugh. "That's all Richard cares about. Sensible chap! He knows you can't have two commanders. They'd spend all their time arguing and never give the proper orders. Richard's army outnumbers Philip's, that's true, but when we get to Acre things will be different. There are a lot of uncommitted people there, you know, people who've been fighting for the past year, knights whose homes are now in Outremer and who have a stake in victory. Things haven't been going too well there.

Somebody's got to take charge. Richard means it to be himself."

"And he prepares for it by undermining poor old Philip," chuckled Pons. "Philip the Lamb! Half his men have already come round to thinking of Richard as the lord and Philip as the vassal. I'll lay you a hundred deniers to five that when we get to the Holy Land King Guy, along with Bohemond and the count of Tripoli, and the rest of his supporters will end by swearing fealty to Richard."

"Done!" said Hugh, promptly. "I don't doubt it for a minute, dear old gossip, but I can't pass up odds like that."

He gave Denys a good nudge in the ribs with his sharp elbow, and winked.

Arthur shook his head. "But surely," he said, "Guy of Lusignan is king of Jerusalem? And surely, if there is a single commander of the army, it should be he?"

He blushed, even as he spoke, for Hugh, Peire Vidal, and Pons had all fixed their eyes on him as if he were a novel and surprising spectacle.

"Child," said Peire Vidal, twisting the point of his small beard between thumb and finger, "you will surely find the Holy Grail, for you are pure of heart. Guy of Lusignan is king of Jerusalem in name only. His claim rests on his marriage to Sibylla, the sister of the former king Baldwin the Leper, who died six years ago. But there is another claimant—Sibylla's half-sister, Isabel, who is married to Humphrey de Toron. So far, Humphrey has remained loyal to Guy. But I have heard that there are many barons who would like to see Guy lose the crown. He could never lead the armies of England and France —he can't even sit on the throne of Jerusalem without strong backing."

"Yes, and Richard is his logical supporter," Hugh put in. "The Lusignans are from Poitou—I suppose you might say that Guy is technically Richard's vassal."

"I'm afraid I'll never understand all this—this intrigue," Arthur sighed. "I thought we were simply going to fight the infidels. I don't see why we can't just go there and attack them and beat them, and never mind who has the power or who's the leader of the army."

Peire laughed, and Pons began to say, "You are as innocent——"

Denys interrupted him. "You're quite right, Arthur, as always," he said, sharply, getting to his feet. "It would be far better for all of us if we remembered that we are pilgrims going to the rescue of Our Lord. Some of us, I fear, think only of our own profit."

"My dear fella," Hugh protested, "you've no need to get so hot. We're all very fond of Arthur. Why, good God, we've been living on his bounty for the past fortnight. We had no intention of insulting him. But you know as well as we that war isn't a matter of knight errantry. Rescue the Holy Sepulchre? Abso-bloody-lutely! But surely you yourself have no intention of turning round after we've done so and trudging home again with nothing but a scallop-shell to show for your pains, eh?"

It was Denys's turn to blush. "That's not the point," he retorted. "The point is—well, damn the point! Just leave him alone. He's right. And he's worth more than all four of us together."

He jammed his hands into his belt and glared at them.

Pons said, with a smile, "Calm down, Denys. None of us will argue the matter. He *is* worth a good deal more than we are."

Arthur said, "Really—I say——!"

"Oh, come on, Arthur" Denys said, turning away. He had understood Pons's double meaning, and recognized the futility of going any further. "Let's take a walk. I want to talk to you."

They strolled together between the tents, and away from the camp towards the shore. The sharp pleated hills rose behind them, skirted with tiers of houses, grey, white, or rosy pink, red-roofed or brown. Before them, the tireless turquoise sea dashed itself against the rock, casting up handfuls of jewels or pearly foam before the swinish fishermen. Hundreds of gulls rose like flakes of burning paper above the rocking masts of anchored ships.

They stood for a while, looking. Denys tossed pebbles one by one into the water. Arthur, straddling a salty log, with his hands clasped behind him, blinked mildly at the blue and gold fog which for him was sea and sky.

At last, Denys said, "I seem to have lost touch with things."

"Oh, I don't know," said Arthur.

"You must have worried about me. I suppose I've been walking about like someone in a dream."

"You did seem a bit distracted. Are you—er—is everything all right?"

"Everything is fine. I've been working on a poem, you see." He glanced sidelong at his friend. "Is that true, what Hugh said?"

"What? I don't know what you mean."

"You're a dreadfully inept liar. You know what I mean. Have they been living on your bounty?"

"Well, no, not exactly," Arthur said, uneasily. "Only, you see, Pons had no money, and Peire Vidal didn't seem to have any, and after Hugh lost everything betting someone that he could toss heads three times in a row . . ."

"And I was going about in a stupor. And so you paid for everything. Is that it?"

Arthur looked squarely at him. "I couldn't let you all go hungry, could I?"

Denys grunted. "Let's go back to camp," he said, abruptly. "What are you going to do?"

"I'm going to visit my lord and patron, the king," said Denys. "Perhaps he'd like to be sung to."

He got his horse and rode out to the villa where Richard was living. On the way, he rehearsed what he would say, muttering to himself, "My lord, you promised I should have eightpence a day . . . one gift of fifteen silver marks didn't go very far . . . not a spendthrift . . . promises and no performance . . . expenses, horses, harp strings . . ." None of it sounded very convincing to him. Where *did* the money go? he wondered. It seemed to flow between his fingers like fine sand. The closer he came to the villa, the less courageous he felt; by the time he reached it he was wishing there were some honourable way for him to turn back.

He gave his horse to a groom, and he was just mounting the steps when Richard came out dressed in a short green hunting tunic edged and collared with weasel fur. A leather cap tied under his chin confined his tawny hair. He was slapping a pair of gloves against his thigh, laughing with half a dozen knights who followed him.

Denys stepped aside with relief, for obviously he could not accost the king when he was just going out. But Richard caught sight of him and called to him. Denys came and bowed low.

"Well, well, my dear Renier, I haven't seen you in weeks,

have I?" Richard said. "And how's that blasted minstrel of yours, the one who can't keep his hands off other people's things?"

Denys mumbled something about having beaten Giraud for his sins.

"I'm sure you must have been living well from his pickings during the last month," Richard said, pleasantly. "How do you like that, gentlemen? He's trained his minstrel to steal for him like a monkey! You ought to buy the fellow, Leicester. Wasn't it one of your chaps I had to hang for thievery? Still, give the devil his due, he sings like an angel. And what new songs have you for me, Denys? Never mind—I'll hear them tonight. Come along with us, we're going riding."

He strode on, and Denys, uncertain whether to feel happy at this mark of favour, or apprehensive over Richard's wicked tongue, joined the group. He knew one or two of them pretty well, and when they had mounted he rode with Baldwin de Carreo, a young man with curly blond moustachios and a happy, ingenuous expression. Although little more than a youth, he had already won fame by going alone to Spain and fighting under the banner of Castile against the formidable Yusuf Almansor. He had been knighted on the field of battle by King Alfonso and had returned to take service with Richard, well able to uphold his knighthood with the rich prizes he had brought home. He was immensely powerful, with a fist like a mace, and as good-natured as he was thick-headed.

He was very flattered at Denys riding with him, and did his best to make conversation. Fixing his prominent blue eyes on Denys's face with delight, he asked, "Er—ah—is it hard to write songs? How long does it take to write one? Er—ah—however do you think of words to rhyme with one another?" Denys did his best to answer in simple language, while Baldwin stared at his lips like a deaf-mute, and exclaimed, "My word! Not really?" and occasionally a more complicated ejaculation picked up during his days in Spain.

Only one road skirted the eastern coast of the island, and that was a rutted cart-track which ran along the coast, from Messina through a dozen villages to Syracuse. A number of goat paths left it and wound up into the mountains to the isolated villages there. Richard led his party a little way along the main road, and at the junction with one of these hill paths they reined in, for a group of French knights led by the count of Nevers came picking their way down. Some had spears and some short bows, and across the cantle of one of them hung a runty wild pig.

"God's legs!" exclaimed Richard, jovially, when he caught sight of this. "What have you there—one of the local peasants?"

"We'd have had better sport if it had been," chuckled the count. "We've ranged all over these damned hills without a sight of anything worth hunting. William only took that thing out of desperate boredom."

"What better way to take a boar?" Richard said, quickly, and everyone laughed heartily.

"Ride along with us," the king continued. "We'll go as far as that great rock which juts out into the sea, and then return to my villa and drink some wine together."

They trotted off, all mingled together, and after a bit Richard turned in the saddle and called, "Denys, my dear, come up here and give us a song."

Denys came up alongside the king. "Something brisk, for God's sake," said the count of Nevers. "We're all pining away with idleness. Give us a song with some action in it, one of the old lays."

"Very well. With your permission, my lords, I'll sing you a bit of Roland and Oliver. You'll have to excuse the fact that I haven't a harp or a vielle with me."

He frowned in concentration for a moment, and then sang them the verse in which Count Roland, commanding the rearguard for the emperor Charlemagne, beholds the great host of the paynim coming upon him at the pass of Roncesvaux. Three times his dear comrade Oliver asks him to sound his war-horn to summon the emperor to their aid, and three times Roland refuses, saying, "Never shall the Franks be shamed by me, nor shall it be said that Roland feared the infidel." Then, with twenty thousand against a hundred thousand, they fight until all the rearguard are dead, Oliver, Turpin the Archbishop, Anseis, Duke Berengier, and all the noblest champions of the French, and Roland too, slain with his sword under him.

When he had finished there was silence, the best applause, and many eyes were wet. The count sighed, and said, "That was beautiful, Sir Denys, beautiful. I don't know when I've been so touched."

Richard leaned over to pat Denys's thigh. "I can't imagine why you bother with that wretched minstrel of yours," he said. "Your own voice is quite sweet enough."

"Thank you, my lord," said Denys.

"Personally, I always thought Roland was an idiot," Richard said, shaking his head. "If he had been one of my barons he'd never have been entrusted with the rearguard. Fancy refusing to call for reinforcements when he was outnumbered."

"But he was gallant, my lord," protested the count. "He was full of courage. Surely, you don't mean to imply that a knight should not be courageous?"

"Count," said Richard, fixing him with a sardonic eye, "a man who is fighting a war needs a cool head and good judgment. Courage is useless when it's wedded to folly. If Roland had listened to his friend, Oliver, and blown his horn at once, Charlemagne would have hastened back with his whole army and there would have been an equally splendid fight, only the champions of France would not have died uselessly. The paynim would have been utterly dispersed, and Charlemagne would not have lost his whole rearguard. Twenty thousand men! What I could do with twenty thousand men! Surely, my dear Nevers, you don't think Roland showed his loyalty to his liege lord by throwing away all those lives for the sake of his vanity?"

The count was fiery red. "My lord," he said, stiffly, "I am not accustomed to being schooled in knightly behaviour."

Richard smiled his most charming smile, reaching across Denys to touch the count's arm. "Not even a king would venture to school you in that, my friend. You are the pattern of honour for the whole army."

The count was visibly soothed.

"Yet the song itself says, 'Roland was brave, Oliver was wise'," Richard added. "That expresses exactly what I feel. The perfect knight may be impetuous, headstrong, bold as you like, but the perfect military commander must be cautious and wise, and know when to risk everything with bravery and when to retreat. To face an enemy with courage—yes, that's a fit subject for the old lays, that's fine and noble! But to win battles is another matter. And it is the province of a commander to win battles, not admiration."

Denys, listening, was deeply moved. In this mood Richard was irresistible.

"My lord," Denys said, "forgive me for speaking for I know nothing whatever of warfare. You are right! But surely, Roland was something more than an idiot—even a noble idiot. I've sung his song more times than I can remember, and yet until this moment I've never properly understood it."

"What do you mean?" Richard asked.

"Roland was a noble vassal," said Denys, warmly. "What he did, he did not from vanity but from love of his lord. Isn't that so? 'Never shall Frankish valour fall by me,' he says. Not his own honour but that of Charlemagne, his lord—that was his chief care. Yes, perhaps he was stupid. But a man ought to know one thing well: how to die for loyalty. Death isn't much. But dying properly, ah, that's something else again."

He stopped, surprised to hear himself speak thus. Behind him there was a murmur of approval from several knights who were near enough to hear him. My God, he thought, I sound like Arthur. It must be catching.

But not all his cynicism could keep his admiration for the king from shining in his eyes. Richard looked down at him.

"Ah, and so you know what loyalty is, Denys?" he said, softly.

Denys met the king's gaze. Suddenly they both smiled at the same moment. He said, more lightly, "I hope to learn under your tutelage, my lord."

It was as though some secret message had been exchanged, so secret that Denys did not even know what it was, yet he felt warmed by it.

Then Richard said, looking away, "I can teach you this, that loyalty and love go hand in hand and they are both hard taskmasters. They repay you more often with blows and kicks than with prizes. Are you man enough to face such a thing?" And more quietly, as if to himself, he added, "Is anyone?"

He rode in silence for a while, his head lowered.

Around a bend in the road he had to rein in his horse abruptly for a wagon was coming. Richard drew to one side and the rest of the party divided to let the wagon pass. It was one of the gaily-painted wooden carts the Sicilians had loved since ancient times, drawn by a patient ass and led by a countryman who stared up at the knights in sullen apprehension. The cart was loaded with long rushes, or reeds, stiff-stemmed and with pithy heads like cat-tails, such as were used to thatch farm buildings.

"Ah! Now we shall have some sport," Richard exclaimed, all at once. He held out a hand to stop the peasant. "Here, tu—vorrei che—voi—vendre—that load of rushes. Damn it, don't you speak French?" He took out a tiny gold coin, a *terrin*, and held it up, pointing with the other hand to the cart.

"You want to buy?" the farmer growled. He shrugged. "Take." He snatched the coin, tucked it away, and dragged the rushes quickly off the cart, grimacing in silent amusement. Nobody would believe *this* story when he got home. He had expected to be cut to bits or thrown over the cliffs into the sea at the very least, and here they had given him a *terrin* for a pile of worthless reeds. It just went to show you could never predict what foreigners would do; they were all crazy, otherwise they wouldn't be foreigners.

When he had driven on, the king said, "No, don't look so surprised, gentlemen, we're not going to build a little hut. Don't you remember the games we used to play when we were children? 'Tilts' and 'knights'? Come on, we'll have a tournament."

He stooped from the saddle and caught up one of the rushes, flourishing it as though it were a lance. "Who'll ride against me?" he shouted.

Sniggering and joking like schoolboys, the knights followed his example. Scattering along the road and up the gentle slope of the hillside, they began to ride at one another, thrusting with their mock lances, pretending to loll wounded in the saddle, crowing with triumph at a shrewd hit.

Denys had paired off with Baldwin of Carreo, whose reed was weaker and broke off short in his hand. "You have vanquished me," he laughed. "I yield arms and armour."

"I didn't know my own strength," chuckled Denys.

Baldwin mopped his brow. Denys, shading his eyes, looked around for the king. Richard had turned away from the count of Nevers, whom he had just defeated, and with a fresh reed was facing a bull-necked young man with bright red hair, whose tunic was striped garishly red and white. It was thus a play on his name, for he was William des Barres, a French knight who stood high in King Philip's favour.

Denys knew him; he had been in command of the French forces in Châteauroux when Richard besieged the city, on the day when Denys had saved the king's life. He had also held Mantes, somewhat later, during the endless bickering between King Henry and the French, and had been captured by Richard but had broken his parole and escaped. Richard had sworn never to forgive him, yet here they were riding against each other in a light-hearted game. Denys smiled, considering how the crusade healed such breaches.

Richard and William trotted towards each other and thrust with their rushes. Richard's reed broke, and William tapped him on the chest grinning with just a shade of insolence.

The king's face changed. In an instant it had grown purple and swollen, his eyes hard and bright as diamonds. He set his horse at William's. They collided, thigh to thigh, and Richard swung his arm. He hit with the side of his forearm, as if it were a club, and the crack rang out clearly. The French knight swayed but kept his saddle. He defended himself with his now splintered reed and slapped Richard across the face with it.

Everyone stood frozen. Denys's smile had congealed.

One of the English knights rode forward, crying, "My lord, my lord!" He attempted unsuccessfully to catch the king's bridle.

Richard screamed, in a shrill voice, "Let me alone! I'll kill him!"

He struck des Barres again and tried to hurl him from his horse. He was shrieking like a woman, in such an abandonment of fury that half his blows missed their mark.

The count of Nevers had joined des Barres. He seized his bridle and dragged his horse away from Richard by main strength. The earl of Leicester had come up on the king's other side and was speaking to him in a low voice.

Richard fell back in his saddle. "The rotten filthy traitor!" he cried. "Whore's son! Oath breaker! I'll castrate him. I'll cut his heart out." He fumbled for his dagger.

"My lord, really—control yourself," gasped the earl.

Richard gulped for breath, as if he were strangling. Between clenched teeth, he said to des Barres, "Get out of my sight. If ever I see your face again it will be the end of you."

Des Barres, very stiff and pale, a red blotch standing out on his white face in a kind of parody of his gay tunic, glanced at the count of Nevers. The count jerked his head. Des Barres turned his horse and rode off. The count opened his mouth as if to speak; then he motioned silently to the other French knights and with a bow to Richard left the field.

Richard sat limply, his hands hanging. His eyes had become glazed and lifeless. After a time, during which no one ventured to move, he said flatly, "Let us go."

He rode slowly up the road, the rest following him. Denys alone remained behind.

That new contentment which had englobed him was shattered like an egg. His ears yet rang with the noise of Richard's hysteria; the king's distorted face hung before him.

Love, he said to himself, and loyalty? Oh, it's too much.

He kicked his horse. The beast's hoof slid among broken rushes. A reed—is that what I am? Denys asked himself, bitterly. Not much to lean on. A noble vassal. Are you man enough? Is anyone?

The back of his throat was sour with bile. He urged his mount forward, up the hill. Up above, not far away, was the ruined temple where he could sit and let his mind empty itself.

"And come for your money some other day," he said, aloud.

The temple looked out serenely at the sea, unmoved, golden in the late sun, as it had stood watching the arrival of the Punic ships, the Roman sails, the Byzantines, the Saracens, and the dragon prows of the Normans. Denys walked to the rocky point from which he could look down on the roofs of Elena's house. He stood there for a time, then he climbed the slope of the hollow in which Giraud had stolen her basket, smiling at the memory, and so to the steps of the temple and there he sat down, chin on fist.

Why should he care if the king lost his temper? He had seen it happen before, and as unpredictably and violently—was it not said that the Plantagenets were descended from the devil? It was a vassal's part to watch, to be obedient, to accept both affection and hostility with no other thought than loyalty.

He shrugged. I am not his vassal, not yet, he said to himself.

Before they had left Vezelay, when he had agreed to take service under Richard for the term of the crusade, he had knelt before the king with the others and had sworn to defend him and take his part, to do nothing to his hurt, and to follow him into war. It was such an oath as was common in many parts of France, but it was not, strictly speaking, either homage or the oath of fealty.

Yet was there not another oath, one taken silently, with the eyes alone, and not an hour ago? He lifted his shoulders impatiently. Nothing of the sort could be binding, nor could he even tell what had been exchanged—whatever he had felt, it might be that the king felt nothing. If the oath of service could not be thought of as an engagement of loyalty beyond merely following Richard to the Holy Land, how on earth could he feel himself bound in any way by a glance and a few obscure words?

And still, he told himself wryly, any oath was nothing more than a few words.

His horse, which had been grazing a little distance away, threw up its head. Denys sprang to his feet. Elena stood there, panting a little from the haste of her climb.

"I saw you standing on the rock," she said. "I knew it was you. I was free; I thought, I go up quick and see."

He almost ran to her. He caught hold of her and pulled her close, burying his face in the hollow of her neck. "Oh, God!" he muttered. "Oh, Christ, what a mess."

She held him a little away. "What is wrong?"

He gave a bark of laughter. "*I* was wrong. King Richard does have a tail, you know."

Her eyes widened.

"Oh, no, I'm just joking. Joking! But he is the devil. I swear it. I saw him go mad today."

She said, "He tried hurt you?"

"Hurt me? *Hurt* me? Dear sweet Jesu, I'm frightened to death of him! And at the same time, I've never felt such love for a man—no, not love, veneration. Ah, that's it. One minute you feel there isn't, never was, never could be a king like him, royal, like a god. The next instant you're cowering terrified out of your wits before a kind of naked insanity."

He let go of her, looking at her helplessly. "You don't understand what I'm saying, do you? Christ, I'd like to get out of here. But I can't go."

"No?" She began to smile.

"No. I have a friend, a man named Arthur de Hastynge.

He won't leave the crusade, and I can't leave him. He's blind as a bat. I daren't leave him. Anyway, if I did, I could never face myself again."

She said, thickly, "Oh. A man. I thought——"

"I'm sorry," he said. "I didn't mean you. I wish I did."

Elena stamped her foot. "You wish," she said. "*You* wish. You treat me like whore. You use me. I have to run meet you because is *your* wish. I lie down, spread the legs, and thank you kiss the hand goodbye. That's all, eh? Is enough?"

"Elena," he said, trying to keep his temper, "let's not quarrel. There's no point in going over all this——"

"No point?" Her voice rose. "Where is point? You love a man, eh? Better than me. *Two* men. For a man you come or go, stay or not—a man, a *man*! Woman isn't good enough for you."

"Shut up, you slut," he snapped.

"Brutto! Bestiaccia!" she screamed. She flew at him. Screeching like a harpy she pulled his hair, tore at his cheeks with her nails, and at last, falling on him, bit his ear until her teeth met in the lobe. He clapped his hand to the wound, dazedly, holding her off with the other hand. There was blood on his fingers——

—and the pain in his ear was unendurable. But worse than the pain was the abominable pleasure.

Below the mirror of the shallow self lies quicksilver, and in it a million fish dart, elusive as the quicksilver, shoals and schools of memories. Or, below that mirror a hundred other mirrors bearing reflections of all the chain of selves, one after another, posturing, making faces, chattering, capering, from now to then where it diminishes in the distance in the curled foetus.

Denys is eight. Here, you, what's-your-name, hold this hank of wool. Come, child, pick up my stool, my linen, my needle. There are the cold dark corners of halls where things may lurk. There is the kitchen, hot and smoky as the painting of hell on the chapel wall, but full of greasy comforts. There is standing behind chairs to serve until your feet go to sleep. There is the sudden slap coming out of nowhere. There is loneliness, the loss of the warm bed and the soft, heavy, protecting nest that mother's body made. There are stable smells, cooking smells, the smells of urine and wool, straw too often slept in, closed shutters in winter, steaming dung heaps in summer. There is metal to be cleaned with sore fingers, dried herbs that captivate the nostrils, and now and then a casual caress, none the worse for being unthinking.

The voice of Dom Felix drones above their timid heads: 'But this is how you learn knighthood, in the discipline of servitude. Young men, your day will come, vel qui tibi offerunt hoc sacrificium laudis, even so you shall offer yourselves as sacrifices to God's work, belted and wearing the sword of justice, thus must you learn to serve humbly now, that you may be stern but kindly masters later.'

Balian snickers. '*His* only master's an onion. Old Onionhead.'

Denys looks up at Balian fearfully, for he is the eldest of the pages, thirteen, practically a squire.

Balian says, 'What are you looking at, snotnose?'

A pang of terror, like a blade, goes through Denys.

Then there is another time, an evening when a famous trouvère comes to the castle of Beaupréau. He sings the Song of Jourdain de Blaivie. There is something in that song which frightens Denys. He cannot listen, but listens; he puts his hands over his ears and lifts them off again; he wants to run out of the room but cannot stir. The tears burst from his eyes and he cries bitterly where he sits on the floor with the other pages.

And afterward, in their nook behind the screens of the hall where the pages are whispering and giggling and settling down for the night like mice, Balian stands over him and says, 'Why did you bawl like that?'

'I don't know,' says Denys.

'You'd better tell me.'

'I don't know,' Denys whispers, and begins to cry from the overwhelming awfulness of being a stranger among all these strangers.

'Cry baby. Look at him—little mama's boy.'

Balian grabs him by the ear and twists it. Denys tries to get away, but moving makes it worse.

Balian says to another big boy, 'Dreux, Dreux, you grab

his ear and hold the little pig. That's how you hold pigs. We'll make him grow up. He'll grow up fast.'

His voice catches in his throat. The others creep closer, fascinated, their eyes glittering around him like weasels. Dreux takes Denys's other ear, while Balian pulls up his shirt.

'No, don't,' Denys begs. 'Don't do it. Please let me go.'

Balian bends over him. Dreux's fingernails are sharp and he is squealing with excitement.

The pain in his ear is forgotten. It has become part of the pleasure, shameful, unholy pleasure, secret, painful, and consoling. . . .

. . . He shoved Elena roughly away so that she staggered and almost fell.

"Get back, you bitch!" he snarled. "You damned weasel, you've torn my ear open. God damn it, get away from me."

For the first time in all their quarrels there was hatred in his face. He did not know why, he remembered nothing, but all at once she had become as repellent to him as a snake.

She threw up her arm as if to ward off a blow. Her face was white as lightning. She bared her teeth at him and there was a smear of blood on her chin; with her hair hanging about her eyes she looked like a werewolf so that Denys involuntarily gave back a step.

She spat on the ground at his feet. "My brothers—they will kill you," she said. "I tell them I am pregnant by you."

She turned and left him to bleed alone.

For the next few days Denys went about in fear of his life. But there were times when he almost welcomed the thought of death. He was rocked by waves of disgust at himself, pity for her, remorse. Yet she had hurt him: his ear was swollen and tender and would bear a scar. Nor did he want to marry her, less now than ever. He walked gingerly about the camp, always on the alert, his hand never far from his weapons.

By degrees, he began to forget. He pushed her out of his mind, thought less about his safety, grew so that he no longer jumped at shadows or sudden movements. It was all over, he told himself. Naturally, her first instinct would have been to threaten him, just as her first action, long ago, at the very beginning of the affair, had been to draw a knife on him. She had had no intention of using it then. His pity turned to a kind of lofty philanthropy: he gave pennies to beggars, looked mildly at the children who swarmed around the camp for scraps, and began to consider how he might, perhaps, make things up to her by sending her some money if it could be done secretly and without risk to her from her family. He did not recognize the fact that he wanted to salve his own conscience: it only seemed to him a worthy and repentant act. He decided to visit the merchant Turhan de Aragona, the friend of that Genoese businessman whose life he had saved on the day of the riot. Turhan, a Sicilian of Moorish descent, must have a hundred tentacles which touched every part of life on the island. He would know how to go about the matter.

He walked into Messina one morning, determined on this errand. Pons of Capduoil came with him, planning to buy a skin of the rough but refreshing wine of the country. Pons had had a stroke of luck after so many arid weeks. Fretting with idleness, the knights of Normandy had organized a behourd, or spear-running, and de Tankarville had summoned Pons, who was very good at this sport, to ride in his party. Pons had overthrown two men and taken ransoms—small ones, but enough to fill his purse.

As they strode along, he said, "Ah, Denys, you don't know how a little money restores my soul. It isn't the money so much as the sense of being able to treat my friends. Poverty is cruel, it's harder for a man of gentle blood than for a base person. One's nature suffers when one must turn to others for assistance. I assure you, it hurt me to accept your friend Arthur's bounty."

He took a deep breath, squinting at the sun-drenched walls which rose before them. "I am a man whose spirit demands to be unfettered. You know me—you've known me for many years. You know that I love to be able to put my hand in my purse. I have never stinted myself or my friends. It's a matter of principle with me."

Denys grinned. It was a picture as unlike Pons as he could imagine. "I know that's true, Pons," he said, in an unctuous voice. "Why, take my own case. I never could have got to England without your assistance."

Pons looked a trifle puzzled, but his mind was on what he was saying, and he continued: "I've heard, now, that in the Holy Land there are baronies the size of whole counties in France, just begging to be taken from the Saracens. Some of the men of Aquitaine and Poitou who went out there without so much as a shirt to their backs have castles larger than any in France, hundreds of servants, orchards, meadows, cattle, slaves. . . . It's a paradise! Humphrey de Toron, the Lusignans, de Châtillon, they've all made themselves counts—even kings. Do you know what I've heard? They have pools in the centres of their gardens in which perfumed water spouts up into the air, and the most beautiful naked Saracen maidens fan them all day long."

"And you believe that stuff?" Denys asked.

"Of course I believe it. Why should they lie about it? You talk to anyone who has fought the paynim in Spain—talk to Baldwin de Carreo, for instance. Even in Spain, wherever the Saracens settled, they brought in luxuries the like of which nobody in Europe has ever seen, not even the emperor, not even Richard himself, and God knows he loves luxury. I tell you," he added wistfully, shaking his head, "those infidel dogs know how to live."

They had passed through the gate and were threading their way along a street filled with tiny booths and shops, among chattering, gesticulating crowds, noisy, odorous, hot and happy, endlessly bargaining. The Sicilians had the curious faculty of being able to look both indolent and industrious at the same time.

Pons said, "Let me just get there, that's all I ask. I'll bustle about! God can take care of the Holy Sepulchre. It's His, after all. He gives us our strength and wit to look out for ourselves, doesn't He? I know this would upset your friend Arthur, hearing me say such a thing. My God, Denys, that boy is wonderful! He's Lancelot and Tristram and the paladins of Charlemagne all wrapped up in one. Now, don't be offended——"

He checked himself, and said in a different tone, "They breed them handsome hereabouts. Yes, my dear, what can I do for you?"

Elena had stepped out of the shadows of an alleyway. She stood before them, the sun on her skin golden as an apricot, her eyes narrowed against the glare.

Denys's heart seemed to turn over in his breast. He stared at Elena, and she looked back at him as if she were seeing him for the first time. Her face softened. Her lips trembled with indecision. Suddenly, she stepped close to Pons, threw her arms around his neck, and kissed him. She whirled and ran off, up the street, into the crowd.

"I never know my own charm," Pons began, with a wide, flashing smile.

And all at once, Denys understood. But before he could move or utter a sound, two men sprang from a doorway. Their knives caught the sun for an instant. They darted up to Pons and one of them stabbed him in the side. As he yet stood staring in astonishment at them, the other thrust him at the base of the throat, tearing the knife free viciously. Pons half turned and caught Denys by the arms. His legs gave way under him and he sagged. Denys held him, stupefied by the speed with which it had happened. Pons tried to speak, but blood jetted from his throat and strangled him.

The two men vanished. There was no more than a stir in the crowd which now closed in, watching. It grew quiet, a quiet which spread away from the spot in shuffles and whispers.

Denys sank to the ground with all Pons's heavy weight in his arms. The faces watched him in a ring, curious, hostile, or compassionate, but no one raised a hand to help him. He remained kneeling, laden, his shirt and hose soaking with the blood of the man who had died, all unwittingly, in his place.

The murder of Pons threw a shadow of gloom over his friends, especially as Denys was unable to explain to anyone why it had happened. It thus appeared to be one of those senseless pieces of hostility on the part of the native population which made Richard angry and provoked him into an exchange of bitter letters with King Tancred of Sicily. One result was that Tancred insisted that Queen Eleanor, who was now in Naples, would not be permitted to enter Messina because her large following would only crowd the city still more and undoubtedly bring on further incidents. Instead, he offered her the use of a small but pleasant castle in Reggio, on the mainland. After satisfying his dignity by sufficient objections, Richard accepted for her. Actually, he was far from put out by the arrangement. His mother could, on occasion, be something of a burden.

The air of Sicily was poisoned for Denys. Consequently, he was overjoyed when Richard summoned him and said, "Denys, my dear, I'm sending you over to Reggio to help amuse the Queen. She can't stand the sight of Peire Vidal, you know, and now that Pons is dead you're the only first-rank trouvère I have.

I'm sure she'll be enchanted with you and she'll enjoy Giraud's voice. Only you'll have to see to it that he keeps his hands to himself. She is less tolerant than I, and she'd have his head skipping off his shoulders quicker than you could say 'knife'."

As Denys was leaving the king's presence, a gentleman tapped him on the arm, saying with a smile, "You don't recognize me, do you?"

"I'm afraid not, sir."

"I am Gian-Maria Scasso, of Genoa."

Denys stared at him. Neatly combed, beautifully robed, clean, affluent-looking, suave, he bore little resemblance to the dirty, blood-stained wreck Denys had rescued from the French archers on the waterfront.

"I'm not surprised you didn't know me," Scasso grinned. "I look a bit more respectable today eh?" He took Denys familiarly by the arm and led him aside. "I have been hoping I'd see you before I left Messina. And now I hear that the king plans to send you across to the mainland. Won't you let me give you passage?"

"You're going to Reggio?" Denys asked.

"I am sailing day after tomorrow for Genoa. However, I'd be delighted to take you across the strait first. I want to talk to you. What do you say?"

"Nothing would give me greater pleasure," Denys replied. He meant it, too, for although he had lost most of his fear and dislike of sea travel he considered that he would be a great deal more comfortable in the merchant's vessel than in one of the king's open galleys.

He said goodbye to Arthur with considerable anxiety.

"You're sure you'll be all right?" he asked for the tenth time.

"Of course I'll be all right."

"You're certain you don't want to come along?"

"No, honestly, I'd rather not. I'll live a quiet, peaceable life here. The queen is much too intellectual for me. To tell you the truth, from everything I hear of her she rather frightens me." He took Denys's hand. "You'll be back before we sail?"

"You won't get away without me," Denys said, affectionately. "And for heaven's sake, stay out of trouble. If there's a brawl, or a riot, keep away from it."

He turned to Hugh, who was watching them with a little smile lifting the bristling corners of his moustache.

"You'll look out for him?"

"Count on me, dear old gossip. He won't have a penny left by the time you come back to us."

"That's what I'm afraid of," Denys said. "In a way, it's a good thing poor old Pons. . . ." He broke off with a sigh and crossed himself. "Goodbye, then."

He embraced them both. Giraud picked up the saddlebags, in which changes of clothing were packed, and followed him.

The Genoese ship was a round, fat, commodious vessel, as solid and prosperous as her owner. They cast off, over the glittering, dancing wavelets, and Denys leaned on the bulwarks feeling like an old sea-dog, with no queasiness to trouble him and the roll of the ship a familiar thing under his feet. He watched the land slip away alongside as they beat around the protecting arm of the harbour: they changed course and headed southward, the seamen hauling on the lines and chanting hoarsely.

Scasso pulled his cloak a little tighter around him for the air was crisp. He looked aloft, and all about his ship, and called something to the master mariner who stood at the tiller. The man nodded. Scasso said to Denys, "Let's go below and have something to drink."

There was a big, comfortable cabin with open shutters which let in the light and air, and Scasso motioned Denys to a seat. Bracing himself against the movement of the ship he skilfully poured wine into two horn cups set on silver feet.

"I hope you'll like this," he said. "It's part of a shipment I sold Richard. He complained that he couldn't drink the Sicilian liquor. I can't really blame him. Their notion of ageing wine is to say, 'Wait a minute.'" He chuckled, and drank, smacking his lips. "Ah, that's the real stuff," he said. "I must send some on my next shipment to Cairo. The True Believers don't drink wine, you know—their religion doesn't allow it—but it's surprising how easy it is for people to find a convenient path between their beliefs and their appetites."

Denys wrinkled his brow. "I'm afraid I don't understand. Cairo—that's in Egypt, isn't it? Do you mean to imply that you actually trade with the Saracens?"

"Trade with them? Why of course, my dear man! Why not? Their money's the best in the world—gold, not silver, and paid on the nose. What's more, they never try to skip out on a contract like some of the European gentlemen I could name. Cheat you? Yes, if they can. They know all the tricks, believe me. They're sharp. But I'm a match for them, have to be to stay in business." He smoothed down his coat, complacently. "Sawdust in the flour, loaded weights, all the tricks in the book. But once they've given their word about something, you can depend on it like iron. Delivery dates, full payment, courteous treatment, and no defaulting. I tell you, it's a pleasure to do business with them. As for their bargaining—well, that's the sort of thing that lends a little spice to life. Things would be pretty dull if you simply gave a price and the other fellow accepted it without argument."

"But I thought they were our enemies," Denys said.

"Oh, *that*," Scasso said, with a shrug. "Well, of course, if you want to put it that way. . . ." He poured himself another cup of wine and nodded. "I'll admit we have had our difficulties with them. But our real rival is Pisa. However, we look forward to some very profitable dealings with Richard now, and by the time we're through I believe we'll have squeezed Pisa out altogether. For instance, we've persuaded Richard to hire two thousand Genoese crossbowmen. And a friend of mine, one of the Doria family, and I have formed a partnership and we're supplying shafts, arrow-heads, bow-strings, bows, short swords, and belts at a very good price. With a little modification, we expect to sell the very same models of belts and swords to the Sultan. Our steel, you know, is better than anything they can produce in the East. We've got the factories working night and day. I just wish we could persuade the Saracens to try some of our crossbows, but they're not interested. Well, that's how it goes, you can't have everything."

"But," Denys began. He had to stop and rub his forehead. Then he tried again, "But don't you think there's something wrong in trading with both sides?"

"Wrong? My dear man, what can be wrong?" Scasso looked genuinely concerned. "I don't know what you're talking about! Trade is trade. If someone comes up to a booth and wants to buy a pair of shoes, do you think the shoemaker asks him what his religion is? Besides, a merchant runs terrible risks for his money. Why, every time one of my ships sets out I have to consider storms, accidents, pirates, all sorts of dangers. You can put everything you own into a venture and find yourself a

beggar because of an unforeseen puff of wind. Don't you think
we're entitled to a little return for our risks? We have to make
arrows of any wood, as the saying goes."

"It's only that we're fighting a war with the infidels," Denys
said rather weakly. "I mean, aren't we?"

Scasso waved his hands. "Well, of course we are! Where do
you think those two thousand Genoese crossbowmen are going?
And Genoese sailors and archers fought right alongside the
Normans and Franks at the taking of Jerulsaem in '99. Some
of us must fight and others must carry on the world's work. I
don't fight because it's not my trade. I don't expect Richard to
deal in spices or timber or arms because that's not *his* trade. It's
all quite simple. Each of us does what he knows best how to do.
God gives us abilities and talents and sets us here on earth in an
appointed station, and then we have to make the best we can of
it. Besides," he added, with a disarming smile, "if I didn't trade
with the Saracens some Pisan would. As a good Christian, I
hate them with all my heart, so we all know where we stand."

He refilled Denys's cup. "And speaking of knowing where
we stand, and making the best of things," he went on, "what
about you?"

"What about me?"

"What are your plans?"

Denys rested his chin on his hand. "I don't have any plans,"
he said, "At least, no particular, well-thought-out ones. I'm
going with the king to Acre. What I'd like," he said, thoughtfully, "is to find a nice little barony over there, a piece of land
with a castle on it. . . . Maybe I could settle down then."

"Hmm. There's land in Italy, you know." Scasso carefully
fitted the tips of his fingers together, looking over the top of this
cage at Denys. "You strike me as a man of decision, as well as a
man of intelligence. I've been asking around about you. I've
heard several interesting things. You saved King Richard's
life, once, by quick thinking, just as you saved mine. You met
his challenge to compose a song in one afternoon. That must
have been something to hear. You're loyal—your friend
Arthur de Hastynge had a good deal to tell me about that."

Denys sat up straight. "Arthur? You've talked to Arthur?"

Scasso nodded. "I don't like leaving things to chance. I
had a long talk with de Hastynge. An interesting young man.
If you don't mind my saying so, he's got what I call Lancelot

fever. I mean, he thinks he's living back in the olden days, in some sort of heroic ballad; he believes in enchanters, and imprisoned maidens, and the duty of a knight to be pure and upright and God knows what else. But these are modern times, Denys. A man like that's an anachronism. No offence meant," he said, hastily. "Don't misunderstand me, I admire him. I have a soft spot in my heart for idealists. But in business we haven't much time for that sort of thing. I admire your love for him, and your loyalty to him. But really, my dear man, you're nothing like that yourself. There's no use pretending."

Denys could not help smiling, although he felt a pang of something like treachery to Arthur when he did so. However, affection often goes hand in hand with a delicious, and secret, sense of superiority. "I'd never pretend such a thing," he replied. "But I don't see what it has to do with you."

"It has this to do with me. I may not be a shining idealist but I'm a man of principle, and one of my principles is to pay my debts, especially when I can find some profit to myself in doing so. I owe you a great deal. At the same time, I can use a man with your abilities. As things open up, with all this movement to the East, we're going to be busier and busier. Transporting the troops, feeding them—have you any idea how much grain is needed for five thousand men a day, for instance—clothing them, arming them, all that's a big job. Whether the crusade is successful or not makes no difference to us, as long as they go on fighting. And new orders are coming in every day from the Saracens as well. Take slaves, for instance. We buy up consignments of Greeks, or Slavs, and sell them in Cairo at three hundred per cent profit. That's going to go on whether there's a crusade or not."

"You sell Christian Greeks to the Saracens?" Denys said, in astonishment.

"Oh, the ones we buy are Eastern Christians. They're sold to us by Byzantine traders. But you mustn't look at it that way. Most of the slaves we buy are wretchedly poor, they live hopeless lives, nothing to look forward to. They'd die of starvation, most of them, in any case. And it's all they're good for, my dear man. They *like* slavery. You know perfectly well that if they didn't like it they'd do something to better themselves. I consider we're doing them a favour by taking them out of the squalor of Macedonia or Serbia or whatever ghastly place they come from, and putting them to work with good-natured masters in a nice warm climate where the living's a lot easier.

"What I'm getting at is that with all this increase in trade, I need agents I can trust. I need a man in Cairo itself, for instance, to look after my interests whole-heartedly. I'm going to need someone in Alexandria—my factor there is a cousin of my wife's, and I'm afraid he's more interested in lining his own pockets than attending to my business. What about it?"

Denys shook his head. "I? Your agent? You must be out of your mind. I don't know anything at all about business. I'd make a botch of things. Buying and selling—? I'd beggar you in no time."

"I don't think so," Scasso said, seriously. "You underestimate yourself. Give you a month, three at the outside, and you'd be a match for the best of the Egyptians. Or, no, perhaps not them, but certainly you could begin by handling my business with the Franks at this end. You're looking for a piece of land and a castle, eh? What's a knight's fee in your country?"

"Oh, well, it varies, you know. Somewhere around twenty-five or thirty marks. About five hides of land, sometimes less."

"Yes. Well, now, I've just finished arranging with the king for the transhipment of supplies for his army to Acre. I acted as middleman for a syndicate which will undertake to have corn, dried fish and meat, wine, and dried fruit waiting there for him when he arrives. Do you know what our profit from the venture will come to?"

"I have no idea."

"If everything goes smoothly, about a thousand marks. I'll get another three hundred for arranging the deal. That's only one of a number of operations I'm involved in. Suppose you had handled it for me? No mystery about it—just some smooth talking and polite behaviour, calculations of the amounts needed, a little gentle dickering over prices, and sign the contracts. You could have put that three hundred marks into your own purse."

He sat back, running a hand lightly over his round, sleek head. "Well?" he said.

"I don't know," said Denys.

He got up and went to the window, staring out at the foaming wake. Sicily loomed behind, blue with distance, the folds of the mountains still visible. It was as though he were leaving more than a camp and some friends behind: his life had changed in subtle ways there, and this was the turning point. He was more than tempted.

What would Arthur say if he were to accept Scasso's offer? Arthur would smile warmly, and say, "If that's what you really want, Denys, then I'm happy for you." It would never occur to him to question his friend's decision. Ah, but what would he say if he knew that Denys would be dealing in Christian slaves, or selling arms to the Saracens? No, he'd say nothing at all, but it would be hard to meet his gaze.

Denys bit his lip. Why should he, of all people, begin worrying about the good opinion of a country knight, a bumpkin from some God-forsaken English county? He would make his decision without considering Arthur, he told himself. Lancelot fever. . . .

And what about Richard? You never knew with Richard. The king might be enraged at his defection, for after all he had sworn to follow him to the Holy Land. On the other hand, a few hints at profitable arrangements, or lower prices, or something of the sort might be enough to make the king embrace him with delight.

But you never knew what Richard would do. His thoughts turned to that unfortunate knight, William des Barres. After the incident of the reed lances, not even the intercession of King Philip could soften Richard's animosity, no, not even the fact that the noblest barons of both England and France had gone down on their knees to ask him to change his mind. Richard could be implacable. And yet he could be yielding and full of grace, too, and charming and bountiful in such a way that no man could refuse him anything. That dainty young chaplain, Dulworth, who had once offended the king by singing a scurrilous ditty and whom Richard had knocked senseless with a drinking vessel, had been taken back into favour, had been nursed and cosseted by the king himself, and now sat at his ease back in England keeping the king's chapel on an allowance of two shillings a day and twenty-four candle ends.

There would be no such unpredictability with Scasso, that was certain. You would always know where you stood with such a man. You would be his friend, his equal, his partner . . . and there might be a little castle somewhere, and a house in

Genoa . . . You would count your money with both fists if you did your job properly.

Yes, he thought, turning to look at Scasso, who looked back at him with a paternal smile, and what a job! You would be an agent—lining his pockets, not your own—juggling accounts, haggling over prices, overseeing the shipping of dried fish or filthy, miserable serfs torn out of hovels somewhere. How could you ever get your hands clean again? And after you had tried to wash the stink of the market away, you'd sit down and write—what? A love song to larger profits, an aubade while waiting for a cargo of belts and swords to be sold to the Sultan? Why, this might be the very answer to his search—a new kind of poetry indeed!

> "Why must the nightingale so soon depart?
> The shipment's here, and profits fill my heart."

He burst out laughing, and in that instant the whole preposterous notion fell from him.

"What are you laughing at?" Scasso asked, in surprise.

"I was imagining myself as a businessman," Denys replied. "No, Scasso, it won't do. It's not for me."

"But why not?"

"I could never keep my mind on the work. I'm a trouvère, that's all I am, that's all I'll ever be. Someone else once tried to turn me into a chivalrous knight, and that didn't work either. Naturally, I'm attracted to the huge sums you talk about, but—well, you said it yourself before: each of us does what he knows best how to do. God gives us abilities and talents and we have to make the best of things. There's no use my deceiving myself, or deceiving you, which would be worse. You'd find it out soon enough. I'm no good for anything but making songs. Besides, there's Arthur. I can't let him go on to the East alone."

"You're as much a romantic as he is," Scasso sighed. "Perhaps you're right. I still think you'd make a good merchant. You've got imagination, wit, resourcefulness, and you aren't afraid of action."

He shrugged. "On the other hand, you might find your scruples getting in the way of hard common sense. That would never do. Your attachment to your friend Arthur, for example. It's unhealthy, Denys. Take it from someone who's interested in you. You may find that it does you more harm than good."

"You don't know the whole story," Denys said. "I owe him a great deal, and like you I prefer to pay my debts."

"I see. Well, if you ever change your mind you can find my house in Genoa without much trouble. Meanwhile, this may be useful to you."

He was untying the strings of his purse as he spoke, and he drew out a folded square of parchment. "I had this prepared in case you refused my offer," he explained, holding it out.

The superscription read: *Rachel Comitissa, in Jaffa*. There was a single line of what looked like arbitrary curlicues with the pen, and below that the signature *Scasso*, and a leaden seal stamped with a fist holding a mace and bearing the motto "Io spezzo".

"I don't understand," Denys said. "What's this? What are these squiggles?"

"Hebrew," said Scasso. "It says, 'I commend the bearer to you as if he were my brother.' "

"And who is Rachel Comitissa?"

"She's a banker. Or rather, her father, Jacob, is the banker, but he must be a hundred years old by now and she runs the house. They handle a good deal of business for me in the East. They're strategically placed between Syria and Cairo. When you get to Outremer, my friend, you can't tell when it may be useful to have someone to turn to in case of emergency."

Denys folded up the parchment and tucked it away. "I don't know how to thank you," he said, earnestly.

"Nonsense! It's the least I can do. You wouldn't take any money, and you won't take employment, but you may find that Rachel is better than either," Scasso snorted with amusement. "I've never seen her, you know. I've only met her agent, Vives, in Genoa. But she's probably a dazzler, big dark eyes, a nice full figure——" He drew a pair of curves in the air with his hands. "That wasn't exactly the emergency I had in mind, but you can never tell." He heaved with laughter.

"Now come sit down and have another drink," he said, patting the table top, "and if you'd like to do me a favour, do tell me the story of that song you wrote in answer to Richard's challenge. Is it true he got Arnaut Daniel to eavesdrop as you were composing it, and then to sing it before you could do so? I hear it was one of the dirtiest tricks Richard ever played. . . ."

* * *

Journal of Denys de Courtebarbe. Extract 8.

For many days I remained in the court of Queen Eleanor,
composing songs which Giraud sang for her pleasure and that
of her ladies, and much flattery was I given thereby. Gay
and lively was this court, for wherever this queen went there
was no idleness or boredom. Her wit is quick and her mind
ever busy with new devices so that it is a great marvel to
behold her, still fair and straight of back in spite of her years,
coming and going, jesting, debating, presiding with bright
eyes over dances and pastimes, or speaking of many matters
with wisdom and penetration. I heard from her own lips
how she had contrived those Judgments and Laws of Love
for which her court at Poitou was famed, and how she had
caused André le Chapelain to write them down. I first
played, too, a new game of her invention called The Queen
Commands, which is merry enough, and I recall how a
certain lady, Guiscarda, who waited on the queen, gave us
much joy by her innocence. For in this game, you go before
one who is chosen queen (or, if a man, king) and do homage
and must then answer her questions truthfully or pay a forfeit,
and often enough these questions are so put that many a lady
and gentleman have made much ado to find a way to answer
them without blushing too much. Guiscarda was chosen out
by the Princess Berengaria who cried, 'Guiscarda, go you to
court!' This demoiselle, then, protesting that she did not dare,
and blushing so that you might have read a breviary by the
light of her face, knelt down and the queen said, 'Guiscarda,
you must now reply as I command. Say, in what place do you
feel love most strongly?' And Guiscarda replied 'In a garden'.
Nor could she tell why we all laughed.

In this way our evenings were filled, with games, dances,
and sports, and the days with riding out or playing at ball
or at tables. I found some favour with the queen and often
she kept me beside her and conversed with me, and she never
wearied of speaking of her son and praising him and hearing
me tell what I knew of him. And often would she speak
strongly of her late husband, King Henry, calling him the
old eagle that had pecked to death his own brood and saying
that but for him she would have four sons, not one and a half
(for often she disparaged Count John, since he had been the

apple of his father's eye). I spoke, sometimes, too, with the Lady Berengaria and found her a worthy and good-hearted maiden, something dull-witted it may be and slow of speech, but exceedingly fair to look upon, which may in most cases excuse all else.

In this month of March, the count of Flanders, a most politic gentleman, at last made peace between King Richard and King Philip over the irksome question of Princess Alysia, the French king's sister, and it was settled that Richard should be free to marry Berengaria and should pay ten thousand marks fine to Philip for Alysia's dower. And when this was agreed upon, then on the third of the kalends of April Richard came to Reggio and brought his mother and Berengaria back to Messina, which was now less crowded for the reason that when peace was made King Philip embarked for the Holy Land. And you must know that before he sailed he besought Richard once more to pardon William des Barres, and the king at last agreed to do so, as long as they both should remain in the service of the Cross. I was not much surprised, for I now knew well how Richard could hate and forgive in the space of a paternoster without ever changing his main purpose, and I thought to myself that were I William des Barres I would come not near Richard again for a thousand pounds, pardon or no pardon.

Four days Queen Eleanor remained with her son, and every day there was feasting and mirth. Berengaria, meantime was placed in the care of Richard's sister, Queen Joanna, she who had been wedded to the old king of Sicily. Upon the third of the nones of April Queen Eleanor departed to return to England, and now we all made our preparations to continue on the long-interrupted crusade. And I have this day brought this journal up to date and now will pack it with my other goods, for I look not to have matter to write in it again until we come within sight of the city of Acre, and do now resign myself into the hands of Providence and hope for a safe, speedy journey across the sea.

*

iv Non. June, mclxxxxi. If I have learned aught in twenty-nine years of walking the earth—and sometimes I misdoubt me of it—it is to beware of certainties. As Hugh has often said, 'Be most on your guard when someone offers you a wager on a sure thing.' As I read over the end of that which I wrote above two months ago, I must laugh, for I thought to have nothing but a sea voyage of ten or twelve days to Acre, and fancied myself a seasoned mariner after all my passage in ships, and looked by now to be fighting upon the soil of Syria. Yet here I sit in a peaceful garden above the city called Nicosia, in the island of Cyprus, yet a long sail from Acre. Now must I tell how all this came about, and how, as the merchant Gian-Maria Scasso said to me before we parted from each other, all ventures may be overset by a mere puff of wind.

On the Wednesday of Holy Week we set sail from Sicily, and I was not sad to see that unhappy island fall behind us, in which there had been so much strife, so many pilgrims perished of discord, and my friend Pons laid in the earth through my doing and Elena's. Near two hundred ships of all kinds, busses, galleys, and the smaller sort, made up the fleet, and a proud sight it was to see all those sails of many colours, and painted shields, and banners, spread over the water. I was in a ship commanded by Robert, earl of Leicester, and with me Arthur, Hugh de Hamelincourt, my servant Giraud, Peire Vidal and his jongleur, Bruno by name, and Baldwin de Carreo, as well as many other knights and squires of good renown. The trumpets blew, the townspeople lining all the water front shouted, and with a gay noise we thus set forth to bring aid to the Holy Land.

However, we got no farther than the coast between Calabria and Sicily, within sight of the great, snow-capped mountain they call Etna, when the wind dropped and we were forced to anchor for the night. The seamen muttered that this was an ill omen, and that we should soon have wind and to spare, The next day a breeze sprang up and we sailed on, but on Good Friday there came such a gale of wind that our ship lay upon its side and the whole vessel was full of the groans and distress of valiant knights. And if such was the case with them, well might you believe that we poor trouvères, Peire and I, with our minstrels, gave ourselves up for lost and lay beneath one of the lower deck beams with a skin of wine among us, now singing dolefully and weeping, and anon pausing to throw up the wine with great illness and drink again. Arthur was somewhere near by, but in truth I was in too sorry a case to know where or to think on him.

But on the next day the weather abated, by God's grace, and all was calm for Easter eve, and for the day of Easter as well, with a fresh following wind. Thus three more days we sped on without delay, and each night there burned a great lantern in the stern of Richard's ship which led us all as chicks will follow a mother hen. So on the Wednesday of Easter week we came to the isle of Crete, and anchored. But on the morrow, all the ships were counted and then we found with great grief and woe that above two score were missing, among them one which bore the Princess Berengaria and the king's sister, Queen Joanna. At this news, so we were told, Richard tore his beard and hair and rolled upon the deck in fury, that in spite of all his precautions the sea should have so bereft him.

We then put in at Rhodes where we rested ten days, and here the king heard rumour that some of his ships had been cast up on the island of Cyprus, which was ruled by a most traitorous and evil tyrant, Isaac Comnenus, who wrongfully called himself emperor of the Greeks and shamefully used all who fell into his hands.

Accordingly, we sailed out for Cyprus. And now we came to a part of the sea in which, the seamen said, four contrary currents met. Strong winds arose to add to our anguish, and all that we had suffered before seemed no more than the blowing of summer breezes over a millpond. Yet at last we won through and came to anchor at the port of Limassol on the coast of Cyprus, although I was so foredone with weariness by then that I would have cared nothing if we had come to rest at the bottom of the sea. It was then the sixth day of May.

The news spread throughout the fleet that three of the king's ships had been wrecked upon this shore and of those who were in them many had been drowned, while those who won safe aland had been captured and imprisoned by the Greeks. The ship in which were Queen Joanna and the Damsel of Navarre had come safely to harbour and the Emperor Isaac had attempted to entice the two ladies ashore, but they had wisely refused to place themselves in his power lest he use them as hostages. As for those who had been imprisoned, they broke out of the fort in which they were held and, although nearly unarmed, having only three bows with some quivers full of arrows amongst them, nevertheless did great scathe to the Greeks, being led by two good knights, Roger de Hardicort and William du Bois. Those who were in the queen's ship sallied out to help them, and they won at last into Limassol where they took shelter. Soon after, came Emperor Isaac Comnenus with soft words and beguilements, and whilst yet he attempted to get the queen and the princess to come ashore, he gathered a great host in readiness to seize their ship. As God willed it, his plans were frustrated by the king's arrival with all our fleet.

Richard, although I could well believe him to be enraged at this trumpery emperor's ill-treatment of his men, his sister, and his betrothed, sent a legate to speak with him, desiring that he should make some kind of restitution for the lives his people had taken. Emperor Isaac, as we were told later, cut short the message by making a discourteous noise with his lips* and drove the legate forth with mockery. To such behaviour, though he were a saint Richard could have made only one reply, and straightway the cry went from ship to ship that we should arm and go ashore.

We, therefore, hearing a garbled tale of how the Griffons in Cyprus had slain many pilgrims and threatened the queen and the princess, quickly drew on our mail and took weapons. From every ship you might then see an innumerable host of small boats rowing to the land all filled with warriors, and as they sprang ashore a great noise of battle-cries caused the very earth to shake.

As for me, I had a clear view of the battle from the high forecastle of our ship. For when the earl of Leicester called upon us to arm and make ready, Arthur inquired of him who those folk were upon the shore, and learning that they were Christian Greeks, said that he had sworn a solemn oath never to draw his sword against fellow-Christians for whatever cause. And when the earl railed against him for a coward, Arthur replied softly that not even for that word would he be foresworn. And I said, 'My lord, bethink you

---

* "Pruht!"—*Itinerarium Regis Ricardi.*
"Tproupt!"—*Estoire de la Guerre Sainte.*
"Phrut!"—*L'Histoire des Croisades.*

that it takes more courage, maybe, to hold an oath in the face of insult than to break it. I have sworn to stand by my friend and for this reason I will not go ashore, but I will prove by my body against you that he is no coward.' With this, the earl turned from us and said no more.

Now we saw the small boats come to the land, and the knights sprang out into the surf and waded to the shore. The king's crossbowmen now showed their worth, for ranging themselves along the bulwarks of the galleys shot clouds of shafts into the Greeks who held the shore, so that they yielded ground. And we saw how, in the forefront of the knights went Richard, taller than any other, hewing about him as a farmer cuts grass, and the Griffons gave way before him and soon we saw them streaming away in terror. Thus was the city won, and the Greeks driven into the plains beyond. And Peire Vidal, who had prudently remained with us in the ship, said that never before had he seen so rapid and so notable a victory.

That night we rested in the city, and the following morning, very early, the king had the trumpets sounded and the host moved out to find the Griffons. Our horses being much wearied with tossing on the sea and standing for so many weeks in the ships, they went at a slow walk. Not long after, they found the whole army of the Greeks which had spent the night in a valley, and these came out and commenced shooting stones and arrows at us. Arthur and I, with Peire and our servants, rode up to a little hill and watched, and so vast and powerful did the Greek army seem, and so small our own by comparison, that our hearts sank and we wondered if King Richard would indeed attack. And as we heard later, a certain clerk, Thibaud de Mara, came to the king and said, 'My lord, it would be wise to retire for the time before such a multitude.' But Richard replied, 'Sir clerk, get you to your profession of writing and leave me to mine, which is the making of war.' With that, putting spurs to his horse, he dashed against the enemy and the knights followed him. And now, behold how timorous were the false Greeks, for they would not stand to fight but ran away. The king, coming face to face with the emperor in the press, thrust him from his horse, but he, helped by his guards, was placed upon another and so got hence. Our horsemen pursued the enemy as best they could, but for the weakness of their mounts gave up after a mile or two and returned. And now our men plundered the camp of the Griffons as they would, and took much rich booty, the tent of the emperor with vessels of gold and silver, sheep, cattle, swine, fowls, and horses, wine and provisions of all kinds, and arms and splendid clothing. As for the Greeks, they retired with their emperor into the strong city called Nicosia, and so matters rested for the time.

While we refreshed ourselves, Hugh came to me and drew me privily aside asking if I could speak aught of the Greek language. I replied that I could speak no more of it than to say *alpha beta*, but that Giraud without doubt knew it as he seemed to know all tongues. Said Hugh, wiping his face, 'Before God, then, call him, for I have captured a Greek nobleman who is like to overflow me with his words but I cannot tell what he means.' I fetched Giraud who said that he knew the Greek tongue well enough, and we went with Hugh and found a man tied up hand and foot and bound by the neck to an olive tree. He was robed in a long, full cloak all oversewn with gold ornaments and gems, the richest I ever saw, but his face belied his cloak, being dirty and un-shaven. He blubbered and wept so that it would have broken your heart to hear him. Giraud then fell to speaking with him in his own speech, as it were the barking of dogs: 'toun, bou, ka ka kis, bou, pou,' and the like, and then said to us, laughing, 'This man says that he is the cousin of the emperor, but I think him a liar, my lord, for I believe he is some common thief who has stolen this cloak. But he says if you will not kill him but let him go, he will give you a great ransom.' To this Hugh said, 'Very well, for of what use to me is his life?' This Giraud told the Griffon, who, when we had untied him, fell upon his knees and embraced Hugh's feet, slobbering upon his shoes. Then he sprang up and led us away from the battlefield to a ravine among the hills, and there we found a good horse, several bundles of cloth tied up, and a woman wrapped in a black cloak with her head covered by a thick veil. The Greek drew out from one of the bundles a collar of gold set with precious stones, of great worth. Hugh said to Giraud, 'Tell him I would see the face of the woman.' Giraud replied, 'He says she is very old, very ugly, and the sight of her would make you sick, my lord.'

'Nevertheless,' says Hugh, 'I will look upon her.' He then stepped forward and drew away her veil. She was exceedingly fair, with large, dark eyes and an olive skin, and she smiled at Hugh very winsomely.

He said, 'I will take the woman, too.' When Giraud had translated this, the Greek fell to moaning and crying out 'agapisa' or some such. Giraud said to us, 'He says that he loves her, that she is bound to him with a chain of love.' Said Hugh, 'Tell him that the best of chains may grow rusty and be broken.' Giraud said, 'He says now that he cannot part with her, but he will sell her to you for fifty gold pieces.' Hugh laughed, and I also, at this sudden death of love. Then Hugh drew his sword and looking loweringly upon the Greek bade Giraud tell him to be off without further ado or he should lose his life. The Griffon, falling down once more upon his knees, begged that he be given his horse at least, but Hugh started towards him, and he, leaping up of a sudden, snatched up the smallest of the bundles and made off like a deer. In the other two bundles we found handsome vestments, plates of gold and silver, and a pair of cunningly worked lamps of gold.

The woman went with us very willingly, and Giraud, after speaking with her, told us that her name was Demetroula and that she was one of twelve who accompanied the emperor and robed him and bathed him and did his pleasure. The man we took her from had been a valet of the kitchen, and when the battle was joined had hastily caught up what he could steal and run off. And he would have got safe away had it not been for his greed, for he had come back to get the emperor's own cloak which had been left behind, and thus Hugh had captured him. As for her, it was true the man loved her and had done so for many days, and for this reason had taken her with him, but she said she would as lief come with us as with anyone.

She was, indeed, the most pliable and obedient of women. And now you shall hear how by means of her Hugh cozened Peire Vidal so that when the story was known it gave much innocent mirth to the whole army.

When we came to the city of Limassol, wherein we had taken up our quarters in a fair house from which we thrust forth the inhabitants, Hugh straightway began to tell of how he had saved Demetroula from some who would have harmed her, and of how she was a princess of the Griffons and the niece of Emperor Isaac, and I know not what besides. All the time he spoke, Peire Vidal was looking upon her languishingly and rolling his eyes at her, and sighing. When Hugh had done Peire asked what he meant to do with her now, whereat Hugh replied that he would keep her to ransom, for certes the Greeks would give a great deal of money to have her back, and that therefore he meant to keep her close and shut her up in an upper room of the house. And so, said he, clapping Peire on the shoulder, if he meant to boast how he had kissed the hand of an Imperial princess, he must do it now for no doubt they would ransom her on the morrow. Peire bowed to her, kissing her hand, and she said something to him privily in a soft voice, on which I observed him start and stare. We dined all together; Giraud and Bruno cooked us a pot of stew with garlic, and when we had done Hugh led the damsel away as he had said.

Now that night, when all was still, came Hugh to my bedside and woke me and bade me keep still and follow him. I saw that he was stifling his laughter with his fist like a schoolboy who has pinned an ass's tail to his master's gown unperceived. 'Come you with me,' said he, 'for a witness,' and when I said that it was a poor hour for witnessing aught, he replied that what I was to witness could best be seen only in this hour. Then he went on and told me how he had had Giraud instruct the maiden how to say in French, 'I love thee, come to me,' and further that she must whisper this only to the lord who would kiss her hand, which was Peire.

He had a torch by him, and with this he lighted me up the stair. Then we burst suddenly into the room wherein he had shut Demetroula and there we found Peire atop the maiden most valiantly playing at brangle-buttocks. Hugh had his sheathed sword in his hand, and he brought it down across Peire's arse with a great show of anger, crying, 'Ha! by God's pain, is this how you betray me and my trust?' Peire scrambled to his feet most sheepishly, beseeching Hugh to pardon him and saying, 'Alas, it is my fate that what damsels see me must love me, nor rest until they have brought me to them, and how can a man overcome fate?' But Hugh would have none of it, but cried that he was shent and ruined, for the

Greeks prized maidenheads in their princesses and he feared to get naught but curses in place of a ransom.

Then Peire said that he loved the woman well and found her very fair, and desired to wed with her that the Imperial blood in his veins might mingle with hers. And the upshot was that he offered to pay Hugh a fair ransom for her, leaving it to me and to Arthur to decide the sum. Upon the morrow, then, we set that he should pay two hundred marks over to Hugh, and since he was careful with his money and a saving man, he could well afford it.

But when this was done, and we had witnessed it, two days later what does he do but go to King Richard with the damsel, offering her to the king for a ransom of a thousand marks, with a great tale of how he had taken her from the emperor's side. But Hugh had meanwhile told all to the king, and Richard said to Peire that he was not that day in the market for Greek princesses and that he might keep her as long as he liked. Whereupon, Peire begged the king at least to repay him the two hundred marks he had spent for her, and that Richard might keep what he could get in ransom from the Greeks. This, too, Richard refused with much laughter.

The story sped about the army that this Greek princess was no more than the emperor's bath-girl, and when Peire knew how he had been gulled he packed up his belongings and went aboard a ship that was sailing for France with the king's dispatches, and so departed. Before he sailed, he embraced me, saying that it was none of my doing and that he held me for a friend, but that he had had a bellyful of the crusade and wished to return to Marseille to show the Lady Azalais de Baux that he had consoled himself for her loss with the daughter of an emperor. Thus I knew that he was irrepressible, and I thought it only good of him that he had advanced Demetroula from a mere niece to a higher and more intimate relation with the emperor. He had his revenge upon Richard, however, for he left behind him a sirvente which many sang, and which begins:

> 'King of England, God and I complain
> That ill you serve us both in this campaign;
> He of His holy war which you evade,
> I of my money which you have not paid. . . .'

Now you must know that on the day after Peire's departure there arrived a ship from the Holy Land bearing King Guy of Lusignan, styled king of Jerusalem, and with him the lords Geoffrey of Lusignan, Humphrey de Toron, Bohemund prince of Antioch, Count Raymond of Tripoli, and some others, all of whom swore fealty to Richard. And Hugh shook his head sadly and said, 'Alack! it is a great pity that Pons lived not to get his money for his wager,' since he had said long since that this very thing would happen and these lords become Richard's liegemen. And now it seemed to me that Richard would aid King Guy's claim to the crown of Jerusalem, and in return win the support of these barons and lords of Outremer that he should be made chief leader of the crusade.

The next day, the twelfth day of May, Richard and the Princess of Navarre were wed in Limassol, and she was then crowned Queen of England by the bishop of Evreux. Soon after, the king rode to meet with Emperor Isaac to make peace with him. Very splendid was the king that day, mounted on a Spanish horse, with a saddle of red and gold, dressed in a coat of rose-coloured stuff ornamented with crescents of solid silver, girt with a gold-hilted sword, and on his head a cap of scarlet orfreyed in gold.

But we were not yet done with this double-dealing emperor, for no sooner had he exchanged the kiss of peace with Richard than he fled off to his city of Famagusta and straightway set about gathering a new army against us. Now Richard put his homagers to the test with deeds, for under the pretence that he was ill he sent out King Guy against the enemy. King Guy took Kyrenia and then laid siege to the fortress of Didemus, whilst Richard went to besiege the castle of Buffavento. But now, seeing that he could no longer make headway against Richard's might, the false emperor commanded his host to lay down their arms—which I guess well they were not slow to do—and came himself to fall at Richard's feet and sue for mercy. He surrendered all in the island to the king, and asked only that for his honour's sake he might not be put in iron chains. And this Richard spared him, for pity, binding him instead in chains of pure silver.

We wait only until Richard has established his governance over the island. It is said that we shall set sail for Acre within the next several days. But I must come to note down one more thing which has preyed long on my mind, nor do I know yet whether it may bring more grief or no and am much troubled by it.

It happened soon after that battle outside Limassol at which the Greeks were so furiously scattered, that King Richard was giving dooms and dealing with sundry business in the castle there. And Arthur and I, with our friends, were present, and the king summoned Arthur up to him, and looking upon him with disfavour said, 'I am told, sir, by the earl of Leicester, that you would not take up arms to fight against my enemies. Is this true?'

Arthur replied that it was true only that he had sworn a solemn oath after the taking of Messina never to draw sword against a Christian fellow, nor to draw it until he came to the Holy Land to fight against the infidel.

Then the king said balefully, 'Little do I heed such oaths, but I think rather that you are either a coward or a knave. For your oath to follow me and do my service should be greater than any other.'

My heart misgave me as I heard this, and I trembled for my friend. But he, giving the king eye for eye, although he blushed like a girl, said, 'Nay, my lord, I came as a pilgrim upon a holy mission, and as far as your lordship is above me, so is God higher than your lordship and has first claim upon my fealty. I took the Cross to do battle with the Saracens and none other, and such was my oath to you. Let you try me in combat in the Holy Land, my lord, before you give me a craven's name. But the oath which I took to God I will not retreat from though you put me to death for it.'

There was in him as he spoke something so good, so much of nobility and honesty that many a one nodded and even Richard was silent for a space. All we who watched knew not whether the king would accept this rebuke or slay Arthur where he stood, and for my part I had my hand on my hilt and sought about me for the quickest door, and was determined that come what may I would do my best to bring my foolish friend safely out of that place.

The king said, at last, 'Whose vassal are you? The bishop's of Chichester, is it not?'

'It is so, my lord,' said Arthur.

'Ha, by God's legs, I know such churchly knights as you,'

said the king with a bitter laugh. 'And am I not your king? Has that clerk not schooled you in obedience to your lord? Or will you lesson me in what is fair and honourable?'

Arthur said, most simply, 'My lord, God forbid I should ever fail in true obedience to you. As for honour, I learned it from the best of models—yourself, my lord. For I have heard it said that when you held your worst enemy in your power you forebore for honour's sake to slay him.'

The king's face grew first red, then pale as death. I knew well that Arthur meant to speak of King Henry, and it was clear the king knew this as well. But I could see, too, that the back of Richard's anger was broken, and I let out my breath again.

He said, in a harsh voice, 'Think not to win me by flattery. For this once I will spare you. Get you gone and see that you draw my attention no more until we come before the walls of Acre. And then look you to it that you perform better than you speak.'

Thus was the matter ended for that time. Well do I know the king was baffled by Arthur's firmness of purpose, for such deep goodness is rarely found, and for a man like Richard hard to deal with. A man may be slain for breaking his oath, but not even Richard might slay a man for keeping all oaths. Yet I know that the king forgets nothing, nor does he overlook aught. I fear that Arthur gave him a wound which will be slow to heal. Whatever may befall when we come to the Holy Land, I must be watchful and wary for him, and on two sides at once. I will go now to burn some candles, that the blessed Mother of God and my good patron Saint Denys may be reminded to have us in their care.

4

ACRE AND JAFFA

To the men lining the bulwarks of Richard's vessels it seemed
that Acre rose out of the sea like a magical city: at first, a dark
projection from the land jutting out across their horizon, then,
as they coasted down upon it from the north, a jumble of grey
and white blocks that stood up out of the water plumed with
feathery smoke. Richard had but twenty-five galleys with him,
for some, separated from the fleet, had been captured by the
enemy, and the main body of sailing ships had been delayed by
contrary winds at Tyre. With their oars dipping in time, the
long, low vessels swept round the circuit of the grim walls and
made for the harbour, borne in on a great wave of cheering.

Acre! The name was a battle-cry stirring the blood like the
clang of a war-horn. Here, the hosts of the Cross had struggled
for nearly two years against overwhelming odds, besieging the
city while themselves ringed by the troops of the Sultan,
Saladin, enduring famine and disease and slowly tightening
their grip upon this stronghold which was, it was said, the
column upon which rested all the Frankish holdings in Outremer. The port was the best on the whole coast, and from it
caravans could go easily overland to Damascus, avoiding the
difficult mountain roads. It had been taken from the Franks in
1187, when Saladin, sweeping victoriously through the Holy
Land, had made himself master of every city but Tyre and had
captured Jerusalem itself. Two years afterwards, King Guy,
with a handful of knights and a few thousand common soldiers,
had valiantly sat himself down before Acre to retake it. He had
been joined by scores of barons whose names were a roll-call of
the greatest houses in Europe: Jacques d'Avesnes of Flanders, a
very Achilles on the field of battle; the count of Brienne, the
count of Dreux, the earl of Derby, the castellan of Bruges, the
counts of Hungary, of Ponthieu, of Clermont, innumerable
others, all gallant, hard-handed gentlemen with their archers
and spearmen. Many performed such deeds of arms that

a hundred minstrels would not suffice to sing them all, and many left their bodies before the desperate towers while their souls ascended meekly with folded hands to Paradise. Soon after the beginning of the siege, Saladin had come bustling up with his devilish followers and had treacherously laid siege to King Guy's camp so that the armies of Outremer had found themselves fighting on two fronts. Yet they held out heroically for twenty months while reinforcements came trickling in to support them and all Christendom prayed for their success.

Rescue was at hand. In April King Philip of France arrived and at once set up his siege machinery. And now, Richard, the lion of England, was here. Acre must fall; it only remained for the Franks to stretch out their hands and give the final push.

The galleys shot past the mole and its ominously-named guardian, the Tower of Flies, and drew to the beach. Trumpets sounded from ship to ship. The king was the first to land, leaping over the side and splashing to shore without waiting for the gangway to be put in place, and behind him hurried his barons, grimacing against the cold water, the spray glistening on their faces.

Tears streamed down Arthur's cheeks, nor was he alone. Denys himself felt a lump in his throat, and even Hugh, hardened campaigner though he was, wiped his eyes and blew his nose in his fingers. King Philip stood waiting under the banner of France. He stepped forward and embraced Richard, and they heard him say, pettishly, "Welcome, Richard, welcome. We have all needed you. I hope you're quite finished plundering Cyprus. That is something we will need to talk about."

The cheering and shouting was continuous. The gangways thudded down and the squires and valets began to lead the horses to the beach and to bring out bales of gear and supplies. Denys, Arthur, and Hugh led their own horses to land, while Giraud brought his nag and the two sumpters. The sun blazed down and the confusion was numbing, what with the men pouring out of the ships and those on shore pushing close to gape, weeping for joy and running excitedly to and fro. Richard mounted and rode off with King Philip, and his heralds came ploughing through the crowds waving their batons and calling upon his followers to keep behind him so that they might come to their camp site. Slowly a kind of order was imposed and they all moved off inland parallel with the city walls.

And now, as they left the waterside, a cloud seemed to descend upon them: a terrifying stink, almost palpable, which stopped the breath in their nostrils and closed their throats. It came from everything and everyone; it was everywhere, so that the ground itself reeked. Hundreds of men and animals had trampled over this stretch of earth, had guzzled, sweated, bled, relieved themselves, died and rotted here. Engines of beams covered with wet leather had been set on fire and had charred with the bodies of their manipulators. Corpses had been thrown into the ditches and had been stamped upon. Men had vomited with illness, had fallen dead upon their own excrement, and had been piled into shallow common graves. The winter rains had churned the bloody, barren ground into mud; the sun had baked this dreadful dough into stone, and by its heat flourished clouds of flies that sipped impartially from the living and the dead.

Of the dead, there were ample evidences everywhere. They were less frightening than the living. These were scarecrows, ragged and filthy, their grins gap-toothed from scurvy, their waving hands mere talons, their faces blotched with pustules. It was easy to distinguish the more recent arrivals: their dirt had a healthier look. The richer knights, the barons and counts, were in somewhat better case, but as there were only ten of these for every hundred of the poorer folk, the general effect was of some hellish gathering of beggars, or of the servants and hangers-on of beggars.

The newcomers made their way through the camp with increasing horror. The pavilions of noblemen, many of them stained and patched, rose among whole villages of tiny huts, some of them mere holes in the ground roofed over with thorny branches and scraps of canvas. There were women as well, some dressed in the most outlandish assortment of rags, and small children, naked and with swollen bellies, who played among the cooking fires as if they were at home in France or England or Italy; but this was "home" for most of them, and their playthings were the cast-off scraps of battles. It was a curiously limited world. Along one side of it ran the walls of Acre, grey and battered, broken open in places and spilling fans of rubble. In these spots the defenders had built up new parapets of the fallen stones. A long ditch ran beside the wall, and this the besiegers kept trying to fill up; they used not only earth and stone but the bodies of dead beasts and men, and at night the Saracens crept out of the fissures in the walls and cut up these poor corpses and carried them off to throw into the sea. On the other side of the camp the same thing happened in reverse, for trenches had been dug between the Christian army and that of the Saracens, and Saladin's men tried to fill up these ditches while the crusaders did their best to keep them open. The Sultan's army lay among the foothills of the mountains and all across the open plain: their tents and banners could be seen plainly, and the smoke of their camp fires smudged the hot sky, mingling with the smoke of the crusaders' camp and that of Acre.

"It's not exactly the way I thought it would look," Denys said, with a shudder.

"Or stink," added Hugh. "It's war, you know."

Arthur blinked pitifully at a couple of children who were dragging a dead dog by the tail. Their arms and legs were as thin as reeds and their hair had fallen out in patches. "Perhaps we shall end it quickly," he said. "Perhaps it will all be done within a few days, now that we are here."

"Don't bank on it," Hugh advised. "I've seen a few sieges in my day, but nothing quite like this. Ah, we're halting. I suppose this is where we'll make camp."

They had come to a place where the city wall turned at a sharp angle. A squat, scarred tower jutted out, defending the corner, and a row of catapults and mangonels stood facing it in the plain. A large area had been cleared of huts to make room for the English king's followers, and they could see Richard's banner planted just out of shot of the walls, and all around it a great stir of activity as his servants began raising his pavilions.

Denys tethered their horses to stakes, while Giraud began unpacking the tents. The others gave him a hand, and they had the first one up when a knight came limping up to them and said, "Is that Hugh de Hamelincourt?"

Hugh straightened from a rope he was making fast. "Who's that?" he said. Next moment, he had sprung forward and clasped the other in a bear hug. "Ivo! By God, it's good to see you," he roared.

"Here, watch what you're doing," cried the knight. "You're breaking my ribs. And I'm not the man I was."

Hugh held him off and looked at him. "You're not, you know," he said. He turned to Denys and Arthur. "This is—or used to be—Ivo de Vipont. Ivo, this is Denys de Courtebarbe and Arthur de Hastynge."

Denys tried not to stare, but Ivo was a grotesque sight. His mail shirt was rusted to the colour of dried blood, and had holes in it where the links had broken apart. His mail hose were not much better, and there were blackened leather rags wound around his feet. Over his mail were belted the shreds of what had once been a white surcoat, and there was a faded bit of red cloth sewn to the shoulder, a scrap of a cross. Perched on his head was a Saracen helm a bit too small for him, jauntily on one side, with a dented leaden medal of St. Christopher hanging by a thread tied to the nasal. His skin was the colour of a well-smoked ham, his cheeks, covered with a silvery stubble, were sunken in so that the cheek-bones stood out sharply. His eyes, deep-set in their sockets and surrounded by a mesh of wrinkles, moved restlessly, showing their whites as he glanced over their baggage, their tents, and themselves, but never met their gaze directly.

"I say, have you anything to eat?" he asked. His hands were trembling and he began to rub them together nervously.

Arthur fumbled with one of their bundles, and produced some hard cheese. Ivo snatched it from him and began to wolf it greedily.

"You be careful of your provisions—any other stuff you may have," he said, with his mouth full. "The camp is full of thieves, damned swine who'd as soon cut your throat for a bit of bread as look at you." He chuckled, without humour. "I remember back in February, two of my chaps were down to a penny, and they were able to buy thirteen beans from some farmer out there, beyond the line. Well, you know, they got back and started to divide the beans between them and found that one of them was rotten. So back they went, all the way through the lines, right up past the wing of the infidel camp—look, you can just see that outcrop of rock to the north, that's where it is—and got the farmer to exchange that bean for them. We all had quite a laugh out of it. By Christ, we were hungry, I tell you. Until supplies began coming in again this spring there wasn't a war-horse in the camp. We'd eaten them. One egg cost twenty deniers. As for bread—well, a penny loaf was three pounds Angevin money, and damn well worth it if you could get any."

"It's been difficult, eh?" Hugh said.

"Difficult? Oh, yes, something like that." The first edge of Ivo's hunger had been blunted on the cheese. He swallowed, his adam's apple bobbing inside his scrawny neck. "Damn good cheese, this. Do you know, even when the supply ships came in there were merchants who wouldn't lower their prices? Corn had been selling at a hundred bezants a sack—the bezant, that's this gold coin they use out here, you know, worth about thirty-five deniers—and it dropped to four. There was one man, a Pisan, who kept his prices up, but God punished him. Yes, struck him down in his pride, He did." He chuckled, hoarsely. "The fellow's house burned down mysteriously one night and nobody 'd lift a hand to help him put the fire out. His warehouse burned, too, but oddly enough no one ever found any burned corn or sacks in the ruins. Curious, wasn't it?"

Hugh sighed. "It sounds as though you haven't been doing much fighting, just grubbing about for food, old boy," he said. "And what a stench, my dear chap."

"Yes, I suppose it is rather awful. One grows accustomed to it, you know," said Ivo, brushing the last crumbs from his ragged surcoat. "You should have been here in February, when we had all that rain. Upon my soul, that was something like stinks. Everyone down with dysentery, you know. The latrines were flooded and we had to use the trenches. It was all you could do to squat down without having some bloody great Saracen bastard come charging down on you with his lance at rest. Richard de Vernon—you remember old Dicky, don't you?—he was nearly killed that way. He brained the bugger with a stone, fortunately."

"Remember him? Good old Dicky! I should say I do. What times we used to have," Hugh said, wistfully. "By God, many's the good fight, eh? What about that time at Lagni, eh? You and I, Bobo and the Marshal, what? By God, you've changed, Ivo. What price gilded helmets now?"

"Ah," said Ivo. He began rubbing his hands together again, and all at once tears burst from his eyes and streamed down his dusty cheeks. "Gilded helmets," he cackled. "Jesus, you old horse-thief, Hughie. You and that silly gold chaplet that kept slipping down over your eyes. The old days . . . the Marshal and Bobo . . . riding to tournaments with never a care in the world. I've been here since last August, you know. I enlisted under the banner of Thibault de Blois; he didn't last three months. Caught a fever and *sst!* he was gone. You wouldn't believe how many are gone. It's been grim, very grim, old boy."

"Poor chap," Hugh muttered.

"Things will be different, now," Arthur put in, fiercely. "King Richard won't give them any rest. He'll take Acre the way he took Taillebourg when nobody thought it could be taken."

"That's right," said Denys. "I've been near the king, I've seen him in action. I heard him say to a meeting of prelates and barons that he'd sweep away the infidels instead of striking bargains with them. He'll do it, if anyone can."

He said it stoutly enough, and more for Arthur's sake than his own. But even as he spoke, his heart misgave him for the blank look Ivo turned on him.

"Ah, yes, no doubt," Ivo said. "You wait until you've been here a while, sir. You've only brought in twenty-five galleys, haven't you? Not much food there, I'm afraid. Well, I must push off." He got creakingly to his feet. "You'll find this a little different from the usual sort of war, Hughie. Not very sporting, on the whole. I'll see you later on, shall I?"

"Where can I find you?"

"Well, just at the moment I'm rather at loose ends," Ivo said. "King Philip has offered pretty good pay to anyone who'll take service under him, but I don't fancy that lad. I don't like the look of his mouth, you know. A penny-pincher; not trustworthy. You don't happen to know whether Richard is looking for knights?"

"I'm sure he'd be glad to get you," Hugh replied. "But you wouldn't do much better with him. He's generous with promises but not much else."

"Ah, well. At least he's a fighter. He might lead us in a raid on Saladin's camp, and we'd find something to eat over there at any rate. Well, I shall look you up later."

"All the best," said Hugh. He looked after Ivo as the other limped away, and sighed. "You'd never believe it," he said, sadly, "but that man used to be one of the most dapper fellas

238

in France. Go through a whole day of tourneying without a hair out of place. Used to gild his helmets and wear a sword with a solid silver hilt. What's the world coming to, I ask you?"

Arthur was biting his lips. He burst out, "How can God allow such things to happen to the army of the Cross? I don't understand it. Do you think he was exaggerating?" His voice died away on the word, for only to inhale was enough to convince anyone of the truth.

Giraud said, "God? What do you know about God? It's the Devil's doing."

They had forgotten him. He stood slackly, with his hands hanging, a strange, empty, distant look in his eyes, but a wolfish grin lifting one corner of his mouth so that a tooth glinted there. "Army of the Cross?" he said, in a cracked voice. "An army of Hell is what it is, fighting for the Devil. I knew it as soon as I smelled the place. All you have to do is look at them."

Hugh made one stride and, seizing him by the arm, spun him around. At once, Giraud's face changed; he seemed to return to himself, regaining his customary impudent expression even as he cringed away.

"Don't hit me, noble sir," he said.

"What did you mean by that?" Hugh barked. "Some sort of damned heresy? Eh? Hit you? You're not worth hitting."

He gave Giraud a shove so that the man lost his balance and fell sprawling.

"We'll have no more talk like that," said Hugh. "Poor old Ivo and the rest of the chaps—starving—grubbing about for offal and spilling their guts out fighting the wogs. You won't talk like that about 'em, my lad, or I'll have your heart out in two shakes."

He was white, as much from the effort of controlling himself as with pure rage.

Denys looked at the man on the ground, and revulsion welled up in him, mingled with a kind of sick pity.

"All right, Hugh, leave him alone," he said. "Get up, Giraud. Go back to your work and keep your mouth shut."

On Giraud's face a look of pure malevolence came and went like a flash of lightning. Then he had scrambled to his feet, fawning and bowing, and in a whining voice said, "Nobile signor, adlige Ritter, cher Seigneur, forgive me, I am nothing but dirt, a poor minstrel whose brain has been turned by hardship. I will be silent, my lord. Mum's the word. You'll hear nothing more from me—until your noble lordship wishes me to sing, of course."

He began unfolding the second tent.

Arthur said, with an effort, "I think I know what Giraud meant. Although we call ourselves pilgrims we are full of sin, and so the taking of this city can't be easy; it must be as difficult as overcoming sin itself. It's God's way of testing us."

Hugh stood spraddle-legged, his thumbs hooked in his belt, his head lowered like a bull's as he stared at Arthur. Then he said, heavily, "Stow it."

In silence, they finished putting up the tents and storing away their gear. Giraud went off to find wood for a fire, while Denys watered the horses. Hugh went to the king's pavilion and made arrangements for them to mess with some other knights beginning on the morrow, and Arthur found the store-sheds at the waterside and paid a couple of men to bring some hay for their mounts. It had been badly baled and was wet from the ships, but they were glad to get it. Giraud got a tiny fire going, of twigs and chips and bits of dried dung, and made a pot of pease porridge which was comforting, if not very appetizing.

All through dinner they barely spoke to one another; the sense of oppression was heavy over their heads. Around them the camp was loud with rejoicing by the old hands over Richard's arrival. They had lighted huge fires recklessly out of the dwindling stores of wood, and wine which had been hoarded for weeks was passed around freely. Richard, touched by the poverty of the camp, had ordered more barrels of wine opened, but he did not dare give away food, and so his own followers were visited endlessly at their campfires by beggars, pleading for scraps and weaving with drunkenness, a little wine going a long way in their empty bellies. Most of the newcomers felt as Denys and his friends did, somewhat on the subdued side.

Denys could not sleep but lay staring at the canvas over his head on which the reflections of the bonfires leaped and danced. A great weight of gloom clouded his mind; he thought of the pleasant lands he knew, of Arthur's home where he had passed such happy hours, of smiling Sicily and that girl whose name was already fading from his mind, of the court of the Dauphin of Auvergne where he had long ago been merry, and of many other courts and castles and towns where it seemed to him life had been easy, and all the bad and bitter times appeared, in retrospect, to have been nothing but slightly uncomfortable adventures. And he thought, clenching his teeth, of his foolish anticipation of how things would be here in Outremer; "A nice little barony . . . maybe I could settle down there"—yes, he had said that to Scasso, imagining the army of the Cross with its banners flying marching up to the walls of a toy city, the trumpets blowing, and the Saracens throwing down their arms to Richard, and a kind of Garden of Eden opening before him in which there would be fountains full of rose-petals and Saracen maidens. . . .

He rolled over, grunting with disgust. Arthur was asleep; he could see his profile against the lighted canvas. Denys got up and went out of the tent. It was nearly as hot outside as within. He stood with his hands behind his back, sniffing the all-pervading stench, now sweetened a bit by wood-smoke. There was still noise in the camp but it was scattered and distant; the singing had become thin and discordant, and the few voices which still yelled pleasantries seemed far apart and lonely. Several large fires burned not far away, in the French camp, but no one seemed to be tending them. As he watched, one of them collapsed and sent a cloud of sparks soaring like fireflies. They faded, and the light dimmed.

Someone came shuffling towards him, singing off-key and hiccuping.

"Giraud?" Denys said, softly.

"Eh?"

"You've been stealing wine."

"You know something? You're right," said the minstrel, with satisfaction.

"Is there any left?"

Giraud thrust his face forward, trying to see Denys, and nearly pitched over. He steadied himself, lifted the wineskin he was holding, and shook it.

"What do you know about that?" he said. "There is. You, Sir Denys, the great tourvère—trouvère—ask me for a drink? Very well. I ginit, giniv, givin it to you."

Denys drank deeply. "Sit down," he said. "It's more comfortable on the ground."

"If I sit down I won't get up again," Giraud objected.

Denys drank again. The wine, strong, coarse, and cheap, went to his head quickly.

"Giraud," he said. "Why did you say that—what you did —about an army of Hell fighting for the Devil?"

"I din say nothing," Giraud replied, with dignity. "I don't mean I din say nothing, I mean I din say anything about nothing."

Denys squirted another thin stream of wine into his mouth from the skin, and smacked his lips. It seemed to him that the most important thing in the world was to pin Giraud down. "You are the most elusive damn fool I've ever met," he said, angrily. "Speak up, now! You must have had something in your mind. God damn it, you can't say that this—the crusade —is the Devil's doing and not mean something."

Giraud gently took hold of his hand. He bent close to Denys, breathing a nasty breath into his face, squinting to focus on him. "Why do I have to mean something?" he said. "Do you mean something? Or are you only a body with a devil inside it, trying to make me believe you mean something?"

"You're crazy," Denys said, uneasily. "I'm Denys de Courtebarbe."

"Oh? Yes? Really? How do you know?"

"Because I am. I was baptized, wasn't I? If there had been a devil in me, it would have flown away."

"Yes, it would," said Giraud, holding him tightly. "If there is such a thing as baptism, it would. Now, listen. Listen to me, Sir Denys de Corburb. You take a look around you. Look at the merry world without end. Have you ever seen anybody do a good, unselfish thing?"

"Of course I have. Arthur, for instance."

"I don't mean Arthur for instance. He isn't real anyway." Giraud brushed Arthur out of existence with a flap of his hand. "No, I mean *anybody*. Have you ever seen anybody who never broke a single one of the Ten Commanits? No, you didn't. Now listen. If God gave us those Ten Commanamas and God knows everything, He knows we can't keep them. If we could keep them we'd be angels, not men. Wouldn't we? Angels. Those Commamem—Comman—they're a joke. Now that's

242

what you would expect from a devil. Isn't it? Tell you to do something you can't do, and then send you straight to hell because you do what he knows you're going to do anyway. Right?"

Denys tried to pull himself away. "I want another drink," he said. "You're crazy. Who's talking about the Ten Commandments? You're wrong. The Archangel Gabriel told me he worried about that and the Voice told him to go fishing."

"Fishing?" Giraud began to laugh, spluttering and drooling. "Fishing! That's just exactly what he would say. What do you expect of an archangel anyway? Now, you listen," he said, becoming serious again. "You believe in the Devil, don't you?"

"Of course I do. Everybody does."

"All right. *All* right. And when you look around you, you can see his works, can't you? Backbiting, stealing, killing, hycorprosy——"

"What's hycorprosy?"

"I didn't say hycopsory. I said hypocropy. And kicking little children, and beating them, and murdering, and adultery, and lying, and gluttony, and everything. That's people. No damn good, right? Now you believe in God, too, don't you? All right, look around you. Can you see his works? Kindness? Love? Humility? Charity? What about that, Sir Denys Barb? If somebody ever gives a penny to a blind beggar, he does it because he's glad he isn't blind himself, not because he feels sorry for the poor bugger. Humble? Only to the man with the biggest sword, and he's humble to somebody with a bigger one. Love? Don't make me laugh. Do you love me? Am I your brother, old gossip, old chum of mine?"

He threw an arm around Denys's neck and kissed him on the cheek. "Of course, you're different," he confided. "You're a real son of a bitch, and I love you. I don't mean you're a son of a bitch, sir. I mean you're *real*. You aren't like some of these gentle knights who knock a poor man down and spit on him. They don't love anybody. But you do. I can see it, the way you love your friend Arthur, and you love me too. I know that."

Denys tore free and staggered back a step or two. He found that he was still holding the wineskin, and he took another drink, a long one.

Giraud was swaying, balancing himself with his legs wide apart. His face was shadowed, but the dying firelight touched his jutting chin and his cheek-bone, and twinkled in one eye. He seemed, suddenly, to loom over Denys and he was laughing in a whisper, a hissing, gasping sound, terrible to hear.

"There you are," he said. "There you bloody well are. Now you know who runs the world. That's what my dear old mother used to say to me when she beat the hell out of me. People can believe in God who have a childhood. But I was sold to a minstrel when I was a kid, and for two deniers. That's all I'm worth, dear old chum of mine. It's not everybody who knows just exactly how much he's worth. Gi' me that wine."

He came closer and snatched the skin out of Denys's hand.

"You know who sold me? My dear old mother, that's who," he said. "I didn't know any better. I was surprised when I found out that that wasn't what all mothers did with their kids."

Denys stammered, "Listen—Giraud—I was sent away when I was a boy, too. They sold me, too. Do you think you're the only one?"

Giraud shook his head, unhearing. "I was damned well surprised. The only man who was kind to me was a man who told me, 'Steal, boy. You are doing the Devil's work. The world belongs to the Devil, he made it, he is the true God. To die is the only way to cheat him.' But I didn't have the courage to die. I had to stay here in this rotten, stinking, dirty world. They killed *him*, though. They cracked his bones with iron rods, and cut holes in him and put hot coals in them, and ripped out his guts and wound them around a red-hot wheel, and he just smiled at them until he died. It took a long time. And all the time they said prayers over him. Those mild, saintly, kind, gentle, loving Christians prayed for him. But I could see their eyes, you know, and those tight, dirty little mouths. They loved it. They *loved* it!"

His voice faltered, and faded. He lifted the wineskin. The stream missed his mouth and the last few drops spattered on his chest. He dropped the skin. He said, thickly, "Then I knew. I knew they were all devils. He was right. I knew where I was. I'm stuck fast here. And so are you. So are you, sir, until the day you die if you're as big a coward as I am."

Denys grabbed him by the front of his coat. The leather

was greasy and slick, and moved like a serpent under his hands. Giraud dwindled, shrank before his eyes and seemed, for an instant, ready to slip through his fingers.

"Don't hit me," he whispered.

"Hit you?" said Denys. "You whoreson, I'll cut your throat. That'll help you out. That'll get you free of this damned place, if that's what you want."

He let go of the other and fumbled at his belt for his dagger. Giraud slumped down and lay motionless, an empty heap of clothing and a snore.

There was no dagger; Denys had put his weapons aside before lying down to sleep. He looked up at the sky and the stars wheeled and swooped over his head. He heard laughter. He found that he was crawling, instead of walking, towards his tent and this seemed funny to him. He reached the coarse blanket that was his bed and lay down upon it, still chuckling, and plunged sickeningly into oblivion.

Denys was not the only one in the camp who awoke with a frightful headache. It was a place of groaning, of men who walked tenderly as if the ground were sharp, of slow motion and sudden snarls. If the Saracens had chosen to attack at that moment, the siege of Acre would have been lifted without a blow struck. Even the leaders of the army had celebrated too joyfully the night before, and Richard's customary temperance had been forgotten so that he, too, found the daylight unbearable. Only King Philip, prim and self-contained, had drunk very sparingly—it was said by those who disliked him that his sense of economy made him count the cost of every cup even when it was someone else's wine. He came to Richard's pavilion, his mouth pursed up tightly, and began to scold. The substance of his complaint was one more of Richard's arrogant gestures. For after his arrival, having been told that Philip proposed to offer three gold bezants a week in pay to any knight who would take service under his banner, Richard had instructed his chamberlain to offer four, and this had been cried through the camp that very morning immediately upon the heels of Philip's announcement.

It was, to be sure, more than mere extravagance. Even Philip could see plainly that Richard intended to be recognized, in fact if not in title, as chief of the army. He began by protesting that this kind of overbidding was not seemly, especially since Richard was his vassal. Richard, pressing his temples delicately between his forefingers, suggested that the king of France should have had more care for his honour, and that after all three bezants a week was less than the rent received by a knight of Outremer from his fief. Philip fumed and fussed, and at last, trying to seize the initiative, demanded that a joint attempt against the walls of Acre be made that very afternoon. Richard, his temper fraying, threw himself face downward on his bed and replied that he would not so much as spit towards the walls until he had made reconnaissances, set up his siege engines, and recovered from his headache. So ended round one.

Round two was brief and consisted of one neat rabbit-punch delivered by Richard. Count Henry of Champagne, one of the most powerful of the nobles, had spent the winter before Acre and, following in the tradition of his father who had been known as Henry the Open-Handed, had given freely of his supplies to the starving soldiers. He now went to Philip, who was his uncle, and begged for a loan. Philip offered £100,000 money of Paris, but demanded the county of Champagne as surety. Henry then went to his other uncle, Richard. Richard said heartily that he never gave loans; instead, he made Henry a gift of four thousand bushels of wheat, four thousand flitches of bacon, and four thousand Angevin pounds. Within a few days' time the king of France had lost face and friends, while almost all those knights who were free to choose—as well as a number who were not—had taken service under Richard.

Philip retaliated by insisting on an immediate assault against the city, attempting to make it appear that Richard was being laggardly in his duty. They had arrived on the eighth of June; five days had passed and nothing had been done except that Richard's wooden fort, Kill-Greek, had been unpacked from the galleys and set up within bow-shot of one of the towers. The French king, on the other hand, had been steadily bombarding the wall opposite his encampment with a great number of short-range weapons and one enormous mangonel, called *Bad Neighbour*, which cast stones weighing well over five hundred pounds.

Richard had two perfectly good excuses for immobility. His fleet, carrying most of his barons and all his heavy siege machinery, was still held up at Tyre by head-winds. And he himself had fallen ill with scurvy, complicated by his recurrent malaria. To Philip's jealous eye the time seemed ripe for an assertion of his own leadership. Accordingly, he ordered an assault, and Richard, gritting teeth which had loosened in his jaws, was too sick to oppose him.

On the morning of the fourteenth, therefore, the host of the French armed itself. Mass was said, and all voices lifted in the singing of *Veni, Creator Spiritus*. Then they moved forward against the walls. Richard's followers, having received no orders from their king, remained at their tents or strolled down to watch the battle.

The French had been concentrating their artillery fire against a section of the wall on each side of, and encompassing, the Accursed Tower, so called because it was said to have been the place in which Judas's thirty pieces of silver were minted. A section near the top of the ramparts had been battered in and this could be reached by relatively short ladders. The catapults were moved closer so that they could cast stones over the parapets and into the press of the defenders. The ladders were raised up and the French knights began swarming up them, led by a valiant and daring young man named Aubrey Clèment who had sworn a solemn oath that he would enter the city that morning if he had to do so alone.

As the French climbed, the people in the city set up a great racket of yelling and beating on drums, basins, platters, or anything else that would make a noise. King Philip remarked on the unholy music which must be, he said, either their way of praying to the Devil their master, or the sign of great fear. A few moments later, however, it became clear that it was neither, for shouts and the clash of weapons broke out at the barricaded trench surrounding the crusaders' camp. The uproar had been a signal to Saladin, who now in his turn attacked the camp.

Fortunately, Geoffrey of Lusignan, brother to King Guy, had been patrolling the trench. Swinging a heavy battle-axe, and with fifteen knights at his side, he held the barricade, personally slaying half a dozen of the enemy, until others from the camp could run to his aid. They beat back the Saracens after a couple of hours of hot fighting. Meantime, the French had fared badly at the city wall. The weight of soldiery had caused several of the ladders to break under them; other ladders had been pitched over by the defenders, and Aubrey Clèment had been marooned in the breach and had fallen gallantly, surrounded by infidel dead.

The French were removing their armour to cool off and eat their dinners, when the alarm was sounded once more. They had left their siege engines close under the wall, and the people of the city had cast Greek fire down in showers and set the wooden frames ablaze. Soldiers rushed up with buckets of sand and earth—for they had long ago discovered that water was of no avail against the burning naphtha—but in vain; by nightfall most of the French artillery was charred and ruined beyond repair. King Philip's secretary noted down in his daybook that the king "overcome by fury and anger sank into a state of languid sickness, and from confusion and discouragement mounted not on horseback".

His discouragement was as nothing compared to that of the rest of the host. For a few days it looked as though all were lost. The heart went out of everyone. Those who had been longest before Acre sat like sacks, motionless and speechless. Others growled against both kings and talked of abandoning the siege and going home. The French said that the English were lazy and cowardly and let other people do the fighting; the English replied that little was to be expected of soldiers who had not enough sense not to overload scaling ladders. Many of the newcomers began to fall ill with scurvy and dysentery, and all that prevented the whole camp from disintegrating in the end was the arrival of Richard's fleet, at last, bringing food, the main part of his army, and the masses of huge wheels, beams, ropes, and weights that made up his siege engines.

These new, fresh fighting men, these barrels of meat and sacks of grain, these speedily-assembled stone-casters creaking on their solid wheels, drew the army out of its melancholy. They also helped put Richard on the road to recovery. He had his bed carried out where he could supervise the erection of his mangonels; he ordered the building of a testudo, or covered shed, which could be pushed close to the walls and from which his arbalesters could shoot in safety; he had his sappers begin intensive digging beneath the tower of Saint Nicholas, which connected with the Accursed Tower, undermining its footings and propping up their tunnel with beams which, when all was ready, would be burned away to let the tower fall. Meanwhile, King Philip assembled wood and cordage and built more engines of his own which began shooting again at the Accursed Tower, and at the breach which the Saracens had filled up and reinforced. Further along the wall the Hospitallers and Templars kept up their own shooting with small catapults good for little but to knock an occasional Saracen off the parapets, but, as the Master of the Temple remarked, "every little helps".

The days blurred into each other, feverish, busy, exhausting. From early morning until sunset men carried stones to the artillery, great smooth rocks which Richard had had brought as ballast in the ships, masses of stone from the shore, or jagged chunks dug out of the plain itself. The arms of the mangonels and trebuchets never ceased their groaning and thudding, and beside them the smaller catapults, tough as bulldogs, whanged away. Buckets of dirt came up from the mines below the towers and were heaped alongside the engines to be used in case of fire. Every day saw fighting at the outer trenches, token battles as a result of which few were killed but nobody got any rest. The sun blazed down out of a bright, dry sky and men dropped where they stood from weariness and heat. Simply to patrol the barricades in armour for an hour was as fatiguing as battle. Those who had helmets packed them away, for to wear a helm was an invitation to suffocation. To all other pains were added the raw sores made by the chafing of metal or leather on the skin. Men sweated until it seemed there could never be enough water in the world to replace what they lost. Lips cracked, eyes hardened like boiled eggs, and the friction of swordhilts wore through the callouses even of tough old warriors like Hugh de Hamelincourt.

Waiting was the hardest part of it for the knights, armigers, and squires, so that in despair many of them took a turn at bringing stones for the engines, or, with borrowed arbalests, tried to pick off enemies who showed themselves above the parapets. They would stand at the trenches in the rear of the camp and shout insults over at the Saracens, hoping to goad the Sultan's men into an attack for the sake of a bit of action. Every morning, they asked each other, "Will it be today? Surely, everything is ready; surely the king will command us to take the walls?" Tempers frayed as the tension increased, and squabbles were common as each day frustrated their hopes.

Denys, at first, had worried about what would happen to Arthur in combat, but after they had once defended the barricades he found that in hand-to-hand fighting his friend could see quite well enough to distinguish the infidels, with their pointed helmets and flowing robes, from the Franks. He was content to defend himself while keeping one eye on Arthur so that he could protect him against an unexpected blow. His mind emptied itself of thoughts. Each day came and went in a simple, mechanical routine: eating, patrolling, waiting, watching, and falling at last into a heavy slumber full of ominous fragments of dreams while the heat of the day slowly evaporated from him in steaming sweat.

And Arthur, too, seemed to have little to say. He drew into himself day by day, brooding and weary, his mild spirit ground down by the abrasions of the life they lived, by heat and smells, monotonous diet, long stretches of idleness, and the irritability of his neighbours. He was only happy when they went to walk the circuit of the barricade; then his face would take on a little colour and he would snuff the air and say, hopefully, "Do you think they'll make a sortie today?" And if, by chance, a daring band of Saracens, themselves bored out of endurance, rushed the barricade, he would met them laughing like a boy, utterly careless of wounds, and Denys would have to follow despite himself. But when all was over he would lapse into silence once more, only saying wistfully, now and then, "What are they doing at home, I wonder?" but, if Denys began to talk of home, or Maude, Arthur would only listen in silence, and on his face the fixed empty smile of one whose thought is elsewhere.

They were breakfasting in their mess one morning, twenty knights and armigers seated in two long rows with their body-squires or servants waiting on them. Giraud, bending over to pour the thin, sour wine was jostled by another valet. Wine splashed on Arthur's sleeve.

"Look what you're doing, can't you?" Arthur snapped.

This was so unlike him that Denys and Hugh and several others who knew him stopped eating and stared.

Denys said, "It wasn't Giraud's fault."

"And you needn't take his part," Arthur said, shaking the drops from his arm. His eyes, smudged below as if he had wiped his cheeks with muddy fingers, were dulled and colourless. Down each side of his face ran an ugly red seam, from his forehead to his chin, where the edges of his mail hood had rubbed away the skin. Denys looked at him as if he had never seen him before, and thought, "My God, is that what I look like? What's happening to us?"

"I know what it is," Hugh said. He tore a chunk from one of the flat, grey loaves and reached for the oil. "He's just bored with sitting about. We're all bloody well sick of it, my lad. That's a siege for you, nine parts waiting to one part fighting. I hate the damned things. Give me a nice free-for-all any day, what?" He nudged his neighbour, Baldwin de Carreo.

Baldwin's blond moustaches had lost their curl and hung as limp as wet hay, but his face was as stupidly amiable as if nothing that troubled the others had ever touched him. "Good Lord, yes," he said. "I remember once when I was in Spain and we were besieging Trujillo—or was it Caceres? No, I think it must have been Trujillo because what's his name was there, you know, that stout chap with the scar across his nose who took the chaplet at the tourney in Azay—oh, Lord, I can't think of his name."

Since he had never yet finished any story he had begun, no one was surprised.

A man across the table, William de la Mare, a rich knight of Suffolk, growled, "What the devil is the king waiting for? That's what I can't understand. I don't see his father sitting here all this while, doing nothing."

"Quite right," said Hugh, laughing with his mouth full. "Nobody ever did see old Harry sitting in the Holy Land, not for five minutes. I never thought Richard would be fool enough to come, but now he's here he'll take the city in his own time and his own way."

Ivo de Vimont shook his head. He was somewhat cleaner and less ravenous than when they had first seen him, for he had succumbed to the lure of the four bezants and enlisted under Richard's banner. He now spent most of his time with Hugh, swapping yarns of the old days. The two of them also ventured out almost every day into the debatable ground between the Sultan's camp and the crusaders' trenches and exchanged lance-thrusts with stray infidels.

He said, "I'd feel happier if I hadn't heard the rumours that Richard has been dickering with Saladin."

"Ha! There it is," said William de la Mare, slapping the

table with a knobbly-knuckled hand. "We've all heard those rumours. Didn't he ask Saladin to send him a few chickens so that he could feed his hawks? Feed his hawks, indeed! It was Richard who ate well that day, not the birds."

His brother, Robert, a darker, shorter version of him, nodded grimly. "What was it Bertrand de Born called him? Richard Yes-and-No. Who can tell what he's up to? I wouldn't put it past him to make his own peace with Saladin, take what profit he can, and be off. Where would that leave us, I ask you?"

Hugh pushed himself back from the table. "Not a very courteous thing to say, Robert. Got the wind up, have you? Afraid you'll be left to do some fighting?"

"I came here to fight, not to sit idle like a damned hawk in the moult," Robert said, frowning. "By God, if I'd known Richard was going to muck about this way I'd have switched my fealty to King Philip. At least, he assaulted the walls."

"Ah, yes, that's Philip for you," said Ivo. "That bloody tight little mouth! Jumped before he was ready, and then even a child would have known better than to crowd those few ladders. Still, if it's action you're looking for, Robert, why don't you come out into the plain with Hugh and me this morning? I don't think I've seen you at the barricades once in the last week."

"Are you calling me a coward, sir?" said Robert, fiercely.

"I'm not calling you anything, sir," Ivo replied. "If the glove fits——"

"By God's bones, sir, I think your intention is to insult us," said William.

"Have it any way you like, sir," Ivo retorted.

Robert was on his feet, his dagger drawn. "I don't think I like your tone, sir," he said.

Ivo at once got up; so did Hugh, both with their weapons bared. Baldwin said, "Oh, I say——" and stood up ponderously. A young Suffolk knight snapped, "You keep out of this, Baldwin." William's dagger flashed in his hand as he made a motion as if to climb over the table.

And suddenly Arthur cried, "My God, must you go on and on?"

He pressed his hands to his temples. "Stop it!" he shouted. All eyes turned upon him. He looked back, seeming disconcerted by his own outburst. "I'm sorry," he said. "It's all this quarrelling. Are we all mad? Maybe Giraud was right, maybe it's an army of Hell. With this kind of talk. Daggers ready for each other's throats. What? Haven't we all taken the Cross? I don't think it's. . . ."

He choked on his words, and sank back upon the bench.

Ivo said, mildly, "Well, upon my soul. What's the matter with *him*?"

"He's right, you know," Hugh said. "But still—Arthur, my dear chap, you mustn't take things so seriously. I mean to say, what else is there for us to do but quarrel? I mean, a gentleman must fight, you know. There's really nothing else worth doing. Isn't that so?"

He blinked round at the others, and they all nodded solemnly.

"Good Lord," he said. "Show us a bit of sport, that's all we ask. If not—well, you know, the best surgeons recommend a little blood-letting for a choleric temperament. Eh? We simply have to think of our health."

There were appreciative chuckles. Hugh stroked his moustache, and added with a grin, "But still, as I say, the boy's right. Not at the breakfast table, what?"

Denys, with his hand on Arthur's shoulder, looked searchingly at his friend. Arthur's face had grown very red, but it was an unnatural colour, not the proper colour of a blush. He sat with his head hanging, and said, in a muffled voice, "I don't know what's the matter——"

At that precise instant there came a rumbling crash from the direction of the city, and afterward yells, shrieks, and cheers. The noise pinned them all to their places.

Then Hugh said, "The tower! They must have sprung the mine."

A herald came running past, shouting, "To arms! To the walls!"

They broke for their tents and began dragging on their armour, tying thongs and laces, buckling on belts, all contention forgotten. From every part of the camp men streamed to the spot opposite that section of the walls between the tower of Saint Nicholas and the Accursed Tower.

Early that morning Richard had commanded the sappers to fire the supports in their mine. By breakfast time the beams, soaked with oil, had burned through enough so that the tunnel collapsed, bringing down with it the face of the tower of Saint Nicholas and part of the wall as well. The stones filled the ditch, dust rose chokingly above them, and amongst the rubble could be seen half-buried bodies some of which still moved. The arbalesters were already lined up, protected by shields made of rough boards, shooting steadily while their captains ran along behind the ranks to correct their aim. The standards of England and Aquitaine had been planted dangerously close to the walls, and as Denys and the others ran up they saw that Richard had had his bed placed beneath the banners. He sat erect, a coverlet thrown across his knees, his face yellow and haggard, an arbalest in his hand.

His heralds were calling, "The king offers two gold bezants for every stone pulled from the tower."

Men at arms began to push their way through the lines of archers, and Richard had to order the arbalesters to move out of the way, some into the shelter of the testudo, others with their mantlets to the rear. The men at arms began scrambling up the rubble, swords, daggers, or axes in their belts. They commenced wildly pulling and digging to get their money's worth of the tower.

French banners appeared to the right of the English. Their stonecasters had never stopped shooting, but now knights, squires, and men at arms, certain that a general assault had been commanded, began to attack their own part of the wall, next to the Accursed Tower. Ladders were thrown up in a dozen places, but most of them were cast down again. French soldiers climbed up towards the breach they had made but the defenders had blocked it solidly at the top, and so they descended and ran to the tower of Saint Nicholas to try for the stones there.

The Saracen engines on the walls began to shoot. Fortunately, most of their ammunition was small, for there was little room up there for anything but catapults or ballistas. A stone the size of his head thumped into the ground a few feet away from Denys. Another went rushing over him so close that he felt the breeze of it. He heard a crunch and a muffled screaming behind him, but did not turn for his attention was fixed, along with everyone else's, on the rampart.

A Turk had appeared on the wall wearing the surcoat of Aubrey Clèment, the knight who had been killed in the French assault. He bore Aubrey's shield, as well, and waved a spear on which an unrecognizable head was impaled. King Richard raised his arbalest, bracing his elbow on his knees. He sighted along the barrel and pressed the trigger. The *chunk!* and clang of the weapon could be clearly heard in the momentary silence. The Turk staggered and toppled backward, out of sight.

The army roared. "By Christ, there's a king for you!" shouted William de la Mare, thumping his brother on the back.

The heap of rubble was black with men, like ants, streaming up and then down again with stones in their arms, some grinning, some cursing broken fingernails, some carrying wounded friends. But most had taken no shields, and the arrow-fire from the wall was too heavy for them; they began to retreat leaving a slimy trail of blood mixed with dust where they retired. Bundles of rags and wood soaked in Greek fire began to fly from the city, dropping here and there to burn with a fearful stench, hissing and crackling in spite of the sand that was dumped on them.

A young squire, holding the banner of Andrew de Chauvigny, ran out into the open. He mounted on a tumbled block and looked back, waving his sword and shouting, "Come on!" A stone from above hit him and tore his head from his shoulders, drenching the banner with blood that spouted from him in a fountain.

Someone yelled, "Take the wall!"

Knights and armigers poured forward. Stones clattered under their iron feet. Arthur plucked out his sword, crying, "Hastynge! Saint George!" He ran forward. Denys followed, caught up in the excitement. "This is the moment!" he thought exultantly. "We shall take the city." He looked up at the parapet above and began to climb, raising his shield over his head.

He slipped and nearly lost his footing among the loose stones. Somebody fell against him and almost knocked him over. When he regained his balance he could no longer see Arthur, but there were mailed men all about him, climbing on. "Courtebarbe!" he shouted, and thought he heard the answering battle-cry, "Hastynge!" Arrows whiffled past, and a lance clanged against the stones under his very eyes, striking sparks. He sprang upward, unconscious of the weight of his mail, his body light and swift as if he were being borne aloft by the wind of battle-cries.

Where the wall and tower had cracked apart, at the top, was a wide breach, and Saracens were clustered thickly in it like flies at a broken honey-jar. Denys saw white eyes in dark faces, spiked helmets above white coats, and he was filled with hatred and jubilation. Baldwin de Carreo was already there with a dozen others; he could be recognized because his head was bare and his blond hair shone in the sun as he hewed about him. Even above the uproar Denys fancied he could hear the grunts that accompanied each furious blow. To come up to the top of the wall! To get into the city! To kill and kill until not one of God's enemies was left alive! Dimly he heard himself growling between clenched teeth, and the hair rose on his neck.

A dark face appeared before him and he thrust up at it and went on. It vanished, and he felt something writhe underfoot, and forgot it, and was caught in a swirl of men who came down upon him. He slashed at them, lost his balance, saw a sword lick out beside him and knew that he was not alone. He recovered and chopped at another face, an arm without a hand pouring blood, teeth that flew from a gaping mouth like fragments of sea-shells. The way was clear. He forced himself on.

They were pushing and shoving all together now, the mailed men and the white-robed ones, with hardly room to swing their arms, stumbling among the rubbish at the breach. For one instant, as they all hung there, Denys could see, beyond the heads and shoulders, the domes and towers of the city. Smoke billowed up suddenly and the crowd broke apart.

More of the defenders had come running to the ramparts. They lighted clay pots of naphtha and oil and began to throw them at the mass of fighting men, heedless of friend or enemy. The pots broke and showered them with blazing liquid. It clung to armour, scorched up surcoats and white robes in a twinkling, ran between their legs and trickled flaming down among the crimson-spattered stones.

Denys, luckily, was not in the forefront. He saw the gout of smoke as the first pots were ignited, and the uprush of flame. He heard them shrieking, "Greek fire!" and without further thought turned to get away, knowing there was no facing the stuff. A man fell rather than ran past him making a horrible crying; his surcoat streamed fire and he flailed burning arms like wings. He dashed headlong and fell, and lay smoking. Denys scrambled down, his heart pounding with terror. He had gone perhaps halfway when he remembered Arthur. He stopped, bracing a foot against the point of a block of stone, trying to hold steady in spite of the men hurtling past him.

"Arthur!" he bawled, at the top of his voice. "Arthur de Hastynge!"

Bitter sweat ran into his eyes. The stink of burning made him cough. "My God," he gasped. "I've lost him. He's dead."

Something gave him a sharp push from behind. Then someone tugged at his arm. He recognized Baldwin de Carreo.

"Let go of me," Denys said. "I've got to find him."

He tried to pull Baldwin's hands away and realized for the first time that he had no sword. He had lost it somewhere. Arthur's gift, and he had thrown it away.

Baldwin was saying something earnestly, but Denys could no longer hear a word. The flesh on one side of Baldwin's face was blistered and raw, one eye was closed, and his moustache was blackened and shrivelled up on one side but still thick and yellow on the other. He looked so grotesque that Denys began to laugh.

An arm was around him and he was staggering downward, lurching among the stones.

He said, "How could I do such a damned stupid thing?" Then he fainted.

A hearty voice boomed, "And how's our troubador today?"

Denys opened his eyes with difficulty, for the lids seemed to be glued together. It took him a moment or two to get his eyes focused and to realize that he was looking at a pair of soft leather boots. They were of good quality, dyed red, fastened with golden laces, but very dusty.

A voice he recognized as Giraud's said, "He's cooler and quieter this morning, Excellent Signor."

He discovered that he was lying on his stomach, and that his left shoulder was stiff and painful and appeared to be much larger than usual. He said, as loudly as he could, "Turn me over, damn it," and was astonished at hearing the thin piping that came out of him.

"Aha!" the hearty voice said. "So he's with us today, is he? *Meraviglioso!* Now just lie still, and let us take a peep at you."

He felt a light, cool hand on his neck and various prods and tugs at his shoulder. "Ow, damn it," he said, and was childishly pleased that his voice seemed stronger this time.

"Very nice. Very pretty indeed," the hearty voice said. "Observe, please, how beautifully conglutinated it is. I think we can turn our friend over and sit him up. I doubt there will be any further bleeding."

It was a slow and uncomfortable process, but at last Denys was able to look about him. He was one of a row of a dozen or so wounded men, lying on filthy blankets or heaps of blackened straw under a canvas awning. Giraud crouched at his feet, and standing beside him was a portly man with a face like the moon, pale, round, and shining. A little round cap was tied over his head and bunches of greasy grey curls escaped from the sides of it like fluffy clouds. He was attended by two young men, silent and efficient, wearing tunics and long, cross-gartered hose ominously blood-spotted. One of them carried a portable medicine chest, the other a cloth bundle from the ends of which peeped out such surgical implements as a saw, a long pair of forceps, and the points of several sinister knives.

"What happened to me?" Denys said.

The portly man nodded to his two assistants. "Please observe," he said, "the distinct difference in his colour today. The sanguinary congestion appears to have vanished from his cheeks, and if you will touch his skin you will note that it no longer seems desiccated."

Both young men obediently bent forward and touched Denys's face.

"Will you please tell me," Denys began.

"Tut, tut, tut!" said the surgeon. "Don't upset yourself, my friend. *Pazienza, sempre pazienza e tranquillità.* You have lost a good deal of blood."

"Why?" Denys asked.

"An arrow wound," said the surgeon with satisfaction. "A perfectly beautiful penetration of the large shoulder muscle. Looked like the doorway of Saint Matthew's Cathedral. Unfortunately, as they were bringing you down the shaft broke off and the motion made it cut several blood vessels. I had to dig the head out. It was a big one—one of ours, you know.

Then, we had a trifle of purulence as well. However, I think we're all nicely cleared up now."

He turned to Giraud. "You've done very well so far. Let him eat a little something if he wishes, some bread, a little fruit. Give him plenty of liquid but no strong wine—about half and half, I think. I'll look in on him tomorrow again, and I think we'll have him on his feet in a day or so."

He beamed at Denys and beckoned to his assistants. "The important thing," he said to them, as he departed, "is to have the patient walking as quickly as possible. Nature is the best healer. And as you have seen in this case the argument in favour of laudable pus is absurd—such a practice does nothing but hinder nature and prevent the normal healing of a wound. Now my master, Arnulfo de Lucca, always maintained . . ."

Denys watched him go and then stared at Giraud. "So you've been looking after me," he said.

"There was no one else," said Giraud, with a shrug.

Denys's heart sank. "No one else——" the words had an unbearably ominous ring. "Was it—was it Baldwin de Carreo who brought me down from the fight?" he said.

Giraud nodded, and began to mix wine and water in a gilt cup. Denys looked at it thoughtfully. He recognized it as one which had been given him at the king's Christmas feast in Sicily. It had been gambled away once, by Pons, and Hugh had won it. After Pons's death, Hugh had offered to return it to Denys, but as a matter of honour he had refused it and Hugh had kept it ever since. It was, actually, all that was left of a number of rich gifts which had long since been lost at dice by Hugh, or sold for money with which to buy food and drink for all of them.

Giraud said, "It was one of our own shafts that hit you, as the surgeon said. The arbalesters had begun to shoot again when we saw that the Turks were driving you all back with fire. A number of our people were hurt before the king commanded the archers to wait until all of you were safely down. That was the king's own surgeon who attended you. When the king heard you were among the wounded, he sent Signor Ambrogio to you. He sent some food and wine also, from his own table, and some money, which was just as well because there didn't seem to be any left in your saddle-bags."

He knelt at Denys's head with the cup. "Now, drink this

down," he said. "You heard Signor Ambrogio—plenty of drink."

Denys sipped, and realized that he was thirsty. He took the cup in a shaking hand and drank it all. He was deeply touched at Giraud's strange, new, protective manner.

Then, holding the cup in both hands, turning it round and round and not looking at Giraud, he said, "You needn't be afraid to tell me. Arthur's dead, isn't he?"

"No, he's not dead," said the minstrel brusquely. "Why should he be? He's had a sprained ankle and dysentery, but he didn't die of either of them."

Denys sank back and closed his eyes. The reaction of relief was so great that his head spun, and for a moment he felt a wave of nausea flow over him.

Giraud was saying, "We used the last of his money. He has gone to see the king's chamberlain to ask for some of the pay which is owing to both of you." He snickered. "He didn't want to. He said that a knight ought to serve God without thought of pay, but I pointed out to him that you were also serving King Richard. And I said you were going to need care and good food, and there was no telling how long the king's gift would last or when any more would come in, and so at last he went for your sake. I think he's mad, you know," he added, casually, taking the cup out of Denys's hand.

Denys barely heard him. "Thank God," he murmured. "Giraud, I think I'll sleep for a while now. But when Arthur comes back, wake me."

"Wake you? No. I think it would be better for you——"

"Never mind that. Just do as I say. And if we need money, tell Hugh to sell that cup and get hold of a cheap wooden one for me. He needn't have been so sentimental."

Giraud said, "Sentimental——?" biting off the word so oddly that Denys opened his eyes again.

"Giraud," he said, with a sigh. "Oh, you swine. You stole it from him."

Giraud's lips were twitching, and he could not meet Denys's gaze. "No," he said. "No, I didn't steal it. I swear it."

A thrill of horror went through Denys. "What are you babbling about?" he said, weakly. "What's the meaning of this? You're lying, you filthy clot. If I could only get up——"

Giraud was looking here and there desperately. He put his

hand on Denys's and said, with an effort, "Don't excite yourself. You'll start the bleeding again. The surgeon will kill
me. Perhaps you'd like me to sing something for you? I'll get
my harp."

He started up. Denys raised a hand to stop him. "Never
mind," he said. "You were always as poor a liar as you were
a thief." He drew a long breath, trying to overcome his giddi-
ness. "How did it happen?" he said, at last. "In the assault?"

Giraud nodded. "I saw Sir Hugh follow you up the wall,
right after Sir Arthur. I saw Arthur fall—we didn't know
what had happened, but a stone had just grazed him and he
lost his balance and fell and hurt his ankle. He couldn't get
up again. One of the sergeants dragged him back. He was
cursing and crying, something terrible to hear. Then he began
vomiting—he was sick, you see. He must have begun to have
the dysentery that morning but he never told anyone. Meanwhile, we saw you all fighting up at the top and it was all
mixed up, nobody could make out what was going on until
we saw the smoke and flames. It must have been up there,
while you were all trying to get down again, that Sir Hugh was
killed."

"I see." Denys was barely able to get the words out. "And
do you know how?"

"Nobody knows. It might have been the fire, or one of our
own arrows, or a Turkish spear. He never came back."

Helpless tears ran down Denys's cheeks. Giraud patted his
hand awkwardly.

"Hell! I should never have told you," the minstrel said. "I
didn't give a damn for him—he never treated me as anything
but dirt—but I promised the surgeon I'd see that you weren't
upset. A lot of men were killed in that assault. It might have
been you, or your friend Arthur. Don't grieve. How do you
think Sir Hugh wanted to die? In his bed with a pair of dice
and a skinful of wine?"

Denys turned his head away. "That's enough, Giraud," he
whispered. "Leave me alone now. I'm tired. Let me sleep."

Giraud sighed, but did not move. He sat in silence and
Denys quickly forgot that he was there.

Behind his closed lids, Denys saw clear, small pictures of
the attack. He remembered the moment when he had missed
his footing and a sword had flickered out beside him to guard

him. That must have been Hugh. He remembered, with a shudder, the man who had fallen past him wrapped in fire. Had that also been Hugh? How had he lost sight of Arthur? How could he have failed to know that Hugh was beside him, or behind him, or with him? All that remained was a sense of the awful confusion of battle, and, far worse, the depression that swept over him at the knowledge that he had lost Arthur's sword, and lost Hugh as well. And here he lay, wounded by an arrow from a Christian bow—a message from a friend, you might say.

It was all madness, as mad as Giraud with his devils and his army from hell. What a heroic song it would make! The images whirled in his mind, mixed with words and the echoes of harping, and soon he slept.

He awoke to find Arthur sitting beside him.

"Ah, you're well again," Arthur exclaimed happily. "My word, it's good to see you looking something like yourself for a change. Giraud told me—I could hardly believe it—he said the surgeon was very pleased, that you'd taken a cup of wine and that this was just a natural sleep."

Denys gripped him by the wrist. He had grown thinner, and the bones stood out under the skin. "So it's you," he said, feebly. "I thought you were dead."

"Not I. Dead? I wished I were, for a while." Arthur shook his head. He looked drawn and very pale, with dark circles under his eyes. "I had a twisted ankle. Did you know? There I lay, and I could hear the shouts up on the wall, and I knew men were dying bravely up there even though I couldn't see that far. I couldn't see well enough to find my way back to the battle," he finished bitterly, "even if I could have climbed among the stones. Even if I hadn't been doubled up with cramps."

"Don't talk that way," Denys said. "You acquitted yourself with honour. You might have been lying up there now, charred to ashes, dead like poor old Hugh——"

His voice broke. Arthur looked at him in dismay.

"Giraud told you!" he said. "I'll beat him, the fool. He has no more sense than a dog—less than some I've had." He clapped his hands irritably on his thighs. "Ah, well, he has certainly looked after you devotedly. I suppose I mustn't be too harsh on him."

"He couldn't help it," said Denys. "I guessed it, and dragged it out of him. Besides, what difference does it make? I'd have learned sooner or later. Poor Hugh. It's hard to think we won't see him again. It's so *final*. You know? I never dreamed Hugh would be killed. He seemed——"

"Tougher than any of us. Yes, I know. I've missed him too, Denys. I had come to rely on him."

Denys smeared his hand over his eyes. "Damn it, what's the good of it?" he said. "If God wanted us to win you'd think He'd be helping us instead of killing off the best of us. We'll never take Acre, that's the long and short of it." A thought struck him. "How long have I been lying here?" he asked, abruptly.

Arthur sighed. "This is the eighth day," he said.

Denys let his head sink back against the folded cloaks that served him for a pillow. "I don't remember any of it," he muttered, in a dazed way. "How can you lose eight days?"

"You were out of your head for most of the time," Arthur replied. "And burning with fever, for a while. When Baldwin brought you back you had fainted from loss of blood. Baldwin is high in the king's favour, you know. He went at once, just as he was, burned and covered with blood, and begged for Ambrogio de Salerno to come and attend to you. He's a marvellous surgeon—always so calm, very sure of himself, full of confidence. And as he works he goes on lecturing to his two students."

"I know. I met him," Denys said.

"Yes, well, you came to your senses and he said he would have to cut for the arrow head and didn't want you squirming around and disturbing him. Baldwin said helpfully that he'd be glad to knock you on the head, which was the way he'd always seen patients kept quiet. Ambrogio delivered a lecture on primitive medical methods, and gave you something to drink—opium and mandragora, I think he said—and you went sound asleep. Can you imagine? Baldwin said he had seen something like that among the Moors, in Spain. Well, then he cut the thing out and sewed you up, and you slept for nearly two days. Then the fever started, and the wound began to look very ugly. For a few days we thought you were sure to die. You were raving and singing—I remember, you kept chanting some verses about someone named Jourdain."

"I did? What were they?"

"I couldn't make out much, mostly it was just gibberish. I heard the name Jourdain, and something about Fromont the fell traitor, but not much else that made sense. Is it one of the songs you wrote?"

"No. Not exactly. Never mind, go on."

"Anyway, I was ill—I suppose Giraud told you that, too; he doesn't seem to have kept much back—and he watched beside you and kept you cool with wet cloths. The surgeon came every day and fiddled about, and then yesterday he looked very pleased and said he thought the worst was over."

Denys lay still, trying to absorb this news. As he forced his memory to the task he thought he could remember, dimly, the pain in his shoulder, wild dreams, waking with his face pressed against the coarse blanket, and many other voices talking, or screaming close by, or singing. "Eight days," he said, at last. "Hugh has been dead all this time, not just since yesterday. How many others have died? What's been happening, for God's sake?"

"I'll tell you everything. But first, aren't you hungry?"

"Now that you mention it, I am. Did you get the money from the king?"

Arthur laughed. "Yes, I got it. Let me fetch that large-mouthed minstrel and see that he feeds you. Then, as you eat, I'll bring you up to date."

After the battle in which Denys had taken part, a number of Pisan men at arms, anxious for glory, had tried the same ascent up the fallen section of the wall and had fought their way into the breach. But they had chosen a time when the rest of the army had gone to eat their dinners, and their unplanned and unsupported assault had failed. That same afternoon Saladin's whole army had launched a major attack against the camp. The fighting had been general all along the barricade, hot and desperate with many losses on both sides, but by evening the Turks had been thrown back.

And then rumours had begun to fly through the camp, at first wild and fantastic, then solidifying into what appeared to be the truth: that negotiations were under way, and in fact had been proceeding for some time, between the infidels and the two Christian kings.

Even before the battle at the tower, Richard had sent an

envoy to Saladin asking for a meeting. Its purpose, he explained, would be exploratory. The Sultan had replied, however, that it was not customary for kings to meet until they had previously settled all the preliminaries and decided on a trustworthy interpreter. "For," said he, "once they have spoken together and given one another the tokens of mutual confidence that are natural in such circumstances, it is not seemly for them to continue to make war upon one another." Soon afterward Richard's messenger went to Saladin again to explain that the king was ill and to propose an exchange of gifts. There was some further talk of an informal meeting, perhaps upon the summit of the hill, Tell el-Aiâdiya, where Saladin had pitched his tents and made his headquarters. Once again the Sultan put aside the notion of such a summit meeting, but sent Richard some snow, tightly packed in skins to prevent its melting, and some citrus fruit which according to the surgeon Ambrogio of Salerno was an excellent treatment for scurvy. These exchanges of courtesies, these preparatory hagglings, had been accompanied by an unending bombardment of the walls by all the siege engines, both French and English, but the armies themselves had been restrained from further assaults.

"So Richard is like all the rest," Denys said, scornfully. "Richard Yes-and-No! I myself heard him swear never to make peace with the infidel. I remember how contemptuous he was of the leaders of previous armies who made truces with Saladin. And even while we were fighting on the wall, he was dickering with the enemy. Was it for that that Hugh died?"

Arthur said, with a troubled air, "I know, Denys. Most of us felt at first as you do. I've been searching my heart to try to understand what's right. And it seems to me that the important thing is that Acre should fall into our hands. Perhaps the king has some hidden plan which we can't understand at present. I think we must trust him."

Denys nodded. "Oh, yes, of course. It's perfectly clear that Richard is only carrying on these negotiations so that it will seem he's the real leader of the army, and empowered to speak for everyone. I don't care one way or the other; I'm only a trouvère who happened to get in the way of one of our own arrows. But I can recognize politics when I smell them."

"But it's gone beyond that, Denys. Envoys have been coming from the city to discuss its surrender. That's the whole point of what I've been telling you."

"Oh?" Denys tried to sit up a little straighter, wincing against his wound. "That's a different story. Then perhaps it will work out. What's happened?"

"Well, apparently the emir Mashtub, who is one of the chiefs in the city, went first to King Philip. I was at the trenches that day but Baldwin de Carreo saw him come with a flag of truce. Mashtub asked for terms, and Philip said that the defenders were nothing but slaves and that they must rely on his mercy. Mashtub grew angry and apparently some hot words were passed and he said he'd die rather than surrender. He went back to the city, but the next day he returned and began to bargain again, and this time Richard came and took part in the discussion."

The meeting, according to all reports, had begun badly with Philip accusing Richard of conducting private negotiations with the Sultan while he himself was trying to deal with Emir Mashtub. This, he said, looking haughtily down his nose, was improper, and disruptive, and unfit behaviour for a vassal. Richard, however, kept his temper very well and said that it was even more improper for the two of them to bicker in front of the Saracen envoy. He then went on to say that according to his information—gathered in the course of just those private negotiations during which his own representatives had been allowed to walk about freely in the Sultan's camp, and observe, and listen—it was evident that Saladin's army was beginning to defect. Although reinforcements had come in, many of the emirs and princes were refusing any longer to send their people into battle. The Sultan, he said, could do nothing more to help the city. He also revealed that a spy within Acre, a Greek Christian, had been keeping him informed of everything that happened in the city, and that after the assault on the tower of Saint Nicholas many of the defenders had begun to desert, taking boats from the walls or swimming around to the northern shore.

It should be clear to the emirs, Mashtub and his associate, the eunuch Beha ed Din Karakush, governor of the citadel, that unless they made peace the city would be taken by storm and everyone within it put to death. This, Richard added, would certainly happen sooner or later, for the might of the

Franks was increasing while dissension grew in the Sultan's camp. He suggested that a mediator be chosen to arrange terms, someone who knew Arabic and was trusted by both sides. In the end, Mashtub agreed to this, and, after some hesitation, so did King Philip. The matter was referred to the council of the army for the choice of such a mediator. Richard had been hoping that one of the Lusignans, either King Guy or his brother Geoffrey, would be picked, but to his disappointment the council chose Guy's rival, Conrad of Montferrat.

"And that's where we stand now," Arthur finished. "The marquis is in the city discussing terms, and we've all been waiting to see what will happen."

"And there's been no fighting?" said Denys.

"None to speak of. Oh, now and then a few hotheads from both sides meet in the plain, but most people feel it's not worth running risks when it seems clear the city will surrender."

Denys nodded and closed his eyes. "At least we're alive," he murmured. "If only Hugh could have been saved. If only he could have waited somehow . . ."

"But, Denys," Arthur said, gently, "it was his death and the death of others which helped force the city to this point. And he died a martyr, fighting like a true knight."

Denys could not help a smile. Arthur's eyes, larger than usual in his hollow face, glittered with earnestness. Looking at him, Denys thought: I don't believe it. He died like the fighter he was, knowing nothing else, wanting nothing else, and as pointlessly as if he had fallen in a tournament. He would have gambled away his immortal soul—his martyr's soul—if someone had offered him decent odds. And while we were making that profitless attack in which he died, Richard was going his own secret, subtle way. We are here to be used by *him*, for his own purposes. We are like the toys children play with, pushing them against each other until one or the other falls from his horse in the game.

Aloud, he said, "I lost your sword, somewhere in the breach."

A shadow darkened Arthur's face and passed away as swiftly as if the wind had blown it. "Why, Denys, that's of no importance. It was lost in a noble cause. We can get you another."

Denys gave a sigh. "Yes," he said. "That's true."

And he recalled the words of that acute and practical man of principle, the merchant Scasso: "Your friend has what I call Lancelot fever." Yes, he's incurable, he thought. But perhaps that's what I love most about him.

The very next day the news was cried through the camp that Acre had surrendered. The terms were good: the city with all its stores, ships, and engines of war was to be handed over to the Franks, along with two hundred thousand gold pieces to be paid in two instalments. Furthermore, a hundred knights and squires who had been taken prisoner by the Saracens would be returned, along with five hundred other soldiers of the common sort. Most valuable of all, the True Cross, which had been in the hands of the infidel since the fall of Jerusalem, would be yielded up.

For Denys, the day was made even happier because he was allowed to get upon his feet. Leaning on Giraud, he walked slowly out of the tent into the blazing sunlight. His legs were at first as boneless as jelly, but, like the soft wings of an insect exposed to the sun, drew strength from the heat until they could support him. Arthur stood close on his other side, shielding his wound from accidents and carrying a folding stool. They walked slowly through the camp towards the walls until Denys, blinking and trembling, felt that he had to sit down. Arthur opened the stool for him and stood behind it so that Denys could lean back against his friend's thighs.

The defenders were already marching out of the city, coming by the gates of the Patriarch's Tower and the portals of what had been the wards of the Hospitallers and Templars when Acre had been a Christian city. Their turbans and helmets could be seen winding among crowds of shouting, cheering soldiers; they bore themselves proudly in spite of their wounds, privations, and illnesses, even greater than those which had afflicted the besiegers, and many a knight, squire, and sergeant regarded them with the admiration and affection given a noble enemy.

As Denys watched, blossoms opened upon the ramparts—white, gold, scarlet, green, silver, and azure—the banners of the chiefs of the army. They took the breeze, snapped, and spread themselves wide from their staffs one after the other, the arms of France, of England, of Aquitaine, Normandy, Champagne, Flanders, and Jerusalem, the blazons of arch-bishops, counts, bishops and princes: Virgins, crosses, bars, saltires, colour upon colour, lions and eagles, hawks and griffons, leaping in splendour against the burning sky to the thunder in a dozen different tongues of "Victory!"

On Giraud's face there was a twisted smile as he crouched beside Denys, watching like a hound. Arthur wept openly, and Denys felt the salt sting his own eyes.

"At last," Arthur said, shakily. "At last! Think of it—after four years. It has fallen to us. It's over, Denys. It's all over."

Denys turned his head with an effort, grimacing as his wound pulled at the tendons of his neck, and squinted up at Arthur. All about him men ran, hobbled, limped to get into the city, to begin the joyous task of looting whatever was not securely fastened down. The earth shook with great claps of cheers. Small figures capered on the ramparts which had been so liberally washed with blood and scoured by fire.

He looked back again at the proud banners. One had already been toppled by a group squabbling over something which could not be clearly seen—it flashed as it was dragged from one hand to another, a souvenir perhaps, a Saracen helm or shield, and the wrangling men trampled the banner as they swayed this way and that.

"I hope to God you're right," he said, softly.

*   *   *

Journal of Denys de Courtebarbe. Extract 9.

My wound heals apace, which is a great wonder and can only be attributed to the solicitude of my good patron, Saint Denys the Martyr, to whom I never fail to address my prayers and who ceases not in consequence to watch over me. Yet also is it in some measure the doing of the physician, Ambrogio de Salerno, who is greatly skilled (and let you not, fair Saint Denys, feel jealousy at my writing thus, for in our lives man's skill and heaven's good will are as sword and shield together). I thanked him much and said that I had naught to offer him, whereat he replied that he cared not a jot since I had provided a good example for his apprentices of his treatment of a suppurating wound, which was worth more to him than money, especially since I had had the grace to live and thus prove his treatment. I have

promised to make a song for him and this, he says, will be
ample payment.

At his direction I have exercised much, keeping myself
active, and thus I find that my muscles have returned quickly
to their use. Often have I walked and ridden out with
Arthur, and gone through the city of Acre to see for myself
the wondrous sights therein, the fair churches desecrated by
the infidel, the rich quarters of the Templars and Hospitallers
made foul by the Saracens living in them and scrupling not
to steal what they would, the fine palaces and houses cast
down into ruin by the violence of war brought thither by
the obstinacy of the enemy. Much booty have our men
taken in Acre, and Giraud's every finger wears a gold ring,
for he has not been behind-hand in his picking.

I have also seen the king, who summoned me before him
only yesterday, the day of the Magdalene, and soon after he
had taken up his residence within the city. For you must
know that the whole city and all within it were divided
between Richard and Philip of France, and by the casting of
lots that part containing the royal palace was given to King
Richard while King Philip received the great palace of the
Templars. I found the king looking somewhat pallid from
his illness but able to walk about once more, and his great
strength returning, although his beard was sparse by reason
of the loss of so much of his hair. Yet nothing did this abate
his kingliness; he gave me his hand to kiss and praised my
wound got in his service, and condoled with me upon the
death of my friend Hugh de Hamelincourt, saying that much
would the Marshal mourn when this news came to him.
Then he asked me if I lacked aught, and I said nay, since we
ate by his bounty, but asked that he give me some of my
wage so that Arthur would not need to come to him again.
At the name of Arthur his face grew stern and I saw that he
had not yet forgiven my friend, and so I made bold to tell him
that Arthur had been first of all of us upon the ruins of the
tower and had been hurt by a great stone. On this, he said,
'Speak to me not of him, for he is one who does not fear to
lesson a king. Too mindful is he of what is honourable and he
no more than a beggarly country knight. As for you, Denys,
take care you know where your loyalty lies. Once you told
me that Roland was a noble vassal who died for love of his

lord. More dear to him than the life of his friend Oliver was his care for his lord's honour. Or was it not so?" I replied humbly that it was so, and this I said not only because that way the wind blew my weathercock but also because I could not forebear to agree in my heart that something of truth there was in Richard's words. Then he let me kiss his hand and said that he loved me well and that so soon as ever I was fully healed I should come with Giraud and sing for him and his queen, who was now lodged in the palace and sickened for lack of amusement. I understood how this might be so, for there is no other trouvère of any note with the army. only a scoundrelly hanger-on of the duke of Burgundy by name Ambroise who writes hobbling verses of small merit. When I reflect on how close I stood near death, I wonder at my being here myself.

While I was yet with Richard, there came in four noblemen of France, to wit the duke of Burgundy, Drogo de Amiens, William de Mello, and the lord bishop of Beauvais, asking audience of the king. I therefore stepped aside into a corner and thus I heard with my own ears what the whole army speaks of today. For they stood hangdog before the king, shuffling and coughing as if not knowing how to begin and all taken with a summer rheum, until at last Richard said that he thought he knew what brought them thither and that they must have no fear but speak on behalf of their master to plead his cause. Then the duke, a courteous and fair-spoken gentleman, said that King Philip had fulfilled all his promises and come upon the crusade and by God's mercy had assisted in the freeing of Acre, and now that was all over he wished to return home to France. And he said, further, that Philip was broken in health as a result of all his sickness, and that if he remained in this land he would surely die. Richard looked upon the duke and the others with a tigerish eye, and replied 'Not by my counsel will he go, for if he do it will be to bring shame and contempt upon his name. But if he must either go or die, let him in God's name do what best pleases him.' And with that, he dismissed them. When they were gone, spying me still in my corner, he cried, 'What think you, trouvère? Say, shall King Philip stay or go?' I replied that it ill became me to speak of such matters, but that to my own mind it seemed the king of France had done little enough to bring about the overthrow of the city and if he were to get him home the army would then have but one leader, and he the best.

Then the king laughed, exclaiming that I was his true friend and that he could see I spoke from the heart. 'But,' said he, 'you do not speak from the head, for you forget that I have my own realm at home, of England, Normandy, and Aquitaine, and he would like well to dispoil me of what he may whilst I am not there. No, no, my Denys, kings must even sit cheek by jowl and dip in the same dish, where in loving friendship each may watch the other's hand.' With that, sinking his chin upon his breast, he waved me away and sat deep in thought.

But today the rumour has gone through the camp like a serpent that Philip intends to depart by the month's end, and great is the unrest and dissension occasioned thereby.

*

v kal. Aug. On this day the two kings and their council gave judgment as to who should reign over the kingdom of Jerusalem. This matter arose long ago as a contention between Guy of Lusignan and the Marquis Conrad of Montferrat, the same who arranged the terms of peace with the Saracens within Acre. And it was decided that Guy should remain king so long as he shall live, but that upon his death Conrad will inherit the crown. This was both victory and defeat for Richard, for Guy did homage to him in Cyprus, while Conrad is King Philip's friend and ally. From all that I hear, this marquis is a subtle and crooked man, full of deceit, and many evils are blamed on him, as that he hindered the passage of provisions to the army from his city of Tyre and that it was he who urged King Philip to demand a portion of Cyprus from Richard, although no French blood was shed in taking that fruitful island.

*

St. Peter's Day. On this morning the King of France set sail for Tyre, taking with him Conrad of Montferrat and such noble hostages of the Saracens who fell to his share. Many were the lamentations and curses when King Philip embarked; for my part, I remembered what Richard had said to me, and wondered to see with what good cheer and an open face he bade the French king farewell, embracing and kissing him as if they were two fond brothers. It was but two days ago that Richard agreed Philip should depart from the crusade only if he swore a solemn oath not to do injury to any of Richard's lands or men while the king remained a pilgrim. This oath was sworn and King Philip brought ten witnesses, noblemen of France, to be his surety. It may be that Richard is satisfied. If it were I, I should think on Philip's meanness of soul, and indeed, watching him go on board his ship, Ivo de Vimont stood beside me and said, 'Little do I like men with small mouths, for of all that such a one says, half is kept back.'

Ivo is much with us these days. He is very like poor Hugh, and speaks often of him telling us tales of the days when they were both in their pride of youth, and lamenting that Hugh should have got his death in the taking of Acre. 'For here had I been,' said he, 'lying before this accursed city all the winter without more than a scratch or two upon me, and he, having just arrived, to be slain so soon. Never would I have thought to lose my old comrade in such wise, and it showed a want of solicitude in him which did not use to be the case. Much had he changed in growing older.' I know not whether he says these things to keep our spirits up, or, as is more likely, because he is of the same hard-headed breed as Hugh.

My wound has near mended, save for a stiffness in the back and a certain discomfort when I lie down to sleep. I have been at work upon a sirvente on the fall of Acre, against that time when the king calls on me.

*

xiii kal. Sep. Much has happened in the past three weeks since King Philip departed from the host. And now, the word has been cried throughout the camp that we must be ready to march on the morrow. I will note down what I can recall of these events, in haste, and then set aside inkhorn and pen. God knows when I shall write again, for who but He can say what perils may lie in wait for us between here and Ascalon, whither we are to go.

After the departure of the French king, our lord King Richard was chosen by the council of the army to be com-

273

mander, although some barons opposed this bitterly, as did some men of Pisa who had sworn fealty to King Philip. But Richard over-rode all obstacles with fair words or gifts, and furthermore caused all the archers of the army (including those of the Pisans) to come before him and hired them into his service. By this means he made himself the most powerful of princes and none could oppose him.

He announced that it was his intention to lead the army to Ascalon, the strong city upon the coast, so that he could win back all those regions from the infidels. But first he must make the exchange of prisoners which had been agreed upon with Saladin, and receive the ransom of Acre, to wit, one hundred thousand gold bezants, with a like payment to be made afterward, and also the True Cross which Saladin held in his camp. Now messengers went back and forth between the king and the Sultan, and every day fresh rumours flew through the camp, and we all waited as if dancing upon daggers like performers at a fair.

And meantime, the king had sent emissaries to the marquis Conrad of Montferrat, at Tyre, ordering him to return to the host, and to bring with him those of the Saracen hostages which King Philip had borne away, so that the proper exchange of prisoners might be accomplished. But the marquis replied that he would not return, and as for the hostages, said he, when the True Cross was returned and he had received half of it for the king of France, he would return the hostages, but not before. Once again Richard sent to him demanding his obedience, and for reply the perfidious marquis hindered the passage of our ships from Tyre, which should have brought fresh provisions, so that we all began to feel the pinch.

Then came the date on which the first part of Saladin's payment for the ransom of Acre fell due, which was the eleventh day of August, and Richard called upon the Sultan to make good his promise. Yet there came neither money nor the True Cross, nor those of our noble barons and knights who were to be delivered up from captivity. Thereupon, our king moved out into the plain and we pitched camp once again and prepared for battle. On the following day the the duke of Burgundy returned from Tyre where he had persuaded the marquis Conrad to yield up the Turkish hostages, but the marquis himself came not but sent only insolent words.

Now there ensued some few broils and passages at arms with some of the Saracens in the plain, but all the while heralds went to and fro between Richard and Saladin, our king urging the Sultan to keep to his word and deliver up money, prisoners, and the Cross, and the Sultan replying with ambiguous words, soft and treacherous answers, and requests for more time. At last Richard agreed that the day should be postponed until the twentieth day of August.

On Monday the king, returning into Acre, sat at dinner with his queen and the chiefs of the army, and I was called upon to sing before them. Giraud that day lay in a drunken stupor, having somehow found a store of wine so that when the time came for us to go to the palace to dine he first spoke to me of devils and demons, and then sang in many different tongues, and at last fell into such a sleep as not even thunder-bolts could rouse him from. At first I was enraged, thinking how I should appear without my minstrel. And then I fell to laughing for I remembered how I had once prided myself that my voice was good and my playing of the harp or vielle fair enough so that I could boast I never needed a jongleur. But now, so strong is custom, it seemed I had never done without Giraud. I went up alone, therefore, and took my place at the low table, and dined better than I had for some days past (nor did I forget to wrap up in my scarf several good bits for Arthur). And afterwards I sang many songs to the pleasure of the company, they having had little enough of entertainment save what could be found in battle. Among others, I sang my new-written sirvente, 'When to the walls of Acre England's king,' after which I observed some of the French barons to look somewhat greenly on me. But Richard, well pleased—as much, I guessed, at their dis-comfiture as at my song—sent me a cup filled with silver bezants.

There was talk at the high table then, and I, sitting right beside it, heard the king say to some of those noble lords that the morrow was the day appointed for the Sultan to keep his word and that not one day more would be given. 'And,' said he, 'I would have you know that it is my firm resolve to march upon Ascalon and the coastal cities to come as near the Holy Land as I may before winter.' The earl of Leicester said to him that they must either be burdened by all those prisoners which were held within the city, or must divide their forces so to leave guards upon them—for there were upwards of two thousand such Saracens of the common sort and several hundred of their barons and knights. Upon which the king replied, 'They are hostages, my lord, and their lives lie between my hands.' Whereupon he commenced speaking of the disposition of the army, of the preparation of the ships, of the provisions that would be needful to take, and of who should be left in Acre to guard its walls and his queen and her ladies.

Thus, this very day, it being the twentieth day of August, after we had eaten our mid-day meal, the heralds cried through the host that we should all assemble with our arms to see justice done. And when we had come out into the middle of the plain the king's heralds cried that the Sultan had by his treachery failed to ransom his prisoners whose lives were thus forfeit. Then all those Saracens were led out from the city save some two or three score of the most noble and wealthiest. And there came forth a procession of churchmen, of whom we had a good profusion in the host, among them the bishops of Bayonne, Salisbury, and Beauvais, and the archbishops of Tyre and Pisa, and they, after giving us their blessings, called upon us to fall to and slay the unbelievers, to wipe them out root and branch and leave none alive, for the glory of God and to the utter confutation of Mahomet and his followers. Then our soldiers, drawing their swords, rushed upon the Turkish prisoners and cut them down, one after another, despite their cries and pleas. Some of us, squires and knights, would not soil our blades upon them, and not only Arthur but many another said that they thought it ill accorded with their honour to slay bound and unarmed men. But most felt no such scruples but slew as hastily as they could, remembering our martyrs who had fallen before the walls of Acre, and all those pilgrims of the host who had perished at the hands of the infidels.

By the computation of one of the king's clerks, Thibaud de Mara, there were slain here two thousand six hundred of the unbelievers, and when all was done their bodies, hacked like firewood, lay heaped up higher than a man's head, and all that space of sandy plain, dry though it had been, was a red quagmire. And shameful as it is in me to write it—nor would I say so aloud—I pray I may never see such a sight again, though it be meritorious in the eyes of God.

* * *

The trouble with life, from a historian's point of view, is that it is anticlimactic. Instead of submitting to the scholarly desire for order it tends to be chaotic; instead of progressing from planned events through a neat series of causes and effects to decisive peaks, it boils and surges as furiously and aimlessly as a vat of oatmeal, and its apparent moments of culminating triumph have a way of bursting as emptily as bubbles. Such was now the case with the crusade. It was two years, lacking a week, since the day Acre had first been besieged by King Guy. Hundreds had died on both sides, hundreds had been maimed, hundreds had starved, lain ill, spent all their worldly goods. And now the city had been taken again by the Christian host and it seemed that a turning point must have been reached, that the war was all but over and all that remained was the victorious march on the gates of Jerusalem and the crumpling into disaster of the infidel power. Nothing, of course, could have been further from the fact. Aside from the flags which now flew over the walls of the city, almost nothing was changed.

Two days after the slaughter of the Turkish hostages, Richard moved the army to the banks of the stream called the River of Acre. The following day they crossed and began to march southward along the coast. The fleet, loaded with provisions and bearing some of the archers and foot-soldiers, kept pace with them on one side, while the armies of the Sultan paralleled them on the other and never ceased their skirmishing. The Turks had a disagreeable habit of avoiding close combat. Unweighted by any armour save their helmets or little, square breast-plates, armed with bows and javelins and mounted on swift horses, they were, says the author of the *Itinerarium Regis Ricardi*, "Like the fly, which if you drive it away will go, but when you cease it will return; as long as you pursue it will flee, but it reappears the moment you desist." They would ride in close to the marching column and shoot a volley of arrows. Then, when the knights and squires cantered out after them, they would be off, jeering, leaving a dead horse or a wounded man to mark where they had struck.

The next two weeks were an unremitting torment for the host. The dry, dusty earth rose in a choking powder under their heavy feet, caking their faces and filling their mouths. The sun heated their armour unbearably, despite their long surcoats. What water they found was usually brackish and disgusting, and they were persecuted by flies which clustered on every moist spot of their bodies, wherever they sweated or bled, and particularly about their eyes. At times they had to break their way through tangles of thorny brush, too low to furnish any shade but just high enough to scratch their faces. And relentlessly, endlessly, the Saracens harried them so that they could never rest. Every evening, when they made camp, there was one man, a powerful serjeant from Beauvais who had a festering wound; half-crazed by pain and the discomforts of the day, he would roar in a great voice, "Help, Holy Sepulchre!" and from pure fear and distress all who heard him were compelled to shout with him; this gave them some relief.

Even at night they had no respite, for scorpions and tarantulas crept amongst them in great numbers, and while few died from their poison, the stings and bites swelled and became infected, and proved as great an irritation as the enemy. All sorts of remedies were tried, and at last a contingent from Provence, which claimed to have some acquaintance with this sort of vermin, persuaded their fellows that noise would drive the creatures off. So, when the sun set, the whole army began hammering with the pommels of their swords, or with maces, on helmets, pots, washtubs, and basins, anything which would make a racket, and this fearful din reached the Sultan's army where it lay around its own fires so that they stared into the darkness in amazement at the insane doings of the Franks. The noise actually did seem to keep some of the pests away, but on the other hand it gave everyone but the most stolid a blinding headache, and prevented sleep as effectively as did the scorpions.

On the 29th of August the army camped by a river in which it was said that there were crocodiles, and the rumour soon went round that two men had been eaten. The following day they arrived before the walls of Caesarea, where the Turkish garrison, after demolishing the defences, fled without a battle.

After the briefest of pauses, they moved on. A little way beyond Caesarea they were attacked again by a strong force of Saracens and lost many horses. When evening came and the enemy drew off, the soldiers gathered around the dead beasts and began offering their owners large sums for the meat. Fights broke out, and at last Richard had to intervene. He settled the matter by offering a live horse to every man who would freely give his dead one to the cook-pots.

The army remained for two days at this spot, beside a sluggish water called the Salt River. It was a marshy, mosquito-plagued region, but they were able to rest and regain their strength. Then they went on, through flat, sandy territory. The ground began to rise, and trees appeared, and at last a real wood, the Forest of Arsûf. Here, it was rumoured, the Saracens lurked, and the army hourly expected an ambush. But nothing happened; they forded a river near a wide, stinking marsh, and came out into an open plain where they made camp.

Turkish patrols had been seen riding along the slopes below the forest, and Richard's scouts went out to investigate. They returned with news that the forest and the whole mountain was full of Saracens, "three hundred thousand of them". Richard, experienced campaigner that he was, knew perfectly well that few of his followers could count above ten in the first place, that it was absolutely impossible to estimate large numbers of men in a forest and at a distance, and that the figure "three hundred thousand" was only meant to express alarm and astonishment. However, he did not doubt that Saladin's whole army was gathering in the wood. Here, if anywhere, was a perfect spot for an assault, which could be launched downhill from the cover of the trees into the open valley plain.

That night, and all the next day, he allowed his men to rest. At dawn, on Saturday, the 7th of September, he roused the army and prepared to march on towards the partly-ruined town of Arsûf, knowing that they would probably have to fight before the day was over. He had already made his dispositions.

He knew that if the army could keep its ranks unbroken the Turks would follow their usual tactics of dashing in for a quick blow and darting away again. If this were endured patiently, they might be enticed to try coming to hand-strokes. The king therefore gave orders that the troops were to move in close order along the road, but to hold their formation without counter-attacking until he judged the enemy was close enough, and committed enough, to be engaged and smashed. His signal would be the sounding of trumpets, two in the van, two midway, and two with the rearguard.

They began the march, but before they had gone a quarter of a mile the forest seemed to open a multitude of gates, and in moments the slopes were swarming with Turkish horsemen. It was as though all that parched soil had burst suddenly into flower: brilliant cloaks, jewelled helms, yellow and green banners, and the deadly silver of weapons, appeared as if by magic.

They swooped down all along the line of march, but the crusaders resisted stoutly and kept on their way. The arbalesters proved their worth that day, for although their weapons could not outrange those of the Turks, they carried more force and emptied many a saddle. The battle wore on for some hours, the Turks pressing in by hundreds, particularly on the rearguard. As Richard had foreseen, they lost their caution and remained a little longer each time they came in. At last, the anger of the rearguard could be contained no longer. Disregarding their orders they broke ranks and charged the enemy. At this, Richard, seeing no help for it, ordered the trumpets to sound and himself led out the rest of his knights. They burst through and over the Saracens like an iron sea. The Sultan's men gave back, then turned and fled in a panic. In moments, all was reversed. That great infidel army was flung apart and scattered, pursued for miles by vengeful men at arms. Many a pilgrim could not raise his arm that night after the hewing of the rout.

It was to be the last full-scale battle of the war, in which all the available forces of both armies were involved. Richard's men continued on to Arsûf where they buried their dead, and from which they sent their wounded back to Acre. One of the wounded was Baldwin de Carreo, who had been the first of those impetuous gallants to break ranks. Denys went to see him, and so also did Richard, who, Denys wrote, "At first chid him with harsh words for his folly in breaking out against the foe, and then rewarded him with a golden brooch for his hardihood."

The next morning the host set out again for Jaffa. They met no more serious resistance. On the 10th of September, they arrived at last at the city, having been three weeks on their way. "All that noble fortress," wrote Denys, "was so thrown down and ruined by the Saracens in their terror at our approach that we could find no lodgings in it for the army. Thus we have encamped among the olive orchards outside the walls, and here we now make shift to rest and comfort ourselves after all our woes and tribulations. God send us a little peace to bind up our wounds."

Denys and Arthur, with Ivo de Vimont and the clerk, Thibaud de Mara, with whom they had picked up a friendship on the march, were taking their ease on the crest of a hill over which ran the dusty road from Jaffa inland to Casel. Somewhere beyond the grey-green plain and the distant mountains lay Jerusalem, the centre of the world. But here, they were shaded by olives, twisted and heavy-limbed, so old that they had seen the first crusaders pass a hundred years before; the scent of oranges from an orchard below spiced the air, and the sun outside their grove fell lusciously, full of indolence. Away from the plain, below them on the other side of the hill, the sea flung up spray from the stone piers of the harbour, and they could hear above its beating the click of hammers on stone, a lulling sound. Ivo, yawning, had remarked that no one would ever guess there was a war going on.

Arthur looked up from the leather thong he was laboriously plaiting.

"Do you know," he said softly, "I've suddenly realized that I must be a father."

"How do you mean, you've suddenly realized it?" asked Thibaud, closing his breviary on one finger. "Either a man is a father or he isn't."

He was a lean man, his skinniness making him seem taller than he actually was. His cheeks, deeply furrowed, were burned from the sun and wind to the colour of the Syrian earth, while his thin, fair hair had bleached out so that his tonsure, almost as dark as his cheeks, seemed to sit on it like a cap. He spoke with a grave, deep voice, and this, combined with his light hair and grooved cheeks, made him seem positively ancient, although he was only a year or two older than Denys.

"That's not necessarily true, old boy," said Ivo, lazily. He spat out a blade of dry grass he had been chewing. "I may possibly be a parent several times over, when I think back to the girls I've known and left."

"That isn't exactly what I mean," Arthur said, with a smile. "Or—well, maybe it is. I mean, I left home before the baby was born. Maude was in her third month when we went to Tours. So the child was born in, let's see——" he reckoned on his fingers "—December. Perhaps at Christmas."

"A good omen, some think," said Thibaud. "But others maintain that this presages death in early manhood, as happened to Our Lord."

"And I maintain that your head is stuffed as full of rubbish as an egg is with meat," said Ivo. "Good God, all you chaps— you know too bloody much. Eggheads—and your brains are about as solid as egg-yolk, at that. What earthly difference can it make to a man what day he was born on?"

"You betray your ignorance," Thibaud returned. He and Ivo squabbled continually, although they were the best of friends. "And what says the noble Honorius Augustodunensis? 'The exile of the soul is ignorance and its native land is knowledge.' Many wiser men than you, Ivo, have written about the influences of the natal day, because of the governance of the stars over the movement of the earth. For example, the worthy Socrates, although a heathen and a Roman, wrote many works concerning the power of the planetary bodies upon the lives of men."

"Oh, well. A Roman! What can you expect?"

"This Socrates," Thibaud went on, ignoring the interruption, "was formerly a knight but became a philosopher. He married the daughter of the emperor Claudius on condition that if she died, he must die likewise. Thus, when she was carried off by a fever, he was put to death by being made to drink poison. He was so full of virtue that if you but put your hand on a book containing his works, you will be cured of fever, the bites of serpents, or cramps. And the point is, he was able to foretell the exact moment of his death by reference to the motion of the stars."

Ivo blinked at him. "Tell me, Thibaud," he said, "is all that stuff in those books you read?"

"It is."

"Then I thank God," said Ivo, sinking back on the grass, "that he saw fit to make me a gentleman and an illiterate."

Denys laughed. He clapped Arthur affectionately on the back of the neck. "You mustn't mind them," he said. "I'm sure an honourable father and a loving mother mean more to a child's future than the day of his birth or the movement of the stars. The stars are far away, after all."

Arthur nodded, sadly. "So am I," he said. "December! My God, the child is nearly a year old. What month are we in?"

"September."

"Nine months. Will he be walking, do you think?"

"Riding by now, I shouldn't wonder," said Ivo.

"He'll still be swaddled," Denys said. "They don't walk until they're a year old . . . I think."

"I wonder what he's like," Arthur murmured. His fingers twitched at the leather braid and he began to undo it, absently. "We settled that if he was a boy he was to be named after my father: Roger. But perhaps he's a girl. Then Maude was going to call him Nesta, I mean *her* of course, after one of her ancestors. It's odd to think that there's a child there, someone to have the land, to hold both Hidehurst and Fitzleroy, and I don't even know what he looks like. Is he fair, like Maude, I wonder? Dark, like my father? Will he be honourable and just, a good lord to the tenants? I wonder what they think of him?"

"You needn't worry," said Denys. "You'll see to everything when you get home."

"When I get home," Arthur said. "Yes. When. . . ."

Denys glanced at him. Arthur sat with his head sunk, his fingers limp among the unravelled leather thongs, his back bowed. He had become very brown from the weather, but instead of looking fit and tough, he had a slenderer appearance, almost of fragility, as if the wind and sand had eroded him.

"Yes, *when*," Denys said, with a sudden sense of desperation. "This war will be over and done with by this Christmas. Why, Acre fell to us in a month, didn't it? And after the other armies had sat before it for two years. We smashed the Saracens at Arsûf and we haven't seen any real enemy force since then. They're scattered, frightened to death of us. I'll bet you anything you like the Sultan is ready to ask for peace right now. It's just a matter of waiting a little longer. And then—home! You'll take ship from Acre and back you'll go, stopping at

Cyprus on the way and remembering all we saw there; remember Peire Vidal and that princess of his? And soon after, you'll be in Marseille and you'll ride across France. By then it will be spring everywhere and the may will be in bloom, and they'll be sowing as you pass the fields of Poitou and ride up into Normandy. And then you'll take ship again and come to your own land. And all this will seem like a dream, the battles, the swamp and dusty deserts, the falling walls and war-cries. And your little boy will sit on your knee and say, 'Come on, Dada, tell us how you fought Saladin and made him run.'"

The other three had been listening with their eyes fixed on his lips. Ivo broke into a laugh, and said, "Jolly good! And Arthur will tell him all sorts of lovely lies then, won't he?"

Arthur, with a dreamy but rather fixed smile, said, "Of course I will. But you keep saying 'you'. Where will you be while all that's happening, Denys?"

"Oh—you forget. I have to carve out a principality for myself over here," Denys replied. "That won't take long. I'll be coming to England sooner than you think, with a troop of servants and men at arms behind me ... baskets full of gifts——"

He broke off. With a jingle and clatter, a dozen horsemen came up the track towards them. Richard was in front, mounted on Fauvel, the beautiful bay he had taken from the emperor of Cyprus.

He reined in before them and grinned. "By God's eyes," he said, "you gentlemen know what it is to make yourselves comfortable. Have you anything to drink?"

Ivo had a leather canteen which was hanging from the branch of an olive. He went to fetch it, while the others got to their feet. Richard's companions drew close, and one or two dismounted and went to ease themselves among the trees. They were all dressed in light tunics and short mantles, but armed with spears and bows as if for a hunt. Denys became aware that Fauvel's red-brown flank was streaked with darker red; he then noticed that a severed head hung by its hair from a long cord looped around the high cantle of Richard's saddle. Ivo handed the canteen up to the king and stroked the horses' muzzle.

"Never seen old Fauvel looking so fit," he said. "An absolute picture. I see you've had a bit of luck."

Richard wiped his mouth with the back of his hand and tossed the canteen to a young man who sat his horse with arrogant grace just behind him. This was John Fitz-Maurice, something of a dandy, who had distinguished himself at Arsûf by killing one of the Turkish emirs. He was a very supercilious man, who affected a drawl and an air of studied boredom.

He said, as if barely able to get the words out, "A seven-mile point without a check."

"Yes, a good old-fashioned gallop," Richard said. "My God, you should have been with us instead of lolling about in the sun here. We put the beggar up near that flat-topped hill among the figs; he doubled back and went through the orchard and then into the open country, and gave us a damn good run. But he couldn't out-distance Fauvel. We brought him to bay at the river and I made the kill myself."

"You were ten lengths ahead of the pack," growled a grizzled knight. "Not much work for us hounds."

Richard laughed. "I'm sorry for you, Walter." He lifted the severed head by the hair. "Ugly-looking devil, isn't he?"

Denys looked into the flat, glazed eyes of the Saracen. The face still bore the faint memory impressed upon it of the terror that must have overcome the man when Richard's lance went through his backbone.

"Poor chap," he said, before he could stop himself.

Richard let the head drop and dusted his hands lightly. "My good Denys," he said. "Sympathy for the infidel? What would our bishops say if they could hear you?"

Denys smiled up at him. "I was only thinking that anyone you decided to go for would deserve sympathy, my lord," he said.

The king crooked one leg over the pommel of his saddle and flexed his broad shoulders, visibly pleased. He pulled off his cap and shook his hair free. The sun made a flame of gold all round his head. Denys, with one hand on the velvety neck of the horse, thought he looked like one of those militant arch-angels one saw painted in Last Judgments above the choirs of churches.

"Well, he gave us a morning sport," the grizzled knight declared.

"Who slays the infidel lays up treasure for himself in heaven," put in Thibaud de Mara, in organ tones.

"Blast treasure in heaven," John Fitz-Maurice said, languidly. "I'd rather have pleasure on earth. A good hour's run and a kill at the end of it, what?" He stared down his nose at Denys. "Of course, I can understand that some gentlemen might have a distaste for bloodshed. . . ."

He put a slight emphasis on the word *gentlemen*. Arthur, who was standing near by with his hands behind his back, glanced up at him.

"Small pleasure, sir, to my mind," he said.

Fitz-Maurice raised his eyebrows. "Don't care for hunting?"

Arthur flushed. "I like to hunt as much as any man," he said, stammering a trifle. "But if you don't mind my saying so, I don't see much sport in twelve knights riding down one man, even if he is a Turk."

There was a stunned silence, and everyone looked involuntarily at the king. Richard, curiously enough, sat quiet. His brows were drawn a little together, but a smile lifted the points of his moustache. There was something inexpressibly sinister about this smile, more chilling than if he had burst out in one of his accustomed rages.

At last he said, "Why, John, will you let him bait you? Twelve against one—perhaps he has a point, eh? Did you have eleven others to help you at Arsûf when you fought with that emir?"

Fitz-Maurice had lost his languor. His cheeks were red, as if he had been slapped, and his lips trembled. He turned from the king to Arthur.

"I don't remember seeing you at Arsûf," he said, hoarsely. "Perhaps you allowed your dislike of sport to keep you safe among the grooms?"

"Oh, that was naughty of you, Johnny," the king said. shaking his head. "To remind this young man of his refusal to fight when we were in Cyprus. *I* remember that; I'd hoped everyone else would be good enough to forget."

"That's not true!" Arthur blurted. "I had sworn—I never held back at Acre—my lord, you know perfectly well."

He shrugged helplessly. He was incapable of speaking of his own achievements, nor could he defend himself against the unfairness of the charge. Denys stood petrified with horror, seeing quite clearly what mischief Richard was up to but unable to think of any way of interfering.

In any case, Richard was already saying, "Acre? Of course. You were ill with camp fever there, weren't you? That kept you from going up into the breach. You remember that, Johnny, don't you? But there—you yourself were elsewhere that day, weren't you, John? I've forgotten where: with a wench at the shore, I seem to recall. Not very nice of him to mention twelve against one, under the circumstances."

Fitz-Maurice shook his head, as if plagued by midges. He edged his horse forward and said, glaring at Arthur, "Just now—when you spoke of twelve to one—were you accusing me of cowardice, sir?"

Arthur straightened. "I wasn't accusing you of anything, sir. I only meant to say that we should be fighting the Saracens —besieging the Holy City—not chasing one poor devil as if he were a stag."

"And you fight by sitting snugly on this hillside?" Richard said, almost in a whisper. "By God, John, he's laughing at you."

He had his feet in the stirrups once more, and he nudged his horse. It stepped forward, crowding Arthur, who thus found himself pinned between the king and Fitz-Maurice.

"I can't love a man who will accept such insults, John," the king said, gazing directly into Fitz-Maurice's eyes.

Fitz-Maurice stared back at him almost with despair, and then looked down at Arthur. "Well—draw!" he snarled. His own blade was in his hand as he spoke.

Richard backed his mount away. "Gentlemen!" he cried. "I'm surprised at you. Will you fight?"

His teeth glinted in his beard. "Well, de Hastynge? You were speaking of twelve to one, weren't you? What are you waiting for? It's only one to one, now."

Arthur's hand had gone to his hilt. It dropped away.

"I—I can't," he said, in a voice full of agony. "I swore a solemn oath——" He raised his eyes to the king, and they were brimming with tears. "*You* know that, my lord. Why will you torment me?"

"I? Torment you?" Richard's tone was gentle. "Dear me, don't shift your burden to me. I know nothing of any oaths."

He darted a sharp glance at Fitz-Maurice. "And you— John? You're as frightened as he is. Well, well, let's go back to Jaffa and I can tell how the valiant Fitz-Maurice let himself be reviled and insulted, and was afraid to wipe out the stain. Twelve to one. You'll be known as Johnny Twelve-to-one!"

He laughed, quite merrily. And on that laugh, Fitz-Maurice, goaded beyond endurance, moved.

Arthur was on his left side. Fitz-Maurice twisted his body and struck awkwardly, over his horse's neck. The point of the blade caught Arthur's sleeve and tore it, but glanced harmlessly away.

Denys shouted like a man drowning. He stepped forward, but there was a horseman in his way. Ivo was holding out both hands impotently, as if to stop the fight. Fitz-Maurice's horse reared and turned; the young knight was trying to manœuvre into a better position for a second blow.

But Arthur was no longer the inexperienced youth he had been. He had seen battles, and had fought for his life. He dodged the pawing hoofs and sprang in close upon the left. He caught the pommel of the saddle with one hand, put his foot on Fitz-Maurice's foot and leaped up high enough to catch the other around the neck. They fell to the ground together, the sword flying through the air. For an instant they rolled beside the horse, embracing like sweethearts; then Arthur pulled free and with both fists clenched together struck his opponent on the side of the head, as if with an axe. Fitz-Maurice lay still.

Arthur staggered to his feet, gasping painfully. He picked up the sword and held it as if he were holding a poisonous snake. Then he threw it from him. The hilt clanged against a stone.

"Kept—my oath——" he panted.

He dropped to his knees beside Fitz-Maurice. "God! I—haven't killed him?" he said.

Fitz-Maurice drew a sobbing breath. Richard said, "Not you."

The king's face was impassive. But when he wheeled his horse the beast felt, in its flesh, its rider's bitter tension and danced restlessly.

"Get him to his feet, Walter," said Richard.

The grey-haired knight got down and helped Fitz-Maurice rise, and supported him against his horse's side. The young knight's fine clothes were smeared with dirt; his cap of gold tissue had fallen back and there was a raw red mark on his cheek-bone.

"Give me my sword," he said, feebly.

"No!" said the king, before anyone could do so. "You've had your chance. The fight is over. Put him on horseback."

He turned in the saddle and cast one long look at Arthur,

who knelt still in the same place. There was speculation in the king's regard, and so much of a kind of brooding hatred that Denys, who saw it, felt himself turn to ice. Then the king rode off. The rest of his train followed, almost in silence. Last of all went Fitz-Maurice, held up by the grey-haired knight who rode close beside him, and as they went the young man wept rackingly and unashamedly.

Denys ran to Arthur's side. He put an arm about his friend's shoulders, and then helped him to stand up.

Ivo, shaking his head, said, "Is he hurt?"

"I'm all right," said Arthur.

"There will be trouble," Thibaud said, in a worried voice. "I wish I had been elsewhere."

"Shut up," Ivo snapped. "All that's happened is that the boy showed his mettle. Unarmed, against a mounted man with a sword——"

Denys said, fiercely, "I wish it were that simple. You don't know the king as I do. Richard won't let it end here. It was he you insulted, Arthur, not Fitz-Maurice. You might as well have slapped the king's face. Ivo—you saw how he twisted everything, how he set them against each other—it was as if they were toys he was playing with. Jesus! I know him; I've felt the weight of his displeasure, I've seen him at work. He will keep on about it at Fitz-Maurice, nag him, jeer at him, tell him what a fool he was, play on his pride, and always deftly, softly, smoothly, turning him like a pat of butter, heating him up until you can burn your fingers on the fool. God! God! If only Hugh were alive. If only William the Marshal were here. He understands Richard. He can manage him."

Arthur said, gently, "I think you're upsetting yourself needlessly, Denys."

"Needlessly——!"

"You're jumping at shadows. The quarrel was between me and Fitz-Maurice, and it's over. The king himself said so."

"Oh, my blessed Saviour!" Denys groaned. "How can a man be such a dear fellow and such a fool?" He seized Arthur's hand. "Listen. You will have to leave the army. At once!"

Arthur blinked at him with a faint smile. "Don't be silly," he said. And as Denys opened his mouth, he went on more firmly, "No, certainly not. Leave the crusade and go home with my tail between my legs because of a ridiculous quarrel? I'm certain Fitz-Maurice is as sorry for it now as I am. Why should it go further? No, Denys. In Canterbury I took my oath to follow King Richard to the Holy Land and to fight in his wars against the infidel. That was as binding an oath on me as that other I took, the one about not drawing my sword. . . ." His voice faltered. "No, I can't leave. Not until we have taken the Holy Sepulchre, or until the king himself releases me. You know that, Denys." And humbly, he added, "I know perfectly well what a fool I must sound. I can't help it. I know that people laugh at me. But it's what I feel I must do."

Denys drew a long breath. "Very well," he said. "If that's how it has to be, that's how it's going to be. Will you be satisfied if Richard releases you from your promise to follow him, and tells you to go home?"

"Why, I—yes, I suppose so. But why——?"

"Never mind. Let's leave it at that."

He hooked his arm in Arthur's. "Nobody will laugh at you when this story gets round," he said. "My God, you're become a fighter. A real thruster. You plucked him out of that saddle as if he had been a straw man. It all comes of paying attention to what I teach you."

He forced out a laugh which he hoped rang more mirthfully in Arthur's ears than it did in his own.

Although the walls and fortifications of Jaffa had been demolished by the Sultan's men so that the Franks should not be able to defend the place without extensive rebuilding, there remained many houses in which lurked an uneasy civilian populace, and several fine manors, actually small palaces by Western standards, set among handsome gardens. In one such, Richard had set up his headquarters. Denys came in rather diffidently but, since he was well known, was passed directly into the hall where the king was dining. Because of the size of the hall, Richard had had to forgo the enormous dinner parties he was so fond of: at the high table there were no more than half a dozen barons, and perhaps twenty knights sat below the salt, all wealthy and powerful men and most of them members of the army council.

Denys waited until the tables had been cleared and sweet-meats and fruits set out in great platters. Then he whispered to the chamberlain, who went up and asked the king whether it was his pleasure that the trouvère, Denys de Courtebarbe, should entertain him. Richard craned his neck, saw Denys at the end of the hall, and beckoned to him.

"You have read my mind," he said, as Denys knelt and kissed his hand. "I was thinking of sending for you. What will you give us tonight? Have you not brought Giraud?"

It could not be guessed from his manner that that very morning he had prodded two men, one of them Denys's best friend, into deadly combat. All affability, he held out a cup of wine to Denys, combing the fingers of his other hand through his tawny beard.

"Giraud is hoarse, my lord," Denys said. "I thought, for your pleasure, I'd give you my own version of one of the old tales. I'll sing, if you like, the Death of Vivien."

"Very good," Richard nodded. "What do you say, gentlemen?"

The duke of Burgundy, beside him, clapped his hands lightly. "Splendid," he said. "And very apt."

Denys tuned his harp, then laid aside the key and began the chant, accompanying himself with expressive chords. He sang of young Vivien and how he was brought up by his uncle, the renowned Count Guillaume, and his aunt Dame Guiberc, wisest of women. He told of how the Saracen king, Deramé, came with his fleet up the Gironde and harried France, and how Tedbald of Bourges went to meet him, followed by Vivien and seven hundred brave knights, all in hauberks of iron and green-painted helms. As he sang, he watched the faces of his audience, attentive, anticipatory, some with chins cradled in their palms, some leaning forward with their elbows on the table, others lounging back with their fingers laced behind their heads. All were silent, seeing in their minds the brilliant gathering of that host as they themselves had gathered before the walls of Acre, marking the clustered spears of the Saracens as they themselves had marked the banners of the infidel at the wood of Arsûf.

Denys told how Vivien urged that Count Guillaume be summoned to bring reinforcements, and that battle be joined at once for honour's sake. But Tedbald, seeing the great numbers of the Saracen army, stripped his banner from his lance and fled in terror. So fearful was he that he rode his horse blindly under a gallows where four thieves hung, and was struck in the face by the foot of one of the corpses; in his fright he soiled his saddle-cloth. But Vivien's honour would not let him retreat. Determined to give battle, he was acclaimed by the Franks who swore to follow him to the death even though he was not their lord.

Then Denys sang of the battle, of the clash of arms and the splitting of shields, the smiting of swords on helms and the raising of war-cries. The eyes of his audience brightened; fists were clenched, teeth were bared, and each man lived over his own combats. Ah, but now, as the day wears on, the Franks fall one by one, and still Count Guillaume does not come. Vivien wrings his hands and weeps over the death of his friends. He sees his weary comrades, their reins blood-spattered, their saddles soaked in blood, their entrails spilling from their bodies. "Alas!" he cries, "I have no leech for you. But will you go home to die in your beds? For God's sake, let us take vengeance upon the infidel, let us attack them once again." "God love thee, Lord Vivien," the men shout, and so once more they charge gallantly, and so one by one they fall.

Denys's voice dropped, vibrant with emotion, and tears sparkled in the eyes of his hearers and ran down their cheeks. For now there are but a score of Franks left, and now but ten. Yet, with these ten, Vivien still gallops against the foe. And now his ten are dead, and he alone is left and the Saracens recoil in amazement before this lone man who still fights on, though they be a thousand to his one. They stand back and shoot at his horse and the beast sinks dead between his thighs. One rides forward (how well known that swift riding, swaying in the saddle, swooping in close to cast a javelin and off again like a gadfly) and hurls a dart which pierces Vivien's side. The rings of mail are sundered and the red blood gushes forth; his white banner falls on the ground. Vivien draws forth the dart and hurls it back again so that it kills the man who threw it. But the rest rush in upon him and beat him to his knees. Dying, he calls upon the Virgin, Queen of the Heavens; a javelin strikes him on the head, his brains gush from his skull and so he falls. Vivien, the peerless, the courteous, is slain. The last chords died away in the hall and Denys, in silence, bowed his head.

He had given one of his best performances, and he knew it. He bit in the corner of his lip, listening to the tempest of applause that broke out, and thought to himself, If that doesn't fetch the king I'll never touch a harp again.

But Richard's eyes were as wet as anyone's, and he called Denys up to him and embraced him.

"By God's legs," he said, "that was magnificent, it was enough to bring a dead man to life. Denys, my dear, what can I give you for that song? What would you like?"

In a very low voice, Denys said, "Only a few moments with you, my lord, in private."

Richard's smile faded and his eyes became slightly glazed and curiously flat, almost like those of the Saracen's head which had hung from his saddle. Then he was smiling again; he said, clapping Denys on the shoulder, "I can't refuse you anything. Tonight is yours. Sit down somewhere and wait for me. I shan't be long."

When dinner was over and the knights and barons had gone off to their tents, Richard led Denys up an outer stair to a large room above the hall, a room with a low dais running across one end of it, and fancifully carved wooden fretwork screening the windows. The raised part of the floor was covered with a thick rug, and there were cushions along the wall behind it so that this whole part of the floor formed a kind of large, comfortable couch. Richard threw his crimson cloak into a corner and stepped up on the dais.

"This was once the house of a prince," he said, "or a rich merchant. We have a lot to learn from the Turks about the art of living. Just look at this rug! Look at the colours in it: a garden! And just touch it—it's like walking on moss."

He sat down, stretching his legs and leaning back against a cushion. He patted the rug beside him.

"Come, sit down," he said. "Tell me why you wanted to talk to me in private."

"Well, my lord," Denys began.

Richard touched his arm. "Would you like some wine? Just a moment." There was a silver pitcher and some cups on a low stand in a corner. "Go pour me a cup and take one yourself."

Denys patiently did as he was told. Richard drank, and sighed.

"Forgive me if I seem distracted," he said. "I've got a great deal on my mind. These idiots!—the French, I mean. You know they insist on rebuilding the walls of Jaffa before we go any further. We should be on our way to Ascalon. But they are cautious . . . . Cautious! They don't realize that the weather isn't always going to be like this. They think there's no winter here. But winter is coming; we should be pressing on, making for Jerusalem."

He seemed to have forgotten Denys. He looked grimly into his cup, and went on, "That fool Montferrat. Fool—or traitor? I wish I knew. Is he thinking of Tyre only, or of his chances of edging out Guy?"

He glanced at Denys and smiled, thoughtfully. "It's not easy to make decisions, sometimes. Tell me, my dear Denys, what would you do if you were chief of the army?"

"I, my lord?" Denys grinned in embarrassment. "I can't begin to imagine such a thing. But I think——"

"You, at least, have always shown your loyalty," said Richard, without letting him finish. "But these dull-witted clowns! 'Jaffa is the best route for pilgrims going to Jerusalem.'" His voice became a tremulous, mocking falsetto. "'Let us rebuild it to the glory of God. Besides, the army needs rest.'" He snorted. "Rest! They are becoming a rabble. No, I'm wrong, they were always a rabble. I know what's happening— whole wagonloads of women are coming down from Acre. The camp is turning into a whore-house."

He held out his cup to be refilled. "Pilgrims to Jerusalem. Oh, how delicious. They have forgotten that we have to fight our way over fifty miles of hills and swamps before we come within sight of the walls of Jerusalem. Now, *now*! We should be striking the Sultan while he's still reeling, while he's anxious only to get away from us. Instead, we are giving him plenty of time to regroup his forces. Isn't that marvellous?"

Denys said nothing. He began to wish he had never come.

"And even the rebuilding of Jaffa is slow because they must have their women," the king continued. "Is it any wonder I look for action? Even galloping about the countryside hunting stray Saracens? And do you wonder at my wanting to keep some of my young hounds keen by taking them out of this place and looking for a bit of sport?"

Denys felt his cheeks growing hot. "I'm sorry," he said. "I never thought of it that way."

Richard tapped him on the thigh, and laughed. "Must I always explain myself to you?" he said. "No, don't look so stricken. I take the trouble to do so because I feel we are more than a king and his trouvère. I have always felt that you loved me as a friend, Denys. Do you remember that day in Sicily when you sang 'Roland'?"

Denys nodded, incapable of speech.

Richard drew up one knee, resting his arm on it. He put his head back against the cushion, gazing at the ceiling with its inlaid pattern of wood and shell.

"Why should I explain myself to you?" he said, softly. "I want to be—loved. That's the truth of it. I want to be understood, you know. I want people to think well of me. I want it to be said, 'There is a great king!' My father never thought of himself that way, but only of his works. But he was always so sure of himself. . . ."

Abruptly he fixed his eyes on Denys, and said, "Do you think of the future when you write your songs? Tell me!"

"Of course I do," said Denys, utterly fascinated by Richard's unexpected candour. "We all do. That in some distant time they'll sing the Song of Guillaume, or the Four Sons of Aymon, and repeat my lines, 'I Courtebarbe, made this song.' It's all I have to live on," he added, with a sudden wrench at his heart.

"And Guillaume? And Aymon himself?" said Richard. "It's all the life they have. But what do we know of them? Nothing but what's in the song. It's yours—not theirs."

They were both silent for a moment. Then Richard went on, "That in some distant time they'll sing your song. Ah, yes. But what if they no longer sing songs? How can we imagine them?

"How will they see us? Have you ever thought of that? As a mere spectacle, with our quaint old-fashioned coats of mail? As barbarians—the way we think of those rough Saxon levies who fought against Duke William at Senlac, with their hairy chests bare, fighting on foot with axes, uncivilized and boorish? Perhaps there will not even be kings in that distant day. We will be nothing but names in songs, unknowable shadows."

"That can't be so," Denys burst out. "You will never be forgotten."

Richard smiled faintly, his blue eyes soft, and for just a moment he resembled Arthur, his face full of gentleness, his eyes frank and soft.

"Not 'forgotten'," he answered. "I said *unknowable*. I went to see a Wise Woman once, Denys, a witch who lived in a cave near Poitiers. I was a youth then; I was staying at my mother's court during that time when she had left my father because of his entanglement with Rosamund Clifford. Well . . . never mind. I had ridden out with a small company, hawking, and someone told me about this witch. I decided I wanted to see her. I climbed up through the woods, leaving everyone behind except William the Marshal—he was my instructor in arms and went everywhere with me or with my brother Harry. He worshipped Harry, you know.

"She was a nasty old woman, that witch. Fat, filthy as a sow. . . . I gave her some money and asked her to tell my fortune. She said, 'No, not for money, my boy.' William was furious, he put his hand on his sword. I told him to get out. There was something about that old woman, something that attracted me, something that made the hair rise up on the back of my neck and frightened me to death, and yet she seemed familiar and darling to me as if she were my own mother. Odd! Yes, I remember that I said, 'If you won't have money of me, have a kiss instead.' I kissed her bristly cheek. It smelled like a mushroom. And she said, 'That's my boy. Yes, you're one of my favourites.'

"And suddenly, everything whirled round before my eyes. And then—I saw a strange world, Denys, a world of madness. Great palaces that shot up higher than any cathedral, with glittering golden plates in the sides of them. Men in outlandish clothes who hurried in great masses through unbelievable cities. Things like scuttling beetles with great white eyes, moving faster than horses; things shooting across the sky; things I couldn't take in, or grasp, or begin to recognize. Then it was gone, and I was in the cave again.

"The old woman said, 'I have let you look ahead a thousand years, my dearie. Will you be content with your fortune if I tell you that they still know your name? They call you Richard the Lion-Hearted. They remember you—I won't say how, but they do.'

"She began to cackle. I stumbled out of the cave. I was haunted by horror. My flesh crept as if I were covered with ants. My God, I had never known what it was to be afraid before; I have never known it since. I was like—like Tedbald in that song you sang tonight, who rode full tilt into the foot of a hanged man. I caught hold of William and said, 'Get me away from here.' We both ran—he was as frightened as I was."

Denys stared at him, feeling something of that terror in himself, without understanding it wholly. "But why?" he said.

"It was too far away," Richard said. "Can't you see? All those years. I couldn't begin to recognize what I saw. How could *they* know *me*?" He snatched Denys's hands between his own. "Think of it," he said, shaking him. "Just think. Fifty years from now and you have faded in people's minds. A hundred, and anyone who might have known you is dry bones. Another hundred, and a hundred after that, and still another hundred. What's left of you? A name? And even that's wrong: Richard the Lion-Hearted! I saw myself mortal, Denys, less than mortal, mouldered away to a pinch of dust, and a shadowy *Richard* still going on, shuddering, squeaking like a bat, amongst those distant strangers."

He fell silent, and they sat looking into each other's face. The king's strong fingers, their knuckles downy with golden hairs, heavy with massive rings, tightened about Denys's hands painfully.

"Do you understand?" Richard said.

Denys had forgotten why he was there. He had forgotten his plan, to beg the king to release Arthur from his oath and let him go safely home. He had forgotten even his fear of Richard, his suspicions, his caution. He was filled with love and reverence for this man who lived beneath so magnificent a doom. His spirit yearned to make some gift, to comfort, to respond in some way to the confidence that had been given him, to the greatness and power of the king.

"Richard," he whispered.

Sitting with his hands between those of the king, he was in the attitude of a vassal swearing fealty. And thus, almost dreamily, he began to repeat, still in a whisper, the ancient formula of homage used in his own land: "Sir, I enter your homage and faith and become your man by mouth and hands, and I swear and promise to keep faith and loyalty to you against all others, and to guard your rights with all my strength."

"I accept it," said Richard, in a low, tense voice. He leaned forward and kissed Denys full on the mouth, not like a lord receiving homage, but like a lover.

The night was blazing with stars when Denys let himself out of the postern door and stood in the garden. It was past midnight; he had left the king sleeping.

He stared at the sky and drew deep breaths. The air was cool, spicy with unfamiliar scents, ringing with crickets.

My God, what have I got myself into? he thought.

The most dangerous of positions: to be a king's minion. But Christ! how do you refuse a king? And especially such a king, a great man, a great and marvellous man. And to have listened to him open his heart——

Perhaps that was the most dangerous thing of all.

He kept thinking that Richard reminded him of someone. Someone he knew well but hadn't seen for years. Someone whose name was on the tip of his tongue: it began with a C.

He found that he was shuddering. He began to walk, under the cool trees heavy with fruit that glimmered in the darkness.

To have accepted his caresses and endearments . . . well, no help for that. But the truth was, and he had to face this, and perhaps it accounted for his shuddering: he had found pleasure in them. Not simply the pleasure of satisfied vanity either. No, a more shameful pleasure, unholy, secret, that stirred him deeper than he dared admit. And the instant he allowed this acceptance to enter his mind he began to shudder again, like one who, treading on a branch, finds an adder squirming under his foot.

Someone familiar, someone whose name surely began with C. Or L. It might have been L. Particularly the eyes, as blue as gentians and made bluer still by golden lashes.

It came to him suddenly: Balian. Balian, the oldest of the pages when Denys had served in the castle of Beaupréau. I must have been about eight, and he five years older, yes, because the next year he was made a squire and began to learn the use of arms. How we all looked up to him! He was so handsome, so popular, a great favourite of Lady Elise. He had just such blue eyes, and he had crisp, curly blond hair that clung all over his head like wool. I was afraid of him, wasn't I? He knew everything, could do anything. I remember him running along the narrow walkways of the topmost battlements, jumping from crenel to crenel, daring us to follow as he climbed over the peak of a roof. He sang beautifully, too. He used to catch sparrows and pluck them alive. He said the feather from sparrows plucked alive made the softest pillows. I remember—what was his name?—Dar—Darrin—his best friend, Dreux, that was it— he made Dreux stamp on one of them as it struggled naked on the floor, trying to flap its featherless wings. Put it out of its misery, he said grinning.

My soul, what a little monster he was. But we all loved him. Did I love him?

I suppose I must have. But there was one night when he tormented me. I did something . . . I was always getting into mischief, wasn't I? Trouble, rather than mischief. I did something that made him angry, and he pinched me, or hurt me somehow. But it made no difference; I still thought he was such a splendid fellow. How could anyone mind being hurt by him?

Just like Richard. King of our little world. I wonder what happened to him? Whatever it was, it was probably good. He was a fortunate one, born to good luck. Things fell into Balian's lap without his even trying for them. Just like Richard. What it is to be a king! You hold out your hand and everything falls into it, even a poor bastard of a trouvère, even me.

He looked up at the diamond-spangled sky and laughed, and shivered uncontrollably, and walked faster to be warm as if it were winter and he would never be warm again.

When he came to the grove of oranges where his tent was pitched he saw a dull yellow crack of light shining from the flap. With a guilty sinking feeling he realized that Arthur must be worried about him, had probably remained awake waiting for him. And he? He had forgotten his friend completely; he had not even asked Richard for his boon. But perhaps there was nothing to worry about on that score now. Surely, tomorrow he could go to the king and ask for any favour, for at least one favour, for this one which could not be refused. He hurried forward, fixing a smile on his face as he thrust aside the tent flap.

"Why the hell did you——?" he began.

His heart gave a great jolt.

Arthur lay on his blanket with his hands folded across his chest, holding a lighted candle. His eyes were closed by silver coins which reflected the light of four candles that stood melting upon pieces of brick, two at his head and two at his feet.

"Christ!" Denys said angrily. "What a stupid joke. You nearly frightened the wits out of me."

Shadows moved on the walls of the tent. Ivo was there, and Thibaud holding his beads and a crucifix, and the earl of Leicester in a long mantle and hood.

"My lord!" Denys said. "What does this mean? What's happening?"

His voice cracked. He felt he had known from the moment he entered that it was no joke, and still his mind refused to accept the reality.

He moved towards Arthur. He could see, now, the grey dullness of his friend's cheeks, the horrid immobility of his face. No blood, no breath, stirred that claylike flesh.

"Oh, dear Christ," he said, and felt his knees loosen.

Ivo caught hold of him. The earl of Leicester said gravely, "We did what we could—we had the king's own surgeon, but it was too late. I grieve with you, Courtebarbe."

It was in the earl's company that they rode customarily into battle.

Ivo said, "For God's sake, Denys, get hold of yourself."

"At least he did not die unshriven," Thibaud said.

Denys flapped his hand before his face as if to brush away pestiferous flies. He licked his lips, and managed to say, "Who——?"

"It was that—it was John Fitz-Maurice," Ivo said. "It seems he challenged Arthur again and when Arthur would not fight, killed him in cold blood. I wasn't here, but Giraud saw it all. He'll tell you about it. He is looking for you; we couldn't find you anywhere, and so we sent him . . ."

Denys nodded. "Where's Fitz-Maurice?" he said, choking on the words as if they were dust.

Leicester said, grimly, "I fear you're too late. I sent to find him as soon as I learned about this, but he had already fled, probably to Acre. He will not escape forever. It was murder. The king will hang him for it."

"Ah, yes," said Denys. "The king."

He shook off Ivo's hand. "Leave me alone here," he said.

They went without more words, although Ivo looked back at him for a long moment from the tent flap, before reluctantly dropping it behind him. When he was alone, Denys sank to his knees on the ground beside the blanket.

"Oh," he said, "why did you ever follow me?"

With that, the scalding tears gushed from his eyes and he fell down across the body of his friend.

He wept for a long time. But after a while there were no more tears. He wiped his face with his hands and sat looking at the corpse. Giraud found him that way.

Denys stared up at him, and then slowly and wearily got to his feet. "Well?" he said.

"I—master, I'm sorry for you," said Giraud.

"What happened? Tell me?" Denys said.

"Why—they must have told you already. A young knight, Fitz-Maurice, came into the tent. Sir Arthur was sitting by the light of a candle, waiting for you. I was—I was singing to him. You had told me——"

"I told you to guard him," Denys said, flatly. "I told you to watch over him while I was gone. Never mind. Go on."

"Fitz-Maurice asked him to fight. He said he would never live down the shame if he didn't. He drew his sword and said to Arthur that if he did not fight like a man, he'd be killed like the coward he was. Arthur smiled at him and said that it was neither worthy nor courteous of him to speak that way. Before he could say anything else, Fitz-Maurice stabbed out suddenly and Arthur fell. And Fitz-Maurice ran. And I——"

"And you ran with him, you filthy gutter-rat," Denys howled, suddenly. He sprang forward and seized Giraud by the front of his coat and shook him so that his teeth rattled. Holding him with one hand, he dragged him to his knees, groping at his belt for his dagger.

Giraud threw himself backwards. His coat slipped from Denys' grasp and he sprawled on the ground. With the agility of an animal he scrambled over Arthur's body, sending the silver coins flying, putting out one of the candles as he went. He cowered in the corner of the tent.

"Kill me," he snarled. "Good! Let yourself go. Why not? I hated him. If you want the truth, I was glad to see him killed. There! Like it? He was too damned good. That's why Fitz-Maurice killed him. It's why the king hated him. You know that. He had no business being alive in this rotten world, among the devils. He was better dead. Better! Do you hear me? Better!"

He was almost screaming. Denys lunged for him and caught

him by the hair. He pulled Giraud's head down, across Arthur's knees. He lifted his dagger blindly, wanting only to shut off that voice with blood.

Giraud, barely able to speak, wheezed, "And where were you? If you loved him—why weren't you here? Liar! Liar—like all the rest of us——"

Denys stiffened and tried to plunge the dagger home in the man's throat, but his arm would not move. He let go of Giraud, who lay still, his breath coming in racking sobs. Ivo had burst into the tent at the noise. Denys clung to him, dragged himself erect, and stood panting. Becoming aware that he held the dagger, he let it fall.

"I can't bear it," he said.

He pulled away from Ivo and staggered out, into the grove. There were men gathering, drawn by the shouting, some with torches. But away from the camp, up the hillside, it was dark and still. He ran into the darkness with his agony clasped to his heart like a bleeding wound.

Arthur was buried in the church of St. Michael, which still bore the traces of Saracen occupation: its walls covered with Arabic scribbles, its saints broken from their niches, and its altar stone cracked. The bishop of Evreux officiated, and the king himself was there as if Arthur had been one of the highest of nobles. After the mass the funeral rites were performed; Denys listened to the clods falling on the coffin and heard nothing else, nor did he speak to anyone but went silently away afterwards and sat alone in his tent, drinking. His friends let him be. After a while he became conscious that Giraud was crouching on the floor beside him. He put his hand on the minstrel's head.

"It's over," he said. "I shall never see him again."

Giraud, looking at Denys like a dog, held up his palm. On it lay a small gold cross on a golden chain. Maude had given it to Arthur before they left; she had hung it around his neck and kissed him, and said, "May God watch over you, my love."

Denys took it. "You stole it from—from the body?" he said, and when Giraud nodded, he laughed broken-heartedly. He unclasped the chain and hung it around his own throat. He went on drinking until he fell asleep.

Then there was a letter to be written to Maude. Denys sat for a long time over the parchment, biting and breaking quill after quill, wondering what to say. At last, in despair, he wrote hastily:

"Lady Maude, I sorrow to send you such tidings but your dear husband, my beloved friend, was slain upon Saint Matthew's Day bypast. He spoke often of you and his last words to me were of love for you and for the child which is born. He was slain upholding his honour as a true and chivalrous knight, and all speak highly of him, the king himself commending him and sending with this letter a gift to you from his own hands of silk and a golden cup. I cannot tell you more being all distraught with woe, but he who brings this letter will tell you all that is needful. Know, that in all ways Arthur has borne himself nobly in this war, fighting ever in the fore and winning the admiration of knights and barons for his deeds. I grieve deeply for I am left alone. Well do you know how much I loved him. I commend you to the mercy of God, and beg that you will pray for me."

And as he signed it, and sealed it, his tears fell once again on his hands and he thought, "I carry death with me everywhere. First Pons, then Hugh, now Arthur. It would be best for me to die also."

The letter was sent, along with Arthur's sword and armour, and all the rest of his belongings, in the care of one of the king's pursuivants who was carrying dispatches back to England. Denys kept only the tent and blankets, and Arthur's horse. When everything else had gone, loneliness truly descended on him. Then, for the first time, he understood that he would really never see Arthur again: his shy smile, his gentle ways, his voice, his blinking, short-sighted eyes, everything was gone, finished, ended forever. That they might meet again in Paradise was small consolation.

The following morning Richard sent for him, and when they were alone said, "You may as well know that I have sent my herald to Acre to see if he can find John Fitz-Maurice. But I'm afraid he has fled to Tyre where Conrad of Montferrat will probably give him shelter to spite me. If I ever catch him— and I will, some day—I will hang him for the murder of your friend, de Hastynge."

Denys could think of nothing to say. In his mind, however, he said, "Did you hold me by you that night knowing that Arthur would be unprotected?"

Richard looked keenly at him. As if answering the thought, he said, "I know you believe it was my doing that this happened. It is not so. I warned Fitz-Maurice that very evening to let the matter go no further. I was angry, yes, but I would have dealt with de Hastynge in my own way."

"I know that, my lord," Denys said, thickly.

Richard stood up and clapped him on both arms. "My dear boy," he said, in his most persuasive voice, "I am heartily sorry for you. But you must not go on mourning this way. Think, if he had fallen in battle. We all go in danger of our lives every day. Consider that it is a risk we all run. I want to see you cheer up. Will you try, for my sake?"

Denys said, "Yes, my lord."

"'My lord'?"

"Yes, Richard."

"Blondel."

"Yes, Blondel."

Richard sighed. "Very well. You may go now."

Denys went. But when he was outside he was overcome by sudden nausea; he was filled with loathing for the king, but even more for himself. He leaned against a wall and wiped his clammy forehead, and with an effort kept from vomiting.

"I'll kill him," he thought, dully. "That's it. I'll kill him and then myself. Let it all end. Sooner or later."

And this resolve fixed itself in his mind and became precious, like a carrion fly embedded in amber.

Several days later the king invited a dozen men to go out hawking with him, and Denys was commanded to be one of the party. They wore no armour, but carried lances and swords so that if they came across any Turkish skirmishers they might amuse themselves with combat.

Denys dressed with care in his best tunic, of saffron linen embroidered with red and blue threads at collar and wrists, as if he were going to a feast. He belted on his sword and made certain that it was loose in the sheath. He knew why Richard had asked him to come, it was part of what was clearly intended to be a campaign to take his mind off his troubles. Very well, he thought, let it be so, I'll go joyfully; when this day is over we will neither of us have any more troubles. He tied on a red leather cap and fastened on his spurs; as an afterthought he took out the thin gold chain studded with rock crystal which Maude had long ago given him and which he had kept safely all this time, never being tempted to turn it into money. He fastened it about his neck, over his tunic, Arthur's chain being beneath.

He said to Giraud, "One never knows about these little hunting parties of the king's. If anything happens to me you can keep everything I own. I've written it down on this paper. Perhaps you'd better hope for my death."

Giraud said, "Be careful."

"What?" Denys replied, with a crooked grin. "That doesn't sound like you. I thought you believed the world was full of devils, and that the most glorious thing was to be released from it."

"Be careful," Giraud repeated, gnawing his lip, and putting the paper carefully away in his worn purse. "I'll pray for you."

"To whom?" said Denys, harshly. He sprang into the saddle and trotted to join the king.

They rode over the hill out of Jaffa into the plain, all laughing and chatting, and made for the river where the king hoped to put up a heron from the reeds. It was rich, lush land they galloped over, but little cultivated, since the war made things difficult for small farmers, who hesitated to grow crops too far from the shelter of a city. Yet, here and there were fields of melons, enclosed by stone walls, or a small hut with a few goats tethered near by among the shaggy olives, dark-green and silver. Near the river were cypresses and feathery mimosas, and a few huge old prickly-pears, their trunks netted with flowering vines. There were no people; at the approach of the horsemen they hid themselves. It was like riding through a dreamlike, deserted land.

There were plenty of birds in the low ground near the river, and the king flew his falcons which brought him some game, and cast at a stork which escaped. They had good sport. When the sun was high, they hobbled their horses and sat down to eat the bread, dried meat, figs, and cheese they carried in their saddlebags. The king asked Denys to sing, and Denys, looking as blithe as he could, sang several gay dansas and other popular ditties. Richard stretched out in the shade at the edge of a little wood and promptly went to sleep; the others dozed also, and a few played dice, betting in whispers so as not to disturb the king.

Denys strolled back and forth a little way from where Richard lay. No one was watching him. He drew close to the king and stopped, finally, under a tree beside him. Slowly and cautiously he slid his sword from its sheath, making no sound.

Richard lay on his side, one leg drawn up, his head pillowed on his arm, his other arm limp behind him, the fingers a trifle curled, palm to the sky. He breathed deeply and slowly, untroubled by any nightmare, his face serene as a child's.

Denys leaned on his sword as if it were a walking stick and he the merest passer-by chancing in some pleasant, peaceful glade to stop and admire the view. It was all pastoral, the other sleeping knights, the cadgers snoring beside the motionless, hooded hawks, the group casting dice on the soft, mossy bank of the river, the whispering reeds bending to an occasional breeze, the clear sky, clearer and higher and purer than any sky at home. Now, he thought, I should stroke my harp and sing, something clear and high and pure, a lullaby to keep him asleep and all of them asleep in an enchantment.

I have only to lift this sword and bring it down, swiftly and surely, right through him, through that thick golden-bearded throat. One spurt of blood and he would lie pinned to the earth, and I'd be finished with him. He would pay, and I'd pay too, for Arthur's life. And for that night, he added, deeper within his mind. The thought made him shiver.

There was a crackling in the underbrush behind him. He spun round, and as he did so a javelin whickered past his ear. There were horsemen among the trees, Turks, their spired helmets shining like dark-blue flowers, their curved swords like moons. One spurred straight for him with lowered lance, shouting, "Ul-ul-ul-ullah!" At the cry, other voices were unleashed, as hounds might give tongue closing in on a stag.

Denys saw the lance coming and without thought leaped aside before it touched him. He swung his sword as the man passed and felt it bite the horse, which stumbled and turned sideways. The rider kicked at it, but its haunches were sinking. Richard was just getting to his feet, his mouth wide open and a look of astonishment on his face. Denys cried out, "Guard yourself!" He saw the king, his sword in both hands, flail out at the Turk who seemed to throw himself sideways out of the saddle. Denys ran around the tree near which he stood. Another horseman made for him and Denys dodged again, playing a deadly hide-and-seek behind the tree trunk. Bending low over their horses' necks, the Turks raced past—there seemed to be dozens of them. A knight fell spreadeagled, his face smashed. The riders wheeled and galloped away among the trees.

Richard was already on horseback, shouting, "After them!" Denys vaulted into his own saddle and followed. He thought of nothing but the excitement and urgency of the chase.

They rode out of the wood, the other knights trailing a little way behind, and saw their attackers ahead of them. There were only a few of them after all. Richard glanced back at Denys, and with a laugh motioned to him with his sword. There was a thicker, darker wood ahead and suddenly, from its shelter, a much larger body of Turks emerged. They spread out in a semicircle as they came, shrieking their high-pitched, whooping war-cry.

Richard saw them as soon as Denys did, and checked Fauvel. The bay rose up, turning like a dancer and sped back. Denys caught up with him and they were in the middle of a whirlpool of men, blades and dust. The king was surrounded; Denys saw him reel and recover himself, and lay about him again so that the Turks gave back for a moment.

All at once, Denys knew what to do. He spurred forward, shouting as loudly as he could, "I am the king!" He remembered what the Saracens called Richard: *Melek Ric.* "*Melek!*" he cried. "I am the *melek!*"

He made for the nearest of the enemy and cut at him roundly. The small buckler of the Turk split and the man went over backward as if he had been pulled from behind. The others closed in, and there were javelin points bristling before Denys's eyes and at his throat. He dropped his arm. Someone snatched away his sword; someone else caught his reins.

The whole troop sped away, with him in their midst. It had happened like lightning. He had no time for a final glimpse of the king, not a moment for regret, or doubt, not even time to be afraid.

5

JERUSALEM

Journal of Denys de Courtebarbe. Extract 10.

As I write these words I can scarce believe that I am in truth within the walls of the Holy City. Yet even the paper on which I write, which is both thick and heavy and of a marvellous smoothness, is of such a kind as consorts well with the wonders of this place. I make the date (reckoning as best I can from the day on which I was taken) to be about the ides of October, but it may well be that I have lost one or two days, so confused and numerous have been the events since I gave myself into the hands of the enemy. And to say true, I have cared little whether I lived or died or what the date was, and only within the last fortnight have I seemed to myself to return to life.

I look forth from this upper window upon many rooftops, most flat or with a small dome and spread about with carpets, built of stone and washed with white or colours like the houses we saw in Sicily. There are cedars and many other trees, fair to see. There are the great, round domes of temples, one among them very large and goodly which I am told is called el Aksa and which was formerly the great house of the Templars until all herein was taken by Saladin, four years agone. And there, too, I am told, lies the great palace of King Solomon whose name was told me by the hermit Gabriel when he spoke certain verses of a song made by this ancient king. And yonder, somewhere to my left hand, lost among houses and streets, lies the tomb of our Blessed Lord, that Sepulchre for the saving of which Arthur and I followed the king to Outremer. So I have come nigh it, but I am as like to rescue it as I am to fly from this city over hill and valley and come again to my own land of Poitou.

But look you, Denys, you ninny, how you have become addled in your wits, setting down things arse-first like that

priest who sat on the well to drown the devil and fell therein
himself. Now must I, for my own sake, write down in order
what has happened and thus, it may be, bring myself in some
measure to my senses again.

When that band of infidels had brought me a long way
into the hills we came to a camp above a town where men
were at work throwing down the walls. The chief of my
captors was a young man clad in fair garments and wearing
a gilded helm and a quilted gambeson over which was a
small square breastplate of steel inlaid with gold, whereby I
knew him to be a prince, for their common sort wear no
armour save a helm. He conducted me into the largest of the
tents wherein sat a gaunt, weatherbeaten man with a long
beard, and attended by many servants, the least of which was
more splendidly dressed than he. Yet, by their deference and
that of my captor, I guessed him to be a great nobleman.
And when I came to look into his face there was such strength
and authority therein that I was not surprised when I learned
this was no other than the Sultan Saladin himself. For there
came an interpreter who told me that this was he, and said to
me, furthermore, 'Well does the Sultan know you are not the
king of England. Therefore, say whom you be and why you
did cry out that you were the king, for which cause you were
taken? To which I replied that I was the liegeman of King
Richard, and that fearing the king would be captured I had
diverted the assault to myself. I saw that when this was told
to the Sultan in his own tongue, he nodded and smiled. I
thought him none so ill-looking a man, for we had supposed
him ugly and grim as the devil his master, but he appeared in
truth very kingly, and more so than some I have seen, as for
example the king of France. Thus I began to look for
clemency at his hands rather than instant death. I was then
asked whether I was of noble birth, or base born, and I
replied that my father was Seneschal of Courtebarbe and I
myself of knightly blood. There ensued some debate amongst
the unbelievers, after which my captor, bowing low to the
Sultan and kissing of his hands, beckoned to me and said, in
French, 'Come.' He led me out of the tent and we went
through the camp to another pavilion where he made me
sit down upon the ground and summoned one who brought
flat cakes of bread, bowls of fruit, and water mixed with the

petals of flowers. Then, in few and broken words of French,
he made me understand that I was his prisoner and would
be held to ransom. His name, he told me, was Ahmad
Abd ed-Din ibn Yusuf, but that he was called el Emeen,
which I preferred as being shorter and easier to remember.

He bade me say whether, as a knight, I should prefer to
give my parole not to escape, and thus have a measure of
freedom, or to be shut up in prison and close guarded, and I
swiftly gave him my word. Nor did I wish to escape, being
content to sit idle or walk about their camp and have naught
to do but bide what might come. Ever in my mind were two
thoughts, one of Arthur, which was woesome and sorrowful,
and the other Why, when, I had determined to slay the king
and myself, I had instead saved his life and now was content
to be still alive? I turned over and over the question, had he
indeed kept me by him that night knowing he would thus
leave Arthur defenceless? Or was it for love of me and naught
else? And how came I to submit to his embraces and find a
loathely pleasure therein? But this last thought I put by.

So I passed some days in that camp, neither keeping track
of the time nor caring what I did. I saw little of el Emeen
who rode out each day to raid my own people. I learned that
he was the son of the Sultan's great-nephew, who was called
Mejed ed-Din, and it was clear that, although he was young,
he was a prince and held in much esteem among the infidels,
and many greeted him whenever he walked about, bowing
and putting their fingers to their breasts and lips, as is their
custom.

At last, one day, it chanced that el Emeen returned from
the business he was upon, and at the close of day called me
and bade me sit down and eat with him. They set before us
platters of lamb and rice and sweetmeats of all sorts, and to
drink we had cups of sherbet, which is water thickened with
fruit and sweetened, and also a very mild sort of wine, for it
appears the followers of Mahound are not permitted by their
religion to drink wine, but this they circumvent by putting
dried grapes or dates into water and letting them ferment a
little; they call this *nebeed*, not wine, and so allow it. In this,
it may be seen, as in other ways, they are not so unlike us,
for on my life I have seen monks who baptize beef into
Lenten fish, and wear haircloth of fine linen.

Afterwards, el Emeen called in one of his servants who spoke some French and thus we could converse more at our ease. And first he asked me whether I was content in all things or lacked aught for my comfort. And when I said I was well content, he began to ask me what my country was and how I lived there. Then I made known to him that I was a trouvère, at which he struck his hands together and exclaimed that it was a delight to him to hear it, for he was himself a poet. He began at once to declaim some of his poetry to me, which, being in their language I could but smile blankly at, nor could the interpreter put it into aught but the most simple of words. Yet I could guess even by some of these that he was not inferior to many poets whose works I have heard in our own land, and who, indeed, would be the better for being rendered into a language none could understand. El Emeen cut short the interpreter with a laugh, and said he would not force me to listen to this lame and blunted version. Then I told him of my travels, and of how I had come on crusade with King Richard, and of Arthur, my friend, and his death. And all this I did because he was of about Arthur's age and my own, and listened to me with great attentiveness and sympathy, and also because I had been silent long and found comfort in speech. When I had done, he said that it seemed to him I should not mourn my friend, for to his mind Arthur had died in such wise as he would himself pray to do, holding fast by his oath and keeping his honour pure. And, looking upon me with large and lustrous eyes, he said further, 'If your friend had broken his oath and had fought with that other knight and slain him, would you have loved him more? For he would have been shamed and blackened, and would not have desired to live. If he had fallen in battle against us, having sworn to your king to follow him, he would have lost his life in pursuance of his oath and nothing less. It is the will of God that all men must die, and it seems to me that a good death is better than an ill life. Or how say you?' I felt lightened by his speech, but said that I felt I would have mourned less if Arthur had died in battle, whereas here it seemed to me that he had perished for a foolish quarrel not of his making. On this, el Emeen, smiling within his black beard, replied, 'Nay, if a man defend his faith there is no folly in it. More courage did it take for him to hold by his oath in the face of insult than to fall in hot blood by an enemy sword.' And when he said this I felt the tears come to my eyes, but my heart was easier than it had been for many a day. Little did I look to come by such comfort from one of God's foes, yet so it was.

Somewhat more we spoke, and all that the infidel said I found much to my taste, and to say truth had he not been a follower of the Evil One I would have liked him well. He told me also that my ransom had been fixed at two hundred gold bezants, and that this low sum had been set because he had taken a liking to me and had so urged it upon the Sultan. When I heard this, I grew downcast, although I let him see none of this but thanked him for his courtesy, yet it is clear to me that I have little hope of ever finding a tenth of that sum. El Emeen said also that ransoms must wait upon the end of hostilities, or else on some occasion when it is agreed that prisoners should be exchanged, but, said he, he felt sure that my lord the king must love me well both for my poetry and for my action in offering myself to be captured in his stead, and so I would not wait long for release. But I, who know Richard full well, know that he will never pay out two hundred gold bezants for me. Nay, he will feel he is well rid of me and has no need now to cheer me, or talk to me of Arthur's death, or look into my eyes to see his own guilty part in it. And as for poetry, for all his love of it he cannot pay his knights with poems, and thus the gold will outweigh my song. And although I care not much at present whether I stay here or go, yet I know that to be a prisoner for long years is not within my power to be joyful at, but restlessness and irritation for me, who have wandered footloose so long.

Some few days after this, el Emeen said to me that we would leave the camp and return to Jerusalem. For, said he, his father Mejed ed-Din was commanded by the Sultan to go thither and see to the defences of the city. Accordingly, the tents were struck and we rode a day's journey to a town among the hills, where we spent the night, and by the next evening we came to the city of Jerusalem which sits upon a height and looks not at all as I had imagined. For thinking of such cities as I had seen, and especially London and Paris, I had thought it would be great and fair, with golden gates and pure walls and palaces and such glories of gold and silver and painting and carving as would become our Lord's stronghold. But I found it to be a place of narrow, mean streets, of shuttered houses, of great filth and stench, and what palaces there are—and this one I live in is surely of great splendour—far outnumbered by hovels. Yet it has great fine walls, very strong, with fair gates in them, and there are spires and round domes of cunning workmanship and may colours, and here, too, I saw many camels, which is a beast humped of his back, with an evil face and disposition, and it is said of him that he never needs to drink water and thus is good to fare in deserts. Within Jerusalem, upon the southern side near the walls, el Emeen has a great house and here we lodged. When we came to it we saw but stern walls with frowning gates, but when we went within I beheld that which reminded me with a sudden pang of the words of Pons of Capduoil, for here was a courtyard with a garden and a pool set in the midst, and all about arcades with pillars and arches, and above, in the upper stories, fretted windows and carved stonework. But where I looked to see naked maidens, there came out women whose faces and bodies were covered in heavy white robes so that all that might be seen of them were their eyes.

I was given a room in an upper corner, very pleasant, with two windows that looked forth over the city and a soft bed with cushions of down, but there are no chairs or benches, for among the Saracens all sit upon the floor on carpets. I was given water to bathe in, and fresh garments of the heathenish kind to wear whilst my own clothes were taken from me to be washed. At sunset, as ever, the infidels said their prayers, with much crying out and mumbling, all kneeling together, or lying flat, or standing up, and only then did we go in to dine. For, as I was told, this is their month called Ramadan which is a most holy time for them, and no man may eat from sunrise to sunset. When we had dined of spicy-flavoured foods which I liked well, el Emeen called before us a maiden who bore with her a stringed instrument, like a round covered bowl of wood with a long neck or handle to it. This he called *al-ood*. She sat down before us and he bade her play on it, which she did very deftly, her fingers leaping upon the strings of the neck while with her other hand she plucked them lower down. The music was brisk and twangling, not at all ill to hear, but when she sang to it, although her voice

313

was sweet enough, it was as the braying of donkeys to my ears, or as the wailing of their priest calling them to their orisons.

Now this maiden was not veiled, but dressed in a kind of tight-waisted, long-skirted coat beneath which she wore full pantaloons of white cloth, the which struck oddly upon my eye. Her feet were bare, the soles painted red, and her hair, the colour of a chestnut horse, was covered by a round, small cap embroidered in gold thread. When she had done playing and singing, el Emeen said somewhat which she translated into excellent French, although with an accent unfamiliar to me: 'The prince asks you, sir, how like you my music?' I said, in surprise, 'Well do you speak my tongue,' on which she replied, 'Wherefore should I not? Seeing that it is mine, also.' El Emeen then smiled, and said, pointing to her, 'She is also Frank.' She then told me that her father had been a knight of Outremer, holding land within the fief of Greater Gerin, near to Nazareth, that very city wherein our Lord dwelt and laboured as a guildsman. But when Saladin came into the land and cast out our people, this fief was over-run and conquered and her father and mother lost their lives, and she herself, a girl of twelve, was taken captive. She was sold to Mejed ed-Din, who gave her to his son since she was pleasing in her ways and played well upon the *ood*, and spoke the language of the Saracens as well as her own tongue, having learned it from her nurse. She had been taught to write beautifully in their script so that her value as a slave should increase, and also to sing, dance, and perform some leechcraft, and to say by heart many verses of their holy writ which they call Koran. Nor, she added, did el Emeen take her to his bed more than once or twice, since his wives satisfied him more perfectly in that way. 'His wives?' said I. 'Yea,' she answered, 'he has two and is allowed four by their religion if he wishes it.' 'Where then are they?' I asked. 'He keeps them in a separate part of the palace,' said she, 'nor may any man behold them. Also, he may have maid servants as many as he wishes. Yet, although he is fond of me, he finds my fair skin and blue eyes repulsive.' All this I thought most strange.

Then she played and sang again and a restlessness came upon my spirit, and when she had done I reached out and took the *ood* from her. Striking the strings, I saw that it was not unlike a vielle as to fingering, and like a harp as to plucking, and soon found several chords. Then I began to sing one of my own *canzos*, that one which goes:

> 'I may not ever fly from love
> Though love itself shuns me,
> Between my heart and my desire
> I am consumed in this sweet fire,
> By death alone set free.' etc.

When I had ended, rapt in my music and solaced by it somewhat, I saw that the maiden was weeping. El Emeen spoke to her gently, and she replied to him, then saying to me, 'I have told him that I weep for the beauty of the song and for hearing my own tongue sung again. Now the prince asks me to translate it for him. I have said that it will be difficult. Forgive me, sir, for I must fail to do it justice.'

She proceeded to speak at length in the tongue of the infidels, whilst el Emeen, his cheek on his hand, listened, nodding. Then he said to me in his broken French, 'Good. It is very good. I see that you have brought tears to her eyes. This I have done also when my songs are good.' And bending forward to me, he said, 'Tell me, how long since you had a woman?' I replied, a great while. He smiled, clapping his hands, and said, 'Very well. I give you this one.'

I thanked him but said that I would not take her save if it was her will, for although she was no more than a slave so far as he was concerned, she was French and of noble blood, which made some difference to me. 'How say you, Leila?' then asked el Emeen, and the maid bent her head saying that if it was her lord's wish she would be well content to serve me.

That night, therefore, I took her to my bed but got little joy of her for first we spoke together and I asked her how she liked living among the unbelievers, and she replied that they used her well enough but that she mourned for her parents, slain these five years, and that it was lamentable a misfortune to be a slave especially to her who had slaves of her own and had been cherished and loved as a child, and although they had not forced her to become a follower of Mahound yet it was a sorrow to her never to see a priest or receive our Lord's body, and so on and so forth with sobs and tears so that my desire went out of me, and I bade her take her coverlet and sleep in a corner.

On the next night, however, when we were alone again, she begged me as a boon that I should sing to her. I made shift with the *ood* to accompany myself, she teaching me some chords, and sang her three or four *canzos* and *dansas*. These melted her and made her more affectionate and thus we passed the night in embraces, and more to my taste was her sweet-scented and compliant flesh than the rough camps of war.

I began, therefore, to live from day to day, putting out of my mind all thought of the past, either of Arthur or of the king, and beginning to look about, to eat and drink with more relish, to find curiosity awakening in me, to converse with el Emeen and others, and to find life none so ill. And I began to think of poetry as well. I wondered of what sort the poetry of the Saracens was and felt a great desire to know how it was written and by what laws, and thought to myself that here, it might be, I would learn another sort of song and perchance come to my goal of making a poem different from any made before. Through Leila (for thus the Saracens called her, although her name was indeed Ysabella de Noriz) I spoke with el Emeen, asking him of these matters. He began to tell me of metaphors, of meters and rhymes, of such things as they call *tawil* and *basit*, of four-line stanzas and six-line stanzas, and very soon I saw that we should go nowhere unless I could speak somewhat of their tongue. He agreed, laughing, and said, 'True is that word, for otherwise what is the meaning of a poem, save to say that it is love, or the dawn, or a mistress's arms, or unrequited desire. But no more sense of the poem will you have than that. How delicate and splendid, as a piece of jewelled carving, to hear the form called *mustazad*, in which are blended skilful rhymes with a meter in which each second line has but half the syllables of the one before, but if I ask Leila to translate the words for you, they are but words: "Alas, my love, we must part for the day appears and the sky grows red . . . and so on."' When he said this, I began to laugh in my turn, and sang:

'Why must the nightingale so soon depart,
And we our scented hawthorn bower fly?
The sun's first ray strikes sadness to my heart,
Ah, love, farewell; the dawn invades the sky.'

And never looked I to be singing it under such circumstances.
And when Leila had interpreted for me, el Emeen appeared
much pleased. So I asked that Leila should teach me the
Saracen tongue, and el Emeen replied, 'Much would it
grieve me to lose your companionship, for as God lives I like
you almost as well as if you were one of the Faithful, but I
hope you will not remain a prisoner so long as that will
require. Yet much joy will it give me if you should learn my
speech for thus we may speak of poetry and song together,
and of many other matters as well.'

And now I come to tell of one of the greatest of wonders,
which befell yesterday, and you shall know why I write once
more in this journal. For as I sat about mid-morning with
Leila practising how to play upon the *ood* there came one to
summon me before el Emeen, and when I came thither to his
hall wherein he sat to do justice (and which they call diwan)
I found none other than Giraud, harp and all, standing
before him. Who, when he saw me, fell upon his knees
crying, 'God save you, master,' what while I stood gaping
like one stricken in his brains. At last, coming to myself, I
raised him up and embraced him all that he was dirty and
travel-stained. Then they told me that he had been captured
wandering in the hills, and had been brought before the
Sultan. And impudent as he was, Giraud had smiled
instead of showing fear. When they asked him why he did so,
he replied that he had at first expected the Sultan to put him
to death, but on beholding his face knew he was merciful
and would not do so when he had heard his tale. The Sultan
was much pleased at this (for it is accounted a virtue among
the infidels to show mercy, they speaking of their God as
The Compassionate One) and commanded him to tell his
story, whereupon Giraud said he was searching for his master
who had been taken captive while defending the English
king. Hearing this, the Sultan exclaimed, 'Would that I had
a thousand such servants, for then not one handsbreadth of
my land would the Franks take from me,' and finding out

my name gave order that Giraud should be brought to me in Jerusalem. El Emeen also was loud in his praise and said that it was written in their Scripture that God loves the steadfast, and that Giraud should remain with me and be clothed and fed, and for his loyalty gave him a piece of silver.

And when I had taken Giraud apart to my own chamber I inquired of him why he had determined to follow me, whereupon he replied that he had no more fear of the great Devil Mahound and his followers than of those who pretended to be Christians but were no more than devils indeed, and that one place was very like another to him. And after some further talk of this sort, he added, sulkily, that he had as lief sing for me as for any other, and that as he had been beaten for his sins in all the great cities of the world he might as well be beaten in Holy Jerusalem. I said that I was right glad to see him and so left the matter. I asked of him also concerning King Richard, and he said that the king had spoken highly of my putting myself in his place to be captured, and had sworn that some day he would ransom me cost it never so much, but I who knew Richard's 'some day' knew that he was glad to be so cheaply rid of me. This made me more certain than ever that he had kept me by him so that Fitz-Maurice might come to Arthur unopposed, for sure if Arthur would not have fought with him I would have done so. And the ugly thought came also to my mind that when he invited me to come with him hawking that day, it might have been that he intended to have me slain. But this thought I put by, reminding myself of what poor Hugh de Hamelincourt had once said, that kings never lie as other men do, but conceal, evade, and equivocate, and thus come by their goals in devious ways.

So am I resigned to remain here among the unbelievers. Giraud sold all my possessions and has brought me some few marks of silver, but what I prize more, all this manuscript of my journal. We are snug enough, with my minstrel sleeping across my door and this fair wench for a bed-mate, and much to do and learn. Last night, before ever we slept, so that I might cut the tie with what is past and done with, I gave to Leila the golden chain studded with crystal which once Lady Maude gave to me, and this I did because she has well comforted me. But Arthur's little cross I still wear for I

318

may no more take it from my neck than tear him out of my memory.

*   *   *

Winter closed in with drizzling cold mists, rain and sleet, with snow on the mountain peaks and a biting wind that sliced through quilted gambesons, chain mail, and surcoats as if they had been so much gauze. The English king's position was now precarious: in addition to the worsening weather he faced defections on the part of his army, desertions to the relative ease of Acre, and, most difficult of all to cope with, an attitude of pessimism and reluctance on the part of many of his councillors. Characteristically, Richard took the offensive. He began by moving the army into the field once more, ordering them to repair and refortify the villages or castles which commanded the road between Jaffa and Jerusalem: St. George, Ramla, Château des Plains, and Maen. There was some opposition from the enemy, and one or two pitched battles on a small scale. At the same time, the king reopened negotiations with Saladin and this time came up with a set of proposals for peace which, if they had been carried through, would have established the most astonishing precedent in history.

Richard's terms were that his sister, Queen Joanna of Sicily, should marry the Sultan's brother, el-Melek el-'Adel, whom the Christians called Safadin. These two would be enthroned in Jerusalem as its rulers, with the cities of Acre, Jaffa, and Ascalon given by Richard, and the lands between the Jordan and the sea given by Saladin to make their kingdom. The True Cross would be returned to the crusaders, all prisoners set free on both sides, and Richard would go home in triumph, having established a joint and lasting government of Mohammedan and Christian and brought peace to the Holy Land.

Naturally, however, so reasonable a solution had no chance whatever of being reached. Joanna was infuriated at the thought of being wed to a Saracen, no matter how noble and chivalrous he was said to be, and el-'Adel, for some reason, refused to become a Christian. The councillors on both sides were indignant or simply amused. Richard did not lose heart. He wrote to the Sultan: "I admire your sincerity and desire your friendship. You said that you would give your brother all the districts on the sea-coast, and I am anxious that you

319

should judge between him and me in the division of the land. But we must absolutely have part of the city of Jerusalem. . . . As for the marriage, all Christians cry out against me for thinking of marrying my sister to a Moslem without the permission of the Pope. I am sending an ambassador to him, and I shall have an answer in six months. . . . It is my wish that you should divide the land in such a way that your brother shall be acquitted of blame by the Moslems, and that I shall incur no reproach from my people." It was a frank and generous letter, and the Sultan received it with promises that it should be considered in the same spirit. Immediately afterwards, turning to his confidante, the learned Beha ed-Din, Chief Justice of the Army, he said, "If we make peace with these people there is nothing to protect us against their treachery. The best thing to do is to continue the Holy War until we have either driven them all from the coast, or we ourselves die in the attempt." On his side, Richard began leading his army towards Ramla where he set up his winter quarters with every intention of pressing on to take Jerusalem if he could.

Thus, in an atmosphere of mutual good will, Christmas approached. Richard marched on the fortress town of Beit Nuba, high in the hills. Rain mixed with hail beat down upon the host, and some of the hailstones were large enough to do almost as much damage as sling-stones. The wind and rain increased; tents and pegs were whirled out of the ground, provisions were ruined, and armour and weapons were thick with rust. The threadbare gambesons and jackets of the soldiers, many times mended, dissolved in the wet. Horses fell down under their riders and died in the icy mud. In spite of all, Richard pressed on, sometimes far in advance of his main body with only a handful of his boldest knights and a Syrian guide to keep him company. One day, coming into a pass among the peaks, he saw far off the glimmer of white walls on another, distant hill. "Jerusalem," said the guide. It was the nearest Richard was to come to his goal.

Early in January, the chief knights of the Temple and the Hospital, most of them residents of Outremer and familiar with the land, urged Richard to turn back. Ascalon should be rebuilt and held, they said, to prevent the passage of the infidel to the sea, and to consolidate the coast. The army council, disheartened by the weather and the slowness of their progress, agreed. Richard was forced to give in. Three days after the feast of the Epiphany he returned to Jaffa.

If the council had known how dismal things were on the Saracen side, they might have decided otherwise. The Sultan had withdrawn to Jerusalem with most of his troops, and now provisions began to run short, while the weather prevented caravans from getting through to them. Worn out by ceaseless campaigning, the emirs departed, taking their soldiers out of the mountains. Melting snow flooded the countryside, and cattle, bogged in the mud, perished and rotted.

But the springtime came at last; the ground dried, the gardens bloomed, kids frisked on the hillsides, birds sang and cooed in the thickets, skirmishes began once more between parties of Saracens and Christians, and Richard began fresh negotiations with Saladin, this time writing: "We consent to the division of the country: each side shall keep what they now hold, and if one side has more than the half that is their just share, they shall give the other side a proper concession." Needless to say, nothing came of this; it was simply another sign of reawakening life, like the stirring of sap in the winter-stricken trees.

On one of the gentle slopes outside the northern walls of the Holy City straw butts had been set up for archery practice, but as it was yet early in the day only two men were shooting. They wore loose tunics with their left sleeves bound up in leather bracers, and small, round turbans to keep the hair out of their eyes. The slenderer of the two, lithe and dark-skinned, was named Abd-Allah ibn Zayd, captain of the *halka* of bowmen of el Emeen; the other, a heavy-boned, thickset man, was nick-named Toz-Koparan, or the Dust Raiser. They were both Seljuk Turks, from Harran in the north.

They shot slowly and leisurely, cursing their misses in the traditional manner of archers all over the world and in every century, making excuses for a slipped serving, a loose fletching, or the fact that the warm sun had softened their bows. Neither believed the other's excuses; they were old friends.

"By God, and by God," said Abd-Allah, after a plucked loose which missed the golden centre of the target face by half an inch, "the wind took that one."

"I know. The wind of your complaining," said Toz-

Koparan. "You should learn to shoot more slowly. I've never liked the *ihtilash* method of snap-shooting. God is great! That was a pretty shot." His arrow had thumped into the dead centre. "I talked that one in. Let's move back twenty paces. This is too easy."

"Your mother was a hybrid camel," said Abd-Allah, without rancour. "I'll move back if you'll go pull my shafts for me. It is too warm to walk that far."

Nevertheless, he went with his friend to draw the arrows and then they paced off a hundred and twenty strides and turned to shoot again. As they nocked their shafts, Toz-Koparan said, "Look yonder, down on the path. Isn't that our beloved master, el Emeen?"

"Yes, it is. With that Frankish knight Cordebar. That's the Kurds for you. That son of a lame she-dog! No Seljuk would ever let himself become so friendly with one of the atheistical devils."

"Two hundred and eighty paces if it's an inch," said Toz-Koparan, dreamily. "If we shot and missed the target, our arrows would drop right down that slope and hit them both. Who slays the infidel lays up treasure for himself in heaven. Isn't that what the Imam always says?"

"Our dear master isn't an infidel," Abd-Allah protested.

"Of course not. But he's a Kurd, isn't he? And we are Seljuks. The horse-piss and the fire."

"Yes, that's true," Abd-Allah sighed. "Still, he's a good master and a fine upstanding lad."

"He certainly is. I'd send my best Frank-killer through the gizzard of any man who says otherwise. But he's a Kurd! It's a matter of principle, Abd-Allah. And a man must live by principles. We'd better hurry. They'll be out of sight around the bend in a minute."

They drew their bows, laying their bodies well in behind the handle, opening the stiff recurved arcs smoothly from long practice until the fingertips of their right hands touched their shoulders. Then they loosed. But they had waited a little too long. A gentle breeze had sprung up. Their arrows soared high, wavered slightly at the top of their trajectory, and thumped into the road at the heels of Denys and el Emeen.

"Camel dung!" growled Toz-Koparan.

Abd-Allah was already running down the slope, shouting,

"Who is that? Son of an accursed Jinni, what do you mean by walking behind the butts? You might have been killed!" Then his voice changed, and he fell to his knees. "It is the prince, Ahmad ibn Yusuf. God is merciful. Come, Toz-Koparan, give thanks that God prevented our bad shots from harming our beloved master."

El Emeen shook his head, looking at his grovelling archers. "Oh, you offspring of disastrous marriages," he said, in a kindly tone, "how could you miss the butts by so much? Is this how you will slay infidels? What sort of archers have I in my bodyguard?"

"Forgive us, master," said Abd-Allah. "We were practising. . . . Just before we loosed our shafts, a crow flew overhead and Toz-Koparan, who is, as you know, boastful, bet me that I couldn't hit it. We both tried for it, and in the same instant saw you and your guest—two strangers as we thought —walking on the road below, but it was too late. Who can hold back the flight of an arrow?"

"Go, you are forgiven," said el Emeen. "Next time, look more carefully before you shoot."

The two salaamed and ran off, snickering under their breath like schoolboys. El Emeen turned away, smiling.

"Did you believe that stuff about the crow?" asked Denys. His Arabic was fairly good, after a whole winter of little else to do but practise language and the lute, and he had been able to follow almost all that had been said.

"Of course not," said the prince, as they continued their stroll. "But a good leader knows when to pretend to believe what he is told. They make an attempt on my life about once every six months, but I suspect that their hearts are not in it. They are loyal fellows and love me, you see, and they enjoy serving under me."

"Why do they do it, then?"

"They are Seljuks, my friend. I, like my father's illustrious great-uncle Salah ed-Din, am of Kurdish descent. They consider us tyrants; we consider them barbarians."

"I see. And which is right?"

"Both, naturally." El Emeen twisted the point of his beard between thumb and finger. "It is the will of God that men should have some reason for their quarrels, and I suppose one will serve as well as another."

Denys said, with a chuckle, "It seems to me that you infidels blame everything on the will of God."

"Is it not the same with you?" asked el Emeen, in surprise. "Surely you justify whatever you do by saying it is God's will. That, I know, is the battle-cry of the Frankish knights: 'God wishes it!'"

"That's true, of course, but I suppose what we'd say is that God directs us towards his City, but what paths we choose to get there are our own affair."

"It is the same with us. In whatever we do there appears to be a choice, but the real choice lies in our intentions. We may will what we please, but we act as God has predestined for us."

"In everything?"

"We say, God has decreed five things for his servants: length of life, actions, dwelling places, travels, and portions."

"That seems to cover just about everything."

"And it is written, 'God tasks no soul beyond its scope. For it *is* only that which it has earned, and has against it only that which it has deserved.'"

"That's comforting." Denys's lip twisted. "Your faith seems to take the responsibility for our actions out of our hands. How happy people are who believe themselves to be right! As for me, I don't know what I believe. Not any longer."

"You are still thinking of your friend's death. You believe yourself to be responsible. But your friend could not act in any other way, don't you see that? Whether you had been with him or not, on that night or any other, his death would have come to him in the same way. He was what he was. It was God's decree. God planted in him the seed of right behaviour, which he then nourished and cultivated for himself."

"Oh—God!" Denys said. He stopped in the centre of the road, his hands behind his back, and stared at el Emeen. "Where is this God, then? What is he? The creator of this world? Then that fool Giraud is right, and he is only the Devil after all. From the birth of Adam he has played us false. I remember the hermit's doubts—did God know that Adam and Eve would eat the fruit of knowledge, or didn't he? Why, the answer is simple. It was a trap, as all the fine promises are traps. Right behaviour, moral rectitude, honour, justice,

love, and all the rest of it—the rotten embroidery over the Pit.
Giraud was right; of all people, Giraud! We are all liars, in
the same boat. And God——?" He bit his lip. "Perhaps he's
nothing but a lie as well. God created Man in his own image.
And Man has been returning the compliment ever since.
Whatever God may have been, he's the reflection of Mankind
now: proud, arrogant, piously hypocritical, with a taste for
bloodshed."

He stopped and shrugged. "You always listen so patiently,
Ahmad. The fact is, I used to believe in the human virtues
and now I'm not even sure I believe in the heavenly ones."

The Moslem regarded him sympathetically. "What *is* it
that's troubling you, my friend?" he said. "The discovery that
men are capable of wickedness?"

"Oh, no, not at all. I am just beginning to wonder whether
God is capable of wickedness. What if we've been deceived?
The good things wither, or turn out to be hollow and false.
The man who really holds to his principles is betrayed by his
friend, and dies. Parents destroy their children; kings crush
their vassals and reward homage with treachery. But that isn't
what most gnaws at me. No, I ask myself, *does it matter?* Does
it really matter? Perhaps there's nothing, either before or
afterward. Perhaps we should pray to the Devil, and open our
hands to our lusts—seize our pleasures, bite, tear, destroy
each other and go crashing down into darkness together."

El Emeen was silent for a long time. At last he said, "I cannot answer you. But it may be that I know someone who can
give you more comfort than I. He has comforted me in the
past. Since we set out to take a walk, would you like to walk
a little further, up to the Mount of Olives?"

"Why not?"

The prince led him down the slope, following a goat track,
until they had passed beyond the angle of the walls. Here the
land dropped steeply and they scrambled down to a rivulet in
the valley bottom which they crossed on stepping stones, and
then they began to ascend the hill opposite the city.

"There," said el Emeen, as they passed a small enclosure in
which grew eight thick-trunked, ancient olives, "is the garden
in which it is said that the excellent prophet Jesus was given
over to the soldiers. This whole place is full of his doings. As
for this Mount, on the Last Day a wire will be suspended from

here to the Dome of the Chain, in Jerusalem. All men must cross over it. Jesus will sit upon the end which is in the city, and Mohammed on the end at the Mount. Good men will cross, and the wicked will fall from the wire into that valley below."

He glanced sidelong at Denys and was relieved to see him smile once again. They climbed on, up to the highest of the four summits which made up the range of the Mount of Olives. Here there was a tiny village of huts surrounding a small mosque where, said el Emeen, was kept a stone bearing the imprint of Jesus's foot. From this very spot he had ascended to heaven. They passed on without stopping and began to go down the other side of the mountain. A little way below the summit there was a rocky cliff, not very high, with a wide shelf of reddish soil at its base on which grew a few stunted trees. A narrow path led from above, around the cliff-face to this shelf. When they had half-climbed, half-fallen down this, Denys saw that the rocky face was full of holes, some only large enough for birds, some like low doorways, and one at the bottom twice the height of a man. From one of the upper holes a thin, shining stream of water trickled down the cliff into a small round pool near the large opening and thence out again to vanish over the edge of the shelf. By the pool there was a statue of a seated man carved from some dark-brown wood, so skilfully that it almost looked alive. It came to Denys as a shock that it *was* alive.

He was naked, except for a cloth about his loins. His extreme leanness had nothing of starvation about it but rather a look of fineness as if all excess had been stripped from him. A sparse, silky beard, pure white, showed that he was not young, but there were few lines in his face—or rather, when Denys looked a second time, he saw that the face was a meshwork of tiny wrinkles which absorbed all lines of age. His hair was concealed by a faded green turban. He sat on the ground with his legs crossed and his hands in his lap, his eyes lowered, utterly motionless, without even a rise and fall of his chest to show that he was breathing.

El Emeen squatted before him and, after a moment, so did Denys. They waited for what seemed a very long time, and Denys thought to himself that perhaps time had a different flow for that silent figure. At last, however, the head lifted and the eyes were fastened upon the two: mild, dark eyes which reflected the light like pools of ink.

El Emeen said to Denys, "This is the Sufi, Nasif al-Akhras."

"Peace be with you," said the Sufi, in a surprisingly deep and resonant voice.

"With you also, peace," replied Denys.

Looking at el Emeen, the Sufi said, "Your father forbade you to visit me again."

"My friend's need was great," the prince answered.

The Sufi nodded slightly. "And I see that he is a Frank. The heart takes different shapes," he said. "Come nearer, young man. How are you called?"

"Denys de Courtebarbe."

"Do you know that the Orthodox, such as this man's father, detest those of us who follow the Tasawwuf?"

"I know nothing, not even that word you just used."

"No man knows nothing," said the Sufi, "for we are all part of God and partake of his knowledge. Words are veils between ourselves and knowing. Give me your hand."

Denys did so. The old man's hand was dry, cool, muscular, and scaly, like the body of a reptile, but it awoke no repugnance.

"You are a prisoner of war?" the Sufi said.

"I am the prisoner of this prince."

"I see that you are troubled. Well, question me."

Denys blinked. "Tell me," he began, and then couldn't think what to ask. At the same time, a dozen questions flooded his mind: Am I guilty of Arthur's death? he wanted to say, and, Do I owe Richard fealty? Why do I feel myself still bound to him? Shall I stay here among my enemies or escape and return to the king? "Tell me——" he said again, and fell silent, staring at the old man's eyes. Serenity came upon him, and the turmoil in him dropped away. It was quiet here, and peaceful, with only the steady pouring of water down the stone to emphasize the silence. The warm air was like a bath of wine upon the skin.

The Sufi said, as if musing, "God has no form. And yet he has many forms. He is beyond form. But it is in man that he sees himself and makes himself known. Man is the eye through which God beholds his creations."

"I can't believe you," Denys said, but dreamily. "If that is so, how God must weep when he looks through that eye."

"Both tears and laughter are his. Why should they not be? Did he not make both honey and salt? Look at me. I will show you where God is."

Denys looked.

The face of the Sufi appeared to be surrounded and pierced by sharp corruscations, like the dazzle which is seen when one squeezes one's eyes tight shut. It began to grow larger, filling Denys's vision from horizon to horizon. He looked, as it were, at the surface of a planet, brown-earthed and pitted with craters among which grew slender silvery hairs like grasses. Then he had plunged within.

There lay about him on every side huge, grey transparent objects in uncountable masses, nourished by fluids in which swarmed strange beings. Multitudes of lives were there, pressed together in communal warmth, eyeless, featureless, simple, and yet unutterably complex. Thousands of delicate shapes, each with its transparent rind, containing a living liquid, palpitating to the pulse of the blood and breath: some, calcareous as cliffs, made up the bone, some the soft tissues, some in rustling stria the muscles, one anchored to another, all interwoven with the strands of nerves which, in their turn, were compounded of lithe living things.

The Sufi's voice spoke. "Meditating upon the wonder of man, I turned my eyes inward. See—of this is every man made."

"Every man?"

"All men, all beasts, all that moves and breathes and has being."

The cellular masses grew larger, expanded and rushed towards him and about him. He hung within them, in immense space, where eyes found nothing to see and the senses no longer operated. But other senses made him aware of vast tinglings, of the motion of essences, of a vibration like that produced by lightning. This space itself was not empty but full of rhythm; it pulsated to the hurtling charge through it of titanic forces, unseen, unrecognizable. And this motion, this commingling of forces, was, Denys realized, itself a kind of life, forever in being, changing endlessly, self-destroying and yet the very substance of self-renewal. Infinitely large, this whole universe lay within the infinitely tiny tissues, itself impalpable: being, but not-being.

"It is——?" said Denys.

"All things alive and dead, breath itself, the earth, the stars, all that we know. Nothing random is in this, but harmony and law. All, once set in motion, endlessly continuing, some day doomed to stillness. But from that very stillness, a new gathering: pressures, heat, weight, a new crucible, another birth of motion."

"Then we are all alike in this?"

"All alike, all unimaginably diverse. God has no form, has many forms, and is beyond form."

It seemed to Denys that he came hurtling back across space, through multitudes of years. He opened his eyes and saw that he was sitting in the same place, his hand still held by that of the Sufi, who was smiling.

After a bit, Denys asked, "Was I asleep and dreaming?"

"Are you now awake?" replied the Sufi.

Denys got slowly to his feet. He felt cold and stiff.

"Thank you," he said. "I suppose, now, like the Archangel Gabriel, I ought to go fishing."

To his astonishment, the Sufi said, "Not so. That was the answer to his question, but not yours. Yours is another kind of search; yours will be another kind of finding."

"You know——?" Denys began.

"Why are you surprised? Did I not say we all partake of One knowledge. I, too, have my own seeking and my own finding."

He lowered his eyes and sat as he had when first they came. El Emeen touched Denys's arm, and together they began the steep ascent, without another word.

For a while Denys held within himself the precious memory of that experience. But as they walked, it began to fade and disintegrate, and partly in the hope of restoring its reality he broke the silence.

"What did you see while I went on that journey?" he asked.

El Emeen said, "Journey? You moved closer to al-Akhras and he took your hand for an instant and smiled. Then you asked whether you had been dreaming."

"My God! It seemed to me that I went whirling . . . I can't describe it. I don't know what to say about it." He shrugged.

"Do you feel comforted?"

329

Denys rubbed his forehead. "I do, but I don't know why I
should. I don't understand what he meant, or what I felt.
That we are all one, or that God is harmony, or that there
isn't any good or evil. . . ." He began to flounder, trying to
find the proper words in Arabic. "Good Lord God!" he said,
lapsing into French. "The more I try to put it together, the
more it escapes me."

"What did you say?"

"What the Sufi said—words are veils between ourselves
and knowing. But I do feel some comfort. I suppose it's what
you infidels would call being resigned to one's fate."

El Emeen chuckled. They hurried through the tiny village
on the summit, and stood on its outskirts looking across the
valley at the sienna-coloured hill where the walls of Jerusalem
showed pale, crowned by gleaming domes.

"Tell me about him," Denys said, as they began the walk
down. "I used to know someone like him in another country.
He's a little crazy, isn't he?"

"I imagine he is. But then, anyone who chooses to live at
odds with the rest of us must be crazy. According to my father
he's a heretic and a free-thinker. But I think I prefer his
madness to the sanity of some I know."

"What is a Sufi? A hermit?"

"Some are hermits. Some live in the world. You know the
word *suf*—wool—those who follow the way of Tasawwuf
usually wear plain, coarse woollen cloaks. They are pious men
who believe that one should give up the vanities of the world
and search for God through meditation. But many good
Moslems hate them because their ways seem to teach that all
men are brothers. This would mean that we ought not to
destroy unbelievers, you see. Surely, you must have holy
men among your people who preach love and simplicity?
You know what happens to them. Neither theologians nor
civil authorities love them."

"Of course not. They would overthrow the foundations of
society if they had their way."

They smiled at each other in perfect understanding.

"Just so. The Sultan Salah ed-Din, may God preserve him,
only last year had a young Sufi named Suhraverdi strangled
and crucified for being a free-thinker and speaking out too
publicly about the mystical nature of God."

"And your Sufi——?"

"Al-Akhras? Well, you see, he only sits in the hills here and meditates. To those of us who seek him out, he gives some words of counsel. But he has no following—no disciples, and so he isn't considered dangerous, not at present."

"Then you wouldn't call yourself a disciple of his?"

"I?" El Emeen burst out laughing. "My dear friend, I am a soldier, a nobleman of Islam, busy with the Holy War and the administration of my household. I haven't time to be anyone's disciple, and I don't understand theology in any case. I am content to repeat, 'There is no God but God; Mohammed is the messenger of God.'"

Denys glanced at him. "You are a fraud," he said.

"Maybe I am," el Emeen said, good-humouredly. "I am also a man who loves the good things of life, and it's much pleasanter to be what you are expected to be, isn't it? Within, I can think what I like. I can speak freely to you because you are a foreigner, an unbeliever, and an enemy. And if all else fails, I can write poetry."

He glanced at the sun. "Nearly noon. Let's hurry. I prefer to pray in my own courtyard if possible, and after lunch I want to show you a new verse-form, the *tarji'-band*. It is beautifully intricate."

He began to stride along. Denys clutched once more, in his mind, at the vision he had had, the truth he had seemed for a moment to approach, but it was gone. He remembered only sitting before the Sufi and dreaming—something confused, fantastically strange.

"Are you coming?" called el Emeen.

Denys glanced over his shoulder at the heights, and then ran to catch up with the prince.

However, there was no time for poetry after all. For, as they were finishing their meal, a messenger arrived from el Emeen's father, who ruled the city for the Sultan. The prince excused himself and went off; he was gone for several hours and when he returned he looked grave. Denys was sitting on a bench in the garden plucking out a melody on his lute, and el Emeen sat down beside him.

"I have heard some news which will interest you," he said. "The marquis of Montferrat is dead."

Denys straightened. "Dead? There's an end to one of Richard's biggest problems. How did it happen?"

"He was stabbed to death by two young men as he was returning home from a dinner party. It's a very curious affair. The man who brought the word to my father says that the French claim the murderers were employed by King Richard. However, the king has denied having anything to do with the matter. It is being said that the young men were of the as-Hassani—you know the cult of Hassan?"

"I've heard of it. The Old Man of the Mountain, he's called, who hires assassins to kill people for him."

"It is not quite so simple. They are a religious order. Richard's supporters insist that the as-Hassani hated the marquis and have been plotting his death for a long time. In any case, you see, it is particularly suspicious that this should have happened just now because, first of all, the marquis has been dickering for a separate treaty of peace with the Sultan (may his name be exalted) and second, he has just been elected King of Jersualem."

"What?" cried Denys, in surprise. "But Guy of Lusignan was made king by the decision of the army council."

"Oh, yes, we know all about that. Here is what happened. Shortly after your festival of Easter, the prior of the abbey of Hereford came to Syria with letters informing King Richard that his brother, Emir John, had driven out the chancellor, forced the emirs of England to yield up the royal castles, and to do homage to him, and—worst of all—had laid hands on the exchequer. The prior urged Richard to return home or, said he, he might lose his kingdom.

"Richard called a council and laid the matter before them. They said at once that a new king should be elected who would be strong enough to lead your host and, given a choice between Guy of Lusignan and Conrad of Montferrat, the majority of them preferred the marquis. Richard didn't like this at all, apparently, but he sent off a delegation with Count Henry of Champagne at its head to summon the marquis to receive the crown of Jersualem. My distinguished father was particularly amused at the way in which this city, which we hold and in which, as you know, all the souls of Islam will assemble on the Last Day, has been handed back and forth among your people," he finished, drily.

"Yes, I see. And so, before the marquis could leave Tyre to become king, he very conveniently got himself assassinated," said Denys. "Now, I suppose, Guy of Lusignan has the crown."

"Oh, no. Count Henry of Champagne has been elected in the marquis's place. He has received Tyre, is to marry the marquis's widow, and through her is to be heir to the kingdom."

"Henry of Champagne—of course! A most satisfactory arrangement. I remember that when the king of France refused to loan him any money for his troops, at Acre, Richard made him a gift of money and provisions. From that time on, Count Henry served under England's banner. And what of poor Guy?"

"Not so poor. It is said that Richard is to give him the rich island of Cyprus to rule over."

Denys jumped up, striking the lute strings with a clang. "Marvellous!" he cried. "Oh, there never was a man like him! How does he do it? His enemy, Montferrat, the French king's friend, is dead. The council has chosen Count Henry, Richard's nephew and ally, to be king. Guy of Lusignan is effectively silenced. Everything has worked for Richard. As you infidels would say—God has decreed it."

El Emeen looked up at him with the ghost of a smile. "Then you think Richard had the marquis murdered?"

"I wouldn't doubt it. He is quite capable of doing anything at all to achieve his ends. He is a monster! A serpent! A— well, by God, he's a king, isn't he?"

"Certainly all of us admire him. The Sultan himself has called him the noblest and greatest of our enemies, and there isn't one of our emirs who does not fear him."

"And now? What will happen now?" Denys asked. "Is Richard going home to England?"

"There is no sign of it yet. On the contrary he has gathered his troops and has begun moving against our stronghold of ed-Darun, on the road to Jerusalem. My father thinks he is now pressed to end the war, either by furious assaults, or by doing his best to conclude a treaty of peace—or, of course, by both. Salah ed-Din has begun to recall his chieftains, and to prepare for battle. My father has commanded me to lead our own men to the Sultan's camp, since he himself must remain here in the city, as governor."

He stood up. "I'll have to go, my friend. I don't know when I shall return. Nothing is certain . . . except, of course, the will of God."

Denys stared at him. It had not occurred to him that this might happen: he had, in fact, completely forgotten that el Emeen would have to return into battle.

"When must you leave?" he asked, finding his voice uncertain and the words hard to say.

"As soon as I can arrange for the supply train and put the men in readiness. Two days, perhaps three."

Denys nodded.

"No more poetry," el Emeen said. He bit his lip. "Well, we have had a good winter together. And you have Leila and your minstrel. You won't be lonely."

"No."

"Perhaps the war will be over soon."

"Perhaps," said Denys. He could not trust himself to say more. At that moment he hated Richard and Saladin, Turk and Christian, the Holy War on both sides, all of mankind with its wars, intrigues, and calamities which meant nothing but the death of friendship. There swam into his mind, unbidden and unexpected, a fragment of the song he had once written at Richard's challenge, the "reconciliation of two opposites in a harmonious whole": *On every hand rise new alarms When men in springtime are well met.* Springtime and battle, new life bursting from the earth, and men striving to thrust one another back again into the clogging earth. And all this, according to the Sufi, was part of the Oneness of God.

Perhaps it was, at that. Honey and salt, tears and laughter. Why should he care, in any case? He was well out of it.

"I'll wait for you," he muttered, reaching out blindly to clap el Emeen on the shoulder. "I've got nowhere else to go."

". . . Of this poet, Jarir, it was said that he could raise running sores upon the skins of his enemies by the sharpness of his satires. Now it is related there was once a king who refused to reward poets. He proclaimed that whoever came before him with a completely original poem would be given the weight in money of the paper or parchment or whatever the words were written upon, but if the poem was not original the poet would be beaten and thrust forth. And the way in which the king saved his wealth was this: he could remember, after one hearing, any poem no matter how long it was. He had a mameluke who could remember it after two hearings, and a female slave who could remember it after three. When a poet came before him and recited a composition, the king would say, 'That is not original! I have known it for years,' and he would then recite it word by word. 'Furthermore,' he would add, 'I have a mameluke who knows it also,' and the mameluke would then recite it, and after him the female slave.

"But Jarir came before the king with an ode he had written full of barbed, hard words which glanced like arrows from the tongue, but also full of such wit that as he recited it the king laughed, writhed where he sat, held his temples, and could remember nothing. 'So be it,' said the king, owning defeat. 'Bring me the written poem that I may weigh it and reward thee accordingly.' Jarir caused there to be brought a camel, on the back of which was fastened a marble column on which he had inscribed his ode."

Leila finished with a smile, and Denys lay back among the cushions of the alcove, chuckling.

Leila had been speaking in Arabic; she now reverted to French. "You understood his poems, when I recited them?" she said. "You missed no word?"

"No, I understood everything. And especially that poem, *Give me back my heart unharmed.* He was a master! *I am ill, I am sick unto death, of hiding my love.* . . . Delightful."

He raised his hand and with a finger stroked her cheek, lifting the auburn lock that curled lightly over one eye.

"Delightful," he repeated. "You are the only thing that makes this prison bearable, my darling."

"Prison?" When she smiled, her face changed, widening at the cheekbones, taking on an impish quality; her eyes narrowed to slits of merriment, and grew darker. "It's a prison some free men might envy, then. There are many Moslems who would call it Paradise—'In gardens of delight . . . On ranged couches, reclining therein face to face; And there wait on them immortal youths with bowls and ewers and a cup from a pure spring, Wherefrom they get no aching of the head.'"

"My God, you know almost the whole of that Koran by heart, don't you?" said Denys. "You are—let me see, how would el Emeen say it? Truly, you are a lotus tree; pearls fall from your lips, and each glance of your eyes sears me like a flame. There, does that satisfy you?"

She threw back her head and laughed. "Who heeds the babbling of a fool?" she said.

Denys sat up, hugging his knees with his arms. "But it is a prison all the same," he said, more soberly. "I can't leave Jerusalem, and with el Emeen away his guards watch me like hawks. Oh, they never let me see them, but I know there are eyes on me. And you——? It is even worse for you. A slave, and the slave of a prisoner. Does it hurt you?"

"I don't mind," she said. "You really aren't bad-looking. And by now I have almost forgotten what life used to be like when I was a child. I miss my parents. Sometimes I find myself longing for them so that I can hardly bear it. But I can't bring them back, nor that life either. *Al mektub, mektub*; what is written, is written." She shrugged. "I've learned that much from Islam."

"I am rapidly learning it. And if I could leave, where would I go? Perhaps it was this the hermit meant when he told my fortune."

"The hermit?"

"I told you about him, don't you remember? The archangel Gabriel. 'You will go further than you think,' he said. Well, that was certainly right. 'You won't find what you're looking for.' I suppose he meant lands of my own. 'However you'll find something else which is equally precious, but you won't know you have it until you come near losing it.' Perhaps he could really foresee the future. I've often thought of what he said. I thought once he meant Arthur, but I *have* lost *him*."

"I wish I could have met your friend Arthur," Leila mused, resting her head on Denys's knees. "'You won't find what you're looking for.' Mmm. Perhaps that hermit meant something else. Haven't you often told me how you have searched for another kind of poetry? But perhaps you've already found that, too, among all these new forms el Emeen and I have shown you?"

"Forms." Denys shook his head. "It's all the same stuff, only in another meter, another shape, another language. I don't know what I want. When the Sufi said, 'Question me,' I couldn't think of a question. I think I realize that it isn't form—or, say rather, form is a way of getting at what I really want, but the thing itself is always just out of reach. Arnaut Daniel once told me he invented the sestina in his search for the right way of saying what he felt, and then he understood that it couldn't be found in that form. It isn't the forms." He moved his hand back and forth as if feeling in the air for something invisible. "You can use any form you like. It's what you *feel* and the right, perfect, lovely words and melodies that somehow give it shape. The image ought to grow naturally out of one's blood and bones and make its own shape.

"Listen, here's something I wrote once—the form is nothing, but it says what I want it to, somehow. I wrote it long ago, before I ever knew you, but I might have written it for you:

> "Oh western wind when wilt thou blow
> That the small rain down can rain?
> Christ, that my love were in my arms
> And I in my bed again."

Leila nodded. "I like that. It's so short, but it has so much in it."

"That time I didn't fit an idea to a form," Denys said, earnestly. "I started with something growing inside, like a seedling in the earth: it opened, and took shape, and became that—cry. It's like a cry, isn't it? What can you call it? It doesn't fit anywhere. I couldn't even write a melody to go with it."

He bowed his head and thoughtfully kissed her on the ear.

"What's the good of my calling myself a trouvère?" he muttered. "I haven't found anything. There ought to be another word—'seeker', or 'searcher', or maybe 'restless, uneasy, dissatisfied muttonhead'."

"You're tickling me," she said.

He burrowed his face in her perfumed hair. "Suppose we escape together?" he whispered. "Get horses, ride off some night, go to the distant East, to the land where the Emperor of the Mongols lives in a palace made of glass and hung with golden bells? They'd never think of searching for us in that direction."

She lifted her head and looked at him. "You can't escape, Denys," she said. "You gave your word to el Emeen."

"What of it? Guy of Lusignan himself, King Guy, he gave

his word to Salah-ed-Din after the battle of Hattin, that he would never take up arms against Islam again. The instant the Sultan released him, he broke his word. Why should I be different from a king?"

"Because el Emeen is your friend. You know now what his name means—the Faithful One. He stood surety for your word that you would not depart until you were ransomed. Could you be less faithful than he?"

Denys was silent.

"I'm answered," she said. "It's one of the reasons I love you."

"So you believe in honour, too?" Denys said sourly. "You and Arthur and Maude. . . ."

"Honour is only a word," said Leila. "I believe that a man is what he does, not what he says he is. When I was a child, my mother used to sing to me of Taillefer, Duke William's minstrel, 'whose heart was noble, and ennobled him'. You're a trouvère, I needn't tell you how it goes."

Denys quoted softly:

"Threw high his sword and caught it by the hilt,
And as he led the van, of Roland sang."

He got up restlessly and went to the window. Resting his hands on either side of the frame, he stared down into the small garden below. Reflecting the sky, a marble pool lay in its centre edged with the upthrust purple and yellow banners of irises. Neatly arrayed in small squares, surrounded by paving, were beds of poppies, fragrant narcissus, and marigold, like rich carpets of crimson, white, and yellow set out as prayer-rugs for the Faithful. Around the edges, near the wall, roses grew, pink and white masses echoing the delicate colour of the marble.

"'In gardens of delight,'" Denys murmured. "A happier promise than Old Onion-head used to offer us. There are times when I'm tempted to turn Moslem. How much simpler everything would be, Leila!"

"Do you think so?" She had risen, too, and stood looking gravely at him, her arms raised to pat her hair into place. She appeared small and rather shapeless today, for she wore a loose, long tunic of saffron linen that came below her knees, and under it a pair of baggy trousers from the edges of which her toes peeped out. Denys felt a stab of tenderness at his heart, for she was like a child dressed in adult's clothing.

But when she spoke that childish illusion was dispelled, for her voice was rich and curiously husky; it gave to the simplest words a kind of glowing caress. "Would it be so simple when you left here to go home again? I don't think you're the kind of man who changes sides lightly," she said.

"No? What kind of man am I?"

She came close to him, touching his chest lightly with one hand. "I think," she said, "a man of principle."

"Principle?" He snorted. "I've heard people use that word so lightly that it's lost its meaning. I knew a Genoese merchant who was a man of principle, too. His principles allowed him to sell Christian slaves to the infidels. I have seen bishops turn their principles inside out and wear them like fools' caps when a king dangled benefices before their eyes. If that's all you think of me. . . ."

She gave a little chuckle. "Oh," she said, "you can twist things. You and I between us know a great many songs about noble knights. For most of those who listen, they are only songs of war and great deeds. But for a few, they're models of life: tales of high purpose, of honourable vassals, of a way of living that shines in a world which stinks. And you, Denys, you're one of the few."

"Knight-errantry again!" Denys cried. He took her gently by the wrists. "There's a lady in England who tried to turn me into a pattern of chivalry. A prime ass I looked, too."

"No, not knight-errantry," Leila said. "Why are you so perverse, Denys? You know what I mean. I can see it in your eyes. You make me want to hit you. Why, not five minutes ago you admitted that you couldn't break your parole to el Emeen."

"I didn't say a word."

"Oh——! Fool! You just won't face up to the man you really are."

He stared at her. "You mean it, don't you?" he said.

"Listen. I am a slave, and used to doing what I am told. When el Emeen gave me to you, that first day we met, I was ready to submit to you. Submission—it's all I've had to do since I was brought here as a child. But you couldn't take me so lightly. It was you who were afraid."

"I? What are you talking about?" Denys said, indignantly. "I remember that night. You wept and told me about your childhood and drowned my desire in floods of tears. I remember it very well. Why, I wrote it all down in my journal."

"Did you indeed? Then you'd better change your precious journal," she laughed. "I waited for you to take me, and you hemmed and hawed and watched me out of the corners of your eyes . . . and then you began to ask me how I liked living among these infidels, and whether I was happy, and what my life had been like before I was taken prisoner. It was *that* that made me cry. You awoke all those memories and wouldn't take things as they were. I saw then what kind of man I had to do with. I wasn't simply a naked, forked women for you but a fellow-creature, someone you had to know before you could make love to her, someone with a soul. Why, you—you *trouvère*. You idealist! You didn't want to have a woman given to you. You wanted her to come to you with a free heart. Do you think I didn't understand that when I thought about it later, lying alone in my own corner of the room?"

She pulled her hands away, and Denys automatically threw up his arm, thinking she was going to slap him. But her ferocious expression was only assumed. She caught his face between her palms and looked into his eyes. "At first, I was startled, even hurt. I thought, He is like el Emeen, and my hair and eyes repel him. But I understood. I have had much time to myself to think, you know. And I'm not ignorant. They made me study, so that I'd be more valuable. I didn't learn the Koran by heart without much pondering."

Her slender fingers, strong from much practice on the lute, laced behind his neck. "The next night," she said. "The next night I wanted *you*. I wanted not to be a slave any longer, but to pretend that we were both free, that I could be wooed, that you could love me. I asked you to sing to me."

"Yes, I remember that," he said softly.

"And with songs, and wine, and kisses——"

He nodded. They stood silently for a little while, pressed close together. And he thought, with wonder, how much she reminded him of both Maude and Elena without being like either of them. Elena's freshness and delight in embraces, and Maude's sense of high purpose—but in Leila turned from romantic notions of chivalry to something deeper and nobler.

He whispered, "You can be my conscience, then. You can tell me always what kind of man I really am."

Her face clouded. "Always?" she said. And her fingers clenched in the folds of his tunic. "I don't know what 'always' means."

Her eyes filled with tears. "No," she said, "I'm wrong. Let's go on pretending that nothing will change. Pretend that there is an *always*."

"When I leave here," he began.

But just then a voice from the garden shouted, "Cordebar!"

He turned away, reluctantly, and glanced out of the window. Down below, a man in a golden helmet was standing among the flower beds as if he had just grown up out of them. He was a Greek, tall and pale in a white and gold tunic, one of the mamelukes of the emir's guard.

"Peace to you, Yezid," Denys called down. "Have you any news of el Emeen?"

"Nothing new." The soldier looked up, hands on hips. "I have come for you, Cordebar. My lord wishes you to attend him."

"Me? What for?"

"I think, to act as interpreter again."

Several times, during the six or seven weeks that el Emeen had been away on campaign, his father had summoned Denys to interpret for him whenever Frankish prisoners had been brought in. Denys threw a light cloak over his shoulders and wrapped a small turban around his head. He let Leila pull his tunic into neater folds, kissed her, and ran down to the court-yard to join the mameluke.

He expected to be ushered into the diwan, the large room in the Citadel where the emir held his court of justice. Instead, he was taken by a narrow alleyway to a rear door and led up a stair to a small chamber in a corner of the tower. Two tall, pointed windows lighted it, and on a low dais at one end sat the emir, Yusuf Mejed ed-Din, a stern, elderly man with heavy-lidded, cold eyes. Denys bowed low before him, touching his heart and his lips as courtesy demanded.

The emir inclined his head slightly and motioned to the floor beside the dais. Denys sat down, crossing his legs; he had grown accustomed to the Turkish way of sitting and no longer found it uncomfortable. Mejed ed-Din asked him several polite questions, as if this had been his only reason for summoning Denys: how his health was, whether he had been able to take enough exercise, whether he had gone out hunting or hawking, whether he required anything. Denys answered patiently, knowing the Oriental custom of approaching any point, by slow, circuitous routes. In his turn, he asked after the health of the emir, and whether any news had come of the young prince, el Emeen.

"Nothing for more than a week," replied the emir. "But I do not doubt he carried forward the war. Your people have retaliated upon us for our ambush of your caravan a week ago. They have now fallen on a great caravan of ours, at the stream of el-Hesi, capturing a thousand camels and two hundred men. It was the doing of your king, Richard, who with diabolical cunning and great strength fell upon them in the morning when everyone was at prayer. Save for this, I have had no other fresh news."

He paused, stroking his beard. Then he went on, "And now that we speak of King Richard, tell me, is it true as I have heard that you are hostile to him?"

Denys blinked. "Why do you ask me this, lord?" he said.

"It has been told me by one who listened, that you, speaking with my son one day cried out that King Richard was a monster and a serpent. And this I thought not the word of a friend."

"I have no cause to love the king," Denys said, rather grimly.

"I questioned my son before he departed," continued the emir, "and he said that you had some enmity against the king and bore him a grudge for the death of one of your comrades."

Denys shrugged. "I see no reason why I shouldn't tell you. It's quite true. I have little love for Richard. And as you see, he has left me unransomed, in captivity."

The emir nodded. "Two visitors are coming this morning to confer with me. I have dealt with them before this, on other matters. But today I desire all that we discuss to be secret, and it may be you can give me certain advice or information that will be useful as you interpret for me. But I wished to learn, first, where your heart lay. For one who has two tongues must have intelligence as well so that the words come clearly as they are meant, and not simply word for word so that the meaning may sometimes be lost. And for your services, now and in the past,

I am grateful; I will cause your mouth to be filled with gold."

Denys bent his head with a rather sickly smile. He knew that the Turkish princes sometimes had a disagreeable way of carrying into literal practice what might otherwise be thought of as flowery metaphors.

The emir clapped his hands. Yezid, who had been waiting outside, opened the door and ushered in two men in soft boots, dark camel-hair cloaks, and turbans. They glanced round the room, and one of them threw back his robe displaying a splendid tunic embroidered with silver flowers, and girdled with a red leather belt from which hung a straight, broad-bladed sword. The other man, slighter, more weather-beaten, and with a sharp beak of a nose, wore chain mail under his cloak and was armed like his companion.

They bowed to the emir in a perfunctory fashion, and the taller of the two said, in harshly-accented Arabic, "Peace be with you." Then, lapsing into French, he added, "Is the interpreter here?"

"I am the interpreter," said Denys.

The tall man looked him up and down. "Greek?" he asked.

Denys grinned, although he was annoyed by the other's arrogant tone. "I am a Poitevin," he said. "A prisoner of war." And as the two looked at each other, he said, "You have no need to fear. Mejed ed-Din has already told me that the matter is secret, and I can guess that it concerns King Richard. You can speak as you like; I am no friend of the king's."

The emir bent forward, and Denys quickly explained to him what they had been talking about.

"Very well," he said. "Bid them sit down, and ask them if they will take some refreshment."

The mameluke had set out two low stools before withdrawing. The knights—for it was clear that such they were—perched themselves awkwardly on these and accepted cups of wine which Denys poured them.

"I trust," the emir said, "that you are not too wearied from your long riding."

"Never mind that," said the tall man, bluntly. "Let us avoid long-winded conversations and come to the point."

Denys could not resist translating this exactly as it came. In Arabic it emerged even ruder than it sounded in French. The

343

emir sat up a trifle more stiffly, and grunted, "Barbarians! Very well. Let them speak on."

"First, then," said the tall man, "let us understand one another. We are not here as traitors. Our fealty was given to the lord of Tyre, the marquis Conrad of Montferrat, who was murdered by the command of King Richard. We are interested only in justice."

"And in the territories of Tyre and Sidon, Balian," said the other man. "Make that plain."

"Be still. Leave it to me," said the tall man.

Denys stared at him. "Balian?" he said. "Is your name Balian?"

"What of it?" said the knight, eyeing Denys suspiciously.

"Were you once a squire in the castle of Beaupréau?"

The knight shook his head. "Not I," said he. "I have never heard of the place."

"Excuse me," Denys said, in confusion. "I once knew someone named Balian."

He translated what had been said for the emir, and Balian continued, "Our lord the marquis would have made peace with the Sultan, as you know. We are concerned with our fiefs; the war is ruining us. And we will not bend our knees to Richard who looks for his own advantage everywhere. If he could, he would take Tyre for his own! But he cannot hold power for long. He has alienated everyone—he can be seen now for the devil he is. Even his dearest friends hate him for the death of the marquis, and fear him as well, for they never know what filthiness he will be doing next."

The emir nodded. "Why, then," he said smoothly, "do you not slay him, or cast him out? Surely, you would be thanked for it."

Balian's face twitched. "It's not so easy to kill a king," he replied. "He is well guarded . . . in any case, the situation is very complex. It's not so certain that if we knights of Outremer, along with the French, turned on Richard, we would be supported by the whole army. No, probably not by the *whole* army."

Denys translated this with a crooked smile, and, observing the emir's eyes, knew that Mejed ed-Din was not at all taken in by what Balian said.

"I understand," said the emir. "Then what can you do?"

"We can weaken him," put in the smaller man, fiercely. "We can sap him, undermine him the way he undermined the towers of Acre. We can ready him so that when you push, he'll fall."

Balian said, "You know that he is about to leave en-Natrun, do you?"

"I know that he was camped at en-Natrun," said the emir, cautiously.

"He was waiting for provisions and siege engines before starting his advance against Jerusalem. Well, he has what he wants. The first supply train has just arrived. Very soon he will marshal the host and move upon Beit Nuba. You know as well as we do how far it is from there to Jerusalem. A day's journey?"

"Perhaps."

"We have already held a private council," said Balian. "The leaders of the French, together with some of the Hospitallers who still hold it against him that he gave them no support in the rearguard at the battle of Arsûf, and many of the knights of Outremer—some of us who were Conrad's men, and others who were friends of Guy of Lusignan and feel he was passed over, we've met and made our plans. We will do this: we will urge upon him as strongly as we can that he should turn back from Jerusalem."

"And if he does not listen?"

"He must listen. He has no choice. In any serious disagreement he must submit the matter to the council of the host. The council includes enough who are with us to carry the decision."

The emir raised his eyebrows. "And then? How does this weaken him?"

"That will be the beginning," Balian said, with a grim smile. "It will be a grave discouragement when we have to retreat within sight of the very walls of the Holy City. Discord can be bred of it. We can so stir matters up that there will be trouble in a dozen places, in Jaffa, Acre, Ascalon, so that Richard must spend his time flying from one place to another, wasting his energy, consuming his talent. And then——"

He paused, to let Denys translate. "And then," he went on, "the day will come when matters are so arranged that in the midst of his ripest confusion he is found with the fewest number of knights and men at arms, in some exposed place, in a camp or outside a city. And when that moment is at hand a swift messenger will go from one of us to you. He will carry the news of where the king is and how he may be attacked. It will be your part, then, to send a strong force and crush him."

". . . and crush him," Denys finished. He remained looking into the emir's face, and then smiled incredulously. "I think they are too hopeful, lord," he added.

"Why so?"

"Their enmity blinds them to the king's strength. They cannot turn the whole host against him. For one thing, too many men depend on Richard's bounty."

"Say that to them, and let us see how they reply."

Denys turned to the knights. "The emir says he thinks Richard's wealth will keep the army loyal to him."

"Richard's wealth?" Balian laughed. "He is scraping the bottom of his war-chest. Do you not know that he himself paid for the rebuilding of three parts of the walls of Ascalon out of his own pocket? When the French troops, in February, said they would fight no longer without pay, the duke of Burgundy was forced to ask Richard for a loan, and Richard had nothing to give him. That was why the French left Ascalon and returned to Tyre. Haven't you heard of the troubles in England? No money—or precious little—comes from there to the king. Richard has been forced to borrow wherever he can. Now that Henry of Champagne is lord of Tyre, he has returned the four thousand pounds Richard gave him at Acre; it is with this money that Richard has purchased supplies and paid his troops. It won't last long."

"In any case," said the other man, whose name Denys had not yet learned, "our plan is not to turn the host against him, but to isolate him by dividing the contingents against each other."

"Just so," said Balian. "If we turn one against the other, the time will come when we can manœuvre Richard into a position where he is relatively weak. Tell the emir that it may take a month or two, but surely we can wait and plan for that possibility."

Denys translated again, and added, "It seems to me, lord, that they want you to cut up the meat so that they can eat it."

The emir permitted himself a twinkle of amusement. "It

346

appears, however," he said, "that the Faith stands to lose nothing and to gain a great deal. It is clear that God has sent a madness upon our enemies so that whatever comes of it, they will be weakened. Therefore, say to these knights that I accept their plan. If Richard indeed turns back from Jerusalem, I will know that they are not boasting and that the plan may come to fruit. At that point, I will reserve my own *halka* of mamelukes to this task, and I will levy a thousand other troops at least, to join them."

When he heard this, Balian gave a curt nod and rose to his feet. "Very good," he said. "I'm satisfied. Tell Mejed ed-Din that I can see we were wise to come to him, with whom we have had dealings before this, rather than to the Sultan, whose hatred and suspicion of all Christians sometimes prevents him from knowing a good thing when he sees it. As for you, sir, we are grateful to you for interpreting so well. Tell me your name, and when Richard is overthrown it may be we can arrange for your freedom."

Denys told him, although he felt quite sure the information would be conveniently forgotten. The knights took their leave without more delay. Denys received the emir's thanks along with a handsome gold ring from his own finger. It was only as Yezid was leading him down the stair that the thought occurred to him that they might have had another purpose in asking his name: he was now a hostage for their secret. They knew who he was, but he knew nothing of them beyond the name Balian. If they were betrayed they would certainly make it appear that he was implicated in the plot; if he were tempted to reveal it, by a warning message for example, his own life would certainly be forfeit. Richard would never rest until he had taken revenge.

Richard? Why should he worry about Richard's revenge when it was his own revenge that might be at hand? The plan might very well succeed. "God has sent a madness upon our enemies," the emir had said. It was the upshot of months of such madness. From the beginning of the crusade the internal conflict had gone on, almost as strong as that against the infidel: English against French, Norman against Poitevin, Pisan against Genoan, Hospitaller against Templar. Out of these divisions a worse chaos might be wrought in which Richard would surely be destroyed. And then Arthur would be avenged, Denys's own weakness wiped out. A just fate for a king so heartless, so cunning, so cruel and selfish.

He tried to feel light-hearted. But a nagging doubt crept into his mind, chilling his satisfaction and leaving it ashen.

*   *   *

Journal of Denys de Courtebarbe. Extract 11.

Thus have I hung in uncertainty, wishing that Richard might be brought low as he has done to so many others, yet mindful that I once placed my hands between his and swore him fealty. Such an oath, I say to myself, was taken from me by trickery and cannot be binding. Yet I hear Arthur say, 'A knight has only his word.' Then says that other part of me, but Richard played me false and so Arthur died. Why, then, should not the king die in his turn? I could not kill him when he lay sleeping near the river of Jaffa. The matter is out of my hands now. I have but to wait (and for a prisoner that is easy) and they will overthrow him. And there is more in my mind, some thought of how I sinned with him, and this too may be reckoned against him so that we will be quits if he is slain. And still, on my life, I know not whether this be right. I scutter forth and back like some old beldame in a flood who knows not whether to save cow or goose and may come herself to drown from hesitation.

But in the last four weeks the army of the Cross has thrust forward to the fortress of Beit Nuba and lies less than five leagues from the Holy City. Great deeds have they done, and I have heard how Richard has come like a whirlwind upon the Saracens and with his own hand has captured Saladin's herald and slain near half a hundred of the infidels. God be praised that so far el Emeen has not been among them—although I ought to feel shame that I should be glad the life of a Saracen has been spared.

The Sultan has caused the wells and springs near Jerusalem to be filled in or fouled, and has withdrawn almost to the city gates. There are now armed men everywhere and within the city great unrest and fear, so that I durst not go abroad but have remained within the palace of the prince. The Sultan himself has come into the city each day to pray in the great mosque called el Aksa, and from my window I have seen his banners and the crowd which surround him as he goes out and comes in.

What will befall now, no man knows. And I know least of all. If Richard besieges the city and we come to meet again, what will happen? Nor do I see how he can fail to besiege it, and well may we see a desperate battle here, worse by far than that of Acre.

I look at that which I last wrote, and understand why these unbelievers say, 'Tomorrow is in God's hand'. For now is it plain that the knight Balian brings his conspiracy to fulfilment. Yesterday, it being the 23rd day of the month Jomada II, which I reckon to be near the 20th day of July, there came home my friend and captor, el Emeen, with the news that the army of the Cross has broken camp and is retreating back towards Jaffa.

Having first reported to his father, el Emeen came to his own palace and embraced me, saying that he had heard much good of me, and that Mejed ed-Din had taken him into his confidence and informed him of the plot against the king. And, said he, spies going into the Christian camp often brought word in what ill case they were, their supplies dwindling and men deserting them daily, and many wounded and sick, but, above all, dissension among them, one party crying them on to Jerusalem, and the other saying nay to that since there was no water to be had near the city. At last, the disagreement growing out of measure, a council was called of five nobles of the French, five Hospitallers, five Templars, and five noblemen of the kingdom of Jerusalem, and these gave it as their opinion that the army should withdraw to Jaffa or Acre, and make speedy plans for carrying the war from our cities which we hold on the coast, into Egypt itself. Very clear is it to me that this is the doing of those whom the knight Balian represented, and thin was their excuse, for if they cannot take Jerusalem being so near it, how can they go against Babylon which is so far away? But as soon as they had made the decision they began to move the supply train, and this very morning, before el Emeen came back to Jerusalem, he saw their knights departing in the rearguard.

And now his father, faithful to the word he gave Balian,

has gathered his bodyguard of five hundred mamelukes under the command of Yezid es-Iskandarun, whom he trusts greatly, and near a thousand of his own Kurdish troops, as well as more than a thousand other mamelukes under the command of a notable Turkish warrior, Kaimaz en-Nejmi, who is a eunuch. All these he keeps at his own cost outside the city, and waits now for the message which is to come from Balian, and which I no longer doubt will come, be it sooner or later.

*　　*　　*

Night, mild, moonlit and peaceful, embraced the hills, enfolded Jerusalem with languor. On rooftops, men and women sat to catch the breeze, and the plucked strings of a lute mingled with distant laughter, plaintive singing. Flower scents lay heavy above the gardens, caressing the earth with sweetness. In his chamber, Denys reclined on a silk rug looking at the silver-tinselled sky, the white night beyond the windows. Leila sat beside him, and a little distant Giraud leaned against the wall, touching the strings of his harp and singing softly,

> "I drink the air that whispers from her lips,
> Thirsty for love but forced to live on sips.
> Ah, love, embrace for dawn is near at hand."

"Who wrote that?" Denys asked, idly. "Is it mine?"

Giraud gave a cackle. "There's an enviable position to be in, by God! To have written so many songs you can't even remember them all. Yes, it's yours."

"I think Denys is fishing for a compliment," Leila observed. "It is written, 'Be modest in your bearing and subdue your voice. Lo, the harshest of all voices is the voice of the ass.'"

Denys propped himself on his elbows and grinned at her. "One of these days I'm going to learn the Koran by heart so that I can give you thrust for thrust," he said. "Doesn't it say something about wise women keeping their mouths shut?"

"The Prophet admired women," she replied, demurely. "But the Caliph Omar said, 'Consult with women and then do the opposite of what they advise.'"

"The Caliph Omar was a boor and not a courteous Frenchman," said Denys. "No, let's leave things as they are." He sighed, and lay back, lacing his fingers behind his head. "Oh," he said, "I'm not in the mood for aubades. Leave things as they are. . . . I wish I could!"

They were silent for a time, Giraud's fingers moving aimlessly on the strings, bringing forth a note, and then another, no more than the merest vibration of the harp.

Leila said, "What is it? Are you thinking of the war?"

"Of the war . . . of Richard. He doesn't know what is being prepared for him. But if he knew what would he do? He'd laugh, damn him, he laughs at everyone and everything. He'll trick them all, somehow. The world's jester. Richard Yes-and-No. Balian had better be careful."

"Who is Balian?"

"A certain knight, whose name reminded me of someone I used to know." He rolled over, resting his cheek on his arm. "It was long ago. Someone I admired and hated and feared and loved. I can't remember too clearly . . . I think he beat me because I cried at a song, a song I've never been able to remember. Jourdain de Blaivie."

Giraud, in a low voice, sang:

> "Listen, my lord, and may God give you grace,
> Hear this good song which ancient is and fair."

"Is that it?" Denys asked. "I might have guessed. Giraud who knows every song. I remember the first day we picked you up, how you sang everything we asked. I haven't heard Jourdain since I was a boy. Not since I was about seven."

He closed his eyes. And suddenly, a shiver went through him, a spasm of dread, as swiftly as a puff of wind that shakes branches and is gone.

Giraud was saying, "Do you want to hear it now?"

"Why not? It has always disturbed me, the thought that although I can remember dozens of other songs——"

"But not your own," put in Leila, mischievously.

"Yes, well, I remember hearing Jourdain but I can't recollect any of it. Isn't there something about a traitor named Fromont whose ear is cut off?"

"If you like, I'll sing it for you."

Once again, the premonitory chill touched Denys, and he almost cried out, "No! Don't sing it!" But his curiosity was

351

greater than this nameless, pointless instant of fright and he swallowed it, so that he sat up and said, "By all means. Sing on, and if I like it I'll follow the example of the infidels and fill your mouth with gold."

"I'd rather have wine, if it's all the same to you," said Giraud. He struck a vigorous chord, and began the chanson again: "Listen, my lord. . . ."

And as he sang, the pointed arches of the moonstruck windows, the walls traced with painted quotations from the Koran, the inlaid floor, the silk rugs and cushions, the house, the houses of Jerusalem, the hills, the whole present—all melted and were transformed. They became a dark, lofty hall, from whose beams hung weapons and the antlers of deer, a hall lighted by some bundles of oil-soaked rags sputtering and stinking in brackets on the walls, and by a great fire of four-foot logs in the pit in the centre of the floor. Smoke and sparks rose from this fire and mingled with snowflakes that sifted in through a hole in the roof. Denys saw this before his eyes as clearly as if he were there; he saw himself, a little boy lying on his stomach on a fleece beside his mother, whose foot rested lightly on his back. His father, in a carved chair, held his chin in his hand and stared broodingly at the fire. And a minstrel in a ragged cloak, from which hung some tatters of fur, sang for their entertainment. His voice and Giraud's blended; the song was the same.

Listen, my lord, and may God give you grace. Here is an ancient song, and a glorious one. Girart, the noble knight, godson of Amis and of the great Count Amile, held all the land of Blaivie, that strong city upon the eastern shore of the Gironde. To him, King Otho gave his daughter Hermenjart to wife, and of this union there was born Jourdain. The child was sent to the house of the brave vassal Renier, the son of Gontelme, to be cared for as a godson. In Vautamise was Jourdain baptized, and there he was raised with Renier's own son, Garnier, both as brothers with the same wet-nurse. Alas, how many tears and how much blood would be shed, how many men would lose their heads, because of this same babe.

And now the tale commences.

There came to Blaivie, Fromont, the nephew of that traitor Hardré, whose head was lopped off in battle by Count Amile. Fromont begged for shelter, and the good and worthy knight,

Girart, thinking no evil, welcomed him in and gave him food and drink. A covetous eye cast Fromont on the keep, and on the strong town of Blaivie, and swore that he would hold it for his own. To him there came two serfs, nourished and raised by Girart, like two serpents, and for gold they led Fromont by night into the bedchamber of their lord. Behind the bed he hid, and at midnight, when all was still, with his fell sword the traitor Fromont slew both Girart and his fair dame Hermenjart. Thus got he vengeance for his uncle's death, slain by Amile in battle, and made himself master of castle and of town.

God's curse on such a guest!

Now those two serfs told Fromont that Girart's son, Jourdain, lived still at Vautamise, in the care of that brave vassal Renier, and of his wife Erembors the wise. Fromont sent for Renier and offered him much gold if he would deliver up the child, for well did Fromont know that if any were left of the blood of Girart his own head would never be safe. But Renier refused. He was thrown into prison but never would he yield up his charge, not for any pain. His lady Erembors come to the false Fromont and pleaded for her husband's life, but she too was cast in prison by that traitor.

By God, great was his anger!

He tortured them, both husband and wife, and much woe had they. They were threatened with death if they would not give up the child, Jourdain, to be slain. Then said Dame Erembors, "Sir Renier, my fair spouse, by God, this traitor will not rest till we be dead," and bitter tears she wept. "Say, lady, what shall we do?" asked Renier. "This is my counsel," Erembors replied. "Jourdain the infant is our true liege lord. We will give up our own son in his place for of one age and one appearance are the babes. Thus shall Fromont be snared and Blaivie live." The noble Renier wept to hear that rede. "Cursed is the father who betrays his child," said he. "Not for the fear of death, nor for all the gold God made would I do such a deed. But for my homage will I do so."

God send every lord such a vassal!

To Fromont the false then these two were brought, and in seeming agreed to do his will. Renier remained in prison, while Dame Erembors returned to Vautamise. All Renier's barons she swore to secrecy. Then her own son, the smiling babe, she wrapped and brought to Blaivie. And as she went up to the keep, she said, "Sweet son, Garnier, by your body is the body of your lord delivered. You shall lose your life, alas. Nine months I carried you in my womb, and never now shall you play like other lads outside the walls, nor ride to the quintain and the shield, nor sing verses, nor fight with rushes, for you shall lose your life. By tomorrow midday much will I grieve; heavy is my heart or ever that day be past. Nor will you see tomorrow's sun descend, for you shall lose your life."

("And will they really kill him, mother?" whimpers Denys. He has risen to his knees, clutching at his mother's skirt.

"Hush, child," says his mother, patting him absently, for she wants to listen.)

Comes Erembors before Fromont the false. "Sir Fromont," says she, "for God's sake have pity on Girart's son." The felon hears but answers not; with his own sword severs the infant's head.

By God, few folk in this or any other age would so do as did Renier and his lady.

(Little Denys buries his face in his mother's lap. He does not want to hear any more. But the song goes on.)

Now Renier is delivered from prison, and Fromont the felon rejoices that the line of Girart has been wiped out. Renier and his lady Erembors to Vautamise they go, and young Jourdain they raise as their own son. He comes to the age of fifteen years, a fair and noble youth. One day, Fromont the traitor to Renier says, "Sir Renier, send to me your son that he may serve me in my court." And this is done.

Jourdain now serves in Fromont's court as squire, and many love him for his courtesy. Upon a day in Easter Fromont holds his feast, and there into the court they bring a goblet made of fine gold, which Girart long ago brought from Poitiers. Filled with wine it goes from hand to hand, but to Jourdain none is given. Then on his knees the young man goes and asks for wine. "Not so," says Fromont, "by my head, I swear. Nothing of mine shall you have any more. For when I look upon your face I see the likeness of the duke Girart. Son of a whore! a bastard must you be, fathered on Erembors by duke Girart." With his great staff he strikes Jourdain so that the blood runs from his head, and cursing loud bids him begone.

By God, great was his anger!

Jourdain rides home to Vautamise and there in shame tells Renier all the tale. "Grieve not," says Renier, "for no son of mine are you. You are my liege the lord of Blaivie, for whose sake my own son was slain. And Fromont the false traitor both your parents slew." Thus all the tale is told.

Homage to Jourdain Renier gives, and all his knights and barons likewise kneel. Then do they mount and ride, all to Blaivie. The castle they surround, and Renier holds the gate. Jourdain the proud goes to the banquet hall, and there Fromont the traitor sits at meat. He sees Jourdain and cries, "Come you once more? May hell flames consume you!" Then says Jourdain, "For that blow which you gave me shall you pay. And for my father and my mother whom you foully slew, yourself shall die."

With his sharp sword he strikes at Fromont. Upon his head the blade descends, but glancing falls and slices off his ear. Fromont springs back. No more of steel he wants. Huistace, his son, is seated close at hand, and with one blow Jourdain strikes off his head so that it rolls among the broken meats.

Thus ends the first part.

(There is more to be sung on the following night. There is the tale of how Jourdain, still too young to overcome Fromont, is driven into exile, and of his long wandering and many adventures, and how he returns at last and, before the emperor Charlemagne, brings his suit to the wager of battle and kills Fromont. But for this night, the story is told, and Denys is carried off to bed. Snug in the warm blankets he throws his arms tightly about his mother's neck, and says, "Mama, would you do such a thing?"

"What thing?"

"Would you give me to be killed?"

His mother smiles. "Oh, what silliness. Go to sleep, little piglet."

"But would you?"

His mother says gravely, "When you are given your

spurs and sword, when you become a knight, as I hope and pray you will, always remember that loyalty is one of the greatest of virtues. To give oneself for one's pledge, to keep one's word—that is commanded of a knight."

"I don't want to be a knight," Denys whines, and salt tears begin to prickle in his nose.

"Oh, I never heard such nonsense in my life."

"But I don't *want* to!" Denys is bawling in earnest, now, half frightened out of his wits.

"Get up at once, you foolish child, and pray to God to give you strength. Do you want to be a coward? Do you want to live without honour or responsibilities like some mucky farmhand?"

She takes him out of bed, but gently—for she is always loving and gentle—and makes him kneel beside her on the floor next to the bed. A cold wind blows across his poor bare bottom and sets him shivering. She folds her hands over his and says in her sweet voice, "Dear, fair, Sir God, forgive my foolish son and fill him with courtesy, humility, and courage, like a true knight."

Then they snuggle down cosily together and Denys seems to feel God filling him with all those good things. But during the night he wakes in the dark from a nightmare, and cries and cries.

And then it is later, it is the following spring, and Denys rides off with his father to the castle of Raymond of Beaupréau to be a page. And there he serves, bereft of his mother and her comfort, patted now and then carelessly like a puppy, the youngest of the pages. And there, one night, ranged with the other pages and squires, he hears a minstrel sing the Chanson of Jourdain and once again hears how Erembors the wise carries her little son to his death in Jourdain's place. And he, Denys, has been sent away as well; he is here, in this cold place, among strangers, sent away perhaps to his death. Perhaps he will be given up by his mother and have his head stricken off by his father's cousin, Raymond of Beaupréau, a huge, fat, wheezing man whose face shines with the oil of good living. He cannot listen to the song; he puts his hands over his ears; the tears burst from his eyes and he cries bitterly where he sits on the floor with the other pages.

And afterward, Balian stands over him, tall Balian with the pimply face and the fierce blue eyes, and says, "Why did you bawl like that?"

"I don't know," says Denys. He begins to cry again from loneliness and terror.

And Balian grabs him by the ear and twists it. Denys tries to get away, but moving makes it worse. This is what Fromont the traitor felt, when his ear was shorn from his head. This too is what it must feel like to have your head cut off.

Balian says to another boy, "Dreux, you grab his ear and hold the little pig. That's how you hold pigs. We'll make him grow up."

His voice breaks and catches in his throat. The other boys creep closer, fascinated. Dreux holds Denys's ear, while Balian pulls up his shirt.

Balian bends over him. Dreux's fingernails dig into Denys's ear.

And then the pleasure, shameful, unholy pleasure, secret, painful as the sharp fingernails in his ear, and yet consoling. And afterwards, when they have all scuttled to their beds of straw and all the room is quiet, Balian, somewhat ashamed, sits beside Denys and says roughly, in a whisper, "You aren't hurt so what are you crying for? Everybody does it."

"Everybody?"

"Until you grow up. Then you can have a woman."

"Oh."

"Want me to teach you how to throw a dagger?"

"Oh, yes, please, Balian."

"All right. Tomorrow I'll show you. I'll loan you my dagger with the silver hilt."

Then night, and silence, and the slow ebbing of memory, and dreams, and at last it is all gone. All but Jourdain, whose life was purchased at the expense of another's.)

"Thus ends the first part." Giraud's voice died away with the last chords. Denys lifted his face from his cupped hands.

"Shall I go on? Do you want to hear the rest of it?" Giraud asked.

Denys did not reply. He got to his feet and went to the

window and stood looking out over the garden at the further rooftops, beyond which the silvery dome of el Aksa rose under the moon like a transparent bubble on the surface of a dream. All that he had remembered had flashed through his mind, far below its surface so that he was hardly sure he remembered it or what he remembered, like the glint of fish-scales perceived in water; it was as if he looked out at life and saw it as the city yonder, a broad silent pool on the surface of which rose men's deeds constructed into roofs and spires, below which swam the lurking fish of hidden thoughts, impulses, and desires: above, domes, and within secret laughter, anger, or the tinkling notes of a lute.

As he thought this, there swam up in his memory the vision the Sufi had shown him of vast empty spaces filled with the silent crackle of gigantic forces in motion, the web of everything that is, being and not-being simultaneously. What held it all in shape if not Law, the essential harmony which God imposed upon chaos? Then all that he was, and did, fell into shape. If men were vile, they were also good; for every evil deed and false apology there was a spine to which humanity clove and from which it derived—loyalty existed, even though it might be perverted, and love, friendship, and justice also existed no matter how they might be warped or wounded by men's actions. Men alone, conscious of themselves, could recognize the harmony and comprehend it. What had the Sufi said? "Man is the eyes through which God beholds his creations."

And this was what the hermit Gabriel had meant, the "something precious which you won't know you have until you come near losing it". It was that which lay in every man, the thread which bound him to every other living and unliving thing, the sense of Oneness. When, in defiance of the urge towards chaos, a man—like Arthur, it might be—acted in accordance with some principle, the Law was upheld.

Then, thought Denys, Renier and Erembors were right although it cost them their son. And my mother was right. And I was right to be afraid because it is certainly very difficult to do what you know is required of you.

He turned to the others who waited in the dusky shadow, watching him. "I am going to have to get away from here," he said. "I've made up my mind. I've got to get back to Richard, and warn him."

These words said, he felt at once lighter and happier than he had since Arthur's death. But when he had explained to the other two about the conspiracy against the king, Leila shook her head.

"You're right, of course," she said. "But how can you go? You can't simply run away and leave el Emeen to face the Sultan's anger, and his father's as well. Or do you think one promise cancels out the other?"

"No. I *am* concerned about el Emeen. If only I could find my ransom! Look, Mejed ed-Din gave me this gold ring." He pulled it off his finger. "How much do you think it's worth?"

Giraud took it, weighed it in his hand, and bit it. "It's good," he said, "but not two hundred gold bezants' worth of gold." He returned it, and went back to leaning against the wall, with a sulky air.

Denys rubbed his forehead. "Haven't I got anything else? None of the gifts I've ever received for my songs? Didn't you bring anything, Giraud?"

"You know as well as I, what I brought," Giraud replied, with a shrug. "A few shirts, some hose, your old leather purse with fifteen marks in it—that's what I got for the tent, blankets, and odds and ends—and your manuscript and writing materials. I rode your horse; the Saracens took Arthur's horse away from me when they captured me."

Denys beat his fist in his palm. He went to the chest in the corner where he kept his belongings, and threw it open. He took out the purse and opened it, shaking the money on the floor. "Ten pounds, silver, in Angevin money. And the ring is worth perhaps another ten. Maybe I could sell you into slavery, Giraud? I wonder how much that harp of yours is worth?"

He felt around in the purse. There was something else caught in the leather stitching, something small, hard, and flat. He drew it out, and his expression changed. It was the parchment Gian-Maria Scasso had given him, addressed to Rachel Comitissa, in Jaffa. He had folded it up tightly and thrust it in the purse, that day on Scasso's ship, and long since forgotten it.

He burst into delighted laughter. "What an idiot I am! Here it is—this may be my ransom, and I've had it all this while and never thought of it. Leila, you're the best one to

359

handle this. Go out tomorrow morning and see if you can find a Jewish banker or money-lender in Jerusalem who knows someone named Rachel Comitissa, also a banker, but in Jaffa. I think this note may bring some money from her."

"Rachel Comitissa?" Leila raised her eyebrows. "I know that name. She has loaned money to el Emeen. I've seen her here, in this house, a little bent old woman no taller than a child. But I doubt that she's in Jaffa. Last year, when the host of the Cross defeated the Sultan at Arsûf and it became clear that they were marching on Jaffa and Ascalon, all the Jews in those cities fled away, most of them to Jerusalem. They were, of course, far more frightened of the Christians who were coming to set those cities free, than of the Moslems who held them in bondage. I suspect that Comitissa is here, as well."

"Then we must find her," said Denys. He caught Leila's hands. "And if I can buy my freedom, have I bought yours, too? What is the law in such matters?"

She looked at him, round-eyed. "The prince gave me to you. Even though it was not before witnesses, he's far too honourable a man to take back his gift. . . . Unless you wish him to."

"Certainly not. But where would you go? Your parents are dead and your land held by the enemy. Haven't you any relations who would be glad to see you?"

"Then you don't want me," she said, in a low voice.

She tried to free her hands. Denys gripped her tightly.

"Wait a minute," he said. "Don't be so damned impetuous. Don't jump to conclusions so quickly."

She fell quiet, but each breath she drew shook her. Denys, smiling at her, thought, "This time I can't get out of it. We're twined together, she and I. I can't leave her behind to be a slave among the Turks, but if I take her with me . . ."

"I haven't anything," he said. "Don't you understand? I own nothing at all, and I haven't any particular prospects. I'm trying to consider what's best for you, Leila. It's not as though I held a fief and could take you home. In a month, or a year, I may be sleeping on the ground without even a blanket."

"Do you think that matters?" she retorted. "Have we been nothing to each other? Well, never mind, if you don't want to be burdened with a woman——"

"Oh, you fool," he said. "I've been burdened with you

360

ever since I got you. I've grown as used to you as if you were a harp I had to carry with me. It's because I am so fond of you that I'm trying to think of your welfare."

"Well, stop thinking of my welfare and just ask me what I want," said Leila. "Not to grow old as a slave here, whatever else happens. I want to go back to my own people. And you, you disgusting man, I've grown to love you in spite of the fact that there isn't even a priest to marry us, or a match-maker, or any dowry, or property to change hands. We have lived together as if we were man and wife for nine months. Doesn't that mean anything to you?"

He pulled her close. "You may regret this," he said, wryly. "A comfortable, sheltered life in a fine palace can have its good points. You'll go with me, and share what I have—or haven't, and complain, and cry, and say you're cold and hungry, and quarrel with me——"

"Yes, that's right," she said, slipping her arms around his neck.

"Well, it's worth it, I suppose," Denys said, and within him joy mingled with resignation.

Giraud's voice, edged, broke in upon them. "You haven't asked me whether I want to go with you or not."

Denys turned from Leila to stare at him. "No, I haven't."

"I think you've lost your mind," Giraud almost snarled. "What do you want to go back for? You've been lucky, so far. You nearly died at Acre, wasn't that enough for you? And you've lived from hand to mouth—you haven't paid me my sevenpence a week since Lord knows when. This is the first place we've been really comfortable, here in this palace. You've been treated like a baron! I've been eating well for the first time in years; I've been so full I haven't even wanted to steal anything. And now you plan to throw it all away and go back to the king. I know him, even if you don't. He'll thank you, and embrace you, and then he'll consider that you probably had a hand in the plot and whip off your head to be on the safe side."

Denys sighed. "Everything you say is true, Giraud. I haven't paid you, and I have no right to ask you to do anything. You must suit yourself. I'm sure el Emeen would be delighted to have you stay and serve him."

"Who said anything about serving him?" Giraud cried.

361

"And what has pay got to do with it? Is that all you think of me—that I'm mad for money?"

"But you said——"

"What's the difference what I said? You've always twisted my words. I *will* suit myself. Damn you to hell anyway!"

He wiped his nose on his sleeve, and added, with dignity, "When are we leaving?"

It proved easy enough, after all, to find Rachel Comitissa. Leila learned, next morning, that she was living on the northern side of the city not far from the Street of Jehoshaphat. Denys went off to see her at once, for now that el Emeen was home again the restraints upon his movements had been eased and he no longer had the sense of being followed wherever he went. She was, as Leila had said, a withered old woman, shabbily dressed, small and helpless-looking, so that at first Denys's heart sank and he thought there must be some mistake. How could such a crone be wealthy and powerful enough to take part in such large-scale banking and business operations as Scasso had talked of? But when he showed her the note she chuckled in a thin, whispering way, like a broody hen, and peered at him with eyes which were suddenly so sharp and intelligent that he began to change his mind.

"What can you have done for Scasso that makes him commend you as a brother?" she said, speaking in Arabic, since Denys had introduced himself to her in that language.

"I saved his life," Denys replied.

"Yes, yes, I understand. Very good. Nothing else would make him so grateful. And now, what can I do for Scasso's brother?"

"I must have two hundred bezants, in gold."

"Hm. A good annual rent for a knight's fief. Not a very large sum, nor yet a very small one. Now why would you want precisely that amount?"

"I don't think that's any of your business," said Denys.

"Don't you? Ah, don't you, indeed?" She gave her little clucking laugh and came up close to him with a sudden brisk hop that made him start, for he had not expected her to move so rapidly.

"Let me see," she said. "You expect me, on the strength of this note from my old friend Scasso who has never yet lost an opportunity of cheating me, to hand over two hundred bezants to you. Well, I might do so. You're a good-looking youngster with a fine, sweet voice. Let me put it to you this way: I'm an old woman, and almost the only pleasure I get out of life these days is gossip. Every little bit of gossip cheers me up, and it also tells me a little something about what's going on in the world. Business rests on knowing the news, my boy. Now if I could know why a young knight who is clearly a prisoner of war, and has been here long enough to learn Arabic as well as you have, should suddenly want his ransom money so that he can clear out, it might be a very useful repayment for me. Especially since, in spite of my old friend Scasso's gratitude to you, I will probably have a hard time recovering my money. There! Is that clear enough for you? Or let me put it another way. If you won't tell me out of pity for my age and my love of gossip, just remember that I don't know you from Adam and this note may be forged."

Denys said, rather uneasily, "It's supposed to be a secret. How do I know you won't betray me to the Moslems?"

"Betray you? To *them*?" She grinned toothlessly. "I am neither on their side nor on yours. Do you know Scasso? On whose side is he?"

Denys, remembering his talk with the Genoan, said, "You mean that you are only concerned with profit?"

He could not help a touch of contempt as he said it.

The old woman's eyes glittered at him. "Ah, this seems very bad to you, doesn't it? You think I ought to love the Christians, perhaps? You and your people have been washing your hands in Jewish blood for a thousand years. The Arabs have been kinder to us, but they, too, hate us and despoil us. I am concerned with realities, my dear young man. My money goes to four children and eleven grandchildren, to the Temple of our people, to charities in the name of my dead father, to the care of needy Jews, and to the protection of our community against your friends and the Moslems alike. And of course, if I choose to give it, to you, too."

Denys felt his face grow hot. "Very well," he said, stiffly. "I'll tell you what you want to know."

When he had finished the tale of the conspiracy, and explained that he felt compelled, by reason of his having sworn loyalty to Richard to go and warn him, the old woman nodded, and mumbled her lips together for a long moment or two.

"Well, well," she said, at last, "this is very interesting. Now I will give you some information in exchange. The knight who visited Mejed ed-Din was undoubtedly Balian of Ibelin, so you may give that news to your king. Do you know where Richard is now?"

"No, I don't," Denys confessed. "I had thought of going to Acre to find out."

"Well, you can save yourself a journey. When he turned back from his advance on Jerusalem, he went to Acre, as you heard. The Sultan then moved with his entire army on Jaffa, which had been left almost undefended, full of sick and wounded. A few days ago, the city surrendered, all but the garrison. You might like to know that at that time King Richard was on the point of embarking for home."

"Leaving the Holy Land?"

"Aha! That surprises you, does it? But he is having a good deal of trouble in his kingdom. His brother, John, is manœuvring to take it away from him. My messenger told me that the garrison in Jaffa sent an urgent cry for help to Richard, and he announced he would go to their aid. The French troops, however, refused to go with him. Either your friend's scheme is bearing fruit, or else it's the natural contradictoriness of the French. I have heard nothing since, and that was four days ago, but I would be very much surprised if the king is anywhere but at the walls of Jaffa."

She nodded again, as if her tiny head were on a spring. "Very interesting," she repeated. "I suspect we shall see the war end before winter, whether you warn the king or not. If he should be taken, or killed, your army of the Cross will fall apart. If he escapes, he will be more determined than ever to do no more fighting with an army council he cannot trust, especially since he must now conclude matters and go back to England. You see, every little bit of gossip is useful for an old woman who can do nothing but sit at home and count out money."

He squirmed under the irony. As with Scasso, he had a vague feeling that there was another level of activity going on in the world which he could neither perceive nor wholly comprehend —a movement of goods and money quite distinct from that of armies and their captains. Scasso and his comrades in Italy, Rachel and her people here, Saracens in Egypt, Greeks in Byzantium, all with a network of information and interests, all bustling about their own affairs, and somehow just out of sight of the world Denys knew, of castles, camps, battlefields, political intrigues, and religious conflicts. The thought crossed his mind, just for an instant, that perhaps that other was the real world, and his only a kind of painted gauze laid over it. But it was too fantastic an idea to entertain; it was gone almost as soon as it had come.

Rachel, in any case, was turning a thick key in the lock of an iron coffer. She pulled out a bag almost too heavy for her to carry, lugged it to the counting table, and poured out a heap of gold pieces. She counted two hundred of them into another bag and secured it with a thong.

"There you are," she said. She brought out an ink-horn and a pen and wrote something on Scasso's note. "Sign this receipt," she went on. "It is for the two hundred bezants. I may possibly get them back some day. However, here is a present for you—another five gold pieces which will help you on your way. I have no love for King Richard, quite the contrary, but I admire your loyalty. You're a good boy. That kind of thing is all too rare nowadays."

Denys tucked her gift into his purse, and took up the bag of money.

"Scasso told me that he thought you were young and beautiful," he said, with a broad grin. "You aren't young, but to me, madam, you are more than beautiful." It was a good speech, he felt, and worthy of a Poitevin.

He returned to el Emeen's palace, worrying on the way about the possibility of being attacked in the narrow streets by someone who might guess what was in his bag. Nothing happened, however. At the palace he asked a servant to take him to the prince. He was brought into the diwan and told that he must be patient for el Emeen was with his father at the Citadel. So there he sat, crosslegged on the *durka'ah*, the lower part of the floor where suppliants waited, with two hundred gold pieces in his lap, for more than an hour.

El Emeen arrived at last, and with him two or three armed men with whom he was speaking very earnestly. He dismissed them when he saw Denys, and came to greet him. Denys stood up.

"They didn't tell me you were in here," el Emeen said. "I'm sorry you should have had to wait so long. The fact is, I'm——" He stopped, looking at Denys's face. "Something is wrong. What's the matter?"

Denys found he had no words. He held out the bag.

"What's this?" El Emeen took it automatically. His face froze as he felt its weight.

"It's my ransom," said Denys.

The prince said, in a strained voice, "I don't understand. How——?"

"I once did someone a favour and he has repaid me."

They stood staring at each other over the money as if they were strangers. A muscle began to jump in el Emeen's jaw, above the line of his beard.

He said, "And now you want to go?"

"Why are you angry? You knew it would come to this some day."

"I'm not angry. Nor do I blame you."

"In any case, it's your own fault," Denys said, a sullen rage growing in him. That it was compounded out of sorrow and even a sort of guilt made no difference. "It's your own talk of honour that has made me see I must go back to my obligations."

"I don't believe you," said el Emeen, harshly.

The fact that it was, indeed, not true—or at least, not wholly true—only made Denys angrier.

"I didn't think *you* would call me a liar," he said.

"I didn't think you would betray a secret. Do you imagine I don't see what you're up to? You want to run to Richard and tell him about the conspiracy in the hope of being well rewarded. The Sultan was right—you and your people are so steeped in treachery that there is nothing in you that isn't crooked. How can I blame you? It's your nature."

He hurled the bag of money from him. It clashed in a corner of the room and burst open, gold spinning and ringing from it upon the tiles.

Denys's fists clenched spasmodically. "And you?" he said, thick-tongued. "You who keep talking about honour? 'The Faithful One.' If you were in my place, having sworn loyalty to your Sultan, what would you do? Or is it just talk, lovely words?"

366

And suddenly, his anger ebbed out of him, leaving him drained. "Ahmad," he said, "for God's sake, help me. Do you really think I'm wrong?"

The prince's eyes, fixed on Denys, brimmed with tears. "How can you ask me that?" he said. "Can't you see it hurts me to think of your going? Fool! You're an enemy, an infidel. I've been taught all my life to hate you. And we have been friends. I have loved you."

He swung away, as if by walking he could rid himself of his emotion. From the other side of the room he said, "Don't you know that I shall be leading my father's troops against your king?"

Denys shook as if he had been struck. "I thought Yezid——"

"Yezid will lead the mamelukes. But my father's own men—our Kurdish soldiers—it's I who will be leading them. And today, this very afternoon."

"Today?"

"How could you know?" El Emeen came swiftly to Denys and seized his arm. "The message came this morning. Richard came down upon Jaffa by sea and took the city again, after it had surrendered to the Sultan. Salah ed-Din had left a garrison and had gone off to Caesarea with his main army. Richard drove out the garrison. He is encamped outside Jaffa with no more than a dozen of his knights and a thousand archers and spearmen. The French refused to go with him to Jaffa. However, some other troops have set out from Acre to reinforce him. They've been delayed, and we are informed that they will continue to be delayed until we can trap the king."

He bared his teeth, but not in humour. "You must go at once, then, if you're to go," he said. "I'll give you a safe conduct saying that your ransom has been paid. I will tell my chamberlain to furnish you with food and two horses."

"Three horses."

"Leila——? Very well. If you leave within the hour you'll have a good start of us. There are only three of you. You should be able to travel swiftly. It is thirty miles to Jaffa. We will be there at daybreak tomorrow, for we are used to night riding and we'll have no supply train, nor anything to slow us.

"And I'll do this for you, as well: some of our men are Kurds and some are Turks. I will insist that the Kurds take the vanguard. The Turks will argue. It may delay matters a trifle.

"Now," he added, fiercely, "are you answered? I don't think you're wrong."

Denys shook his head. Silently, he opened his arms and embraced the prince; they clasped each other tight, and broke apart.

"Go with God's blessing," said el Emeen. "May we meet again."

"We will meet again. Until then, God protect you," Denys said.

From Jerusalem to Beit Nuba the track was rough and steep and the going slow. Denys and his companions urged their horses on as best they could, but they dared not take chances. The pressure of haste was upon them, but also the sense that they must not be halted by an accident. This was the worst part of their journey, through a long, stony valley, then over precipitous hills, between ragged, overhanging cliffs where trees hung above them like clouds. They had no sooner climbed one difficult path to a summit than they saw another uplifting to be climbed. The sun seemed to race down the sky; the dust rose around them and parched them. The first crystal stars hung in the darkening air behind them when they reached Beit Nuba.

They found no troops there, neither Saracen nor Christian, but only a handful of peasants who had hung on despite the war which had levelled their walls and swept them from one master to another. These gave them shelter; they ate a hasty meal of the dates, dried meat, and bread el Emeen's steward had given them, rubbed down their horses and let them rest for a while. They themselves hardly dared lie down, lest they should fall asleep.

From Beit Nuba to Ramlah the road was like the dry bed of a mountain stream, narrow, bevelled, and full of pebbles. There were great ridges of limestone, shining grey in the starlight, which had to be crossed carefully. It was easier travelling, and the air was fresh and cold, but the pale, deceptive glimmer of the stars and the depth of the shadows kept them at a slow pace. Their comfort was that the soldiers whom they knew to be behind them could not go much quicker.

Near midnight they came down out of the hills into the plain of Sharon. There lay before them fifteen miles of relatively flat, open ground, and here they rested again.

Denys said to Leila, "There's no need for you to ride so hard. If you're tired, you and Giraud can drop back and follow more slowly."

She faced him, straight-backed in spite of her aches, looking like a boy in the tunic, hooded cloak, cap, and boots she had worn for the journey. "I'm not tired," she said. "It's only that I'm not used to being in the saddle so long. I'll stay with you, unless it seems I'm slowing you."

"Well," said Denys, "the prince plans to halt his troops at Ramlah, to let them sleep for a couple of hours so that they and their mounts may be fresh for the attack. We can go more easily now, trotting and walking our horses. When we come to the camp, I will go in alone. Giraud, you remember Jaffa; take Leila to that olive grove on the hill above the city. We'll meet there."

They set out again. And now there was nothing to mark the time for them. The pale road passed endlessly beneath them, while about them the featureless dark land seemed never to change. They saw black clumps of trees, or passed through villages of mud huts, all silent. They heard the yelp of jackals now and then, or the distant calling of owls, but no other sound. Then, suddenly, ascending a rise they saw ahead of them twinkling lights, like fallen stars lying on the land: the dying fires of a camp. To one side they could make out the loom of a hill.

"Jaffa," Giraud said.

"That is Richard's camp. And there's the hill. Go on. I'll join you when I can," said Denys.

He started ahead, then reined in and turned back. He rode to Leila's side, bent to her and kissed her. Then he kicked his weary horse into a heavy trot and went on towards the camp.

There were no sentries. But as he rode noisily in, men awoke on all sides and rose up around him. Someone called out in a language he recognized as Italian.

"French!" he shouted. "Francia! Francese! Damn it, how do you say it?"

Someone caught him by the back of the cloak and pulled him off his horse. He hit the ground headfirst with a burst of flaming, brilliantly beautiful pinwheels.

He came to his senses abruptly, soaking wet. Shaking his

head to clear it, he gasped up at a man in a leather gambeson, with dirty woollen hose hanging in torn wrinkles about his shanks. The man had curly brown hair and a wide, amiable, gap-toothed smile. He was holding an empty bucket.

"Bene, bene," he said. "Tu sei sveglio, eh?"

"Richard," said Denys. "I must see the king."

The man nodded, smiling indulgently as if to a drunken friend. He patted the air in front of Denys and called to someone behind him. Denys staggered to his feet and stood swaying, fingering the back of his skull where there was a knot that felt as if another head were budding. A man wearing armour under a pleated surcoat sullied with blood-spots and mud came striding up.

"You are awake?" he said, in heavily accented French. "You are lucky. Who are you?"

"Denys de Courtebarbe. A Poitevin."

"You were nearly killed, friend. My archers had begun to strip you, when one of them saw that you wore a cross around your neck."

Denys fumbled at his throat; Arthur's gold cross still hung there on its chain.

"Nothing has been stolen from you," said the other, haughtily. "Why do you come riding in the night, making so much disturbance, waking everyone?"

"I must get to King Richard. At once!"

Already the sky was paling in the east, above the hills of Judea from which he had come.

"I've lost too much time," he said. "For the love of God, take me to the king. And rouse your men. The Turks are coming; they'll be here by sunrise."

"Rouse the men? Who the devil do you think is sleeping by now?" grumbled the Italian. He snapped out orders, and the arbalesters' camp began to seethe with activity.

The king's great pavilion was still dark, but the captain of the arbalesters called for torches and himself went in to wake Richard. When Denys entered, the king was seated on the edge of his camp-bed, a crimson gown wrapped about him that left his chest bare. He was raking his tawny hair with both hands.

Through a yawn, he said, "Denys . . .? Denys! By God's legs, it *is* my blasted trouvère. I never expected to see you again. I thought you'd find life among the infidel so luxurious that you would never return."

He sprang up and caught Denys in a hug that almost crippled him. He held him off, and laughed.

"How did you escape? And what's all this about the Turks coming?"

Denys glanced at the captain of the arbalesters. "I ought to tell you privately, my lord."

Richard waved the captain out. "It's no good, you know," he said, when he and Denys were alone. "They'll all have their ears clamped to the canvas. However, you can pretend we're alone. Go on, then, tell your story."

As quickly and succinctly as he could, Denys explained as much as he thought pertinent to Richard's understanding of the conspiracy, and how he had come to know of it, as well as how he had purchased his freedom. As he talked, Richard dressed, pulling on shirt and hose, diving headforemost into his coat of mail, buckling on his sword.

"Scasso, eh?" said the king, taking up his spurs. "You're the first to have profited by knowing him." He went to the tent flap and shouted outside, "Call the camp to arms. Tell Leicester to arm and come to me." Then returning, "Buckle these on for me," he said.

Denys knelt and strapped the golden spurs around the king's ankles. Richard put a large hand lightly on his head.

"I'm in your debt again," he said. "I seem forever in your debt. From that first time you helped me—so many years ago —at Châteauroux."

Denys looked up in surprise, wincing at the twinge of pain from his bruise. "You remember that?" he said.

A corner of Richard's lip lifted. "I know that it must seem to you I often forget. But you see, my dear Renier, a king must forget nothing. He ought only seem to forget whenever it's necessary. In the case of Balian of Ibelin, that wood-louse, and his wretched friends and their nasty little plan . . . I will forget that, too. There's no profit for me in accusing them. I have too many other things to worry about, including my kingdom and my poor, naughty brother, John."

He lifted down his shield, which hung from a peg on the tent-pole. Denys sank back on his heels, watching him.

"Ah, he is royal!" he said to himself.

The tent-flap was raised, and a knight peered in. "Richard!" he cried. "One of the bowmen has just seen the glitter of sunlight on helmets. And Leicester is here."

"Excellent," said the king. "I'm coming."

He swung round to Denys. "Up!" he said. "I'll make a baron of you. Have you no sword? Come, you can ride beside me."

"No, my lord," Denys said, softly. "I'm not coming. I don't want to be a baron. I'm not fitted for the trade of war. I won't fight in this battle, nor in any other."

The king looked at him impatiently. "Oh, you poets!" he said. "What do you want—money? Later, then. Off with you, to a good safe place."

He started for the tent-flap, but Denys barred his way. "You said you were in my debt, my lord," he said, firmly. "I know now that you remember everything. I want only to be released from my oath of fealty."

Richard's face darkened. "Don't you know," he said, "that it isn't wise to cross me? Will you throw your loyalty in my teeth? Or are you still thinking of Arthur de Hastynge?"

"Of nothing," said Denys, "except to be free. I think I've proved my loyalty several times over, and without asking anything. But I have come as far along this road with you as I can."

Richard went past him. He turned, with one hand on the canvas flap, and said, "You've hurt me, Denys. Be free, then, if that's your wish. And we are quits. Don't let me see you again."

He was gone. Denys could hear him shouting to his barons, roaring out commands above the noise of the camp.

"How like him, this parting," Denys murmured smiling. "He was relieved, I suppose, not to have to pay anything to be rid of me."

He glanced around the tent. An ivory-hilted dagger in a red leather sheath lay in a corner among a heap of clothes carelessly flung down. He picked it up and thrust it into his belt.

"I think I'm entitled to a trivial souvenir," he said, wryly. "Somehow, he made it sound as if I were at fault. 'Shall I teach you how to throw a dagger?' 'Yes, please.' 'I'll let you use mine with the silver hilt.'"

372

He laughed, and went out to find his friends.

From the olive orchard on the hill, Denys, Leila, and Giraud had a perfect view of the battle. Standing among the shaggy trees along with half the population of Jaffa, they saw the long uneven lines of the Saracen horsemen coming across the plain. Richard had set out his little army in a way that showed his military genius, making the best possible use of what he had. His foot-soldiers, no more than a few hundred of them, were stretched in a single rank, kneeling, the butts of their spears planted in the ground, the heads forming a bristling hedge beyond their shields. Behind these, half of his Genoan arba-lesters stood, each with a bolt on the string, and behind each of them another arbalester with his weapon cocked and ready. There were only ten knights with Richard, some of them mounted on mere wrecks of horses; these, his pitiful cavalry, Richard placed on the left, with the right wing of his archers and spearmen anchored against the steep rise of ground where the orchard began. The older and more experienced of the civilians from Jaffa pointed all this out to their neighbours ignorant of war, while children ran and screeched underfoot, and other people took out their breakfasts and began to munch.

As the Saracens came closer, the little figures of the arba-lesters could be seen to raise their crossbows, and a shower of bolts arched up and dropped in among the horsemen. Now the reason for the double line of archers became clear; the instant the first rank had shot, the second rank passed loaded arbalests to them and, while they shot again, drew and cocked the strings of the discharged bows and loaded again. Thus, an almost continual rain of shafts buzzed like a vengeful cloud of hornets across the plain.

The toy horses fell kicking, and the toy soldiers rolled amongst them. A snotty-nosed child grabbed Denys by the leg, scream-ing with excitement, not for the battle but because another child was trying to catch him. A man in a striped cloak, with a filthy turban knotted around his skull-cap, was eating dates with a steady, mechanical gesture, and spitting out the stones explosively, while his companion kept up a stream of admiring comment: "Look, there goes another with a banner, now he's down, now look, someone else is picking it up, and some of them are in among the knights. . . ."

Denys shaded his eyes; the tiny men scampered to and fro, the tiny shafts drew their black arcs against the dust. Here and there roiling knots showed where warriors had come to handstrokes with each other despite the arrow-fire.

"I can't see him," Denys muttered.

"There—over on the left," said Giraud, pointing. "He's so much taller than the rest."

"Not the king," said Denys. "I can see the king. I'm looking for el Emeen."

Leila took his hand and held it, pressing her shoulder against his. She said nothing.

The day advanced. Some of the townspeople were making bets on which side would win. The Saracens had drawn off, had come on again, had recoiled leaving more crawling or silent bundles like ant-eggs on the plain. The noise of the battle was a steady and confused roar, rising and falling like that of the sea, click-clattering where now and then swords met on shields, and groups swept together and flew apart again.

Denys said, suddenly, "They're retreating. See? They're drawing off."

The Turkish riders, bending low over their horses' necks, were rushing away, fanning out from the spot, leaving smoking plumes of dust behind them.

"Are they retreating or is it just a feint?" said the man with the dirty turban, who had finished his dates and was tearing with relish at a hunk of bread smeared with oil.

"No, it's true, they're leaving. They've had it," said his friend. "There go their banners. Look—you can see the king. There's his standard-bearer behind him. Look, he's waving to his knights. Now they're riding out into the plain. Look at that—he's just chopped down a Turk. Look, there he goes again."

One of those miniscule men down there was el Emeen, either lying dead or wounded on the field, or riding away towards the hills. Denys sighed, and slowly sat down on the grass. The long ride, the lack of sleep, the tension, only now began to crush him; until this moment he had not thought of them. Leila sank down beside him. Her eyes were rimmed with red, her face haggard and grey. She clearly kept herself awake only by an act of will. Giraud, too, was pale and limp, but his spare frame, toughened by many beatings, could endure much.

"Is it over?" Leila whispered.

"It's over. When the people leave here, we'll find a safe, quiet spot and sleep. I feel as though I could sleep for a week. And you, my dear, you must be exhausted."

"I'm well enough."

Giraud said, "Another victory for Richard. And now what?"

"He'll go on," said Denys. "He will make peace with the Sultan eventually, I'm sure of it. He will somehow turn any defeat into victory, even his own death. He told me once that he would still be renowned a thousand years from now. How can you help admiring him and fearing him? He's not so much a man as a kind of force, like the wind or the lightning."

"He released you from your oath?"

"Yes."

"What will we do now?" Giraud asked, rubbing his bloodshot eyes. "How will we live?"

Denys sat with his knees drawn up, his arms wrapped around them, his chin on his chest. Some of the townsfolk had gone down into the plain to scavenge for whatever they could snatch from Richard's arbalesters and spearmen; the rest were returning to the town, cuffing their children or shouting for them, laughing, discussing the battle with their arms linked together, paying lost wagers and making new ones.

"I haven't found any of the things I came here for," he said, only half aloud. "If the Sufi asked me, now, I know what my question would be."

"What are you talking about?" Giraud said, petulantly. "What question?"

"Where am I going?"

Denys looked at Leila. She had fallen fast asleep, her face half covered by her hood. He smiled, and moved the cloth so that it should not annoy her.

"I suppose the answer is that it doesn't matter, as long as I go on seeking," he mused.

In the field below, the dust had begun to settle over victor and vanquished alike.

Other Historical Novels by

JAY WILLIAMS

THE SIEGE

An outstanding historical novel of Mediaeval France
"In my opinion this novel has broken quite new ground in its
creation of the world of the professional soldier, on the level, not
of the mercenary, but of the knight occupied in warfare, either
for a livelihood or for the sake of adventure, or both. And it
seems to me that the individuals in this company of young men
are presented by a method and style which, simple and, as it
were, roughly chiselled, give an admirable effect of life and
period."—H. F. M. PRESCOTT, author of *The Man on a Donkey*.

THE WITCHES

"His tale concerns the terrible smelling-out of witches . . . by and
on behalf of King James VI (who became James I of England
later), in the year after the defeat of the Armada. . . . The tale is
told briskly yet with profound and passionate understanding.
The whole achievement is masterly."—JOHN CONNELL in *The
Evening News*.

THE GOOD YEOMEN

*A novel of Robin Hood which presents a striking new interpretation of the
most famous of English legends.*
"His world is consistent and well-imagined. . . . The military
detail is scholarly and the accounts of battle most exciting."—
The Times Literary Supplement.

THE ROGUE FROM PADUA

" *The Rogue From Padua* is by an American writer who combines
good scholarship with good story-telling and real imagination. . . .
A very accomplished book for the more serious reader, excellently
written in a stately and attractive style."—PAMELA HANSFORD
JOHNSON in *The Bookman*.